BY

STEPHANIE DECAROLIS

The Perfect Sister

Deadly Little Lies

The Guilty Husband

THE
PERFECT
SISTER

THE
PERFECT
SISTER

A NOVEL

STEPHANIE
DECAROLIS

BANTAM

New York

The Perfect Sister is a work of fiction. Names, characters, places, and incidents are the products of the author's imagination or are used fictitiously. Any resemblance to actual events, locales, or persons, living or dead, is entirely coincidental.

A Bantam Books Trade Paperback Original

Copyright © 2024 by Stephanie DeCarolis

Book club guide copyright © 2024 by Penguin Random House LLC

All rights reserved.

Published in the United States by Bantam Books, an imprint of Random House, a division of Penguin Random House LLC, New York.

BANTAM & B colophon is a registered trademark of Penguin Random House LLC.

RANDOM HOUSE BOOK CLUB and colophon are trademarks of Penguin Random House LLC.

LIBRARY OF CONGRESS CATALOGING-IN-PUBLICATION DATA
NAMES: DeCarolis, Stephanie, author.
TITLE: The perfect sister: a novel / Stephanie DeCarolis.
DESCRIPTION: New York: Bantam, 2024.
IDENTIFIERS: LCCN 2023056261 (print) | LCCN 2023056262 (ebook) |
ISBN 9780593726013 (trade paperback; acid-free paper) |
ISBN 9780593726020 (ebook)
SUBJECTS: LCGFT: Thrillers (Fiction) | Novels.
CLASSIFICATION: LCC PS3604.E2383 P47 2024 (print) |
LCC PS3604.E2383 (ebook) | DDC 813/.6—dc23/eng/20231208
LC record available at https://lccn.loc.gov/2023056261
LC ebook record available at https://lccn.loc.gov/2023056262

Printed in the United States of America on acid-free paper

randomhousebookclub.com

9 8 7 6 5 4 3 2 1

Book design by Barbara M. Bachman

For my girls:
Never forget how lucky you are to have a sister—
you'll always have each other.

And for Ali:
You'll always be my sister by choice.

A sister can be seen as someone who is
both ourselves and very much not ourselves—
a special kind of double.

—TONI MORRISON

THE
PERFECT
SISTER

PROLOGUE

They say that in the instant before you die, your entire life flashes before your eyes. But that's nothing more than a myth. Or at least it was for me. I didn't see a film reel of my life unspooling out before me. Rather, my mind unearthed one single, seemingly inconsequential, memory. A long-forgotten moment plucked like a diamond from beneath the fallen sands of time.

Suddenly I was back there. I could feel my sister's skin warm against my own, see the flashlight bobbing in her hand. Our threadbare comforter—the filling lumped, the cotton pilling—was tucked behind our heads, propped upon our knobby knees that were exposed in the nightgowns that had grown too short that summer.

She read to me, her voice magnetic as her finger scanned the pages, and I snuggled in so close to her that I could feel her breath sticky on my cheek.

"Girls?" Mom called from her bedroom. "Come in here, please!"

Maddie tossed her edge of the comforter aside, a rush of cool air entering the snug cocoon we'd built. "Coming!"

"How do I look?" Mom asked as we filed into her room

and climbed atop her bed. She glanced back over her shoulder, checking her reflection in her bedroom mirror. She was so beautiful, her hair set in long golden curls, her lips stained a deep, velvet red.

"You look incredible, Mama," Maddie gushed.

"The dress isn't too much? What do you think, Alex?"

At six years old I wasn't sure what made a dress "too much." All I knew was that my mother looked like the height of glamour to me, the sequins dotting her gold dress catching the warm light from the lamp on her vanity, making it appear as if she was glowing. *Your mother is larger than life,* Dad used to say. And in that moment, I finally understood what he'd meant. "I think it's perfect."

Mom reached into the little wooden drawer of her vanity and produced two tiny chocolate bars, pressing one into each of our palms with a wink. "It'll be our little secret."

The wrappers were printed with the logo of the restaurant she was working at that month. I'd never been there, but I knew it was a fancy place on the other side of town, the kind of place where the bill came in a leather fold and meals were finished off with chocolate mints, one of which was now softening beneath my curled fingers.

The owner of the restaurant occasionally let Mom take home leftovers after her shifts, and Maddie and I would spread Mom's good Christmas tablecloth over our kitchen table and pretend we were at a restaurant. Maddie was always the server, taking orders from Mom and me and writing them down in a notebook with a businesslike seriousness. Those were our favorite nights, but, even back then, I could tell that Mom enjoyed them the most: the times when she got to pretend she was the type of woman who got to place orders instead of filling them.

"I'll take the filet mignon," she'd say with a haughty air, even when the only thing on the menu was overcooked steak tidbits on a stale heel of garlic bread.

But that night we weren't pretending. That night Mom had a real audition, for a role on a prime-time TV show. I watched her smooth her dress over the gentle curves at her hips as I peeled back the wrapper of the chocolate bar and nibbled deliciously at the corner.

When she was satisfied with her appearance, Mom turned to us, the smile that lit her face as bright as sunshine. "My girls. My beautiful twins."

Maddie rolled her eyes and giggled. "You know we aren't twins, Mama."

We were used to it, Maddie and I. Strangers were constantly mistaking us for twins. But Maddie was a year older than me, which felt like a lifetime back then, and she was always quick to correct them; to claim her rightful place as the oldest sister. I'd nod along wholeheartedly, as if I, too, needed the distinction, the degree of separation from my sister. But the truth was that I loved to think of us that way, as twins, as belonging to each other. I never tired of wearing her hand-me-downs, copying the way she stood with one hand propped on her hip. She was mine and I was hers. Two halves of a whole.

Mom laughed as she spritzed a cloud of perfume. The misty droplets caught the light, sparkling as they fell—it reminded me of a winter frost. "Never forget how lucky you are to have a sister. Because that means that you'll never be alone in this world. You'll always have each other."

I felt her words wrap around me like a quilt.

"Where are my favorite girls?" Dad called from the living room. It was the same thing he always said when he got back from one of his trips. I didn't understand where he went in those days—I just knew he drove a big truck and that sometimes he'd be gone for a really long time. And that when he came back, he'd have presents for Maddie and me. A cap from a truck stop in Iowa, a plastic palm tree from a corner store in California. Maddie and I collected the trinkets he offered us like treasures, displaying them proudly on a shelf in our room. "Viv, you're gonna be late!"

"We're coming!" Mom called back. She reached for our hands. "Come along."

Dad was waiting in the living room with a spatula in his hand. I could tell from the charred scent hanging in the air that he'd burned the grilled cheese sandwiches he'd set out to make. But I knew it meant something that he'd tried—I couldn't remember him cooking anything for us before—and so I reminded myself not to complain.

"Are you three going to be okay on your own?" Mom asked as she tucked her lipstick into her evening bag.

"We'll be just fine," Dad replied. He knelt down between Maddie and me, pulling us close to him. I breathed in the woodsy smell of his aftershave as the rough stubble on his chin grazed my cheek.

"Someday soon you're gonna see your mama on the silver screen. Her name in neon lights. She's going to *be* somebody." He made a frame with his hands and watched our mother through it, his eyes glittering with adoration. "Vivienne Walker: The movie star."

Mom laughed as she pulled open the front door. "Wish me luck, my darlings." The words were sent off with a kiss blown from her palm.

It's one of the last memories I have of the four of us together, happy, a family. That was before they were all gone. Before I was too.

1.

ALEX

WELCOME TO THE HAMPTONS. The old clapboard sign made of tastefully aged driftwood greets me, its white letters gleaming in the afternoon sun as though they'd just been given a fresh coat of paint. I take in my surroundings as my old sedan rumbles down the main road that snakes lazily through the town. Much like the welcome sign, the town itself is a dichotomy of aged elegance and vibrant freshness. The stately colonial manors wear wood shingles weathered to the color of rust, edged with neat white trim, and they sit upon sprawling gardens of Technicolor-green lawns. Bushels of blooming hydrangeas appear lush and flourishing, despite the brutal summer heat.

How the hell did my sister end up in a place like this? I don't know much about the Hamptons, other than the fact that it's the place where all the rich people in Manhattan retreat to escape the soaring urban temperatures every summer. The two-bedroom cottage where we grew up could easily fit inside the garage on some of these houses. I pick at the chipping red nail polish on my thumb as my car idles loudly at one of the few stoplights in the center of town. Outside my window, elegant women in floral sundresses and wide-brimmed hats stroll along the sidewalks with luxury shopping bags dangling from satin ribbons at their elbows. Couples sit outside small cafés sipping from wineglasses with delicate stems, and men in linen shirts lean lazily in their wrought iron chairs, tanned legs stretched beneath the tables. *Don't any of these people work?*

I look down at my phone once again, at the last photo my sister sent me. It shows a grinning Maddie, arm outstretched, the image of her phone reflected in her sunglasses, and the ocean, a deep sapphire blue, sparkling behind her. It came with a short text:

Found a summer job! Looks like I won't be making it home this summer after all. Sorry, but I need the $! I'll call you on your birthday. We'll still make it special. Xoxo

I hadn't responded at the time. I was still tetchy about the way we'd left things after Mom's funeral. The spiked jabs we'd exchanged, the anger we'd spilled like red wine. It had changed the fabric of our relationship, left a stain that couldn't be lifted. And so we'd ignored it. Letting it weave its way between us, setting into something hard and permanent.

It was just like Maddie to pretend it hadn't happened, to smooth over the past and go on with life as usual. But things had changed, and her text was only further proof. Maddie wasn't coming home. How could she leave me alone in that house? Where the memories wandered like lost souls, floating sullenly through the empty rooms.

And so I stubbornly ignored her. I thought that's all it was—each of us refusing to speak the words we knew needed to be said: *I'm sorry.* But four days ago, when my birthday passed and she didn't call as promised, I knew something was wrong.

I understand that Maddie has her own life. One that looks nothing like mine. Unlike me, she got out of Dogwood Grove, that forgotten place in Middle-of-Nowhere Pennsylvania where nothing ever changes. She went to college, made something of herself. But even if she couldn't make the trip home this year, she would never ignore my birthday, not unless something was very, very wrong.

I think back to my tenth birthday, the first one Mom had forgotten. She'd left to work a shift at the diner that afternoon with a promise of a birthday cake, balloons. But the sky grew dark and she still hadn't returned. By that time, we should have known better. We should have known that she'd stop for a drink on her way home, and that one would become many until all of her good intentions drifted away from her as light as clouds. But we didn't. For some reason, maybe because it was my birthday, we thought that night would be different. And so we sat at the kitchen table, the chipped Formica sticky under our fingers, waiting for a party, until it became obvious that she wasn't coming.

I felt my chin start to wobble. As many times as I told myself that I didn't care, that I was too old to need my mommy, her absence that night felt like it tore open a black hole inside of me, sucking up any last remnants of my childhood.

Maddie wasted no time. She jumped up from the table ready to set things right.

"Pancakes for dinner? With chocolate chips?"

"Do you even know how to make pancakes?" I asked sulkily, slouching in my chair.

She shrugged. "How hard could it be?" She pulled out

Mom's frying pan, a bag of flour, and a stick of butter, and got to work.

A half hour later, she slid a lopsided stack of lumpy pancakes in front of me.

"Oh wait!" she exclaimed, just as I lifted my fork, my stomach rumbling in anticipation. "Close your eyes!"

I put my hands over my eyes and listened to the clatter of the kitchen drawers opening and closing.

"Go on," she said. "Open them."

The pancakes were topped with a pink candle, half melted from birthdays past, and Maddie stood behind it beaming, her face awash in the candle's soft glow, a trace of flour dusting the tip of her nose. "I know it's not a real birthday cake," she said, "but pancakes will do, right?"

"They're even better." I couldn't help but grin as I blew out the lone candle.

When our bellies were full, we dragged our fingers through the melted chocolate smearing our plates, and Maddie grew thoughtful.

"I'll never miss your birthday," she said solemnly, her voice soft and tender. "You'll never be alone."

"Because we're twins?" I asked.

"Yes. And we'll always have each other."

"Can we have pancakes every year?"

Maddie nodded, a smile edging onto her face. "Yeah," she said. "We can. Let's make a pact. Even when we're all grown up and have our own families or whatever, even if we live a million miles away from each other, we'll always spend your birthday together."

"Swear?" I extended my pinkie.

"I swear," she replied as she looped her little finger around mine.

And she kept her promise. It was a tradition we'd held sacred: standing side by side in the kitchen as we mixed up pancake batter, adding chocolate chips by the handful before pouring them into Mom's old frying pan. Every summer, Maddie dutifully returned home for my birthday. Even when life got complicated; when the stories she brought with her turned from college parties and dancing, to waiting tables in New York City to save money for medical school, Maddie always came back. Until now.

A horn beeps, and it pulls me from my thoughts. I edge the car forward, following the directions on my phone's GPS. *"In one mile, the destination will be on your right."*

I wonder how long I'd been idling there, lost to the past. It's something I've found myself doing a lot lately, in the months after Mom's death. Trying to unpack the messy tangle of memories she left in her wake. Some days, all I can feel is the anger. The burning weight of it sitting like a stone in my chest. But on the clear days, when resentment isn't clouding my memories like a hanging fog, I can still see her as she was before: beautiful, vibrant, certain that it was only a matter of time until she landed the role that would change our lives forever. That was before she'd given up, before all of her dreams, all of her youthful ambitions, left her empty-handed and bitter, just as our father had when he walked out of our front door one frigid winter night. And now Mom's gone too. It seems almost surreal that all that she was, all that she could have been, is just . . . erased, gone, as if she'd never existed at all.

I look out at the winding road ahead of me, at the green-and-white-striped awnings that hang over the storefronts, at the lemon-yellow umbrellas propped outside an ice-cream shop, children licking cones while ribbons of melted chocolate drip down their wrists. As I round the next curve, the place I've been searching for finally comes into sight. The Lobster Shack, which, despite its name, is far from a shack. The white stone facade stands out like a watchtower in the bright sunshine, and the restaurant's logo, a lobster relaxing in a hammock, sunglasses pulled over its eyes, is visible from the main road.

I pull up alongside the restaurant, squinting against the sun as I size up the scene before me. Seagulls wheel lazily against an azure sky, gliding above the tranquil ocean, and outside the restaurant, smartly dressed patrons queue up, presumably waiting for a table on the seaside deck. There, the tables have been spread with crisp white tablecloths, and water glasses, filled from frosty decanters, are topped with bright lemon wedges.

I pull my car into the parking lot, my tires bumping over the crushed shell drive, and look down at the picture of Maddie again. I'm struck by a familiar feeling—the same one I've experienced every time I've seen my sister in the last few years—like I'm looking at an alternate version of myself. One in which I've left our hometown and become something. Where I'm not just the faceless girl behind the register at Nate's Hardware. Where I'm polished and worldly and important. Where I wear trendy outfits and spiky heels instead of thrift-shop band T-shirts under Nate's hideous canvas apron, which is the unfortunate color of split pea soup. But that's Maddie's life. It was never meant to be mine.

I zoom into the photograph. Comparing the logo on Maddie's shirt, which is just barely visible in the corner of the frame, to the one on the restaurant in front of me. *Could she really be here?* None of the waitresses whizzing by on the outdoor deck look like my sister, but it's possible that she's inside.

I know it's a long shot, but I don't exactly have a lot to go on: half of a logo that may or may not be a lobster in sunglasses. But I have to try. After all, I've come all this way to find her.

I tried to reach her before making the trip, the tally of unanswered calls and text messages piling up as the days rolled by:

Hey.
Maddie?
Is everything okay?
I'm getting worried.
Call me.

Each met with silence. I even tried calling her roommates, but they hadn't heard from her in weeks. Eventually, I couldn't take the waiting anymore. I told Nate I needed to take some time off, and I followed the only lead I had.

It's almost depressing how easy it was for me to leave my life behind. My job, Nate assured me, would be waiting for me when I returned. Which didn't come as a surprise. Nate has known me and Maddie since we were kids, always trimming down our bill when we'd go into his shop to buy something to fix up Mom's house. Tar for a leaky roof, cement mix to patch the deteriorating front porch. Somehow, no matter what we brought to the register, the total never amounted to more than the crumpled bills in our pockets. But it wasn't just work I was walking away from. There was also the Ben of it all. Arguably the nicest guy that's ever lived, and probably the closest thing I've ever had to a best friend aside from Maddie. Hot shame creeps up my neck as I think of the last time I saw him. The hurt on his face, the words I didn't say.

But I can't deal with that now. I shake off the memory and look up at the restaurant's logo one last time. At the lazy, knowing smile hanging from the lobster's face. It's time to go inside. My sister is all I have left in the world. And I have to find her.

2.

ALEX

I weave my way into the Lobster Shack, ignoring the sideways glances tossed in my direction from the line of people waiting for a table.

"Sorry," I mumble. "Excuse me."

The inside of the Lobster Shack smells of sizzling butter and briny fried clams. Waiters and waitresses hustle across the crowded space, sliding white ceramic plates in front of customers who barely acknowledge their presence. I scan the room looking for Maddie, but I still don't see her anywhere. *Maybe the hostess will have some answers.*

"Hey," I begin as I approach the perky young woman standing near the entrance.

"Do you have a reservation?" she asks, her high ponytail falling over her shoulder in a shiny black ribbon.

"Er, no, but—"

"I'm sorry, ma'am, but we're only seating reservations today." She's already looking over my shoulder, her kohl-rimmed eyes searching for the next customer.

"I'm not looking for a table, I just had a question."

"Oh. Sure." The words are punched out in an efficient staccato. "How can I help you?"

"I'm looking for my sister. Maddie. I think she works here?"

"I'm sorry, but I don't know anyone by that name." She looks down at the clipboard in front of her. "Greco!" she shouts. "Party of four!"

I hear footsteps approaching behind me. Probably the Greco family who will be wondering why I'm still standing in their way.

"Here," I say as I fish my phone from my pocket. "Can you just look at a picture? Maybe you'll recognize her?"

"I'm sorry, ma'am, but we're super busy today. Maybe you could come back tomorrow around—"

I shove the phone in front of her before she can finish objecting. "This is Maddie."

"Oh," she says, her adorable teenage nose wrinkling. She looks down at the photo and then back up at me. "She does look familiar, but the name . . ." She taps a glossy, manicured nail against her lips. "Madison! That's it!"

Madison? My sister hasn't gone by her full name since she was a kid, which always bothered our mother, who was so fond of it.

"Madison," Mom said, as she applied a slick of her favorite red lipstick to Maddie's pouted lips. We couldn't have been more than seven and eight years old, and it felt like such a rare and fortuitous treat that Mom was letting us try on her special audition makeup that was usually off-limits. She was in one of her moods. The kind that felt like magic, where her eyes sparkled and we never knew what was going to happen next. "Such a beautiful name for such a beautiful girl. As glamorous as Madison Avenue in New York City."

New York City. The name rang in my head like a struck bell. It sounded like the most magical and elegant place. I imagined the soaring skyscrapers, the yellow cabs, men in suits, and women in dinner dresses, their heels clicking down the sidewalk, on their way to the theater.

"What about me, Mama?" I'd asked hopefully, squeezing in next to my sister on the vanity bench, waiting for my turn with Mom. I'd always wondered why she'd chosen my name. It wasn't short for Alexandra or Alexis, it wasn't like any of the flowery names given to the other girls in my class, the kind that twirl sweetly off your tongue with a delicate flourish. I'd always just been Alex.

"Why did you pick *my* name?" I was hoping she'd tell me I was named after a famous actress, her favorite author, something as beautiful as the sugarplum visions of New York City that danced in my head.

"Alex," she'd replied, "is a strong name for a strong girl. You, my darling, will never need anyone." She turned to face the mirror, applying the lipstick to her own lips instead of mine. "Especially not a man."

I watched her reflection, watched as the light in her eyes dimmed, as the magic ended. It was only later, in the quiet hours of the night, after we were tucked into our little twin beds on opposite sides of our shared room, that Maddie explained that Alex was our father's middle name. I was named after the man who'd left us and never looked back, the man who'd broken our mother.

"I'm sorry," the hostess says, grounding me back in the moment. "But Madison isn't working today."

"Er, thanks. Can you tell me when she was in last? See, I can't get ahold of her and—"

"Excuse me," a gruff voice says from behind me. "But we're waiting to be seated." *Mr. Greco, I assume.*

"I'm sorry, ma'am," the hostess says again. "I really don't

know. But listen, if you can wait a little while, until after the lunch rush, I'll have Luca give you a call. He usually handles the scheduling. Just leave your number here." She hands over her clipboard.

"Thank you," I respond gratefully, scribbling down my name and number. Mr. Greco lets out an exaggerated sigh and it takes all my self-control not to deck him as I turn and walk back to my car.

————

A rumbling sound startles me awake. It takes me a moment to orient myself: the scent of salty sea air gently blowing through the open car windows, the sound of the ocean lapping against a rocky shore. *The Hamptons. Maddie.*

I snatch my phone out of my cupholder. At first I think it's Ben, my memory returning to the pile of unanswered voicemails accumulating in my inbox:

Alex, it's me. Can we talk? I feel like we should talk.

Come on, Alex. Just call me back . . . please.

But it isn't Ben. Instead, an unknown number flashes across the screen.

"Is this Alex?" The voice on the other end of the line asks after I swipe to accept the call.

"Yes, is this Luca?"

"Yeah. From the Lobster Shack. Sorry it took me so long to get back to you."

I look out the windshield, registering for the first time how late it's gotten, the sun hanging low in the sky, dark clouds growing on the horizon.

"I heard you were looking for Madison," Luca continues. "She hasn't been in for a few days. And to be honest," he adds with a touch of annoyance in his voice, "I'm not sure I'll be putting her on another shift for a while."

"Why is that?" I make an effort to tamp down the deep-rooted instinct to defend my sister.

"She was scheduled to work this weekend, but she hasn't shown up for the last three days. Didn't even call in to have someone cover her shift. She just didn't show."

"Oh . . ." This time I can't keep the surprise out of my voice. That doesn't sound at all like Maddie, the girl who has carried a color-coded daily planner with her since middle school.

"Don't sweat it though," Luca says, much more casually now, probably sensing my alarm. "This kind of thing happens a lot. She probably got a better offer for the weekend. The summer people, they don't tend to take the job too seriously."

"Summer people?"

"You know. Not locals. The ones who only plan to stay out here for the summer."

But he's wrong. He doesn't know Maddie. She isn't some entitled rich kid working a few shifts because her parents want her to learn the value of a dollar. Maddie and I, we've always known exactly how valuable every dollar is. There's no way she'd blow off this job.

"She's not like that," I snap defensively. "She needs this job."

"Oh . . ." Luca stumbles. "Sorry. I just assumed . . . given the address on her file."

"What do you mean?" I ask, my stomach in free fall. I hate feeling like I'm on the back foot, like this stranger knows something about my sister that I don't.

"It says here that she's staying up on Seacliff Lane."

I scramble for a pen from the center console of my car. "Seacliff Lane. Got it," I say, scribbling the street name down on the back of my hand. "What's the house number?"

Luca laughs, a breathy huff. "Don't worry. You can't miss it."

I hear the grit of the sand-swept asphalt churning under my tires as I slowly drive down Seacliff Lane. The winding one-lane road follows the rolling coastline, and the sides of the street are lined with sloping sand dunes dotted with wisps of seagrass that twist in the mounting wind. The clear blue skies of the afternoon have turned dark, daunting storm clouds whipping in off the Atlantic Ocean. Between the dunes, I catch glimpses of the restless sea. It's hard to believe that this is the same ocean I saw earlier; the serene sparkling blue is now menacing, fierce—jagged jade waves capped in white.

As I near the end of the road, the house—the only one that occupies Seacliff Lane—slides into focus. It's set atop a bluff, a shingle-style mansion with gambrel roof lines, a sprawling veranda supported by classic white pillars, and rows of tall windows facing out toward the open ocean. It is all at once breathtaking and intimidating as it looms above me. The house itself seems to keep a watchful eye as I park outside the iron gate at the end of the long, gravel drive.

I step out of my car and look up at the gate, its iron bars twisted into scrolls capped with gold filigree. Beside it sits a plaque with the name BLACKWELL MANOR etched into the gold plating, and below that, a call pad. I debate whether it's too late in the evening to ring the bell. I don't even know who lives here. The front porch is well lit, but most of the house is dark, save for a few upstairs windows that glow with warmth. For a moment, I have the overwhelming desire to turn around. To leave this place. But I shove the feeling aside. If Maddie is in there somewhere, I have to know.

As if to cement my decision, a clap of thunder booms in the distance. A storm is coming, and I have nowhere else to go. Without thinking about it any further, I lift my hand and press the buzzer.

3.

—————

LILY

The tiles are cold on my bare feet as I pour myself a glass of water from the pitcher in the refrigerator. The kitchen always feels cold, even in the height of summer, with its stone floors and sleek granite countertops. Mother had insisted upon its recent renovation. I suppose I was the only one who saw the irony of a chef's kitchen being built for a woman who never cooks. Though I do imagine the chefs appreciate it when they cater Father's business dinners. He regularly hosts his corporate functions here, Blackwell Manor being the crown jewel of his real estate holdings. On those evenings, the house is full of people: caterers carrying trays of canapés, men in bespoke suits vying for a moment of Father's attention. The sounds of polite laughter and clinking champagne glasses float up to my room where I usually hide out until the house is quiet again, empty. Like it is now. I prefer it like this: Mother upstairs attending to her strict evening ritual of mineral oils and under-eye serums that promise eternal youth, Father working late, Theo . . . Lord only knows where with his group of obnoxious friends . . . and me, alone. Without the weight of my family's expectations, without feeling like I'm being examined under the cold press of a microscope. Finally, for a moment, I can breathe.

The sound of the intercom makes me jump, the icy water in my glass splashing onto my toes. I pad toward the front door, curious about who would be ringing our buzzer. Mother hadn't mentioned that she was expecting company, and it's very rare that Blackwell Manor has an unannounced visitor. I tap the security panel, which has been recessed into the wall of the front hall, and the screen comes to life. There's a person standing at the front gate, though it's started to rain and the droplets on the lens of the security camera stretch and distort the image. It appears to be a woman. A girl. Long hair shielding her face. *Why is she here? What does she want?* Behind her, just visible along the edge of the road, is a car. I don't know much about cars, but I can tell it's old, its frame boxy and outdated. *Maybe she's broken down?*

"Can I help you?" I ask into the intercom.

The girl looks up into the camera, her eyes squinting as her face is pelted by fat drops of rain.

My vision starts to swim, the world sliding in and out of focus, and it feels as though the blood is draining from my body.

It's Maddie. She's come back.

———

I walk out the front door in a daze, hardly noticing the rain which is now pouring down in a steady stream. It's like that here on the coast. A violent storm can blow in seemingly out of nowhere, whipping the ocean into a frenzy. I can hear it crashing behind me now, the waves slamming into the rocky bluff. My hair slicks to my neck, and my bare feet crunch over the stony path, but I only barely register the pain. I see her standing there at the end of the drive. Maddie.

I squeeze my eyes shut, just the way Dr. Watkins taught me to do. Ground myself in the moment: feel the sensation of the cold rain on my skin, hear the sounds of the ocean, breath in the thick salty air carrying the brackish scent of the storm-tossed beach. This is what's real. Maddie coming back here, now, is not. I let out a long, controlled breath and slowly open my eyes. But she's still there.

For a moment it's all too much. It's too much like the last time. The rain, the wind, the girl. I feel my stomach pitch, my vision begin to narrow.

"Hey! Can you help me?" Maddie calls out, her voice reaching out to me through the pelting rain, pulling me back to reality.

I edge closer to the gate as if in a trance, the sight of her drawing me in like a beacon in the dark. I start to see it then, this isn't Maddie after all. My eyes had shown me what I wanted to see.

"Who are you?" I ask, my voice muddled, clumsy.

The girl grips the gate and we appraise each other through the bars.

"My name is Alex," she says. "I'm looking for my sister."

"Maddie," I reply. It comes out as more of a statement than a question. There is no denying their relation. My mind overlays an image of Maddie with the girl standing before me, the two women shifting and blurring like a twisting kaleidoscope.

"Yes! You know her!" Alex exclaims, excited now. "Is she here? I haven't been able to get in touch with her. I was starting to get worried."

"No. She's not."

"Can I come in? Maybe I could wait for her inside? It's pretty bad out here and I have nowhere to go."

I know it's a bad idea. I should turn her away. But she's looking at me with Maddie's eyes, with Maddie's face, and I know I can't leave her there alone, in the pouring rain.

I flick the release for the gate and it slowly opens until Alex and I are face-to-face, no prison-like bars left to distinguish our grounds.

"Thank you. Seriously," Alex says with a crooked smile. "I really appreciate it."

I nod, struggling to find the right words to say to her. Maddie's sister. I've never been good at this. Meeting new people.

We trudge up the path to the house, Alex breaking into a light jog to escape the elements, and I follow her lead. She bounds up the steps to the covered porch shaking the rain from her arms. She combs her fingers through her long honey-blond hair and looks up at the house, her face bathed in the amber porch light.

I'm instantly transported back there. To the bonfire on the beach with Maddie. The way the firelight danced across her tanned skin as she threw her head back in laughter, her hair a burnished gold waterfall trailing down her back in a tangle of salty waves. She was so beautiful in that moment, a tableau of summer nights, and I found that I couldn't look away. And then her eyes met mine, and I felt my embarrassment spreading across my face. *It was a mistake to come here. And now she thinks I was staring at her like some sort of weirdo.* But she didn't turn her back like the others had before her, she didn't draw attention to my humiliation. Instead her eyes softened, and she smiled at me, as though she was genuinely happy to see me.

"Lily!" she called over the pulsing music, waving me over to where she was standing. "I'm so glad you came!"

I'd only met her earlier that day. At the Lobster Shack, where Mother had insisted we go for a family lunch. As if we were a normal family, as if we ever did things like that. I don't know what had gotten into her, but she demanded that we all spend the day together. It felt forced, the tension of the togetherness almost suffocating.

"So," Father barked. "How are you making out in your new role, Theo?"

My brother seemed to shrink in his seat. When Father offered him a full-time job at Blackwell Properties, I think he'd envisioned a corner office, a company car. Not another summer in a cubicle among the other interns.

"It's fine," Theo grumbled.

"It's about time you made something of yourself," Father replied pointedly, his contempt for his wayward son only thinly veiled. "Started earning your own money rather than traipsing around the world on my dime."

I could see the muscles in Theo's jaw twitching. The issue of Theo's employment had long been a hot-button issue in the Blackwell family, ever since his failed start-up venture right out of college. A luxury travel concierge service that catered to the young and rich, a business had been funded by our father, an advance on Theo's promised inheritance, and had quickly, and spectacularly, failed.

"And what about you, Lily?" Mother asked, likely an effort to divert the course of the inevitable argument that was about to ensue between Father and Theo.

"Me?" I was surprised to find them all looking at me. It was so rare that the men in this family noticed me.

"Yes, Lily," Father added. "What are your plans?"

I'd taken a year off after high school. A "gap year" Mother had called it. After everything that had happened, she and Dr. Watkins had agreed it was for the best. But we didn't talk about those things with Father. Not that it had ever been expressly forbidden, but it was understood that, while he would pick up the tab, he didn't want to hear about "all of that nonsense," as he'd referred to my ongoing therapy.

"Um, I'm still considering my options," I mumbled. I picked at my cuticles, watching as a bead of bright red blood bloomed against my pale skin.

"Stop fidgeting," Mother corrected, stilling my hands in my lap.

"What's left to consider? You've had a year to 'find yourself' or whatever it is that you've been doing."

"I—I—"

"Can I refill anyone's drinks?"

I looked up to see that our waitress had materialized at the side of the table, her hair, the color of burnished gold, pulled back from her pretty face, her smile bright and open.

"Yes. Please," Father responded.

I felt my shoulders loosen, a flood of relief that I was no longer the focus of his attention.

As Father gave the waitress his order, I excused myself from the table and started walking toward the ladies' room. But at the last moment, I slipped out the back door of the restaurant onto the loading dock, into the fresh air. I leaned against the rough stucco of the building's exterior and squeezed my eyes shut, exhaling a long breath, as the seagulls squawked overhead.

"You okay?" a gentle voice asked.

I opened my eyes to see our waitress standing in the doorway.

"Oh, yeah, fine," I said, straightening my posture and smoothing my face, years of private-school training kicking in. "Sorry, I probably shouldn't be out here."

"It's no problem," the waitress said, stepping outside. "As long as you don't mind if I join you. I could use a break too."

We stood there together, this stranger and I, looking out over the ocean. Normally this type of situation would be stressful for me, my anxiety rising as I struggled to find the right thing to say. But not with her. The silence felt natural, her presence comforting, as if we were already old friends. I stole a glance in her direction from the corner of my eye. She seemed so calm, so at ease, as she leaned over the railing, her face tilted up toward the sun.

"I'm Maddie," she said. I'd noticed it was less formal than how she'd introduced herself to my family earlier, with the name "Madison" printed on her name tag. It was the smallest gesture, but I felt myself opening to her, as if the offer of her name was an invitation.

"Lily."

"This is probably none of my business but . . . things seemed a little intense back there."

I looked away, ashamed. "I should probably get back . . ."

"No, I'm sorry." She reached out and lightly touched my wrist, stopping me in my tracks. The gentleness of her touch, the feeling of her skin on mine, felt so intimate. I couldn't remember the last time anyone had touched me.

"It's just . . . there's this party tonight," Maddie explained. "Down at the beach. A few of us are going. I thought maybe you'd want to come. Blow off some steam."

"A party?" I repeated lamely. I knew of the beach bonfires. Everyone who lived here did. But I'd never been to one. I'd never had a reason to go.

"If you want to. No pressure or anything. I didn't mean to overstep. I just thought it'd be fun."

"Uh okay," I replied. "Maybe." I couldn't understand it—why this beautiful, confident girl wanted to be my friend. She seemed to be a few years older than me, in her early twenties maybe. Surely she had her own friends to hang out with on a Friday night.

"I hope you do come," Maddie said, smiling brightly. "I'm the new girl around here. I haven't met too many people yet. It'll be nice to see a familiar face."

And so I'd gone. Feeling out of place in my sundress and sandals once I saw her, her bare feet in the sand, her long, tan legs below cut-off denim shorts, a faded surf-shop sweatshirt hanging loose on her frame.

She looped her arm through mine when she spotted me in the crowd, pushed a red Solo cup into my hand, the top brimming with frothy beer. I never drank, not beyond a sip of wine at dinner here and there. It was one of Dr. Watkins's rules: Don't lose control of any situation. But that night I didn't care about the rules. I drank that first beer, and several more, until I felt my body, my mind loosen. The thoughts that usually crowded my head melted away until it all felt so far away, so inconsequential. All that mattered was the feeling of the sand beneath my toes, the sound of Maddie's laughter. We danced on the beach, giving ourselves over to the music, to the magic of the night.

It had almost ended badly. She received a phone call. She was upset, afraid she'd have to leave the Hamptons. But I'd come to the rescue. I found a way for her to stay. She'd been so happy then, throwing her arms around me and holding me tight.

"Thank you, Lily," she said, breaking the embrace and

sliding her hands into mine. "I don't know how I'll ever be able to repay you."

"It's nothing," I replied shyly. But it wasn't. Not to me. I'd only known Maddie for one day, and I already hated the thought of her leaving, walking out of my life as quickly as she'd come into it. Maddie had been the best thing that had happened to me in years. Since . . . before.

The music changed and Maddie's face lit up, her smile growing wide. "I love this song!" She closed her eyes and moved to the music, the curves of her body swaying to the rhythm. I watched her, my new friend, my chest filling with warmth that I'd been the one to make her so happy. I've held onto that image of her, twirling beneath the stars, awash in the orange glow of the bonfire, as though she's been frozen in time, a golden, glittering moment I can always return to, and it will always be perfect.

But this isn't Maddie standing here with me now. It's her sister. And she's looking for answers that I can't give her.

"I'm Lily," I say quietly, my voice cracking, my eyes trained down at my feet. "I don't think I told you before."

"Hi, Lily," Alex replies amicably, as she folds her arms across her chest, warming her rain-prickled flesh.

"Look, Maddie isn't here. Not anymore. She was staying here for a while, but she left a few days ago. I wish I could help you, but—"

The front door swings open, revealing Mother in the frame. Despite the late hour, she's dressed in trendy wide-legged pants and a pressed white blouse, her chic platinum bob looking perfect as ever, almost as if she'd been expecting a visitor. She looks at us standing there on the porch, rain dripping from the ends of our hair, her eyes flitting from me to Alex. If she's at all surprised to find us there, her face doesn't show it. Instead she's all polished manners and icy charm. As usual.

"Hello there," she says by way of greeting. "I'm Katherine Blackwell. Please, come inside, it's far too dangerous to be out in a storm like this." A crack of lightning streaks overhead, as if to punctuate her point.

4.

KATHERINE

I've just finished drawing a bath when I hear it. The ring of the front gate, the security system flickering to life. *Who would be out in a storm like this is beyond me.* Probably a solicitor. Those people never tire of trying to win James's business. I decide to ignore it, leaning over the free-standing tub to run my fingers through the soapy water instead. It's one of my rituals, part of my beauty regimen, the regular soaking, exfoliating, waxing, applying of lotions. It's not easy being a woman, all of the little fixes, tweaks, plucks, and pulls that are expected of us. We live in a world where we're constantly reminded that our bodies must be altered, improved, in order to be appealing. Whisk away that unsightly hair, smooth the imperfections, cover the signs of age. We're told to be less, to have less, to take up less space in the world until we've nearly disappeared. And it only gets worse as you age, mind you. The pounds are harder to keep off, the flaws in your skin harder to conceal, and despite all of your efforts, no one sees you anymore. Not really. They don't look at you the same way they did when you were in your twenties, all soft curves and pillowy lips, a woman worth wanting. But you try. You deprive yourself of the rich foods that make meals worth eating, you punish your body with Pilates and spin classes until you feel faint. Until one day you wake up and realize that you've made yourself so small that even you can't see yourself anymore.

But James will be home for dinner tonight, a rare occurrence, especially as of late, and I'm determined to look my best. I haven't eaten all day, so that when I slip into my little black dress, the one he'd complimented at that charity auction last year, he'll notice how I haven't let myself go. Not like some of the other wives. How I have the discipline it takes to keep myself looking the way I do. It's all part of the price I pay for the life we have, for the family I've built.

I see the pride in James's eyes when we attend his corporate functions, when his colleagues, his clients, tell him how lucky he is to have such a lovely wife. *A lovely wife.* A *society* wife. That particular compliment always brings about such a strange mixture of emotions for me. Satisfaction, at first, that someone should think James the lucky one. (For my husband is never more interested in owning a thing as when it is something someone else covets.) But the rush of it is quickly followed by shame. Shame that my worth is reliant entirely on my ability to look beautiful on my husband's arm. A currency that seems to be slipping through my fingers ever more rapidly as the years pass.

There was a time in my life when I thought I'd be something more, when I thought James would think more of me as well. I went to college. Got a degree in interior design. Back when I thought James and I would be a team. He with his real estate acquisitions, and I with my talent for bringing out their hidden potential. But it never came to pass. It seems that James saw my career ambitions as more of a . . . hobby, at best.

"You can decorate Blackwell Manor however you'd like, spare no expense," he'd told me, "but you certainly don't need to work." The last word fell distastefully from his tongue, as if the very suggestion of his wife having a job was something indecent, gauche . . . As if my success might somehow diminish his. *You don't have to worry about money.* Words so many women of our social standing long to hear. Until you hear them. Until your dreams, your aspirations, are made smaller and smaller, just like you. Until they, too, disappear.

Voices float up through the house now, Lily and our unexpected visitor, and I know I can ignore it no longer. I quickly dress, smooth my hair, and make my way to the front door.

When I see her, the girl in the rain, I have the most irrational thought that she must have come for James. This young thing standing on the porch with our daughter, her wet shirt clinging to her breasts, highlighting the curves I no longer have, must be here for my husband. Because while I have become less, an apparition of my former self, James has become more. The gentle way he's eased into middle age amazes me. The gray that peppers his once jet-black hair, and the soft laugh lines that have appeared around his eyes, only serve to make him even more attractive, distinguished, as the years roll past us. I haven't missed the way women still look at him, the way their eyes linger a beat too long, the way he smiles indulgently, inviting the attention. That's the thing about being invisible, you learn to observe the little things, the things other people overlook.

But I don't protest, I don't cause a scene. Instead I slip on the mask I'm expected to wear—a skill I've refined to a sharpened edge—and I smile at our unexpected guest, inviting her inside. I play my part, and I do it well.

The girl follows me into the house, doing her best to wipe her sopping sneakers on the entry mat before giving up entirely.

"This is Alex," my daughter explains, in that timid, shrinking way of hers, her eyes not quite meeting mine. "She's Maddie's sister."

I see it now that she's stepped into the light. The resemblance between the two sisters is remarkable, uncanny even. But there's something decidedly different about Alex. She doesn't have the same practiced poise as Madison, as she stands here dripping onto my hardwood floors with her muddy shoes and chipped drugstore manicure. Yes, it's impossible to miss the resemblance between Madison and her sister, but once you see the difference between them, it's all you can see. Alex's eyes are not quite as blue, her lips not quite as full. But it's not just the physical differences that stand out to me now. There's an edge to Alex, a hardness about her that I didn't see in her sister. *Not at first anyway.*

"I apologize for my daughter's manners," I say, as I usher this surprising visitor into the open foyer. "Letting you stand outside in the rain like that."

She gazes around her with wonder, eyeing the sweeping staircase, its curved, polished banister, the orblike chandelier suspended two stories above her head. "You have a lovely home."

Lily looks up at me with her dark eyes, her pixie-like features etched with worry.

"Lily, would you please fetch our guest a towel at least?"

"Right. Sure. Sorry," she replies before scurrying up the stairs toward the linen closet.

I watch Alex's eyes widen as I escort her through our

home. She clocks the art on the walls, pieces James and I have carefully curated over the years, the black-and-white family portraits in their heavy silver frames. But it's the great room I most want her to see. I designed this space myself and I take tremendous pride in it. I smile to myself as she reacts exactly as I'd expected her to, the way nearly every newcomer to the manor responds to this room, with its soaring cathedral ceilings and its glass wall overlooking the bluff, offering panoramic views of the sea. Even during a storm, perhaps *especially* during a storm, it's an awe-inspiring sight. Alex's lips part in surprise and her feet stop in their tracks.

"Wow," she utters, her wide eyes roving slowly across the room. "This is really something."

"Thank you," I respond casually, "that's very kind of you to say." I can almost see it, the wheels in Alex's head turning, calculating what it must cost to live in a place like this. And it does come at a cost. Though she could never understand the price I've paid for this life I have.

Lily returns with a fluffy white towel and hands it to Alex.

"Thanks," she says, as she uses it to tousle-dry her hair. "So Maddie was staying here?"

"She was. In the pool house," I respond. "Though I'm afraid you've missed her."

Alex chews her bottom lip. "If you don't mind me asking, how did that come about? I mean, I can only assume that the rent here, even on your pool house, was a bit out of her budget."

"She wasn't a tenant, she's my friend," Lily replies, her voice soft and reverential. "She had an issue at the apartment she'd rented for the summer. A flood or something. I was with her when she got the call from the landlord. He said that she was being evicted until it could be fixed up or whatever. Maddie was, like, so upset, and I just offered her the pool house." My daughter looks to me for validation, as she so often does.

"Yes," I add. "And we were more than happy to have her. I have to say, I was quite disappointed when she said she'd be leaving. She's been such a wonderful companion for Lily these past weeks."

"When was the last time you saw her?" Alex asks, picking at her nail polish. I resist the urge to correct her, the way I so often have to do with Lily.

"Let's see, it was . . . about four days ago now," I respond. "Yes, Thursday morning, when she thanked me for our hospitality. I believe she said that she was intending to return to Manhattan?" I look over at my daughter, inviting her to join the conversation. She's never had a natural aptitude for navigating social situations. She sometimes requires a bit of guidance in that department. Though I had hoped she'd have grown out of it by now.

"That's right," Lily adds. "Maddie said she had to get back to her life in the city."

"Interesting," Alex says, her eyes narrowing in thought as she processes the information. "It's just that I called Maddie's roommate in Manhattan before I made the trip out here, and she told me that she hasn't heard from her."

"Oh my." I press my lips into a hard line of concern. "Now I understand why you're so worried about her."

"Would you mind if I checked out the pool house?" Alex asks. "To see if maybe she left something behind? Something that might tell me where she was headed?"

"Of course," I say. "I couldn't possibly let you leave in this storm anyway. You're more than welcome to stay the night, if you'd like."

"That would be great," Alex says with a sigh of relief. "Thank you so much."

"Lily, will you please find the keys to the pool house?"

Lily hurries off to retrieve them, and I turn my attention back to Alex. "I'm sure everything will be okay." I gently reach out and hold her wrist, giving it a reassuring squeeze. "There's probably a simple explanation for all of this."

Alex smiles politely, but worry lingers in her eyes.

"Here are the keys," Lily says as she bustles back into the room, dropping the key ring into Alex's outstretched palm. "The pool house is just outside." She points at the modern glass structure on the opposite side of the pool. "Just follow the paved path."

"Got it," Alex replies. "Thank you again."

I walk over to the French doors at the back of the great room and push them open, the howling wind bursting into the room, cold rain dotting my forearms.

Alex takes one last look back at Lily and me before she holds the towel over her head and runs toward the darkened pool house.

I was wary of Madison from the second my daughter brought her home, this stranger she'd found at a party on the beach. But if I was wary of Madison, I need to be even more suspicious of her sister. There's something about Alex, something wild and reckless hovering just beneath the surface . . . something that cannot be trusted.

We watch Alex disappear into the pool house, the lights flickering on, the curtains pulling closed along the glass walls.

"Why did you invite her to stay?" Lily asks, disbelief straining her voice.

"Because, darling, we're going to need to keep an eye on this one."

5.

ALEX

Wow. This place is just . . . wow. I drop the towel onto the cold, tiled floor of the pool house and slowly spin around. The walls are made entirely of glass, trails of rainwater running down the panes like so many rivers. The interior is of minimalist modern design: a sleek white kitchen, a cream-colored sofa bed, and a glass coffee table. I walk through the space, running my fingers along the cool countertops as I pass, toward the back wall, where I find a marble bathroom complete with a waterfall shower and a small dressing area tucked into the corner. *Maddie really hit the jackpot here.*

I try to imagine her lounging on the leather sofa or perched on the edge of the pool dipping her feet into the water, which now glows an ethereal blue. But I can't conjure the image of my sister in this place.

What I see instead is Maddie in black, her face solemn and pale, mascara smudged beneath her watery blue eyes. It was the last time I saw her. After Mom's funeral. My mind takes me back there now. To the harsh words that were exchanged, the bitterness we released, the things we couldn't take back. It was the first time I ever felt like maybe I didn't know Maddie as well as I thought I did. I remember staring at her, wondering who she was, when she'd changed.

In many ways, it felt like Maddie and I had raised each other. When things got bad with Mom, it was Maddie who packed my lunches and signed my permission slips for school, forging our mother's loopy signature with surprising ease, and it was me who sat in the crowd when Maddie cheered at her first homecoming game, who hugged her in our kitchen, tears of joy streaming down my face, when she opened her college scholarship letter.

But as time passed, things started to change. I sensed a chasm opening between us when she went off to college and I stayed behind taking the job at Nate's, but I told myself we'd build a bridge. We'd find a way to cross it. Maddie may have been going out into the world, her life on an upward trajectory while mine remained stagnant, suffocating in its familiarity, but she was my sister—the topography of her would always be familiar to me, like the beaten path we walked as children carving a shortcut through the woods. And for a time it was, we always found our way back to each other, even as Maddie moved farther and farther away from me and the life she left behind. But after the funeral, I could see that something had shifted. The map was different, the directions back to her had changed. Every road I tried seemed only to lead to a dead end. Part of me suspected this was the reason she'd canceled her trip home. Maybe she couldn't get past it, the impasses we'd hit, the distance we'd felt. Maybe we'd grown too far apart, the bridge back to the people we once were no longer able to close the gap.

But now I know that something is wrong. I can feel it here. In this place. I may not know my sister as well as I once did, but I know this. There's something about Blackwell Manor that's set me on edge, a cold dread that's been building beneath the surface of my skin since the moment I arrived here.

I look back up at the house, its lights all aglow, and I can't shake the feeling that I'm being watched. The glass walls of the pool house make me feel like a trapped animal, a specimen on display. With a shudder, I draw the white curtains across the windows.

My phone buzzes in my pocket and it nearly makes me jump out of my skin. *I need to calm down.* I pull out my phone and check the screen. Another text from Ben.

Alex? Would you please just answer me?

My thumbs hover over the keyboard. What could I possibly say? What combination of words will rewind time, bring us back to how we used to be?

Ben and I met at Nate's, where Nate asked me to train him on his first day at work.

Nate gave us our instructions and just before he shuffled down the paint aisle, he leaned toward me, rough hands in the pockets of his apron, and added in a loud whisper, "He's a smart kid. Gonna be a lawyer and everything. Wouldn't be a bad catch."

There was no way Ben hadn't heard Nate's sales pitch, but he was kind enough not to acknowledge it. Mortified, I barely made eye contact with Ben as I showed him how to work the till, how to lock up at the end of his shift.

After that, it seemed that Nate always assigned Ben and me to work the same hours. I'd spent three straight weeks working side by side with Ben when I decided it was time to give Nate a warning. "If this is your idea of playing matchmaker or something . . ."

"Nothing like that," he said with a wave of his hand, the skin stretched paper-thin over his arthritic knuckles. "I can take a hint. But you two work well together."

And we did. I came to love the friendly banter that made the once monotonous hours at the store seem to fly by. I loved the nerdy, wire-rimmed glasses he always wore, the way he kept his hair slightly too long, so that one rogue curl flopped over his forehead, and how he never seemed to mind when I teased him about it, calling him Clark Kent. There was so much I loved about Ben. Until I ruined everything.

I respond to his text:

I'm out of town for a few days, I'll call you when I get back.

He types:

Everything okay? You didn't tell me you were taking a trip.

There's so much I haven't told him. *If only he knew.*

But I don't have the energy to think about that now, about Ben. Right now, there's only room in my life for Maddie. I shove my phone back into my pocket. *One problem at a time.*

The exhaustion hits me all at once, and suddenly I want nothing more than a hot shower and some dry clothes. I'm not going to find Maddie tonight, not with this storm, and not without getting more information from the Blackwells.

There's something off about them, something as unsettling as this house. Lily with her nervous skittishness, and Katherine's frosty formality. I rub my arm where Katherine Blackwell held it, her long, bony fingers encircling my wrist, and it sends a shivering chill up my spine. I can't seem to shake the feeling that there's more here. Something they're not telling me.

I make my way to the bathroom and turn on the shower, steam quickly filling the room. I step inside and feel the muscles in my shoulders loosen as the warm water sluices over my skin. I try to think through it logically. Everything I've learned so far. According to the Blackwells, Maddie abruptly left on Thursday morning, planning to go back to New York City. But it doesn't feel right. Maddie would have told her boss at the Lobster Shack if she was quitting, if she didn't intend to return. And her roommate, Jessie, told me that she hasn't heard from her. If what the Blackwells say is true, it's been four days since Maddie left Blackwell Manor, and as far as I know, no one has heard from her since.

I shut off the water and reach for one of the towels that sit folded beside the shower. After patting myself dry, I wrap myself in a terrycloth robe I find hanging behind the bathroom door. This place is like a hotel, the kind I could never afford to stay at. Tying the sash of the robe around my waist, I pad into the dressing area, hoping Maddie left behind something that I can wear until the storm breaks and I can retrieve my overnight bag from the car. I pull open each of the dresser drawers, but I find that they're all completely empty.

Frustrated and exhausted, I make my way back to the main living area and drop down onto the sofa. But as my weight shifts the cushions, something falls out from beneath the seat and clatters to the floor. I lie on the floor, the tiles cool against my stomach, and reach under the sofa, feeling around for whatever it was that I'd accidentally unearthed. My fingers graze something hard, just out of my reach. *Maybe it's the remote for the TV?* I stretch my shoulder and reach farther beneath the couch, pulling the object closer with the tips of my fingers until I finally get ahold of something cold and plastic. I slide it out to find that it's not a remote. It's a phone. With an I ♥ NY phone case that I instantly recognize. This is Maddie's phone.

6.

ALEX

My pulse quickens. There's no way Maddie left without her phone. Not if she had a choice. My mind begins to spin out. Maybe she had to leave in a rush, maybe she didn't have time to look for her phone. *But what could she have been running from?*

The phone screen is dark, and I hold down the power button but it won't turn on. The battery must be drained. I check the charger port, but Maddie doesn't have the same kind of phone as me, and so the charger in my car will be totally useless. I'll have to pick up a charger first thing tomorrow.

Thunder booms outside, the storm battering the glass walls of the pool house. It seems to be gaining momentum. The sky is dark now, almost black, and I can hear the ocean lashing violently against the nearby bluff. Another crash of thunder, so close that I can feel the ground shake beneath my feet, is followed by a streak of lightning. For a moment, the yard is illuminated in bright, white light. And that's when I catch something out of the corner of my eye, something that causes my body to freeze, my breath to catch in my throat. A shadowy form, just visible through the curtains, was momentarily exposed by the flash of lightning. There's someone outside. Someone is watching me.

I move toward the curtains slowly, methodically, scarcely breathing, my heart pounding in my chest. I carefully wrap my fingers around the edge of the curtain before abruptly pulling it back. At first all I see is my own reflection, wide-eyed and pale, staring back at me in the darkened glass. And then, through the sheet of rain, I make out a shape, a lumbering form huddled in the doorway. A black umbrella. Rain boots.

"Alex?" a voice calls. "It's Lily. Can I come in?"

"Yes, yes, of course," I reply, relieved, as I slide open the door.

"Sorry to bother you," she says, her words small and soft, as she closes the oversized umbrella.

"You're not bothering me at all." I smile warmly, feeling the need to move cautiously, as though trying to approach an animal in the wild, gain its trust. Maybe this will be my chance to talk to her, away from Katherine's watchful gaze. I noticed the way Katherine was so quick to answer my questions earlier, scarcely giving Lily a chance to speak, and the way Lily constantly looked to her mother for reassurance. "It's your place, after all."

"Yeah. I guess." She looks down at the floor, tucking a lock of her dark hair behind her ear. She's pretty, in an unusual sort of way. Unlike Katherine's hard edges and sharp angles, Lily is petite, with delicate, almost elfin features, and fair skin set against dark almond-shaped eyes. The combination of which makes her interesting to look at, like a puzzle that's nearly been solved.

"Have you had dinner yet?" she asks.

"Er, no, I haven't." I can feel my empty stomach churning, my mouth beginning to water at the thought of a hot meal. "But I'll be fine, seriously. I wouldn't want you to go to any trouble."

"It's no trouble," Lily replies. "Mother insists that you join us for dinner. She said to tell you that she's set a place for you at the table."

Run. A voice whispered from the back of my mind warns me away. Tells me to leave this strange place, this strange girl, and never look back. "Dinner would be great," I find myself saying instead. Right now Blackwell Manor is the only connection I have to Maddie. I can't leave without finding some answers.

"Oh. I brought you these," Lily adds, holding out a small duffel bag. "Just some clothes and a spare toothbrush and stuff."

"Wow, thanks. I really appreciate it."

"No problem." Lily's eyes finally meet mine, where they linger just a moment too long. She opens her mouth as if she wants to say something, but quickly closes it again.

"I wanted to ask you," I start, my voice honeyed and coaxing, "if you know of anywhere else Maddie might have gone, anyone else she might be staying with."

"I don't." Her reply comes quickly, her eyes darting toward the door. "I have to go. But dinner will be ready in fifteen minutes. See you inside."

7.

LILY

The silence in the room is cut by the clink of silverware against porcelain as Mother serves thin strips of turkey, shiny with grease and gravy, onto our plates, intentionally avoiding looking at the two empty place settings left by Father and Theo.

"Thank you again for this," Alex says. Her voice sounds tinny and small in the large dining room that is intended to hold far more than three people. "And for the clothes, Lily."

I nod in reply. My skirt and blouse are a bit snug on her, but in a way that flatters her. The clothes don't hang off her frame as they do mine.

"I know it's late," Mother cuts in, leaning over the table in attire far more formal than dinner at home typically requires, "but I *had* expected my husband and son to be joining us tonight. However, it seems they've been held up, and I thought it a shame to let all of this food go to waste."

She says this as if she's spent the day slaving over a hot stove, as if our housekeeper, Mariana, hadn't been here earlier preparing the meal that my mother intended to serve to my father. But I bite my tongue. I don't tell her that Mariana is the one who should be angry. Not her. Instead, I watch a drip of wax slide down the length of one of the tapered candles and solidify onto the cut-crystal base. I picture Mother sitting alone at the head of the table in her fancy dress, the turkey glistening with fat under the lights of the chandelier, waiting for Father to arrive. For a moment I feel sorry for her, but I know she would hate that, and so I push the thought from my mind. My mother has never been a woman to be pitied. She knew what she was getting into when she married my father.

She'd come from old money with a dwindling legacy. Which meant that she was used to a certain level of comfort in her life, but the only way for her to maintain it was to marry a man on the rise. A man like James Blackwell. None of this, of course, did anyone ever tell me, because no one in this family ever tells me anything, but I've pieced it together from snippets of conversations I wasn't intended to hear, by the way Grandmother looks at my father as though he's captaining a lifeboat, and by the way my mother pretends not to notice when my father disappoints her time and time again. I've come to see my parents' marriage as something transactional, its clauses negotiated and delineated with careful precision so that both parties can extract what they need from it. I wonder if they ever loved each other. If there was ever a time when they felt as though they couldn't breathe if they weren't together.

I risk a sideways glance at Mother as she pours ruby-red wine into each of our glasses. No, I don't think she's the type of woman to have ever lost her senses. And that's what love is, isn't it? Losing yourself in someone else. At least that's how I've always thought about it. But what do I know, really? Only what I've read in romance novels, seen in movies. I've never been in a real relationship. Maybe love, the kind of love I'm imagining, isn't real. Maybe once you tease it out of a fictional world, ground it in reality, it becomes something harder, duller. Something practical instead of magical.

I could have asked Maddie. If she was here. I'm certain she would've known. Maddie was exactly the type of girl people fall in love with. She was beautiful, perfect. But it was more than that. She had this aura about her. This charm that pulled you into her orbit. It wasn't just me. The others felt it too. I could tell. Maddie was special.

The day after the bonfire, Maddie arrived at Blackwell Manor with her things. I watched from my bedroom window as the taxi dropped her off. She raised her hand to her brows, shading her eyes as she looked up at the house, the afternoon sun shining in her hair. I wondered what she thought of it, Blackwell Manor. What she thought of me that I lived in a place like this.

When I was a child, Mother used to arrange playdates with other children, children from my private school whose mothers she wanted to socialize with. I had difficulty making friends on my own, and she thought it important that I learn to socialize with someone other than Theo. So once a week, a friend would be brought to Blackwell Manor for me to play with. Little girls with golden curls and with fancy mommies who would sip chilled wine with Mother on the patio while we were left to play. I could always tell that they didn't want to be there, forced to befriend this strange, dark girl who lived in the mansion alone atop the bluff. I could tell in the way that they were afraid to touch anything in the house, scarcely looking at the room full of toys that were supposed to entertain me so my parents didn't have to. They'd tiptoe down the empty halls, their footsteps echoing as they went, to hover near their mothers until it was time to leave. Few ever came back to Blackwell Manor, and at school, they'd barely look in my direction. I didn't know what it was about me, about this place, but other children seemed to feel as unsettled here as I did.

Not Maddie though. When she looked up at Blackwell Manor, she seemed awed by it, transfixed. I watched her wheel her luggage, one lone suitcase, up the cobbled path. Maddie arriving here was the most exciting thing that had ever happened at Blackwell Manor. At least to me. After all, Maddie was the first guest that was here for me. Not by my parents' invitation, not for my brother who always seemed to be surrounded by a pack of laughing, rowdy friends. Maddie was mine. And for the first time, the house didn't feel so empty, the dark clouds that seemed to hover over this place in my mind parted. Maddie's arrival felt like a burst of fresh air that threw open the shutters of Blackwell Manor, flooding it with light, chasing the shadows away. There was a reason I'd met her, that she'd happened into my life. I thought she was meant to be here, that the universe had sent her to me. But I'd been wrong. So very wrong. Maddie coming here wasn't a new beginning—it was the end of everything.

I grab my wineglass and greedily take a gulp to steady my nerves, but I fumble with the stem and a drop of wine splashes onto the white linen tablecloth, blooming like a drop of blood. I swallow down the bile rising in my throat and shut my eyes, willing away the visions that threaten to consume me: the rainwater tinged with blood, the silver moonlight giving it all an otherworldly haze, as if maybe it had been a dream, maybe it never happened after all.

Dr. Watkins says it's a defense mechanism. These tricks my mind plays on me, where it blurs fantasy and reality, weaving them together into tight knots that I can never seem to untangle. She says it stems from the earliest days of my life, the ones I was too young to remember, when I was still at the orphanage. When my mind had to find a way to transport me away from the hopelessness of my reality. But sometimes I'm not so sure. Theo was there, too, and he was older than I was when we were finally adopted. He spent more time in that place, and yet he doesn't seem to have the same problems. I can tell by the way he looks at me at times that he sees it as a weakness that reflects poorly on both of us. Maybe I'm not a product of my circumstances, maybe this is just who I am.

"Are you okay, Lily?" It's Alex. She's looking at me with a mix of emotions playing across her face—curiosity, concern, pity.

"I'm fine," I mumble, setting my glass back down again. I don't know how I'm going to do this. How I'm going to make it through dinner sitting across from her, this girl who is almost a holographic version of Maddie. They look so similar, and yet I know that if I were to reach out and touch her, the illusion would shatter at my fingertips.

"Well then," Mother cuts in as she flairs out the hem of her dress and perches on the edge of her seat at the head of the table. "Let's enjoy a nice meal, shall we?"

She picks up her fork and knife with her long, lithe fingers, cutting the sliver of meat she's served herself into minuscule bites. My mother doesn't eat. Not more than is absolutely required to sustain life. It's as if the act of chewing, swallowing, is a burden for her, a chore to be checked off her endless to-do list. I don't think anyone else in my family has noticed the way she moves her food around her plate, an illusion meant to conceal the fact that she's hardly eaten. No one pays that much attention to anyone else here. They don't notice the details, the storms brewing on the horizon until it's too late. I thought I did. I thought I was different. But I'm not. I know that now. After Maddie.

The thud of the front door slamming closed makes me jump in my seat.

"Ah," says Mother, sounding rather pleased. "Perhaps we won't be dining alone after all."

8.

THEO

I close my eyes, the cold rain pounding against my face, and lift the champagne bottle to my lips, the crisp, bubbling liquid mixing with rainwater as it slides down my throat.

Hutch takes a sharp turn, and my rib cage slams against the edge of the sunroof.

"Get down, you moron." Mick laughs, tugging on my shirttails as lightning slices through the inky-black sky. I ignore him. By now my shirt is soaked through, the thin cotton near translucent at my shoulders, and my cheeks sting against the cold, but I don't care.

Hutch accelerates down the one-lane road, his tires squealing against the pavement. It's a heady rush: the danger of it, the bite of the expensive champagne. I shake my head like a dog, water winging from the ends of my dark hair, feeling wild, primal, and I tilt my head back and howl at the moon.

"You've really lost it," Mick calls up. I can hear the smile in his voice. He's enjoying the show. I'm always good for that. Upping the ante, pushing the limits. The others get a rush out of it too.

Tonight was just what we needed. A night on the town,

just the boys, feeling like we hold the keys to the kingdom. In many ways, we do. Mick and me, our families are hailed like local royalty out here in the Hamptons, and Hutch's father was just elected governor. There's no velvet rope we can't cross, no VIP list we aren't on.

"Later, bro," Hutch says as he pulls to an abrupt stop outside Blackwell Manor.

"I don't think I'll ever get over this house . . ." Mick adds.

I clap Hutch on the shoulder as I slide back down into his car, bumping my fist against Mick's before I hop out onto the long stretch of my driveway.

I stroll up to the front door, the half-empty champagne bottle dangling from one arm, my fist clamped around the neck, and let myself inside.

"Good evening, family," I call out as I set the dripping champagne bottle on the entry table and make my way toward the dining room. I can hear the slight slur in my words, my tongue cumbersome in my mouth.

Now that I see the set table, the flickering candles, I vaguely recall Mother mentioning something about a dinner tonight, but I'd forgotten about it entirely when Hutch had called, said we were going out.

And then I see her. The shock of it sobers me quickly. I'm caught off guard—and rarely am I ever. For a moment, I think she's someone else. I can tell it registers on my face by the way they're all looking at me. But I recover quickly. I flash her a smile, the one where I tip up one side of my mouth and tilt my head ever so slightly.

Despite what most people think of me, I'm keenly self-aware. Everyone sees the rich kid, the jet-setter, the life of the party, but what they don't see is the intention behind it all. The orchestration of these tiny movements, the practiced smile that is just the right blend of winsome and disarming, but not so enthusiastic that it appears disingenuous. I walk with my chin held at just the right angle to portray confidence, but never arrogance, my handshake is assertive but not aggressive. Maybe these things come naturally to some people, but they didn't to me. Not at first. These are skills I've acquired, refined over years of studying other people. How they interact with one another, the faces they make, the gestures they use. I remember standing in front of the mirror as a teenager, rehearsing this very smile, knowing I'd found the winning combination, the one that would open so many doors for me.

"Hello, there," I say, turning up the wattage on my smile. "I'm Theo."

"Alex," the girl replies, studying my face in a way that makes me feel like she sees right through me to the hollow at my center.

"Pleasure to meet you." I toss her a wink before sinking into my seat at the table. I don't know why she's here, but I'm certain it has something to do with Maddie. *Maddie.* She was problematic from the moment she showed up. I don't know exactly how she managed it, but she somehow got herself an invitation to live here. Not that I should have been too surprised. It's Lily, after all. I just thought she'd have been smarter, after all that embarrassment at her last school. She's my sister, the only blood relative I'll ever know, and it's my job to look after her, but does she have to make it so damn hard? Here she was, following around this perfect stranger like a puppy, lapping up her attention, inviting her to move in. It was absurd. Sickening even. I could barely stand to watch it. But Father could, couldn't he?

The first night after Maddie moved into the pool house,

we sat down for a dinner a lot like this one. With the notable exception that my father deigned to show up that time. And so did Maddie. I have to say, she cleaned up rather nicely. Gone were the scruffy tank top and denim shorts I caught her sporting as she unpacked her belongings in our pool house. Not that I was spying on her, by any means. But I was understandably curious about this newcomer. With my father away from home so often, I felt it my duty to keep a watchful eye on everything that went on in the house. But when she showed up for dinner, she looked like an entirely different person. Her face was scrubbed clean, and she wore only a light touch of natural makeup, a rosiness to her cheeks, an added blush to her bowed lips. Her hair was pulled back from her face into a neat, shiny bun, and she wore a loose-fitting blouse with pearl buttons that made her look demure, sensible beyond her young age. When she introduced herself to Father as "Madison," I scoffed to myself. It all seemed so transparent to me. I assumed the others would see it as well, this poor girl reaching above her station, playing dress-up at our table. But then I saw Father's face. He looked at her with something akin to wonder, his eyes sparkling as he welcomed our new houseguest to the table, standing to pull out the chair next to his.

All through dinner he could hardly keep his eyes off her. It was disgusting, especially that he should behave in such a way in front of Mother. For some reason that I couldn't fathom, he seemed fascinated with the mundane details of this girl's life.

"Medical school, huh?" Father asked her as he swirled the bourbon in his glass. My father is a man who is rarely impressed, but this information seemed to have struck a chord with him.

"I've only just started," Maddie replied humbly, sliding the tiny gold charm on her necklace up and down the chain at her throat. "I always knew I wanted to be a doctor, but it took me some time to save up the money for tuition."

"There's no shame in that. You're a self-made woman. I respect it," my father said, lifting his glass in a sign of tribute.

I felt my blood pressure rising, my jaw tightening. It was a barely concealed dig at me and Lily, and the injustice of it grated on my nerves. It wasn't our fault that we'd been handed the lives we have. He brought us to this house, offered us the best of everything, and then resented us for having accepted it. I looked over at my mother to see if she was as irate as I was, considering she, too, was not a "self-made" woman worthy of Father's respect, but she seemed too preoccupied fussing with the scraps of food on her plate to notice that he was basically tripping over himself to get acquainted with Lily's new friend.

"I paved my own way, too, you know," Father added. "All of this"—he gestured at the house around him, his arms like unfurling wings—"was the result of hard work. Something most people of your generation don't understand."

My hands curled into fists under the table.

"In fact, when I was Theo's age," he continued with a cast-off nod in my direction, "I'd already started buying up land out here. It was nothing impressive then, mind you, but I had a vision. I knew someday the investment would pay off."

It was a story Lily and I had heard hundreds of times over the years. James Blackwell, the savvy businessman, buying up cheap land and spinning the sand into gold.

"That's very impressive," Maddie replied, the appropriate dose of deference in her voice.

Father looked pleased with himself. "Do make yourself at home here, Madison. You're welcome to stay as long as you'd like."

"That's very generous," she responded reservedly, her hands folded neatly in her lap.

"If you'd like, I'll even take you down to the office one day. I'll give you a tour, show you some of the projects we're working on."

"I'd love that," she said with a smile so sugary sweet that it turned my stomach.

How easily he'd invited that girl into his world, into our lives.

I thought it was all behind us by now. But it looks like I was wrong.

9.

ALEX

When I wake up the next morning, it feels like I've been transported to a different world. Golden sunshine filters in through the drawn curtains, giving the room a warm, honeyed feeling. I slide out of bed and pull open the curtains. The yard, which I couldn't fully appreciate last night, is breathtaking. A massive pool sits at its center, a pink flamingo float glides lazily over the water's surface, and beside it are cream-colored lounge chairs and an array of canopied sun beds. If not for the maintenance crew in gray polo shirts busy clearing the ground of the remaining debris, you'd never have guessed the severity of last night's storm. Today, the tropical flowers and open umbrellas seem to sparkle under the sprinkle of the raindrops that have not yet dried in the morning sun, and the ocean beyond the bluff stands at a glassy calm, as if it's exhausted after the exertion of its rage the night before.

I imagine what it must be like to wake up to this view every morning, if the Blackwell family has any idea how fortunate they are. Somehow I doubt it. I think back to last night, to what had to be the most uncomfortable dinner ever. It all felt so . . . forced. Like they were actors playing a role. Some better than others. There was something about the brother, Theo, that I didn't like. And it wasn't just the arrogance, the swaggering bravado. It was something deeper. When he first looked at me, when he thought, for a moment, I might have been Maddie, I saw a flash of something pass across his face . . . not just surprise, but anger. He gathered himself quickly, whisked all trace of it away, but it was too late. I'd already seen it, seen him.

I drum my fingers against the plate glass of the window. I don't know what to make of the Blackwells, of what they've told me about Maddie and her sudden departure. I stare down at the phone in my hand. Willing it to ring. *Where are you, Maddie?* I can hear my mother's voice as clearly as if she was standing next to me. *A watched pot never boils.*

I remember when she'd first said it to me. It was after homecoming freshman year of high school. Maddie was a sophomore, and she'd already made the varsity cheerleading squad, her new friends suddenly an all-consuming part of her life. I'd gone to the game to watch Maddie under the Friday night lights—her shiny hair in a bouncy ponytail tied with an oversized bow, glitter spread across her cheeks, which had turned a rosy pink in the crisp fall breeze. She looked so happy out there, so alive, so far from the darkness and gloom that had settled over our lives at home. By then it wasn't even a question that Mom wasn't coming to the game. Maddie hadn't asked her, and Mom wouldn't have come even if she had. She didn't like to go to school events anymore. She didn't like having to face the other mothers, the ones that ran the school bake sales, chaperoned field trips.

And so that night, I sat alone in the bleachers watching Maddie smile and cheer. It was the version of her I loved the most, the one where she was unbound by the responsibilities she usually carried on her shoulders.

After the game, as she ran off the field, pom-poms shaking, I waved from the stands. "Maddie! Over here!"

She'd smiled at me, waved back, but before she could pick her way through the crowd, she'd been surrounded by the other cheerleaders, a pack of pretty girls in matching pleated skirts, riding the high of having finished their first big performance of the year.

I watched as she talked with them, laughed with them, before she pulled herself away to come find me in the bleachers.

"Sorry, Alex," she'd said, wrapping me in a hug. "I'm so glad you came." I could feel the cool autumn air still clinging to her skin. "Are you cool going home on your own though? Trish is having an after-party for the team at her house and I thought I'd go. But if you'd rather I walk you home first, I totally will."

"No," I'd said, looking back at the huddle of girls, all vibrating with excitement on their big night. "Go have fun, I'll be fine."

"You're the best," Maddie said, giving me one last squeeze before she dashed back over to her friends.

But as the night wore on, Maddie still hadn't come home. When Mom came back from her shift at the diner, she found me staring out the front window. I wondered what Maddie was up to, whether she was okay, whether I should have let her go off on her own.

"A watched pot never boils," Mom said, pulling me from my thoughts.

"Huh?"

"Time passes pretty slowly when you're just standing around waiting for life to happen to you. And staring out the window isn't going to make your sister come home any faster. She's a teenager. This is what she's supposed to do. It's good to see her finally getting her nose out of the books, living a little. There's no need to look so worried. She'll come back."

But what if this time she doesn't? I brush the thought away. I won't let that happen. And I know someone who may be able to help.

I reach for my cellphone, swiping it off the coffee table, and pull up Jessie's number.

Jessie has been Maddie's roommate in New York City for the last two years. I'd called her three days ago hoping she could help me get in touch with Maddie before I made the drive out here to the Hamptons, and I was surprised to learn Maddie had stopped taking Jessie's calls as well. But if Maddie really did go back to the city, surely Jessie would have news by now.

"Hey, it's Alex."

"Hey, girl," Jessie chimes as she accepts the call. "Have you heard from Maddie yet?"

"No, I haven't. I'm out in the Hamptons with the family she was staying with, but they said she left on Thursday to head back to the city."

"Why would she come back here?" Confusion lances her words.

"They said she had to get back to her life there, or something like that."

"I, uh, I guess she didn't tell you . . ."

"Tell me what?" My grip on the phone tightens.

"Look, Maddie didn't exactly have a life to come back to here. When she left, she told us she didn't know when she'd be coming back. We couldn't afford the rent on this place for long without a third roommate, which Maddie knew, and so she told us to rent out her room."

"But what about med school?" I ask, shocked at this latest development.

"She really didn't tell you any of this?" Jessie responds, sounding uncomfortable. "Maybe it's not my place."

"Jessie, my sister is missing. No one has seen her in almost five days now. So if there's something you know—"

"No, no, you're right. It's just that I'm shocked that she didn't tell you herself. Maddie took a leave of absence from school."

"What? When?"

"It was right after your mother passed. I'm sorry for your loss, by the way."

My mind goes back there. To the state Maddie was in. To the surprising weight of her grief. To the argument we'd had. I knew she was having a hard time, but I didn't know she was struggling that badly that she'd derail the life she'd worked so hard to build for herself.

"Thanks," I reply. Because that's really all I *can* say when I hear those words *I'm sorry for your loss*. So many people around town said those same words to me. When they'd find themselves in line in front of me at the supermarket, or when they'd see me behind the register at Nate's Hardware. *I'm sorry for your loss.* The same people who'd pretended not to notice when Mom got sick, the cirrhosis, her body's inevitable retaliation after years of abuse, eating away at the person she once was. They were sorry for my loss, but they didn't understand what it was that I'd lost. In truth, I'm only just starting to understand it myself. Dogwood Grove is a small town and the people that lived there thought they knew my mother, who she was, what she was worth. Mad-

die and I, we'd heard the whispers all of our lives. The judgment passed about the things she wore when she sang at the
open-mic nights at the local tavern (Vivienne Walker never
met a stage she didn't like), the amount she drank, the state
of disrepair she'd let our house fall into, the lawn growing
into a shaggy carpet of green. But they didn't know who
Mom really was—the fact that she loved watching black-and-
white films and hated the taste of coffee. That she'd always
kept a romance novel tucked away in her purse, or that she'd
once studied classical ballet. All of the things that made her
who she was.

"Jessie, do you think it was because of our mom? Was
that why Maddie left school?"

"I guess." She pauses. Seems to mull over the question.
"She was different when she came back after the funeral."

"Different how?" Maddie stayed home for only two days
after Mom's burial. After our falling out, the two of us shuffled around the silent house like ghosts. We were each pro-
cessing Mom's death in our own way and found it hard to
reach out to each other. But it feels like a stab to my heart to
realize that I didn't know how poorly my sister was coping. I
should have been there for her instead of pushing her away.

"I don't know. She just wasn't . . . herself, ya know? She
was quiet. Didn't want to talk about any of it. The girls and
I, we did our best to be there for her. And she told us that she
was doing okay, that she was fine, but she's my best friend, I
could tell that she wasn't. Not really. She just seemed kind
of . . . lost, I guess."

Lost because of me. Because of the way I'd treated her.

"Thanks for telling me, Jessie. I'll let you know when I get
ahold of her."

"No problem. And Alex? There's something else I wanted

to mention. I know you're not into social media and stuff, but Maddie deleted all of her profiles when she left. I thought it was super weird."

"That *is* strange. Thanks for letting me know."

"You got it. Call me the minute you hear from her."

"I will."

Another dead end. As frustrating as it is, at least I know what I have to do next. I'm going to buy a charger for Maddie's phone today. Right after my visit to the police station.

10.
___

ALEX

The village police station looks more like a nod to security than it does a place where actual criminals are investigated. Its coastal design and clapboard exterior allow it to blend in seamlessly with the other downtown shops, offices, and restaurants. I imagine the most serious crime that occurs in a place like this is a member of the public trespassing on the stretches of pristine private beaches. It baffles me that something so wild as the sea, the sand, the air, could be owned by just one person.

I step inside to a blast of cold air-conditioning. Although it's nice to have my own clothes back, I've quickly realized that nothing I've packed, hell, nothing I *own,* seems to fit the dress code around here. I feel oddly underdressed in my shorts and flip-flops, even in the police station.

"Can I help you, ma'am?" a young officer behind the front desk asks. He's thin and wiry, his lanky arms poking out of the sleeves of his blue uniform shirt, which appears about two sizes too big, and he peers at me through thick-framed glasses.

"Yes, I, uh, my name is Alex Walker, and I'm in town looking for my sister, Madison Walker."

He nods slightly, as though waiting for me to get to the point.

"She was staying with a family who lives in town. They said she left a few days ago, but I haven't been able to get in touch with her."

"So . . ." the officer says, slowly. "Your sister left town then?"

"I mean, maybe. That's what the family she was staying with told me. But no one has seen or heard from her since Thursday. I'm worried something's happened."

The officer raises one eyebrow as though his curiosity has been mildly piqued. "Where did you say your sister was staying again?"

"With a family who lives nearby. The Blackwells. At Blackwell Manor."

There's a visible change in the officer's demeanor. His spine seems to snap to attention, and he stops fiddling with the pen on his desk. "The Blackwells. Oh."

Clearly the Blackwell name opens doors around here.

"I didn't . . . My apologies. Please come wait in the chief's office." The officer hops down from his chair behind the tall desk and points down the narrow corridor. "It's the first door on your right. Chief Gilroy will be in to see you right away."

"Thank you," I say, feeling validated, as I march past him.

It's not long before Chief Michael Gilroy strides into the tiny room, holding two Styrofoam cups of coffee. After brief introductions, he places one of the cups on the desk in front of me, the liquid inside still steaming.

"I hope you like it black," he says with a half smile, which reveals a dimple in his right cheek. "I wouldn't even venture a guess as to how long the milk has been in the refrigerator in the break room." He pulls his large hands through his wheat-blond hair, which is tinted silver with age.

"Black is fine. Thank you," I reply as I lift the cup to my lips and blow gently across the surface of the coffee inside.

I can't help but notice the mosaic of framed photographs hanging behind Chief Gilroy's desk. One shows a much younger version of the chief kneeling on one knee, with a Hamptons High football helmet tucked under his arm; one is a shot from his wedding day, his broad shoulders in a white tuxedo, his arm draped over a petite brunette; and the others seem to show a time line of his children's lives. Two tow-headed boys building a sandcastle, a little girl with her mother's big brown eyes hanging upside down from a jungle gym.

He smiles warmly as he follows my line of sight, turning to appraise the photos himself. "A whole lifetime up there on the wall," he says with a sigh. "Though the kids are a bit bigger now. I should probably get around to updating those one of these days. Anyway," he continues, swiveling to face me, his long legs stretching beneath the table, "what can I do for you?"

I fill him in on everything I know about Maddie's disappearance. That she'd been staying at Blackwell Manor, that no one has seen her in nearly five days, that she'd left her phone behind, and even that she'd given up her apartment back in New York City. As I speak, Chief Gilroy nods and takes notes on the legal pad in front of him. His brow furrows with each new bit of worrying information.

"I understand your concern," he says, his sympathetic eyes locked on mine. They are the most interesting shade of celery green. "We can certainly file a report if you'd like, but I will tell you, in most cases like these, the missing person turns up within a few days. We see this a lot around here, young people taking spontaneous trips, meeting up with friends, that sort of thing."

"I don't know . . ." I start uneasily. "None of that sounds like Maddie."

"I'll tell you what," Chief Gilroy replies, "I'll write up a report, I'll start asking around. James Blackwell is a respected member of the community. If a guest at his home has gone missing, I can assure you that we'll do everything in our power to locate her. In fact, I'm certain he'd *insist* upon it." He gives me a conspiratorial wink as if to say: *Rich people, am I right?* "Leave your contact information with me, and I'll call you if we find anything at all."

"Thank you." I exhale with relief as I write down my cell number. This feels like the first real progress I've made toward finding Maddie since I arrived in the Hamptons.

———————

When I leave the police station, the afternoon sun is high in the sky, and the temperature seems to be steadily climbing. The sidewalks sizzle in the heat, and I squint my eyes against the blinding sunlight. Somewhere in the distance, a seagull cries, and between the pastel-painted shopfronts, the blue-green sea twinkles. For a moment, I'm tempted to take out my phone and snap a photo for Ben. And then I remember that I can't do that anymore. Not after what I did.

We'd gone out for a drink after work at the local pub. A routine that had become something of a standing date on Friday nights—the one weeknight that Ben didn't have class for law school—where we drank frothy pints of tap beers and shared a plate of greasy fries smothered in melted cheese.

But that night, the bar was more crowded than usual, our favorite booth taken over by men in basketball jerseys angling for the best view of the game playing on the overhead televisions.

"Sit at the bar?" Ben asked.

I shrugged. "Fine by me."

I shouldn't have had so much to drink.

"You okay there, kid?" Ben asked as I ordered another vodka soda. "Seems like you're on a mission tonight." He called me "kid" even though I was only four months younger than him. What started as a running joke had, somewhere along the line, transformed into an affectionate nickname.

I didn't want to tell him what was on my mind, that I was replaying the argument I'd had with Maddie in my head. I hadn't told him about our falling out, and the idea of explaining it all in that moment felt daunting. Maddie had left Dogwood Grove years before Ben came to town. And as much as I talked to Ben about Maddie, told him how close we were, he'd never seen it for himself—he couldn't understand the bond we had. I didn't know how to rationalize to him that I just had a feeling in my gut that something was wrong. That I was growing increasingly concerned with every day that passed without hearing from her. Besides, was it too much to ask to have one night? I wanted it so badly. Just one night away from my real life, untarnished by the guilt that had started to corrode everything around me.

"I'm fine," I replied, the words tumbling messily from my lips, before I took a long sip.

"Well, bottoms up then," Ben said, raising his own glass to me before drinking it down. After a year of working together, he seemed to be able to sense when I was shutting down. When pushing the issue would only push me further away. I appreciated him in that moment, his silent, sturdy solidarity.

By the time we got to the last fry, Ben and I both sloppily grabbed for it at the same time. His large hand shot out and got there before mine.

"To the winner goes the spoils," he teased as he popped it into his mouth.

"No fair. A gentleman would split it," I quipped as I leaned in close as if preparing to snatch it from his mouth.

"Who said I was a gentleman?" Ben replied, just as I began to lose my balance on the barstool.

He caught me in his arms. "I gotcha."

"See?" I said with a giggle. "Gentleman."

The words seemed to melt on my tongue as I registered how close our faces were, closer than we'd ever been before. Suddenly, I realized how safe I felt in his arms, how *good* it felt to be held by someone. I could smell the bitterness of the beer on his breath, combined with the saltiness of the fries, and I began to wonder what it would feel like to kiss him, how my lips would fit against his. And without thinking about it anymore, I leaned forward and did it.

"Whoa, you are drunk," Ben said, righting me on my stool.

"I'm not," I insisted. "I want this."

"Alex, I don't know . . ." He pushed his glasses up the bridge of his nose.

"Tell me you haven't thought about it," I said, my hand creeping up his thigh.

"Of course I have, but I just didn't think . . . I thought you didn't—"

I quieted him with another kiss, and I could feel his body relax with want as I slipped my tongue between his lips.

We'd ended up in his bed. The rest of that night feels like it happened in fragments, puzzle pieces my mind doesn't want to put together: me on top of Ben, his eyes wide with wonder; him peppering kisses down my neck, tender, gentle; me waking up the next morning with his arm slung over my waist; the lurching feeling in my stomach when I realized where I was, what I'd done.

I tried to sneak out, to quietly and shamefully pull on my clothes that were scattered on the bedroom floor, but he began to stir.

"Good morning, beautiful."

It felt like a knife twisting in my gut.

Ben rolled onto his back, his arms folded behind his head, a serene smile hanging about his lips. "You have no idea how long I've wanted this. Us."

But the truth was that I did know. I'd always known. But it was a line I'd never crossed because I didn't feel the same way. Or maybe I did. I wasn't sure. I had too much going on in my life, between losing Mom and then the falling out with Maddie, that I hadn't been able to sort out how I felt about Ben. All I knew was that he was my safe place, my soft spot to land. And I didn't want to do anything to change our relationship, to put that at risk.

Sleeping with Ben had been a mistake. I'd been craving the comfort, the closeness, the connection. I just wanted to stop feeling so . . . alone. It was dizzying how lonely I'd become since Mom's passing. With Maddie and I not speaking, Ben was all I had left. But I hadn't stopped to think about what sleeping with him would mean for us. How it could destroy the friendship that meant everything to me.

Ben looked at me then, as I zipped up my jeans, and he realized. It was as if he could read my mind. He knew all the words I couldn't bring myself to say. The hurt that was splashed across his face made my heart feel like it was breaking in two. I'd never meant to hurt him. But I'd ruined everything.

I lift my hand to my eyes, blocking the sun that glares at me angrily, knowingly, and try to push thoughts of Ben and the tangle of emotions from my mind. I might have made a mess of things back home, but right now I have to focus on Maddie. Feeling determined, I take off in the direction of the convenience store on the corner.

11.

ALEX

I'm almost tingling with anticipation when I get back to the pool house at Blackwell Manor. I can feel the weight of the phone charger like a secret talisman in the bag looped around my wrist. As soon as I charge Maddie's phone, I might finally get some answers.

I rush to unlock the door, fumbling with the key in the lock before it finally turns over. As soon as I get inside, I tear open the plastic packaging around my new purchase and plug the charger into the wall, jamming the other end into Maddie's phone. The screen remains black at first, staring up at me blankly from the end table, and I have a sinking feeling that the phone is broken, that I won't be able to get into it after all. But after a minute or two, a symbol of a battery with an electric bolt running through it flickers onto the screen. I sigh with relief. *It's charging.* I guess there's nothing to do now but wait for answers.

I turn around, my back to the phone, and drum my fingers on the kitchen counter. I can hear it again, my mother's voice in my ear: *A watched pot never boils.*

Suddenly, movement on the other side of the curtain

pulls my attention. But unlike last night, during the storm, curiosity rather than fear draws me to the sliding door.

Just on the other side is a man with salt-and-pepper hair in a finely cut suit. A "silver fox," Mom would have called him, with his square jaw and a smile that can only be described as "dazzling" as he shakes hands with one of the landscapers.

"Thanks for coming out, Antonio," he says, pumping the man's arm. "Yard looks great, I really appreciate you fitting us in on such short notice."

"Not a problem, Mr. Blackwell. We were happy to do it," the landscaper replies before taking his leave.

So this must be James Blackwell.

As if he could sense my presence, he turns to face me, his pastel blue eyes meeting mine, and he smiles warmly.

"And you must be our new houseguest," he says, offering me his open palm.

His large hand wraps around mine like a glove. "Yes, I'm Alex. Thank you for allowing me to stay the night."

"Of course, of course. You're welcome to stay as long as you'd like. I'm told that you're out here in the Hamptons looking for Madison, is that right?"

"Yes," I manage to squeak out, "she's my sister." There's something intimidating about being in the white-hot spotlight of his attention. His presence is formidable, with his tall stature and intense gaze, despite his cordial tone and easy smile that crinkles the corners of his eyes. "Ms. Blackwell told me that she had been planning to head back to New York City, but it would seem she never made it, and no one has been able to get in touch with her."

"I see," he replies, the corners of his mouth pulling down

in concern. "That is worrisome. Have you filed a report with the police yet?"

"I have. Just this morning."

"Very good. I'll reach out to some of my contacts there and see to it that this matter is given top priority."

"I appreciate that, sir."

"Call me James," he says with a chuckle. "I like to think of myself as far too young to be a 'sir.'"

I offer him a halfhearted smile. After all, he's probably older than my father. Wherever he might be. If he's even still alive.

It's almost shocking how raw the betrayal still feels, how just the memory of my father walking away is enough to knock the wind from my lungs. It was cold that night, so cold that I shivered under the quilt in my little twin bed that sat under one of the drafty windows at the front of the house. I climbed out of bed, tiptoeing across the room so as to not wake Maddie as I snuck into the living room to collect an extra blanket, the one Mom always kept draped over the back of the couch, big enough for all of us to huddle under on movie nights. But as my fingers reached the doorknob, something gave me pause. I could hear voices coming from the back of the house. The kitchen. It was my parents, their voices strained and hushed as if they'd wanted to be yelling, but knew it would wake me and Maddie if they did. I remember being confused; I hadn't even known Dad was back from his latest haul. I hadn't heard the familiar sound of his bellowing voice at the door: *Where are my girls?* There'd been no presents, no stories of rest stops in Minnesota or towering cacti in Arizona. I listened at the doorway to the bursts of hoarse whispers that wound through the quiet house.

". . . not working anymore, Vivienne . . . constant fighting . . . wasn't cut out for this . . ."

And then my mother's voice: ". . . supposed to be a family . . . don't do this to us . . ."

Eventually I heard the front door creak open and pull closed. I felt my tears before I even realized I was crying; they fell down my face in shivering trails. I was only six—I didn't fully understand what was happening. Not yet. But I knew that everything was about to change, almost as if the ground beneath my feet had already started to crumble.

My father and I had a special relationship. Or at least I'd thought so, up until that night. He'd always hug me a little longer, squeezing a little tighter when he came home from his trips. He'd take me fishing, early mornings spent on the lake, our breath coming out in frosty puffs. Maddie had never wanted to go. She hated the smell of the fish and the brutality of the hooks. Truthfully, I didn't enjoy the act of fishing either, but I'd enjoyed the time with Dad, the stillness of the water, of this man who was never still. In those early morning hours, he belonged only to me. I remember staring at him, as though trying to memorize his features, to bottle the tranquility of those moments.

But then he'd left. I'd watched him walk across our front lawn, his boots crunching over the frosted grass, leaving a trail of footprints in his wake. He'd looked back, only once, as his hand reached the handle of his truck. He caught sight of me in the window, my face a pale oval in the glass. I could see his heart breaking as he looked back at me, his head hung in shame. I raised my hand to the windowpane, silently begging him to stay. But he didn't. He turned away and drove off into the night.

We never spoke about him after that, not in front of

Mom. It was as if he'd never existed. It was too painful for her, more than she could handle. I could see the curtains being drawn across her eyes as her world grew darker and darker. She closed us out and retreated deeper into herself with every passing day.

As for Maddie, as much as she missed Dad, I think she could see how badly I was struggling without him. How desperately I needed to make sense of it all. And so, late at night, when we were sure Mom was asleep, she'd tell me stories.

About how Daddy was a soldier fighting overseas. How he'd left us because he was a top-secret spy and he'd had to keep our identities safe. I'd fall asleep listening to Maddie's tales. All the pretty lies she'd told, as light as spun sugar, transforming our lives into something beautiful.

"Alex?" James's voice pulls me back to the moment, the memories dissolving before my eyes.

"I'm sorry, what?"

"I asked if you'd like a tour of the grounds. I'd be happy to show you around." There's that smile again, so dazzlingly bright that it's hard to say no.

"Sure, yes, a tour would be great."

James walks me across the property, narrating its history as we go.

"The land was originally used as a whaling port, purchased in 1652 by a corporation that used the animals to produce oil and candles. But by the late 1800s, after the whale population in the area had significantly diminished, making the port a relic of the times, a manor house was built here for a prestigious New York family so that they could summer in a place that *The New York Times* was calling 'as close an approach to Eden as can be found in a long journey,' and 'exclusive—in the best sense of the word.' The manor house was owned by generations of the same family, until, following a slew of bad investments, their wealth dwindled to the point where the house sat empty and decaying for many years."

James goes on to explain how he, seeing a prime opportunity, sought out the current owner and convinced him to let go of the family's long-held estate on this coveted piece of land, for what he assures me was a price they "simply couldn't refuse."

"The original manor was then razed, and from the debris rose Blackwell Manor, a nod to the land's lineage with a modern finish befitting of the Hamptons of today. So what do you think?" he asks, as we approach the bluff, our feet mere inches from the edge.

I look down over the verge, at the sharp, rocky face of the cliff below me, at the spindly wooden staircase that clings to the side of it, creating a zigzagging path to the beach, and I feel myself getting dizzy. I force myself to gaze out across the ocean instead, concentrating on the feeling of my feet on the ground.

"It's incredible," I reply. And it is. The view, an expanse of blue dipping into the curved horizon, is breathtaking. It makes me feel so small and yet wonderfully powerful to be standing above it, the world at my feet.

"It is, isn't it?" James asks, as he turns to look at me. And for one terrifying, irrational moment, I wonder whether he's going to push me.

12.

KATHERINE

I watch him through the upstairs window, a chilled glass of Chardonnay in my hand, rolling the stem between my fingers. I see him as he takes that girl on a tour of the property, gesturing here and there as he walks. I see as she nods along enthusiastically, feigning interest in the history lesson I'm certain my husband is delivering at this very moment. As they reach the edge of the bluff, the girl seems nervous, her shoulders stiffening, her posture rigid. They stand there for a moment, talking. And then she's shuffling backward, nearly falling in her haste. James's arm shoots out, anchoring around her waist, steadying her on her feet. In my mind I imagine her falling. *Falling, falling, falling.* Disappearing into the vastness of the gray-green swell until she's no longer a problem that I'll have to deal with. But that doesn't happen. Instead, she's in my husband's strong arms, offering him a coquettish smile, surely thanking him profusely for being her knight in shining armor . . . The knight who had led her to the edge of a cliff in the first place.

I can't help but feel that James manufactures these moments. The ones where he walks away the hero, the champion galloping in on his white horse to save the day. And when he can't, he'll simply bend the truth, mold it to his liking, and state the facts as he sees them with such confidence that it's hard not to buy into his narrative. It's how he retells the story of our courtship. Me, the daughter of a failed financier, and he, the up-and-coming real estate developer who offered me the world like an oyster on a platter to save me from a life of financial ruin. But there was so much more to it, so much more to us.

The truth is that James and I met as children, with our knees in the powdery sand of the Hamptons beaches while our parents sipped mojitos on the veranda of the country club. (You see, for all his blustering about being a "self-made man" he often forgets that his own beginnings were far from humble.) But it wasn't until the summer I turned eighteen that James started to see me in a different light.

It was something I'd awakened to slowly, the knowledge that I'd become beautiful in the eyes of men. It was still new to me then. A power I was only just learning to wield. James's eyes sparkled when he saw me in the soda shop that summer, my lips wrapped around a cherry red straw.

"Katherine Clarke?" he'd asked. "Is that really you?"

"Hello, James."

"Wow . . ." He'd pulled his hands through his thick dark hair. "You've really . . . grown up since I last saw you. What's it been, five years now?"

"Give or take," I'd replied casually.

"Can I . . . take you to dinner or something? Catch up on old times?"

We started dating that June. James had just moved into his parents' summer home while developing his company, and it felt like the world was ours for the taking. It was two months of moonlit walks on empty beaches, lunches spread on picnic blankets. It was blissful. Perfect. And by the following summer, James was talking about rings. Telling me how beautiful I'd look with a diamond on my finger, one that would tell the world I was his.

Our parents were elated, already planning the wedding long before James slipped his grandmother's ring onto my hand at the same restaurant where he'd first taken me to dinner almost exactly two years earlier. We stood barefoot on the beach that night, full of love, full of hope, my head on his shoulder, the reassuring weight of his promise around my finger, as we watched the sun slip below the horizon.

It wasn't until later, days before we were to be married, that I started to hear my parents' hushed whispers, the words that floated through my bedroom wall. *"It's over . . . bankrupt . . . time to sell."*

I'd told James. I told him that maybe it wasn't the best time for us to marry, that maybe we should call off the wedding. But he didn't care.

"All I need is you, Katherine," he'd said, taking my hands in his. "Your parents, the money—none of that matters. We'll make our own way, me and you. We're going to be so happy, Katherine. I promise you."

And, for a time, we were. We'd find any excuse to be alone, to touch each other, stealing away from James's stuffy corporate events to make love, to lose ourselves in each other. We were passionate in a way that seems so distant to me now that it feels like a story I once read and only half remember. Something that happened to some other woman in some other life.

And now here he is outside our bedroom window having

found an excuse to put his arm around someone else. I scowl at the pair of them: James guiding Alex back across the yard, his hand hovering protectively near the small of her back.

Of course she'd fall for his act of gallant chivalry. She's probably laughing at her own clumsiness right now, peering up at her rescuer with big doe eyes from beneath long lashes. I take a sip of my wine, feeling the welcome bite at the back of my throat.

The thing most people don't know about James Blackwell is that he is everything to everyone. The ruthless businessman in the office, the charming socialite who will delight you with funny anecdotes at cocktail parties. I saw it with Madison. How he transformed into someone new, a version of him I thought was lost. With her, James became a younger man, passions that had lain dormant between us for years floating back up to the surface.

I don't know exactly when it happened. When the emotion seeped out of our marriage. When it became something dull, complacent, tired. Perhaps it started when I couldn't conceive a child. When my body failed me, failed us, couldn't provide the one thing we wanted most in this world. Or maybe it was the treatments. The cold sterility of scheduled sex, needles, paper gowns, and pregnancy tests. I'd spent years so consumed with the efforts of having a child that I hadn't noticed when the fire that once burned in James's eyes slowly diminished, until the last glowing ember grew cold.

But James seemed to rise from the ashes when Madison arrived on our doorstep. He came back to life in those early days, he seemed invigorated, imbued with a new vitality. He reminded me of the boy I fell in love with, the young man with hungry ambition and starry eyes—but it was no longer me he was looking at.

I'd felt uneasy since Madison dropped, unceremoniously, into our lives, but the cause of my hovering dread slid into focus for me, as though the lenses of my rose-tinted glasses had been adjusted, the day of the sailing trip.

James had woken up that morning and stretched his arms over his head, a lazy smile easing onto his face. He'd traced his finger along the curve of my shoulder, trailing it feather soft down the length of my arm. His touch set my nerve endings ablaze. *When was the last time we'd been intimate?* Not sex for the sake of sex: routine, marital, rote. But *intimate* where we lost control of our senses, fell into each other. When was the last time my husband truly wanted me?

He began to kiss my neck, his lips full and warm against my skin. "Let's take the boat out today," he'd purred into my ear.

The boat? It had been ages since we'd spent a day on *The Heart's Desire,* a gleaming sailboat with billowing white sails and a royal-blue hull that had once been James's most prized possession. When he'd first purchased it, I imagined James teaching me to sail, picnic lunches on the deck, making love on sandy shores. In reality, James rarely had time for *The Heart's Desire.* She spent most of her time in port, as neglected as our marriage. It seemed James never cared to sail his beloved boat. He desired merely to own something so beautiful. Just like me, *The Heart's Desire* sat waiting, maintained in pristine shape, in case someday the tides of James's fickle attentions turned back toward it. And it seemed, that day, they had.

"Will you have Mariana pack us a picnic?" he'd asked. "I'll take the entire day off." *A rare occurrence.*

"Of course," I'd replied, visions of champagne toasts and sun-drenched romance once again filling my head.

"Let's see if the kids want to join us as well," he'd added.

The image shifted then from James and me rekindling our marriage, lying side by side under the shade of white sails, to a day of family bonding. Though the picture was different, it was just as pleasant. I imagined us all together, like we were when the children were little. James and I watching Lily and Theo run from the frothy waves along the shoreline, a spray of freckles stretching across their sandy noses, waving to them from our checkered blanket beneath a luminous blue sky. My memories of those days are frozen like Technicolor photographs in my mind, so bright, so crisp, that I wonder whether I can trust my own recollection, or whether I've embroidered the past in a palette more vivid than reality.

James's relationship with the children has somehow shifted over time, a steely coolness settling between them. It happened so gradually that I can't pinpoint where it started, when they began to let him down, to disappoint him, but I suppose it was inevitable. James has always expected so much of them, perhaps because they didn't come to us through birth. He makes them prove themselves over and over, setting the bar so high that they stand little chance of ever reaching it. I can see how it's affected the children. Theo contorting himself to fit the mold his father expects of him, and no matter how many times he's rebuked he always comes back for more. James faults him for his failed business, but can't he see that Theo only started that doomed venture to impress his father? And Lily, poor, sweet Lily, so intimidated by the heights her father expected her to reach that she retreated into herself, stood paralyzed at the base of the mountain, as though she was so afraid of falling that she couldn't even start the climb.

But that day, when James decided to put his work aside so that he could spend time with his family, I saw a glimmer of hope that perhaps it wasn't too late. Perhaps we could divert the worrisome course our family had wandered down. And then he spoke again.

"Have Lily invite Madison along as well. I bet the girl has never been sailing before. I'm sure it would be a real treat for her."

Immediately my mood soured. That fragile glimmer of hope extinguished like a cigarette ground into an ashtray until all that remained were the smoky wisps of dreams I couldn't quite grasp.

We set sail that afternoon, with me putting forth my best effort to keep a smile on my face, for the sake of my children. The sky overhead was clear and bright, the only clouds like tufts of cotton against the expanse of blue, and the ocean was as smooth as glass, *The Heart's Desire* cutting a path with a gentle ease.

Madison stood at the stern, watching the trail of our wake as we sliced through the still waters of the open sea.

"Do you think we might see dolphins?" she asked, with a childlike wonder that curdled my stomach.

"We might!" Lily replied eagerly. "We've seen a few pods out this far in the past."

Madison seemed giddy with the excitement despite having barely touched the champagne James had poured for us all.

Theo, on the other hand, was already draining the dredges of his first glass and rooting through the bar cart for a refill.

"Maybe it's best to slow down," I cautioned him quietly, my fingers gently resting on his forearm.

"I'm fine," he snapped, yanking his arm away and tipping the bottle toward his empty glass, foam quickly meeting the rim.

I don't know when he became this way. Surly, hardened, angry. He'd been such a sweet, sensitive little boy once. I cling to the golden memories of him then, the way he'd pick the velvety red roses in our garden, the stems clutched in his chubby hands as he'd offer them up to me, the way he'd cried the time we'd come across an injured seagull as we combed the beach one summer evening looking for seashells; how he'd asked me about the pitiful creature as I'd tucked him into bed that night, distraught that its family would leave it behind.

There was a time when I knew my son, when his thoughts were written in a language I could read. I knew how to heal whatever was hurting him just by looking into his eyes. But as I watched him then, he felt so far away, so foreign, that I was left to imagine what was going on beneath the surface, behind the hard set of his eyes, as he threw back another heavy swig of champagne and leveled his gaze at Madison.

"I'd like to make a toast," James announced, calling all of us to attention. "We closed a pivotal deal this week. We acquired the old Seahorse Motel, and we're about to turn it into a five-star resort."

"But I thought old man Hawthorne wouldn't sell," Theo responded, awed as ever by his father.

"It would seem that he's changed his mind, son," James quipped with a conspiratorial wink. "And that was all Madison's doing."

"Madison?" I couldn't help it. Her name leapt from my lips like an assault. The girl at least had the good graces to blush, her cheeks turning a sweet ballet pink.

"Yes, Madison," James replied proudly, his large hand coming to rest on her delicate shoulder. "She's quite a natural in this business, as it turns out. She happened to be shadowing me at the office earlier this week when Mr. Hawthorne came in, kicking up a fit at our latest proposal. But Maddie here . . ." The intimacy of the nickname made me wince, but James, oblivious, beamed at her, "she talked him down, convinced him how wonderful it would be for him to let go of the old motel, to finally stop working and start living, to spend his time with his real legacy: his grandchildren."

"It was nothing," Madison replied, appropriately humbled. "I was just in the right place at the right time."

"It wasn't nothing," James was quick to correct. "You know how to relate to people, to win them over. And that's something we often forget in my line of work. At the end of the day, we aren't just dealing with a bottom line, we're dealing with people. And that," he said, lifting his glass in the air, "is why I'd like to raise this toast to Madison." He looked at her, his eyes soft with adoration. "To you, my dear."

I risked a glance at Theo. He glowered as he knocked back the rest of his champagne, a small trail running down his chin before he swiped at it with his forearm. Lily chewed at her bottom lip, always sensitive to the changing tides of her brother's mercurial temperament. The only one who didn't seem to notice the tension was James.

"How about a sailing lesson then?" he asked Madison.

"Oh, I would love that," she gushed.

I had watched them together, James standing behind her, placing his hand over hers as he taught her how to work the rigs. He was too close, whispering in her ear, laughing with delight as she maneuvered the vessel under his guidance. He never took his eyes off her, never saw his wife's heart grow colder, never noticed the way his son had started to stumble on his feet or the fact that his daughter sat lonely and dejected.

My family was everything I'd ever wanted. I'd given up so much—my youth, my education, my ambitions—for this family. I'd carved away piece after piece of myself to get us here, and Madison and James were pulling at the fragile seams that held it all together. I hated her in that moment. I hated them both.

But she's gone now. And this should have been over. But as I watch James escort Alex back to the pool house, it dawns on me that this will never be over. We might be rid of Madison, but there will always be someone else waiting in the wings to take her place.

13.

ALEX

"You're sure you're alright?" James asks as we approach the pool house door.

"I'm fine, really. Thank you again for the tour." I don't know what came over me back there, the way my knees gave out, my head swimming. We'd been so close to the edge of the bluff, and the way he'd smiled at me . . . I could have sworn I saw something predatory in the rows of white teeth. I'd panicked, stumbled as I tried to back away from the edge. But then he'd come to my rescue, his hand gentle on my waist, and when I looked up at him, whatever I'd thought I'd seen was gone.

"It was my pleasure," James replies with a small wave as he makes his way back toward the main house.

I step into the pool house and close the door behind me, pressing my back against the cool glass. I close my eyes for a moment, resting my head against the door, feeling the last trickle of adrenaline draining from my tensed muscles.

The phone. The recollection hits me like a lightning bolt, and my eyes snap open. I lunge across the room, unable to wait one more moment to open Maddie's phone. But when

I reach the end table, I find that the cord dangles from the outlet like a useless limb. The phone is gone.

I spin around, instinctively looking for who could have taken it, but I can tell from the stillness of the space that whoever was here is long gone.

I drop down onto the sofa, pressing the heels of my hands to my eyes, willing myself not to cry that I've lost my one potential lifeline to my sister. One of the Blackwells must have taken it. Was the impromptu tour a means to distract me while one of them slipped in here and snatched the phone? Someone must have been worried that I'd find something on that phone, something they didn't want me to see. But now I may never know.

All I can say for certain is that Maddie didn't leave this place on a whim. There's something more here. Something the Blackwells don't want me to find out. I can feel it, the malevolence here like a scaled beast that slithers through the ground. It occurs to me now that Maddie might have felt it too. Perhaps she knew she was in danger. And if, as I suspect, she didn't leave of her own volition, there may be more secrets yet to be unearthed.

When you grow up the way Maddie and I did, there are certain things you learn quickly. Things that felt normal to us that would probably make other people raise an eyebrow or two. You see, when you live in a constant state of uncertainty, the few things that belong to you feel like everything. Maddie and I, we didn't have much, but our meager possessions, probably junk in anyone's eyes but ours, had been treasures to us. And we'd learned to protect the things we held closest to our hearts. A plastic pony hidden in a hole in the wall, crumpled dollar bills slid beneath the floorboards, scraps of ribbon, woven bracelets, a lucky penny—precious childhood trinkets—tucked away in the hollow of the old oak tree in the yard. It's a habit that, even now as an adult, I haven't been able to break. Even though Mom is gone and I live alone in that quiet empty house full of nothing but dusty memories, I find myself tucking my wallet under my mattress at night, stowing the few simple pieces of jewelry I have in the darkest corner of my closet. It's something that is so ingrained in me that I doubt it'll ever change. And if I had to guess, I'd bet anything that it's the same for Maddie. *But where do you hide things in a glass room?*

When we were kids, I knew all of Maddie's favorite hiding spots. I knew that she stashed her savings from her part-time job at the Penny Mart between the pages of her biology textbook on the third shelf or behind the picture frames in our room. I knew that the gold stud earrings Dad had given her for Christmas, the last before he left, were hidden in the case of an old cassette tape that had long since been lost. But now, here, I don't have the first clue where to start.

I decide that anywhere is better than standing still. I begin with the kitchen, pulling out the drawers, opening all of the cabinets, even checking inside the freezer. Next I scour the living area, patting down the sofa to see if anything has been slipped inside the cushion covers. Nothing. I search the dressing area, reaching into the corners of the tiny chest of drawers, and finally I comb over the bathroom. Peering into the medicine cabinet, rummaging under the sink. Still nothing. And then I remember. *Maddie's journal.*

It was a short-lived phase. Something she had only kept for a few months in junior high school at the suggestion of the school counselor, as a way to help us make sense of our "complicated home life." The counselor had handed each of us a little purple notebook. Encouraged us to write about our feelings. I didn't take it seriously, laughing about it with Maddie as we left her office.

"Writing down all of the shitty things in our lives isn't going to make them go away," I'd scoffed dismissively.

"Seriously. Like a journal could fix this train wreck," she'd replied with a roll of her eyes.

When I got home from school that afternoon, I slid the empty notebook onto my side of the bookshelf without giving it a second thought. But, a few days later, I woke up in the middle of the night to find Maddie sitting up in bed, the lamp at her bedside pulled close to her, casting a puddle of warm light across her lap. And there sat the little purple notebook, a perfect match to mine, its lavender pages splayed open in front of her. She was writing something, chewing the inside of her cheek as if in deep thought. I wanted to ask her what she was writing about, whether it was helping her "cope" or whatever it was the counselor had said it was supposed to do, why she'd felt that she had to hide it from me. But I knew better than to ask anything of her in that moment. Instead, I closed my eyes and pretended to be asleep, listening to the sound of her pen scratching across the neatly lined paper. When I heard her switch off her lamp, I opened my eyes a sliver, just to see whether she was going back to sleep. But to my surprise, Maddie crawled out of bed and stood in front of our tiny, cluttered desk. I watched as she ripped off a strip of masking tape and affixed the notebook to the back of the headboard of her bed, a place I'd never have thought to look.

It was so tempting knowing that notebook was there, but I'd never opened it. If writing was helping Maddie in some way, I wanted to let her have that. Especially after I'd belittled the idea, made a joke of it in front of her. But every once in a while, I'd peek behind her headboard just to see if it was still there, if she was still keeping this secret. A few weeks later it was gone, and neither of us ever mentioned it again. I wish now that I'd asked her about it. Maybe, if I'd taken the time to listen instead of being so quick to judge, she would have shared her inner world with me, maybe I would have understood her better, maybe we'd be closer now.

But I hadn't. And now I'm afraid it's too late. Though that little purple notebook has given me an idea. *The sofa bed may not have a headboard but . . .* I run back to the dressing room and slide my hand behind the one piece of solid wood furniture in this pool house. My fingers feel something, a soft material, stuck behind the dresser.

My heart racing with anticipation, I lean my shoulder against the dresser and use all of my weight to shove it forward, inching it away from the wall. Just far enough for me to peer behind it and pull down the canvas bag that's been stuck to the back side of it with packing tape.

The bag is simple: similar to an oversized pencil case, and surprisingly hefty for its size. I pull open the zipper and stare down at the contents of the bag. For a moment I'm unable to move. It's as if my brain and my body have frozen in shock. For inside the bag is more cash than I've ever seen in one place at one time. Bundles of neatly stacked bills. Probably several thousand dollars in total. *What the hell was Maddie doing with all of this money? Where could it possibly have come from? . . . And why would she leave it behind?* It's this last thought that drips like ice down my spine.

I kneel down and shake the contents of the bag onto the floor. In addition to the stacks of bills, a gold necklace tumbles to the floor. I recognize it instantly; the delicate heart charm, the gossamer-thin chain that has been repaired countless times, the scrolling cursive engraving of the letter V—for Vivienne. This necklace belonged to our mother. She wore it every day of her life. Sliding the charm along the chain when she was anxious, rubbing the thin metal between her fingers when she was lost in thought. For a moment, just holding it in my hand is enough for tears to prick at my eyes.

My emotions surrounding my mother have always been complicated, but since her passing, the murky waters of my love for her have become even more turbid. Because I do love her. I always have. She was my mother, after all. And despite her flaws, no one is all just one thing. Good or bad. Dark or light. Sometimes the good is indistinguishable from the bad, the two extremes lapping over each other like softly rolling waves, mixing and blending until it's impossible to pry them apart. Sometimes I hated my mother. Resented her for the childhood we didn't have. The burdens she tossed at our feet. But other times . . . other times I adored her. When she was happy, no one shined brighter than Vivienne Walker. I loved the way she laughed. Like a Coca-Cola ad come to life, her head thrown back, her mouth open wide, face tilted toward the sun. I loved the way she danced while she cooked, spinning around our kitchen like a ballerina as she'd cut and toss ingredients, dropping them into a sizzling pan with a swish of her hips. And I loved the way she'd loved us. Maddie and me. How, when the fog cleared, she looked at us with wonder, as though she could scarcely believe we were real.

Everyone always told me and Maddie that we looked like her. "Clones of your mother," they'd say. When I was small, I'd spin in front of the mirror, one of her sparkly dresses held against my chest, hoping it was true. Hoping I'd someday be just like her. The drinking didn't just take my mother away from me, it took away the essence of who she was.

I hold the necklace in my hand, rubbing the charm between my thumb and forefinger, just as Mom used to do, the metal smooth and weathered from years spent beneath her fingers. She must have given it to Maddie. In those final, painful days when we'd had to say goodbye, before she was gone.

I pick up the stacks of bills, start shoving them back into the bag. I don't know where this money came from, but something, instinct maybe, tells me that I need to hide it away again before anyone else finds out about it. As I push the last of the cash through the zippered opening, a small white rectangle flutters out from between the notes, landing on the floor at my feet.

I pick it up, turning the card stock over in my hand. On the other side, printed in raised black ink:

LUCKY JACK'S
A Gentlemen's Club

Somehow, this discovery is even more shocking than the cash. *Why on earth would Maddie have a business card for a strip club?*

14.

ALEX

I don't know what I expected Lucky Jack's to look like, maybe some run-down dive crouching shamefully at the end of a dark alley, but it certainly wasn't this. The broad white building, which stands proudly on a stretch of road just outside of town, looks more like a nightclub than anything else. Now, in the off hours, red velvet ropes stretch across the front entrance, and the neon sign, *Lucky Jack's* formed in pointed script, is turned off. I walk up to the front door, cupping my hands around my eyes and pressing my face to the dark-tinted glass. They're clearly closed for business this early in the day, the chairs stacked atop the tables, their legs pointed into the air like dead roaches.

I'd wanted to rush over here last night, the moment I'd found the business card in Maddie's things. But I'd dialed the number on the card, the phone ringing incessantly into the night. When someone finally picked up, I could hear the thudding bass of dance music, the jeer of catcalls and howls crowding the line.

"Lucky Jack's," the speaker shouted, their words rushed and clipped, barely audible over the cacophony of sounds. I ended the call. There was no way I was going to get the kinds of answers I needed while the club was in full swing. I thought it best to pay them a visit before opening hours.

Instead, I spent the night pacing the floor of the pool house, trying to think of all the ways Maddie could have ended up with a pile of bills hidden behind a dresser, but I never came any closer to finding an answer. When I finally slept, it was fitful, tortured, filled with visions of Maddie being tossed about in the ocean, calling for me to help her. I dreamed that I was in a small wooden boat, paddling toward her, but I couldn't fight the tide; she was always just beyond my reach. I extended my oar, screaming for her to grab on, but she didn't. Instead, she slowly began to sink beneath the water's surface, her hair fanning out around her head like a halo before she was gone.

I shudder with the thought, shaking off the nightmare. I should have known it was too early to come here, that a place like this wouldn't open their doors until the evening, when men with leering eyes and lascivious intentions can prowl under the protection of darkness. But then again, just looking at Lucky Jack's, with its lush velvet booths and sleek marble floors, I imagine the men who frequent this place are unabashed in their desires. I can envision a line forming outside, shined oxfords tramping on a stretch of red carpet.

I'm just about to give up when movement at the back of the space catches my eye. I press in closer to the glass, straining to see through the tinted door. There's a woman struggling to carry a cardboard box, the foiled necks of champagne bottles peering over the top. I bang on the door, raise a hand in greeting. The woman looks in my direction and scowls, her arms straining against the weight of the box. With a heft, she slides the box atop the bar and dusts off her hands. I bang on the door again, waving her over.

"We're closed, doll," she shouts.

"I know, I'm sorry," I call awkwardly through the door. "I just wanted to ask you a question. It'll only take a minute."

To my relief the woman walks toward the entrance, an exaggerated sashay in her hips as she does so. When she pulls open the door, I can see that she's older than I'd thought, her bleached-blond hair teased up in an '80s-style fashion, her face heavily made up. The midmorning sun reveals the cracks in her foundation, the deep lines that form around her mouth liked closed parentheses.

"What can I do for you?" she says, draping herself against the doorframe and crossing her arms below her ample breasts, which threaten to spill over the top of her black tank top.

"I'm in town looking for my sister, and I was hoping to talk to the manager, or, well, anyone who works here really. Anyone who might have known her."

"Would the owner do?"

"Sure, yeah, of course."

"That'd be me. Come on in then, honey," she says as she heads back into the club. "But I'm gonna have to work as we talk."

"I'm Jack by the way," the woman calls over her shoulder as I follow her inside. "As in Lucky Jack's. This is my place." She struts her way through the space, the silver chain belt hanging around her waist dipping as she walks. There's something decidedly sensual about Jack, something almost catlike in the way she moves. She flicks on the overhead lights and Lucky Jack's comes to life, as though awakening from a deep slumber.

At the center is a white stage rimmed with neon blue lights and shining metal poles under hazy purple spotlights.

Surrounding it are high cocktail tables made of clear glass and rounded booths, where I can picture bottle-service waitresses delivering chilled buckets of champagne. Huge projector screens positioned around the dimly lit space display black-and-white images of women in various states of undress. Artistic, suggestive poses: fingers splayed across a bare stomach, an arched back draped in black lace lingerie, a curved throat beneath a tilted jaw.

"I've . . . never seen anything quite like it," I remark as I pull out a barstool upholstered in black leather.

Jack steps behind the bar and begins wiping down the surface with a lemon-scented rag. "Yeah, well, Lucky Jack's isn't just some small-town titty bar; it's a true gentlemen's club. We cater to a certain kind of clientele, if you know what I mean. The kind that expect a little more than keg beer and strung-out girls in pasties."

I nod. It's clear this place is different from the average strip club, it's high-end, exclusive. The girls that work here probably make a killing in tips. My blood runs cold as the thought occurs to me. *Could this be where Maddie got all of that money?* And what, exactly, did she have to do to bring in thousands of dollars?

But no. That couldn't be. I try to picture my sister up on that stage, her feet strapped into towering heels, her body writhing under the glow of the lights, and I just can't see it. That isn't Maddie.

Jack pours herself a finger of amber liquid into a whisky glass that she pulls from beneath the bar. She tilts the glass in my direction, one eyebrow raised as if to ask if I'd like to join her. I shake my head.

Jack shrugs. "Suit yourself," she says as she throws back her drink.

I pull my phone out of my bag, bringing up the picture of Maddie in front of the Lobster Shack. It was taken only a few weeks ago, but it already feels like it was from another lifetime, an image of someone I used to know. In a way, the thought rings true. The more I've learned about Maddie over the last few days, the less it feels like I ever truly knew her.

I slide the phone across the bar, turning it so Jack can inspect the photo. "This is Maddie. My sister. She's been missing for a few days. I was wondering if you knew her."

"Nah, I don't think so, doll. She's real pretty though. Would have loved to have her as one of my dancers. The guys go crazy for that wholesome, girl-next-door type."

I feel my stomach unclench. So Maddie wasn't working here after all. "But has she ever been in here? As a guest maybe?"

"Not that I remember, honey, but this place gets packed. I certainly don't remember every face that comes through my doors. Why are you looking for her here anyway?"

"I found a card—"

"Hey, Jack?" I hear from the back of the club. I turn to see a girl with a short black bob and blunt bangs peering out from a back room. Her eyeliner licks up into pointed wings at the corners of her eyes, and her silver-sequined halter top sparkles under the spotlights.

"Just a sec, Cleo," Jack yells back, holding up one finger. "I'll be there in a minute. Look," she says, turning her focus back toward me. "I've gotta go. We're setting up for a private party tonight, and I've got my hands full." Jack walks around the bar and ushers me toward the exit. "Best of luck with your sister though. I really hope you find her."

"Yeah," I mutter as she closes the door behind me, the lock clicking into place. "Me too."

I turn away and head back toward my car, parked in the shade on the side of the building. It's only midmorning, but already the sun is blaring down heavily upon my shoulders.

"Hey," a voice calls.

I look around, unsure where the sound came from.

"Over here!"

I look to my left, to the lot behind Lucky Jack's, where the overgrown grass sits in shaggy tufts around a metal staircase, rusted in the sea air. There, at the top the stairs, is the girl I saw inside. The one that had come looking for Jack. Cleo, I think she'd called her. She waves me over with a flick of her wrist.

I cross the sizzling blacktop, stepping over the cross-hatched cracks that run through it like fault lines.

Cleo squints into the sun, her silver top sparkling like a disco ball, a cigarette perched between her fingers.

"Hey," she says as I approach, picking my way over the cluster of weeds at the bottom of the stairs.

"It's Cleo, right?"

She laughs. "Actually, it's April. But yeah, Cleo's my stage name. You know, like Cleopatra." She gestures vaguely to the dramatic eye makeup, the black hair that I suspect might be a wig upon closer inspection. "All the girls here have their 'thing.' This is mine." She shrugs. "Anyway, I overheard you inside. You're looking for your sister?"

"Yeah," I reply. "I am."

"Mind if I look at that picture? Jack means well, but she's not on the floor with us, working the crowds. She doesn't know the guests like we do."

"Of course." I pull out my phone and unlock it, the photo of Maddie still shining out from the screen. "I really appreciate this."

"Sure. I've got a little sister of my own. I'd want someone looking out for her too." She takes the phone from my hand and studies the photo. "Yeah," she says with a nod of her head, her black locks swishing against her face. "I recognize her."

"Maddie? She's been here before?"

"Yeah, but she wasn't a guest or anything. She's Becca's friend. I thought the name sounded familiar when I heard you talking to Jack back there. Had to see a picture to be sure though."

"Becca?"

"Well, Natasha around here. She does this whole Russian spy thing." She rolls her eyes. "Anyway, Becca and Maddie are friends. I think they work together at Becca's other job, over at the Lobster Shack. I've seen her hanging around outside the club a few times, waiting for Becca to get off her shift."

"Do you have a number for Becca?" I ask eagerly.

"Nah, I don't. We don't talk much outside of the club. That's kind of what it's like here. We only exist inside these walls," she says, nodding to the building behind her. "As Cleo, Natasha, or whatever. We don't like it to cross over too much into our real lives. Or at least that's how it is for me." She pulls a drag of her cigarette, blowing the smoke into the air in a long plume.

I nod. "Do you think Jack would give me her number then?"

"Doubt it. It's, like, a rule, ya know? She'd never give out a girl's personal info."

"Can I at least give you my number then?" I all but beg. "The next time you see Becca, would you give it to her? Ask her to call me?"

"Yeah, I guess that wouldn't be a problem. Becca is scheduled to work tonight anyway."

"Thank you," I say, searching my bag for something to write on. I dig out a pen and a crumpled receipt. Smoothing it on the handrail, I scribble down my number and hand it to April.

She takes it with a nod and tucks it into her top.

"Seriously, April, thank you."

"Sure thing," she replies as she yanks open the door and disappears back into the club.

15.

MADDIE

"Heads up, new girl!" the busboy shouts as he whizzes by, nearly crashing into the oversized platter that is precariously balanced on the palm of my hand. I hear the plates rattle as he weaves around me. I stop, regain my balance, steady the platter. I can't afford to drop this order. If the owner, Scott, decides to take the cost of these surf and turfs out of my paycheck, I'll be working it off for a week.

I take a deep breath, tilt up my chin, reapply the smile to my face, and make my way to table twelve to deliver the meals.

The family seated at this table, the Caroways, regulars at the Lobster Shack, seem even more miserable than usual today. I winced when Luca told me he was seating them in my section. *How could they be so unhappy while being served a lobster dinner?* That's something I've noticed about the Hamptons in my brief time here thus far: The people here seem to have the best of everything, but it's never enough. Not enough to make them happy. It seems that the more they have, the more they want, as if their contentment is a fire that needs constant stoking or else it threatens to burn out. Alex and I, we didn't grow up going to places like this. I'd never even tried lobster before I started working here and Jose in the kitchen snuck me a lobster tail at the end of my first week. I try not to resent the customers, even on the days when I want to shake them, to ask them if they have any idea how fortunate they are, but some days are harder than others. Especially with the Caroway family. The two teenage boys slouch in their seats, their noses absorbed in their cellphones, and Mrs. Caroway fusses with the napkin in her lap, smoothing it over and over again, all with a pinched look on her face that makes it appear as though she's just tasted something sour. The lipstick she's wearing, a shade of pink that is too pale for her complexion, is smeared at the corner of her pursed lips. But it's Mr. Caroway who makes my stomach jitter as I approach the table. His ruddy cheeks hang like jowls, with the kind of deep lines cutting into his face that result from years spent frowning. He bounces his thick leg under the table, the heel of his leather driving shoe colliding with the floor in a rhythmic pattern. *Tap, tap, tap.*

"Here you go," I say in my brightest the-customer-comes-first voice, sliding the first plate in front of Mr. Caroway.

As I deliver the other plates to the rest of the family, the two boys never even pulling themselves away from their phones long enough to muster a "thank you," I hear the clatter of falling silverware.

I turn to find that Mr. Caroway has tossed his fork onto the table, raising his hands in disgust.

"I ordered my steak medium-rare, and this is *clearly* medium-well. And I specifically asked for an order of crab cakes, and you've brought me . . . whatever the hell this is."

I look down at the salad on his plate, at the leafy greens

and plump cherry tomatoes. *Definitely not crab cakes.* I must have put the order in wrong. This isn't like me. I'm usually better at my job. I take it seriously, unlike some of the other girls, but it was just so busy today, and I dropped the ball.

"I'm so sorry, sir. I'll take it back to the kitchen right away."

"It's too late!" he shouts, his face growing redder. "The rest of my family already has their meals. Am I really supposed to just sit here while they eat and wait for you to learn how to do your job correctly?"

I stand shocked into silence, my mouth agape, unsure what he'd like me to do or even how to respond to his outburst.

"What are you, a moron or something?" Mr. Caroway sneers.

"Again, sir, I apologize for—"

"I want to talk to Scott. This is unacceptable."

I gulp. "Of course," I force out between clenched teeth. God, Scott is in a mood today, after the shipment of wine he'd ordered wasn't delivered before opening. If he finds out I messed up, that I pissed off one of his regulars, one of the big spenders, he's definitely going to fire me. And then . . . then all of this will have been for nothing.

"Scott?" I knock on the closed door to his office at the back of the restaurant. I'm greeted with a grunt in reply. "There's a customer here that would like to speak with you personally."

"Not now," he snaps back.

"It's, uh, it's Mr. Caroway. What would you like me to tell him?"

I hear Scott sigh dramatically, followed by the sound of

his rolling office chair being pushed away from his desk. A moment later, he bursts through the door and strides past me. I jog at his side like a puppy nipping at his heels. "There was a mix-up with his order and—"

"I'll handle it," he grumbles, raising one hand and stopping me in my tracks.

I watch from the drinks station as he confers with Mr. Caroway, nodding his head apologetically. I only catch bits of the conversation. *"Our apologies . . . unacceptable . . . on the house."* I cringe. I need this job. The Lobster Shack is the most popular restaurant in the Hamptons right now. It apparently became known as "a place to be seen" after several A-list celebrity guests were spotted here in summers past. It's the best place to make the big tips, and I need every cent I can gather if I'm going to be able to afford to stay out here for a while. The rate at the motel I'm currently staying at, a musty "seaside resort"—both an insult to the word "resort" and nowhere near the seaside—is already eating into what little savings I have. I'm going to have to find somewhere more permanent to stay. And I'll also have to somehow convince Scott not to fire me. A tall order, to say the least.

I see Scott turn from Mrs. Caroway after a hearty handshake, and I busy myself at the drinks station pretending to be refilling the water pitchers resting at its side.

"Madison. My office. Now."

"If I could just—"

"Madison, I'm *so* sorry," a voice from behind me gushes. I turn to find one of the other waitresses standing behind me, her long chocolate-brown hair hanging in loose curls, her full lips pulled into a dramatic pout. The name on the tag pinned to her breast reads "Becca." I've seen her before here at the Lobster Shack, but we've never officially met, and I certainly don't have the first clue what she's apologizing for.

"I just heard that the order I put in for you, the one for table twelve, was wrong."

My brows lift at the lie, but she continues. "Honestly, Scott"—she turns her big brown eyes on him—"it was my mistake. Madison was swamped with her other tables and I told her I'd put in the Caroway order, and I must've screwed it up."

Scott snorts.

"Oh come on, don't be mad." She bats her mascaraed lashes.

"Fine," he relents. "I'll give you a pass. But from now on"—he turns his scowl toward me—"put in your own orders."

As he stomps off toward his office, Becca winks at me and snaps her gum against her teeth, a wave of spearmint drifting in my direction.

"Thank you for that," I say, my voice a breathy sigh of relief. "I really appreciate it."

"No worries," she replies with a shrug.

"I'm pretty sure he was going to fire me. I hope I didn't get you into too much trouble."

"Meh, I'm not worried about it."

I wonder if she's one of the rich girls, the ones who come out for the summer and pick up a few shifts at their parents' behest because it looks good on their college applications to have worked at least one day of their lives. But somehow I doubt it. I've seen Becca here too often for that to be the case, and the scuffed leather at the toes of her shoes and the tiny fray at the cuff of her blouse tell a different story.

"You're new, right?" Becca asks.

"Yeah, I've only just moved out here and I've already nearly lost my job." I roll my eyes.

She slings her arm over my shoulder. "Welcome to the Hamptons."

16.

THEO

What is she after? I watch as Alex steps out of Lucky Jack's into the bright morning sun, tucking a lock of hair behind her ear as the glass door falls shut behind her.

Interesting. I slide down in the front seat of my car, even though I'm certain she'd never notice me parked discreetly across the street. I wonder what could have brought her here, to this place. Lucky Jack's isn't the kind of establishment people typically wake up and decide to visit on a sunny Wednesday morning. Something must have driven her to make this trip, but I can't fathom what it might have been.

I saw her this morning, the shadow of her figure moving about the pool house behind the drawn curtains, buzzing with energy. I watched her burst through the door, her feet shoved into a pair of foam flip flops, her hair in a loose tangle as she strode across the yard, a woman on a mission, toward the rusted Toyota Corolla that's been parked outside of our front gates. I don't know exactly what it was, but something about her, about the determined clip of her gait, told me to follow her.

My eyes trail after Alex as she rounds the corner of the building making a beeline for the hunk of scrap metal that serves as her car. I don't know what she's up to, but I can already tell she's going to be a problem. Just like her sister. *What is it about the Walker women that compels them to stick their noses where they don't belong?*

Maddie had a particular talent for it. Winding her way through our lives like creeping ivy, her poisonous vines reaching into every crevice. After her triumph with Mr. Hawthorne at the Seahorse Motel, wherein she managed to convince him to give up his grandchildren's inheritance, it was alarming how quickly she became a staple at Blackwell Properties. It seemed to me that she was dropping into the office with increasing frequency, asking my father all manner of questions about his business. He, of course, was delighted to have a fresh audience to whom he could boast about his successes.

"Is it only commercial properties you're interested in?" Maddie asked, her eyes sharp and keen as she looked up at Father, her hair tied back in a neat braid. She did her best to match his long stride as he carved a path through the office.

"Good question. But no, our portfolio is widely diversified these days. When I was first starting out, I was mostly on the residential side of things actually, flipping little seaside shanties into vacation homes, luxury rentals, but in recent years I've found a lot of success in the commercial sector as well."

Maddie nodded, seemed to absorb his words like a sponge.

"I think it's wonderful you're so keen to learn about the business world. I know you have your eyes set on a medical degree, but real estate is never a bad investment. It certainly can't hurt for you to learn the ins and outs."

"Absolutely," she concurred.

"Theo." Father beckoned, as if he'd finally recalled my presence in the cramped little cubicle he'd provided me. I'd worked at Blackwell Properties every summer for the last five years, and he still couldn't scrounge up a more suitable workstation when I started here full-time. I popped my head around the side of the thin partition.

"Theo, why don't you show Madison some of the concept sketches for the new hotel? After all, none of it would be possible if it wasn't for her assistance."

Maddie beamed at his side. "I'd love to see them. If you're not too busy, Theo."

I forced a smile, but annoyance churned in my gut. "Of course."

"Excellent," Father said with an efficient clap of his hands. "Then I'm off to my next meeting. I'll see you both this evening."

Father left, leaving Madison to hover in the opening to my cubicle, which suddenly felt even smaller than usual.

"I hope I'm not interrupting your work," she said, a picture of round-eyed innocence. But I couldn't help but wonder if her words carried an undercurrent of sarcasm. Father was always insinuating that I didn't take my job here seriously, that I didn't understand the value of a hard day's work. I couldn't be sure what vicious words he'd already whispered in Madison's ear during all the time they seemed to be spending together.

Father clutched his opinion of me tightly in his fist, and no matter what I did, I couldn't seem to pry it away from him. But he was wrong. I'd wanted to make my own way, to prove to him that I could be more than a drain on his resources. I'd started my own business, Bespoke Travel, as soon as I'd graduated college, the ink on my business degree still wet, because I knew I had something to prove. For my entire life, I'd been regaled with stories of my father's greatness. And so I tried to follow in his footsteps. I put together a business proposal, an elite concierge service that would cater to the likes of my friends: young people with endless budgets and insatiable wanderlust. I told my father I wanted to sit down for a meeting and I presented it to him, asked him for a loan.

"Are you sure this is the avenue you'd like to pursue?" he'd questioned, peering at me with a scrutinizing glare above the pamphlet I'd given him.

"I've looked at it from every angle and I think there's a gap in the market for this type of service." I'd done my research, I knew exactly what I'd wanted to create. I just needed the cash to get it off the ground.

Father had gently laid the papers down on the conference room table, spreading his hands on top of the glossy pages. "I'll tell you what. Instead of a loan, what I can offer you is an advance on your inheritance. I have some savings set aside for you and your sister. If this is how you choose to spend your share, I'll cut you a check today. You'll be investing your own money into this."

"Yes," I'd said without hesitation. This was my chance to prove to him, once and for all, that I could amount to something. That I wouldn't always be standing in the long, cool shadow he'd been casting upon me for most of my life.

But life had different plans for me. I signed a lease on an office space in Manhattan, prime real estate on Fifth Avenue, that stretched the seams of my start-up budget. I outfitted it for the type of clientele I needed to attract; everything had to give the appearance of being high-end for this to work. My clients had to feel like they were part of something exclusive, that they were special. But then the pandemic hit. COVID-19 swept through the world, running the travel industry into the ground. It was a complication I never could have anticipated, despite all my careful research. I was overextended, stuck in contracts I could no longer fulfill, with a staff I was paying out of my own pocket. And Bespoke Travel died on the vine.

But I doubt Father told Madison any of that, choosing instead to clutch to his belief that I'm a fuckup. I shoved the thought aside and pulled up the plans for Father's new hotel on my computer screen for Madison to inspect. He'd had his eye on this property for quite some time, and had put a lot of thought into what he'd do with it if he was ever able to convince Mr. Hawthorne to sell to him. Madison leaned over my shoulder, clicking through the images of a sparkling-blue swimming pool, the onyx-topped bar, the steakhouse that would eventually be home to a chef from a Michelin-starred restaurant.

"It's amazing," she said, her breath falling softly on my ear. I could smell the hints of blueberry in her shampoo, feel the heat of her cheek so close to my own.

Suddenly, my blood began to warm beneath my skin, and I became hyperaware of our proximity, the tantalizing closeness of her body. *Perhaps I'd been too quick to judgment. Perhaps I should give her a chance.*

"Maybe we could . . . have dinner or something sometime? Get to know each other?" I'd asked, the question falling awkwardly from my lips before I'd even had a chance to think it through.

"You mean, like, at the house?"

"No, I, uh, I meant more like at a restaurant. Just the two of us."

"Oh . . ." She straightened her posture, the energy that was crackling between us like static electricity now gone, as though it had never existed. "Oh . . . I . . . it's really kind of you to ask but . . . I . . . I don't—"

"Just forget I asked," I snapped, my voice tight as a snare.

I shake my head and let out a huff at the memory as I push my aviator sunglasses onto my eyes and turn the key in the ignition, the car rumbling to life beneath me. I need to get to the job site, to oversee the progress on the new hotel. The foundation has already been dug out, and the concrete was supposed to have been poured three days ago. I have to get down there and see what's causing the delay. Make sure there are no surprises.

I take one last look at Alex in my rearview mirror as I edge the nose of my car out onto the main road, watch as she disappears around the side of Lucky Jack's. I'm going to have to keep a closer eye on her before this gets out of hand.

17.

THE WHARF

I wait at the old fishing wharf, cloaked in the anonymity of darkness, away from the street lamps and glittering shopfronts, away from the restaurants, their decks strung with twinkling fairy lights, soft music filtering out into the night, away from the tourists and summer revelers whose laughter echoes down the cobbled roads nearby. Here, the boats bob in their slips, the sea gently lapping at their hulls like a lullaby; fishing nets, frayed and worn, lie in knotted piles; and discarded crates sit forgotten on the pier, the softening wood slowly yielding to the ceaseless sea air. It's quiet here. Still. Until I hear his footsteps, the weathered planks of the docks groaning in protest beneath his weight. He walks in the way men do, when they know they have the world at their feet.

"Here," the man says. "It's what you asked for."

He shoves an envelope into my hand, the sharp daggers in his eyes glinting under the silver moonlight. There had once been more in the way he looked at me, a warmth, a fondness. But that's long gone now. Now that he knows what I'm capable of.

I say nothing as I accept his offering, folding it into my coat.

"This will be the last time," he decrees. As if that decision is his to make. As if he holds any power here. People like him, they wear their confidence as casually as their clothing, an incontrovertible truth that's been draped over their shoulders since the day they were born.

"No," I reply, an icy smile slowly cracking across my face. "It won't."

18.

LILY

The thudding bass of the DJ's music rattles the frames on my bedroom walls. I toss my book aside and flop back on my bed, pulling a pillow over my head, but it's of no use. I can still hear the raucous laughter of Theo's obstreperous friends, the cheering and the chanting, the party that's spinning further out of control with every passing hour.

Theo throws his Summer Bash every year, like clockwork, always ensuring that it coincides with the East Hampton Charity Gala, so that our parents will be otherwise occupied for the evening, and he can swan about like he's lord of the manor.

With a groan, I lift the pillow off my head. I might as well take a peek outside. I tell myself that I'm just checking to see whether Theo and his friends have completely destroyed the yard yet, but it's not really them that I care about. It's Alex. I want to see if the commotion of the party has drawn her out of the pool house, where she's been shut up all day, ever since she returned home early this afternoon. I wondered where she'd gone off to so early in the morning, what, if any, progress she's made toward finding Maddie, but I haven't been able to bring myself to ask her. It's probably best if I just avoid her altogether, and yet . . . I can't help watching. I'm drawn to her, the same way I was with Maddie. As though her presence here is pulling me into her orbit, consuming my thoughts, even though I know this can't end well.

I pad over to the window and push aside the curtains. There's a woman in a bright pink bikini draped over the inflatable flamingo floating at the center of the pool, as if she's posing for the cover of *Sports Illustrated*. Glow sticks have been dropped into the water around her, giving it an otherworldly radiance. At the far side of the yard, a DJ booth has been set up, the DJ diligently spinning at a turntable with oversized headphones slung around his neck. All around the yard, Theo's friends, posh boys with private-school educations, chug from plastic cups, and girls in string bikinis lick salt off their hands before throwing back shots of tequila and sucking seductively on slivers of lime.

That's when I see Hutch stand atop a table, a glass raised in his hand. *"Per unitatem vis!"* he shouts.

Through unity, strength. It was once the motto of their school, Buckley Prep, where Hutch, Mick, and Theo seemed to have formed an impenetrable union. The bonds of their brotherhood stronger even than the blood that binds Theo to me.

"Hear, hear!" a group of boys calls back, all of them falling to one knee and draining the contents of their glasses in response to Hutch's call.

The party seems to grow more boisterous after that, the music creeping louder, the drinks being filled faster.

I look down at the bracelet tied around my wrist. A simple thing, made of an intricate series of knots, a gold charm, a starfish, fixed at its center. Maddie gave it to me. Not long after she moved into the pool house.

She'd found a flyer attached to a light post on her walk home from the Lobster Shack. I never minded giving her a lift home, and I'd even given her the spare key to my car in case she ever needed it, but sometimes she preferred to walk. She said the time alone helped her to unwind after a long shift. But that day, she'd found the flyer advertising a craft fair that was taking place the following afternoon on the boardwalk.

"Do you want to go?" she'd asked me that night as we sat side by side on the sofa in the pool house, applying shimmery licks of pink varnish to our toenails. Maddie propped her feet on the coffee table, wiggling her still-wet toes.

"I guess," I replied. "Could be fun."

The next day, Maddie and I set off together. I wasn't sure how I'd find the experience, whether it would be overwhelming to be surrounded by so many people, whether Maddie and I would find enough to talk about that we'd be able to fill the empty silences as we passed between stalls. This, having a friend, someone to go places with, to have *fun* with, was still new to me. But I shouldn't have worried.

We bought ice cream cones, swirling clouds of vanilla atop rolled sugar cones, that we licked like children as we walked through the fair. Local shops and restaurants had set up booths alongside the boardwalk, their hand-painted signs advertising pickle chips, fried Oreos, handcrafted silver jewelry. Maddie and I walked slowly past the colorful displays, running our hands over gauzy beach cover-ups in tropical patterns, silky scarves, sparkling crystals soldered into silver rings.

By midafternoon, the temperature was nearly unbearable, the heat rising off of the wooden planks of the boardwalk in spiraling waves. We took a break from walking and plopped down on a bench that faced out toward the ocean.

"How about I grab us some lemonades from the stand we passed a few rows back?" I offered, wiping away the sweat at my temples.

I was treated to one of Maddie's sparkling smiles, the kind that made it seem as though she was lighting up from within. "That sounds absolutely perfect."

I dashed off to get the lemonades, and when I returned balancing two plastic cups rattling with ice, I caught sight of Maddie quickly shoving something into the small woven purse she'd been carrying all day.

"What was that?" I asked, nodding toward the bag. It wasn't like me to pry, but perhaps I was feeling emboldened after the wonderful day we'd spent together. Maybe I felt like we had finally become close enough that I could ask her to share more of herself.

"Well . . ." Maddie replied sheepishly, "I was going to surprise you with this later but . . ." She reached inside her bag and then unfurled her fingers to reveal two delicate string bracelets, matching gold starfish glinting under the sun. "I got one for each of us. To remind us of this perfect day."

I couldn't find the words to tell her how much that bit of string meant to me. More than all the gold and diamond jewelry resting in velvet cases in my room at home. "I love it," I said instead, as she tied it around my wrist.

I spin the bracelet on my arm now, my fingers mindlessly toying with the starfish as I watch Theo's party, wondering when it will end, when all these people will finally leave. And that's when I see her: Alex, hovering at the fringes of the festivities, her phone in her hand, the bright screen illuminating her face in a blue-white glow.

I watch as she turns the phone around, showing it to a huddle of Theo's guests. They shake their heads in reply before turning back to their conversations, hardly giving Alex the time of day. She must be asking about Maddie, trying to get them to look at the photo.

I toy with a lock of my hair, picking at the split ends, as I watch her move through the crowd. Theo hasn't noticed her yet, as he's too busy holding court beside the bar. He leans on it languidly while a crowd gathers around him, laughing at whatever story he's regaling them with.

When I turn my attention back to Alex, my jaw tightens. She has her phone out again, showing the screen to Hutch this time. He hardly reacts but for a slight shake of his head before he slings his arm over Alex's shoulders, gesturing to Mick, who saunters up to them with two shot glasses in his hands. Hutch can't be bothered to care about something as tiresome as a missing girl, not during a party where he's meant to be having fun. Alex seems annoyed, shaking her head at Mick, who shrugs and downs the shot himself. She's playing with fire now, talking to the people who are closest to Theo. It's only a matter of time before she gets burned.

She needs to stop. The thought shakes loose from my brain as a shout, reverberating inside my skull. If Theo finds out what Alex is up to, that she's been nosing around, asking questions, he's not going to be happy.

19.

ALEX

I clench my teeth and shrug Hutch's arm off my shoulders. *Self-important jackass.* At least the other one . . . Mitch, Mick, or whatever, had the decency to look ashamed while offering me a shot of tequila as I was asking about my missing sister. *These people.* I can feel the anger pulsing through my body, radiating out through my skin.

"What kind of name is Hutch anyway?" I grumble, more to myself than to him, but evidently he feels compelled to respond.

Hutch tosses his head back in laughter, a deep guffaw. "It's short for Hutchinson—my last name. You know, like *Governor* Hutchinson?"

I didn't think it was possible, but somehow I dislike this guy even more now.

"Well, it's been real . . ." I toss my hair over my shoulder.

"Leaving so soon, love?" He asks as I turn to go, a sardonic smile slung across his face.

I draw my hands into fists, feeling my nails dig little crescent moons into the soft pads of my palms as I walk away from him. *Moron.*

I pick my way through the crowd of trust-fund brats

shotgunning beers on the back lawn and head toward the house. I step inside the great room and pull the French doors closed behind me, happy to dull the pounding blare of the dance music that was beginning to make my head throb. Inside, the party feels tamer. It's less crowded here, just a few couples lounging on the sofas, long tanned legs draped across laps, hands roving over exposed skin. I avert my eyes and head toward the stairs.

If anyone should ask, I'll say I was looking for the restroom, but what I'm *really* after is Maddie's phone. This may be my only chance to look around the main house while most of the Blackwell family is otherwise occupied.

At the top landing, I'm met with a long hallway, white doors lining either side. The first door I reach is closed, a strip of light shining out from the gap beneath it. *That must be Lily's room.* I tiptoe past, hoping she doesn't choose this moment to decide to join the party downstairs.

I come upon what I assume to be Theo's room next. At the center is a four-poster bed in a deep cherry wood set against an accent wall painted a rich navy blue. The room looks exactly like it should for a man Theo's age, but yet I can't dispel the feeling that it's all an act: an empty facsimile of normalcy. Much like the feeling I got when I first met Theo himself. I quietly step into the room and walk past the rows of aged leather-bound books lining Theo's shelves; classic novels: *East of Eden, Crime and Punishment,* titles I suspect are more for display than actual reading. I open the closet and carefully pick through the built-in drawers, between the rows of pressed shirts that smell of starch and a faint trace of expensive cologne. *Nothing.* I decide to move on, pulling the door to Theo's room nearly closed behind me, leaving it exactly as I'd found it.

The next two doors I pass lead to guest rooms—fluffy white duvets, long cream curtains, standing mirrors angled in the far corners, almost sterile in their simplicity. Across the hall I find a linen closet and the bathroom I'm meant to be looking for. I walk by it pretending not to have noticed.

When I come upon the master bedroom, I quickly duck inside. *Wow.* My eyes are immediately drawn to the vaulted ceilings transected by exposed mahogany beams. The space is painted a gentle dove-white and features an enormous bed topped with a cloudlike duvet, the type I'd expect in a five-star hotel, and a marble ensuite with a freestanding soaking tub. I pad across the luxurious white throw rug, my feet sinking into the deep pile, wondering what it must be like to live in a place like this. I open Katherine's bedside drawer first. Nothing of note aside from a couple of night serums and under-eye creams. James's side isn't much more helpful; just some loose change, a set of gold cuff links, and an old dry-cleaning ticket. I'm beginning to feel like this was a waste of time, like I'm not going to find anything of Maddie's in this house.

I make my way back into the hallway, where there's only one last door left to check. This one is closed, and I lean my ear against it, the painted wood cool against my cheek, making sure there's no one on the other side before I push it open.

The door creaks open on metal hinges to reveal an office—an imposing desk built of a rich, solid wood, an up-holstered wingback chair stretched with supple leather, and towering bookshelves, tastefully arranged with thick volumes and nautical curios of all manner: model sailboats, a brass compass, a wooden lighthouse. *This must be James's home office.* I slip inside, pulling the door closed behind me until I hear the soft click of the latch engaging. I flick on the desk light, a vintage-style banker's lamp with a frosted green shade, and rummage through the desk. The top drawers hold nothing but a jumble of office supplies: loose rubber bands, rogue paper clips, an assortment of pens. But when I tug on the bottom drawer, it holds fast. I inspect the front panel and find a tiny silver lock, the kind that can only be opened with a key. Or, if you've worked in a hardware store that also doubles as your town's only locksmith, with a well-placed paper clip.

I grab a paper clip from the top drawer and set about unwinding it until the twisted metal forms a small hook. I wedge it into the lock and poke around for the internal mechanism that will disengage it—but something outside the door makes me freeze, my hand hovering in midair. A shuffling sound on the stairs. Someone is coming. It could just be one of Theo's drunk guests stumbling toward the bathroom, but I can't risk being found in here. *I need to hurry.* I rattle the clip in the lock, my palms slick with sweat, and mercifully, it turns over with a click. I exhale, blowing a lock of hair out of my face, but I'm still not finished. I haven't found what I came for yet.

Inside the drawer are rows of manila file folders, each labeled with property addresses, business names. I hastily flip through the first folder: drawings, designs, receipts. The rest of the files seem to be much of the same. Nothing of use to me. Nothing that will help me find Maddie. I'm about to close the drawer, duck out of here before whoever I heard on the stairs finds me where I shouldn't be, when I notice something interesting. At the back of the drawer is a large envelope, sealed with a metal fastener. It doesn't match the other files in the drawer, the size slightly too large to conceal it. I snatch it up quickly, listening to the sound of approaching footsteps treading down the hallway. *I don't have much time.* I rush to open the envelope, tearing the flap in my haste, and shake out the contents onto the desk, rectangular papers fluttering onto the leather blotter.

It's Maddie. It's all Maddie. Photos of her taken from every conceivable angle: Maddie placing a dish in front of a customer at the Lobster Shack, her face lit up in a smile, her hair tied back in a low ponytail that trails down her back; Maddie on the beach at dusk, her toes in the white foam that trims the shoreline, a pair of flip-flops dangling from her fingers; Maddie with another girl, a pretty brunette with a mischievous smile and a leather miniskirt, their arms looped together at the elbow as they traverse a cobblestone walk in spiked heels, falling into each other with laughter.

I hear the creak of a door along the hallway, and I hastily shove all the photos back into the envelope, stuffing it into the drawer, and slamming it shut. I wince at the sound, freezing as I crouch behind the desk. I don't hear any noise from the hallway anymore, no footsteps echoing down the long hall. It's possible whoever came upstairs is in the bathroom. *Or, it's possible, that they're waiting for me just outside the door.* But I have no choice. I have to get out of here. I can't cower behind this desk like a sitting duck.

My knees feel weak with nerves as I cautiously cross the room, my hand shaking as I reach for the doorknob. The hallway remains silent. *It's now or never.* I peer around the edge of the door, scanning the hall. *There's no one here.* With a sigh of relief, I slip out of the office, quietly pulling the door closed behind me, and hastily scurry down the hall toward the stairs, toward safety. But one of the bedroom doors swings open, nearly knocking me off my feet as I rush by.

Theo. He levels me with an appraising glare. "What are you doing up here?"

"I was, er, just looking for the bathroom." I offer him a watery smile, the best I can muster with my heart bashing against my rib cage.

"It's just there," he says, pointing to the open door a few feet from where we stand.

"Oh," I reply with a clumsy laugh, "can't believe I didn't see it . . ."

But Theo isn't listening anymore as he gazes over my shoulder, his features hardening with scrutiny. I follow his line of sight to the closed door of the office, the warm glow of the lamplight flickering underneath. *I'd forgotten to turn out the light.*

"Anyway, thanks," I say, squeezing past him. "I'll just use the one in the pool house."

I don't wait for a response. I rush down the stairs, my feet tumbling down the treads as fast as they can carry me.

———

Back in the pool house, with the door safely locked behind me, I begin to calm myself down, sucking in deep gulps of air. I settle down on the couch, pulling a Chantilly throw blanket around my shoulders, wrapping myself in the security of its warmth. *Those photos.* I hold them in my memory, my mind tracing over the details. There was something about them . . . a haunting intimacy that gave me the impression that James Blackwell is very much in love with my sister. That's probably why he hid them away as he did. Anyone who saw those photos would immediately recognize them for what they were: homage to the woman he loves. But what bothers me the most, the thought that claws insistently at the back of my mind, is that Maddie didn't appear to have known those pictures were being taken. Just looking at them felt like an invasion of her privacy, stolen moments of her life.

Where are *you, Maddie?* Was she having an affair with James? Does that have something to do with why she's gone missing? I would give anything to be able to ask Maddie all of the questions that have been swirling in my head these past days. I would give anything just to be able to talk to her. To tell her that I'm sorry.

After Mom's funeral, after the handful of mourners left, depositing casseroles and condolences on our doorstep, Maddie and I were left alone for the first time in days. With no distraction of planning the services, choosing floral arrangements, sorting through Mom's dresses, debating which had been her favorite. It was just me and Maddie. In the cool silence of a house where memories of our mother settled like dust over every surface.

"Are you okay?" Maddie asked, breaking the silence as the two of us sat, side by side, in our funeral clothes on the faded floral-print couch that sagged in the middle.

"Yeah. I guess so. You?"

Maddie shrugged. "It's a lot to take in. I still can't believe she's really gone."

I looked around the house that still smelled of her jasmine perfume and her favorite bourbon. "I know what you mean."

"I'm sorry, you know. That I wasn't around more. At the end. I wish you would have told me how bad things had gotten."

Now it was my turn to shrug. I hadn't told her that Mom's drinking had gotten to the point where she could barely keep a job, that she hardly left her room anymore, that the upkeep of the house had fallen entirely on my shoulders. If I had, I knew Maddie would have come home. She'd have given up everything and come back here to rescue me. But I didn't want that for her. She'd built a life for herself. She'd just started medical school, and I could hear it in her voice every time she called. How excited she was, how happy that she was finally making her dreams come true. And I knew that if she came home, back to that house, to the dull, lifeless place that it was, it would have extinguished that light in her forever.

"Mom was really proud of you," I tell her instead.

And it was true. Mom had been proud of Maddie, even at the very end. "Your sister," she'd tell me, stars in her clouded eyes, "was always meant for more than this. She's going to *be* somebody." Every time she said it, I could feel my heart harden in my chest. I knew Maddie was the smart one, the perfect one, the prodigal daughter, but did it mean nothing to my mother that I stayed when Maddie had left? That I'd given everything up so Maddie could be free of the tar-like stickiness of this life, so that she could go out into the world and "be somebody"?

"She was proud of you too," Maddie said, but the words rang hollow to my ears. "It's just"—she continued as she wiped a tear from the corner of her eye—"she had such a hard life."

"Maddie, *we* had hard lives. *Because* of her." The angry spikes in my voice surprised us both.

Maddie turned to face me, her eyes widening in shock. "You can't really mean that. You're just upset."

"Of course I mean it! Don't you remember? Don't you

remember what it was like for us? All the times she left us on our own, forgot to pick us up from school?"

Maddie winced, her face falling at the memory of me and her sitting on the curb outside of our elementary school, watching as our classmates were whisked away in shiny cars by smiling parents, waiting to see the headlights of Mom's station wagon that would never come.

The principal spotted us and ushered us inside to call our mother. We tried to protest, but he insisted, calling our home phone several times before Mom finally picked up, her voice raw and hoarse on the other end of the line. I could tell right away that she'd been asleep, recovering from the night before.

Fifteen minutes later Mom pulled into the circular drive at the front of the school, tires screeching against the asphalt as she made the turn.

"I'm so sorry, girls," she'd said as she all but fell out of the car, enveloping us in a hug that smelled of fresh perfume with undercurrents of sour booze. "I worked a late shift last night," she offered by way of explanation to the principal, Mr. Demmerle, who stood behind us, his arms folded stoically over his chest.

"I see," was all he said, but Mom pounced on the frost framing his words.

"What's that supposed to mean?" she snapped. "You think you know me? You think you know what kind of parent I am?"

"All I'm saying," Mr. Demmerle replied, his hands fanned out in a placating gesture, "is that this isn't the first time the girls haven't been picked up at dismissal."

Mom glared at us then. As though we had betrayed her

somehow. "They're old enough to walk, aren't they? I certainly did at their age!"

By then, other students, other parents, who had been at the school for after-school activities, got wind of the commotion and gathered around the front entrance. It was the first time I really saw Mom as everyone else did. Saw how different she looked from the other mothers. Her top too revealing, the V-cut neckline amplifying her cleavage, her hair wild and matted from midday sleep. It was the first time I remember wishing to myself that I had another mother. The kind that wore sundresses and made cookies for school bake sales.

But Mom wasn't finished. "I'm a single mother! And you"—she poked Mr. Demmerle in the chest—"have no idea what my life is like, trying to raise two kids on my own! You with your fancy suit and your fancy job! How dare you pass judgment on me!"

My ears burned with embarrassment, and my eyes dropped to my sneakers, focusing my attention on grounding the toe of my shoe into the pavement instead of the tension growing around me. I was almost grateful when Mom grabbed Maddie and me by the wrists and pulled us toward the car.

"Ms. Walker," Mr. Demmerle called after her, his tone almost hesitant, "are you in an appropriate state to drive with your children in the car?"

Mom whirled around, her eyes hard, angry slits. "Don't you dare presume to tell me how to raise my children!" She spit the words through clenched teeth, unrestrained rage etched across her face.

Maddie and I dutifully climbed into the back seat of our car, not daring to look out the window at Mr. Demmerle and the crowd that was probably staring open-mouthed at the scene they'd just witnessed. I didn't have to look to know that they were whispering about us, about Mom, already.

Mom marched to the driver's side and got into her own seat, slamming the door behind her. "The nerve of that man!" she exclaimed, her fingers so tight on the steering wheel that her knuckles blanched.

She turned to face us then, Maddie and me cowering in the back seat, her features softening. "You girls know I'd never do anything to hurt you, don't you?" she asked, her voice pleading, begging us to agree with her. "I just lost track of time, that's all."

"We know, Mom," Maddie had said, serving her the validation she'd been looking for. It had pained me that she did it, that she'd given Mom that gift of forgiveness when I wasn't ready to hand it over.

Maybe I still wasn't. Even after we'd buried her.

"She was doing her best!" Maddie chided me, chasing away the painful memory. "She had no one to help her. Her parents gave up on her, Dad walked out on her . . . And she wasn't always like that, Alex. Why do you choose to remember only the worst things about Mom? She deserves more than that."

"What else was there, Maddie?" I can hear my voice growing louder, years of hurt, resentment boiling to the surface.

"What about the beach day?" Maddie crossed her arms over her chest, raising an eyebrow as if daring me to disagree.

As soon as she said it, the memory came crashing back. I remembered being confused when Mom pulled us out of school early under the guise of taking us to the doctor, wondering if I'd somehow forgotten about an appointment, but when we got into the car, she was all smiles.

"I have a surprise for you, girls," she'd said, mischief dancing between her words. It was one of her good days, during one of her stretches of sobriety, which could last days, weeks, or even months at a time. But Maddie and I never knew when things were going to take a turn for the worse again, and so we'd learned to savor those days with Mom, when we had her at her best.

She drove us to the beach, with nothing but a few bargain-bin paperbacks, rolled-up towels, and sandwiches stacked in a brown paper bag, but it turned out to be one of the best days of my life.

I remember standing at the shore, watching as Mom dove beneath the waves, Maddie splashing along beside her.

"Come on, Alex, sweetie," Mom had called. "There's nothing to be afraid of!" She flopped down into the water, floating on her back, her face soaking up the sun's rays.

"I just . . . I think I'll stay here!" I yelled back.

Mom stood up then, and walked through the surf toward me, her salty hands outstretched. "Come, baby. I won't let anything bad happen to you, I promise."

I looked up into her big green eyes, at the tenderness I found there, and it warmed me more than the sun. "Okay," I said bravely, tilting my chin up just as I'd watched her do so many times before. "Let's go."

"That's my girl."

We'd spent the afternoon splashing in the waves together, the three of us lying on our bellies in the sand, breaking off pieces of the cheese sandwiches Mom had packed. And it was a perfect day. A golden glittering memory that rose above the rubble.

"I knew you would remember the beach day," Maddie said, looking satisfied.

"Yeah, I do, but that doesn't make up for the rest of it."

"You're being really unfair to her, Alex." A glint of gold flashed at her throat. Mom's necklace. Looped around Maddie's neck.

It took me by surprise, that Maddie and I had such different views of our mother, of our shared childhood. And it stung like a betrayal. All my life I'd assumed Maddie and I were on the same side, allies fighting the same battles shoulder to shoulder. But in that moment, I realized that the war was over, the dust had settled, and it was only ever me on the battlefield, alone in my armor.

"That's easy for you to say," I snapped. "You weren't here! You just . . . left us!"

Maddie looked as though she'd been slapped.

"You packed up your things and you left me here to take care of Mom, to take care of everything!" My words surprised even me. This ugly resentment had never been a conscious thought. I'd never blamed Maddie for going to college, for succeeding where I'd failed. Or at least I thought I hadn't. Because there it was, hanging between us. "You're so . . . selfish! You've only ever cared about yourself!"

"You don't mean that," Maddie offered lamely. "You're just upset."

"I do mean it," I insisted, even though I wasn't sure that was true.

"I didn't leave you, Alex. But I had to go. I had to make a life for myself. And you made a life for yourself here too!" She held it out to me like a consolation prize. "You have your job at Nate's, that guy Ben you're always talking about . . ."

"Don't you dare bring Ben into this. Don't use him to

make yourself feel better about what you did. You don't know the first thing about him, about this wonderful life I supposedly have. Because you're not here. You're never here!"

"I couldn't stay, Alex. You know that. And if you were so unhappy, you could have come with me. How many times did I ask you? You didn't have to stay here, all these years, you could have had more."

"Someone had to stay, and it sure as hell wasn't going to be you! But do you know what hurts the most, Maddie? That no matter how much I did, how much I sacrificed, you were still Mom's favorite. Her perfect daughter, the one thing she might have cared about more than booze."

"I had to be perfect, just to get her to notice me!" Maddie shouted, her voice rising to meet my own. "She always expected so much of me. All of her hopes and dreams pinned to my back. Do you have any idea how much pressure that is? No. Of course you don't, because you were the one she loved no matter what."

I stood up from the couch, anger in my eyes as I leveled my next words at her like a blow. "Even if I was never going to be as good as you, right? Is that what you're getting at?"

"Of course not!" Maddie yelled, standing to meet my eyes. "You know that wasn't what I meant. Why are you trying to pick a fight right now? Our *mother* just died, Alex!"

"I'm not! I just . . . I don't know why you're defending her, after . . . everything!"

"You know what," Maddie said, a sigh of defeat in her voice, "you don't know what you're talking about, okay? Let's just drop it."

"Fine!" I shouted at her retreating back.

But what I should have said was that I was sorry. For lashing out at her, for sharpening my grief into a weapon to be used against her. And I should have told her that she was right. Because I'm beginning to see that now. Vivienne Walker may not have been a perfect mother, but she'd loved us the best she could. After Dad left, it was just the three of us. Maddie, Mom, and me. Mom's parents, my grandparents, had cut her off when she was nineteen, when she got pregnant with Maddie. Maddie and I never even met them. Mom became a mother too young; she didn't know how to handle it, how to do this on her own after Dad walked off into the night, leaving behind all of the responsibility of parenthood at her feet like forgotten luggage. Maybe she was doing the best she could. After all, she'd given us each other, and that was the best thing she ever could have done for us. If only I hadn't pushed Maddie away, if only I hadn't taken her for granted.

I drop my head into my hands and let the tears fall. Tears for my mother and for my sister, for the family I wish I could surround myself with now. And then a buzzing sound from inside my bag yanks me from my self-pity.

I pull out my phone and stare at the screen in disbelief, pushing away the tears drying on my cheek. One new message from Maddie Walker. I swipe my finger across the screen with a shaking hand.

You need to get out of there. Now.

20.

MADDIE

BEFORE

"Have another one!" Becca yells over the music as she lifts the bottle of vodka, in its expensive frosted bottle, from the ice bucket in the center of our table. She pours a serving of the clear liquid into a shot glass and hands it to me.

My head is already swimming, the lights of the club blurring around the periphery of my vision. "I think I'll pass," I yell back.

Becca winks at me and lifts the glass to her lips, her pale throat bared as she tosses her head back.

The bottle-service waitress for the VIP section approaches our table. "You ladies need anything else?"

"No, thanks," Becca replies, swiping a shimmering drop of liquor from her bottom lip with her thumb before licking it off her finger. She smiles, white teeth behind red lips. "We're good here."

I wonder, not for the first time, how Becca can afford her lifestyle. Bottle service at exclusive clubs, closets full of clothes, designer handbags, her Louis Vuitton clutch tossed casually on the sticky seat of our booth.

Could it really all be from Lucky Jack's? She'd told me about her second job the first time we'd closed at the Lobster Shack together, the two of us working in tandem to wipe the tables and stack the chairs as quickly as we could.

"The tips here are decent," she'd told me, "but they weren't enough. I was barely making ends meet each month, and so when I heard about an opening at Lucky Jack's I auditioned."

I concentrated on wiping a sticky spill from the table in front of me, heat blooming under my collar. I knew what it was like to feel desperate, to feel like you'd never get on your feet. I'd waited tables for years to save up for school, as I was too afraid to take out loans. The way Alex and I had grown up made me fearful of spending money I didn't have, of finding myself trapped in debt the way Mom had been, bill collectors hounding us over the phone line and in our mailbox. But stripping? It wasn't something I could ever imagine doing.

"I'm not ashamed of it or anything," Becca added, as though reading my thoughts. "It's a job. A business transaction. I have something the men in that club want and they're willing to pay for it. It's all on my terms. That's key for me. Besides . . ." She paused, waiting for my eyes to meet hers. "It's actually really fun." A feline grin crept across her face.

The closer I've gotten to Becca, the more I'm starting to understand the appeal of a place like Lucky Jack's to her. She has this fire in her. I've seen the way her eyes sparkle when she's teetering on the edge of danger. She drives too fast, her little red MINI Cooper weaving in and out of traffic. She flirts with men she meets in bars as if it's a game. I've watched her as she lets them ply her with drinks and compliments, allows their hands to linger on her body, their hungry eyes to rove over her roller-coaster curves, before she turns them down, anger and disappointment hardening their faces. It's as if she wants to see how far she can reel them in before pushing them away, how close she can bring them to the edge before leaving them in free fall. I worry about her and the dangerous games she plays, but I know there's nothing I can do to stop her, to keep her safe. Becca gets a rush out of pushing the limits, finding out just how close she can fly toward the flames without getting burned.

"Let's dance!" Becca says now, grasping my hand and pulling me through the throngs of people to the dance floor.

Her body moves slowly, sensually to the music, her hips, wrapped in black leather, dipping rhythmically with the beat. I feel awkward, stiff next to her, unsure what to do with my limbs.

"He's cute, isn't he?" Becca asks, nodding toward an older man with salt-and-pepper hair wearing a custom-tailored shirt, his initials embroidered on the cuffs.

"A little old to still be clubbing though."

Becca laughs. "You know I like older men . . . Especially rich ones." She says it with a wink, as though it was meant to be a joke, but I suspect that there's an element of truth hovering beneath the surface of her words.

"I'm going to the ladies' room," I shout, leaning in close to her ear to be heard. "You okay here on your own for a few?"

"Totally fine," Becca replies, her eyes closing as she tilts her head back, letting her dark hair sway behind her.

I pick my way to the bathroom, trying not to bump into anyone along the way. Once inside, I close the door and lean against it, the music still buzzing through the hollow wood. I let out a slow breath, feeling my chest fall. I love going out with Becca, but sometimes it gets to be too much. Even when I was living in Manhattan, surrounded by some of the most famous clubs in the world, I never did things like this. My roommates and I, we preferred quiet nights in, bottles of wine and reality TV. But nothing about Becca is quiet. It was exciting at first, exhilarating, to step into her world. But sometimes I feel as though I can't keep up, and I'm not sure that I want to try.

I pull my phone out of my bag, a silver clutch that Becca lent me for the night, and check my phone, hoping for a response from Alex. It's been a few weeks since I sent her a message canceling my trip home for her birthday. It was the coward's way out, and I knew it. But I couldn't handle the thought of a phone call, of having to hear the hurt and disappointment in her voice. Someday—hopefully soon—I'll explain why I had to do it. I only hope that she'll understand. But it's not my sister who has been trying to reach me. Instead I find four missed calls and six text messages from Lily:

> Hey!! Do u want to hang out??
> Where are u? I didn't think you had work tonight
> Everything ok??
> Maddie???
> Can you just let me know where you are? I'm worried about u:(
> ???????

I close my eyes and try to shove down the annoyance. Lily is a sweet girl, but she can be so overbearing. And lately it's been getting worse. It seems that everywhere I turn, she's there. Showing up at my job to offer me a ride home, knocking on the door of the pool house, joining me when I have to run to the supermarket. I feel like I can't breathe when she's around. And I don't know if it's my imagination, but I've been noticing that she's starting to dress more like me, wearing her hair like me. Even her mannerisms, the way she stands, the cadence of her voice, seem to be morphing into a facsimile of mine. But maybe I'm overreacting. She's just young, she hasn't found herself yet, and I get the impression that she doesn't have many friends. Besides, Lily is the least of my concerns at Blackwell Manor.

I'm starting to think that it's time for me to move on. I know I got myself into this mess, but it's probably best if I find somewhere else to stay while I'm in the Hamptons, until I finish what I came here to do. There's just something wrong with that place. Or maybe it's the family that lives there. I've seen the way Katherine looks at me. The way she watches my every move with a hard set to her eyes. It's almost as if she wishes me dead.

21.

ALEX

Watery sunlight begins to filter through the pool house, a tangerine gradient that spreads across the room like a warm blanket. I shut my eyes against it, turning away in frustration, my legs tangled in the knotted sheets. Another day has started, another day without Maddie.

I couldn't sleep last night, not after the text I'd received.

You need to get out of there.

I'd called Maddie's phone immediately after I'd read it, but, as always, my call went straight to voicemail, Maddie's chipper recording on the other end:

You've reached Maddie's phone, please leave me a message . . .

I tried her again and again, hoping she'd switch her phone back on. Even for a second, just long enough for me to get through, to hear her voice, to know that she's okay. But the only voice I heard was the same tired recording:

You've reached Maddie's phone, please leave me a message . . .

I try her again now, the screen warm against my face from being held in my hand all night. I'd been afraid to put my phone down, afraid to miss another message from her. Again, my call goes straight to voicemail.

With a frustrated sigh, I end the call and scroll through the series of texts I sent her last night instead, none of which she replied to. I wonder whether she's even seen them.

Where are you?
You need to answer me. I'm freaking out.
Please, Maddie
Is this Maddie?

It's that last one that's been running through my mind since late last night, spinning like a record I can't turn off. It's the thought that kept me awake with a cold worry creeping through my veins. *It may not have been Maddie on the other end of the line at all.* After her phone was taken from the pool house, it could be anyone sending those messages. While it's possible that Maddie came back for her phone and is now warning me against the dangers here, it's also possible that one of the Blackwells took it and is using it to try to frighten me off.

There's no way I can leave now. If there's even a chance that one of the Blackwells was behind the message, that means there's something more here, something they're desperate not to let me find.

The phone buzzes in my hand, the vibration beneath my fingertips startling me so much that I nearly drop it. I fumble to flip over the screen to see who's calling, but the caller ID shows a number I don't recognize.

"Hello?" I venture, my breath held in my throat, praying to hear Maddie's voice come through the line.

"Hey, it's April." *Not Maddie after all.*

I stop myself from sighing in disappointment, my heart hanging heavily in my chest. "Oh, hi."

"Sorry for the early call."

"It's fine. I was up."

"Listen," April begins, "I don't know if this means anything, but Becca didn't show up for work last night."

"Is that normal for her?"

"No, not at all. She always comes in when she's on the schedule. And I heard Jack talking to one of the other girls, and she was real pissed because apparently Becca didn't even give her a heads-up or anything, and she had to scramble to find someone else to cover Becca's shift. Jack is usually pretty cool about it if you have to call out, but all the girls know you can't just bail on a shift. She'll cut you from the schedule for that, bump you from your VIP tables where you get the big tips."

I wait for her to continue, unsure how to respond. First Maddie goes missing and now her friend. I don't know what to make of it yet. My brain is scrambling to slot the pieces together, but they don't seem to fit.

"I got Becca's number off Jack's records and tried calling her this morning. She's not picking up. The calls go straight to voicemail. I don't know if this has anything to do with your sister, but I thought I should tell you."

"Thanks," I reply. "I don't know either, but I'm going to look into it."

"Look . . ." April lowers her voice. "I'm not supposed to do this, but I took Becca's address from Jack's file too. Just in case you wanted to go over there, see if you can get ahold of her."

I stand up, already searching for my car keys. "Text it to me. I'll go right now."

I pull my car onto Becca's street and park in the first open spot I find. I check April's message again, comparing it to the row of townhouses across from me, making sure I've come to the right place. The sandstone-colored buildings each have second-floor terraces facing a small but picturesque park. It's a short walk to the beach, and I imagine that if you were to stand on one of those balconies and look at just the right angle, you might be able to catch a sliver of an ocean view. These weren't exactly the accommodations I was expecting from a girl who waits tables and dances at a nightclub. It seems Becca must be doing pretty well for herself at Lucky Jack's. *Unless she has another source of income that I don't know about.* It strikes me then how little I know about Maddie's supposed friend, about what she could have dragged Maddie into. For all I know, Becca could be a drug dealer and I'm about to ring her doorbell.

It wouldn't be the first time my impulsiveness landed me in trouble. It was a rite of passage at our high school for the upperclassmen to go to the swimming hole after the last day of school. Each year, the junior and senior class would hike through the woods along a path beaten by the footsteps of hundreds of students before us. Everyone knew about the swimming-hole parties thrown by the football team, but only the upperclassmen were invited. By the end of my junior year, it was all I could think about. Maddie, of course, had gone the year before. She always did everything first.

"I'm telling you, it's just gonna be a bunch of idiots from school shotgunning beers and jumping in a lake." She sighed with a roll of her eyes as I tried on the tenth outfit option of the evening. "It's not going to be nearly as cool as you're building it up to be."

"I know, but I really want to go," I responded, sizing myself up in our bedroom mirror. It was easy for Maddie to be cavalier about it. She was invited to everything, by everyone who mattered. She'd always let me tag along, but I wasn't a part of my sister's crowd—the popular kids—not really. Most of them barely even noticed I existed.

It wasn't easy being the unremarkable Walker sister. Constantly being compared to Maddie and always coming up short. Since we looked so similar, everyone naturally expected me to be just like her. They expected me to sparkle like she did. I'd tried, for a time. I'd wanted so badly for it to be true. But it quickly became clear that I was not my sister. And then, well, I might as well have been invisible. The problem was that I didn't know who I was outside of Maddie's shadow, how I was going to navigate the world without her. She was about to leave for college, and I would be left behind in Dogwood Grove to figure it out on my own. Being invited to this party felt like it could be a turning point; it made me feel like I belonged to something for once.

I held up two swimsuits. "Do you like the pink bikini or the black?"

Maddie lifted her eyes and peered at me above the paperback she was reading. "Black," she replied laconically before returning to her book.

When the day of the party finally arrived I was giddy with excitement. Maddie and I carried our towels out to the swimming hole and spread them out on a flat rock, claiming our space. The small clearing was packed with kids, jumping from stony ledges and crashing into the water with dramatic splashes, making out in shady crevices, dancing to the music that blasted from portable speakers.

The party carried on for most of the day, and Maddie and

I had fun swimming in the cool water, sipping from water bottles filled with pink lemonade and vodka. I was glad to have the time with her, since I knew it was limited. I kept trying to put it out of my mind—that Maddie would be leaving soon—taking swigs of my drink to dull the thought. I ended up indulging more than I intended to, a languid warmth spreading through my body as the crowd began to thin, the sky turning an inky black.

"We should go," Maddie said with a yawn.

"Can't we stay a little longer?" I begged. I wasn't ready to leave. It was a perfect summer night: fireflies dotting the air, music floating through the trees, the swimming hole lit with portable camping lanterns set up around the perimeter. I couldn't understand why Maddie would want to leave all of this to go . . . home. Where everything felt heavy, where we had to return to reality like Cinderella faced with the stroke of midnight.

She looked over the remaining handful of partygoers. Her friends—the cheerleaders, a few guys from the football team—passing a joint around, the lit embers glowing an orange-red in the darkened woods.

"Alright," Maddie relented. "I guess we can stay a little longer."

I squeezed her hand in appreciation.

Just then, Jason Adler, captain of the football team and reigning king of our high school, stood up and surveyed the crowd. "Who's up for skinny-dipping?" he asked, his smile mischievous, almost menacing in the flickering light from the lanterns.

A few of the girls squealed with high-pitched giggles as he dropped his swim trunks, his bare skin pale in the moonlight before he dove into the lake. Some of the other guys followed suit, pulling off bathing suits and cannonballing into the water. They called to the girls who looked at one another and exploded into a fit of laughter before untying their bikini tops and wriggling out of the bottoms.

Soon, it was just Maddie and me left standing on the shore.

"You coming?" Jason called.

"No thanks," Maddie yelled back.

"Come on, Walker!" he moaned.

A few of the girls joined in. "Yeah, Maddie, come on."

"It's senior year," Jason yelled. "And you know this is, like, a tradition. Live a little for once."

"I'm just fine living with my clothes on," Maddie responded, seemingly unfazed by the pressure from her friends as she lay back down on her towel, propping herself up on her elbows.

"What about you, Little Walker?" Jason added.

"Me?" I'd asked, perplexed. No one from Maddie's crowd had ever included me in anything before. They'd hardly even spoken to me. For so long I'd lived on the periphery of their world, but they'd never welcomed me in. Until now.

"Yeah, you. You down?"

I looked over at Maddie, who raised both eyebrows at me. We could still do that then, have entire conversations without saying a word. I knew what she was thinking. That the decision was mine to make, that she wasn't going to tell me this was a bad idea, even though she thought it was.

I looked away, pretending not to hear her thoughts as I pulled my top over my head.

"There you go!" Jason hollered while a few of the other guys whooped in delight. I felt my entire body warm with shame, my stomach clench. I'd never been naked in front of a boy before. And here I was practically standing in front of the whole football team. I dove into the water, more to cover my nakedness than anything else. The shock of the cold water sobered me quickly.

"At least Little Walker is fun," Jason remarked, loud enough for Maddie to hear.

I felt myself trembling as he moved closer to me, as he slid his hand, slippery beneath the murky lake water, over my body. He'd kissed my neck. Drunkenly, sloppily, his hands reaching for my breasts. And I'd let him. Even though he didn't know my first name. Even though every fiber of my being wanted to shove him away. There was a time when I thought I'd have done anything to be noticed by Jason Adler, to have him choose me, to want me, but not like this, never like this.

"Come on, Alex," Maddie called. "We've gotta go."

I leapt from the water, leaving Jason wide-mouthed and confused. "You're a real buzzkill, Maddie," he remarked as I pulled on my clothes as quickly as I could.

Maddie picked up our towels and shrugged. "And you're a creep," she said pointedly.

Jason laughed her off, sidling up to Trish Davis instead, his arm snaking around her bare waist much to her giggling delight.

The walk home was quiet, Maddie and I trudging through the woods as I soaked through my clothes, but I wasn't cold. My body was still flaming with shame. *Why had I done that? Why hadn't I just stayed with Maddie where it was safe?* It was as if I'd just announced to the world, "See? I'll never be like my sister. You can stop expecting more of me now."

As we reached our house, we came to a stop in the driveway, both of us looking up at the cottage, but neither making a move to go inside.

THE PERFECT SISTER 153

"You know," Maddie said, her soft voice cutting through the silence, "you don't have to compromise yourself to get other people to like you."

I said nothing. I just looked down at my feet, willing the tears to stop building at the back of my eyes.

"You're perfect just as you are, Alex. I hope you know that. And anyone who doesn't see that, the Jason Adlers of the world who think they're entitled to something from you, well—they don't deserve to know the real you."

I rolled my eyes. "Okay, Mom." My words dripped with sarcasm. I'd hoped it would be thick enough to coat the self-loathing lurking beneath.

"I'm serious." Maddie held my arm, waiting for my eyes to meet hers. "Maybe you don't want to hear it right now, but life is all about choices. I need you to remember that. You get to choose who you want to be."

I step out of my car, closing the door behind me. *I wonder what choices Maddie made that led her here.* I walk down the street toward unit number four, but as I reach Becca's address, I'm surprised to find a man already standing on her porch. His broad shoulders stretch the fabric of his navy-blue collared shirt as he knocks on the door assertively.

I stand perfectly still, unsure whether I should stay or go, but something holds me to the spot. I need to see if Becca will answer that door. I inch closer, listening for a response, but all I hear is the chirping of birds, the buzz of cicadas, the distant hum of a lawn mower.

The man turns to leave, and suddenly it feels as though I've come unglued. I need to move. Now. I don't know this man or what he wants. *I shouldn't be here.* I turn on my heels, ready to sprint back to my car.

"Alex?" a deep voice calls from over my shoulder.

The sound of my name makes me jump, my skin prickling with nerves. I whip around, my hair fanning out behind me. And then my shoulders fall, my body softens. It's Chief Gilroy.

"Oh," I say, my voice airy and breathless, my hand clutched to my chest. "I didn't recognize you."

He looks at me quizzically. "What are you doing here?"

"I could ask you the same," I respond, still trying to catch my breath.

"Jack, the owner down at Lucky Jack's, asked me to come out and check on one of her girls. Said she didn't show up to work last night. I'm sure it's nothing, but Jack's an old friend and I told her I'd swing by and check it out on my way to the station."

"*Jack* is an old friend?" I don't mean to ask it out loud, but the words are out of my mouth before I can stop them.

Chief Gilroy laughs, tilting his head back, crinkles forming at the corners of his eyes. "So you've met her then. And I guess I wouldn't call her a friend so much as a longtime acquaintance. She's a local. Just like me. And it's a small town when the summer folks pack up at the end of the season. We all know each other pretty well around here. Well enough to know that Jack wouldn't call down to the station if she didn't think she had a damn good reason."

"And does she?"

"Doubtful. Though seeing you here does make me curious. Do you know Ms. Jones?" He nods toward Becca's front door.

"No, but I'm told she's a friend of my sister's. I came to see if she might know where Maddie is."

"Still no word from your sister then?"

"None," I lie. I can't tell him about the text. About the

message from Maddie's phone. If he's going to help me find her, he has to believe that she's really missing. And I know if I tell him about the text, it might plant a seed of doubt in his mind.

"Hmm . . ." He looks up at Becca's townhouse thoughtfully. "Let's give it one more try then." He bangs on the door again, his fist thudding heavily against the wood. "Ms. Jones," he calls authoritatively, "it's Chief Gilroy. If you're in, could you please come to the door?"

We stand on the porch in silence, waiting for a response that doesn't come.

"Nothing." I throw up my hands in frustration.

"Well, that doesn't mean anything," Gilroy reassures me. "She could just be out."

"You don't think there's more here? First Maddie goes missing and now her friend." My voice rises in pitch as my worries mount.

"Whoa now," Gilroy says, laying his heavy hand on my shoulder. "Let's not jump to conclusions. We don't know that either of them are missing. Just because Ms. Jones isn't home at the moment doesn't mean she's missing."

"But—"

"Or maybe they've gone off somewhere together, since they're friends, as you say."

But Gilroy doesn't understand. He doesn't know Maddie. We may not be as close as we once were, but I'm certain that she'd never leave me to worry about her like this. Not if she could help it.

"Yeah," I reply, defeated. "Maybe."

If the police aren't going to help me find my sister, I'll have to do it on my own.

22.

KATHERINE

I grip the wooden handle in my fist, the silver blade catching a spark of sunlight as I plunge it downward, burying it to the hilt. The dirt turns over easily once it's been tilled, my trowel breaking through stubborn roots and clumps of dry earth. I dig into the soil, carving out a hole in the dark moist earth beneath the surface. A perfect place for my new dahlias to bloom. I lift the pink flowers from their pot, carefully exposing the roots before placing them in the hole, filling it with the upturned dirt.

I'm certain that our landscaper, Antonio, hates it when I do my own gardening, but I find it relaxing, empowering to create something beautiful where there once was nothing. To bring life to a stretch of barren earth. Antonio maintains the rest of the property, but this patch, this corner of the world, is my own.

I push back the brim of my straw sun hat, wiping my forehead with my wrist. Standing, I brush the soil from my knees and pull the gloves from my hands, feeling the rough granules of dirt that somehow still managed to find their way under my fingernails. I collect my things, ready to stow

them away in the shed, but the sound of the front gate sliding open gives me pause.

I stand in my garden, craning my neck to see down the
long drive, watch as Alex's old Honda Civic rumbles into
sight. James had insisted on adding her license plate to the
security system so that the gates to Blackwell Manor would
part at her arrival, as though welcoming royalty.

"We can't have her feeling like a prisoner here," he'd said
dismissively when I'd asked if he thought this wise. "As long
as she's a guest here, she needs to be able to come and go as
she pleases."

It astounds me how a man as ruthlessly successful as my
husband can be so naïve when it comes to the matter of
women. How easily he's taken in by a batted lash, a breathy
laugh. One might have thought he'd have learned his lesson
with Madison, but here he is again, cracking open our world,
inviting Alex into the fold.

She parks her car and steps out onto the drive, pushing a
pair of sunglasses over her eyes. She waves when she sees
me, and I lift my trowel in response, baring my teeth in an
approximation of a smile.

I can hardly stand to look at her. It feels like a penance, a
punishment for the things I've done, that I should have to see
her face, which looks so much like her sister's, inside the
gates of Blackwell Manor.

I was hoping she'd pass me by, that she'd hide herself
away in the pool house, but she doesn't. Instead she brazenly
walks toward me, and I've no choice but to stand here and
endure it.

"Hello, Alex," I start, "I was hoping to run into you today.
Might you have any news about your sister?"

"No." She shakes her head, her pretty blond hair swaying at her shoulders. "Not yet. But I wanted to ask you, did you ever meet any of her friends? Maybe a girl named Becca?"

"No," I respond, feigning thought. "The name doesn't ring a bell."

"Alright. Well, thank you anyway."

"Of course, and if we can be of any help to you, please do let us know. The whole family is quite concerned about your sister."

"Thanks." Alex sweeps her sunglasses atop her head, holding back her hair. "There was actually one other thing I wanted to ask you about."

"Sure." I nod, encouraging her to continue, though I wish she wouldn't.

"I know you mentioned that Maddie and Lily were close, but was she . . . did Maddie spend much time with anyone else in the family?"

"I'm not sure what you mean, dear."

"Was she friendly with Theo too? Or maybe . . . James?" The pause between her words tells me all I need to know.

"Well, she did express an interest in learning about James's business, and he showed her around the office, I believe, but that was really the extent of it. And I don't recall Theo and Madison having much occasion to interact with each other. Is there a reason you ask?"

"Oh, no, not really. I was just wondering about how Maddie spent her time while she was here."

"Well, then, I'm sorry I couldn't be of more help, but I'm off to wash up." I raise my hands as if offering proof. "Please do let us know as soon as you hear from Madison."

"I will." Alex waves and heads toward the pool house.

I walk to the shed, tossing my gardening gloves and trowel to the ground with a clatter, letting out a huff of frustration.

Why was she asking about James and Madison? How much does she know? When is this going to end?

I close my eyes, lean against the shed door, willing away the memories that flood my head unbidden: James in tennis whites, Madison's long, tan legs beneath a pleated skirt.

I came home from the Ladies Auxiliary Luncheon at the club to find them on the clay court. A court that had sat unused, forgotten, at the far side of our property for as long as I could remember.

I watched them together, the muscles of James's shoulders rolling smoothly beneath his skin, the sinews of Madison's arms, the flexing of her toned thighs. I listened to the way my husband grunted as he hit the ball, a sound so guttural, so primal, that a warm flush bloomed across my chest. It felt almost voyeuristic to watch them together like that, like I'd stumbled upon something intimate, private. The stroke of James's racket, the thwack of the ball as Madison effortlessly returned his serve, her youthful agility, the sheen of sweat glistening on their sun-kissed bodies. They matched each other, stroke for stroke, step for step, a perfect pairing.

Madison hit the ball, a blur of neon yellow-green sailing toward James. He ran to return the volley, his legs pumping furiously. He lunged, swinging his racket wildly, nearly falling to the ground as he sent the ball sailing back over the net, where it bounced once and flew out of bounds.

"That's game," he huffed, bent at the waist, hands propped on his knees as he struggled to catch his breath.

"Up for another match?" Madison called back with an easy laugh.

James chuckled. "Not for this old man."

"Oh, you're hardly an *old man*," she retorted with a sly grin.

I had to look away, to leave, unable to listen to them any longer. That's the problem with peering into other people's private moments. More often than not, you won't like what you see.

"Katherine? Is that you?" James called after me, my foot freezing midair.

"Oh, yes!" I pushed a convincing smile onto my face as I turned to face them. "I've just gotten home and I was wondering where you'd wandered off to. But you two looked so wrapped up in your game that I didn't want to interrupt." I was rambling and I knew it, the words churning out faster than I'd have liked, but I couldn't seem to stop myself. "I'm glad to see the old court getting some use though."

"It's been a while, hasn't it?" James raked his fingers through his hair, sweat sparkling at his hairline. "Maddie here has a hell of a backhand. She's been giving me a run for my money all morning."

I offered a tight smile, feeling the muscles in my jaw twitch beneath my skin at the thought of them alone together for hours.

"James works too much," Madison said, her tinkling laughter floating through the air, light as a song. "I thought he could use a break."

How often had I said those same words? How many times had I begged James to slow down, to take a break, to make time for his family? But he hadn't. Not for years. Not since I'd looked like Madison.

"Well, you two enjoy yourselves," I called with a wave. She probably thought I was so naïve that I couldn't see what was right in front of my face, that I'd served my husband up to her as casually as a ball hit over a net. But she was wrong. She was so very wrong. I wasn't going to let her break up our family without a fight.

"I think it's time for Madison to move out," I'd said definitively as James and I lay in bed that evening, he browsing emails and I rubbing lavender cream onto my hands.

"I disagree" was his only reply, hardly looking up from his phone to acknowledge how strongly I'd felt about the matter. My opinion was of no consequence to him. If he wanted her to stay, there was no way I could force her to go. *Or so he thought.* I knew that if I challenged him in that moment, it would only push him further into her waiting arms. And so all I could do was bide my time, wait for the perfect opportunity to present itself.

I bend over, picking up my gloves and trowel and return them to their rightful places. If Madison told Alex about her involvement with my husband, it could be a problem. But it's not one I can't handle. My more pressing concern at the moment is my daughter, who seems to be deteriorating before my eyes. I step out of the shed and look up at her bedroom window, just in time to catch the rustle of a curtain as it falls back into place.

I rinse my hands in the outdoor sink and make my way back into the house. I'm growing increasingly concerned about Lily. She's hardly left her bedroom in days, and when I tried to check in on her this morning, she refused to open the door. It's something I can no longer abide. I climb the stairs once more, and rap gently on the wood of her bedroom door.

"Lily? It's me. Can I come in?"

"I guess," she replies, her voice faded and frayed.

I find her wrapped in her duvet, a knot of matted hair strewn across her pillow, her complexion ghostly pale.

"Are you feeling alright?" I ask.

She blinks at me, as though I should already know the answer.

"Are you sick, I mean." I press the back of my hand to her forehead, just as I did when she was a child. When I used to be able to right all the wrongs in her world. Her skin feels clammy beneath my fingers. "Perhaps you should see a doctor."

"I'm fine," she mumbles, turning away from me.

"Maybe you could call Dr. Watkins . . ."

Lily huffs, shuffling deeper into the duvet, the blanket a barrier between me and my daughter. "What's the point?"

I can hear the words she doesn't say. *What's the point . . . if I can't tell her the truth? What's the point . . . if she can't help me?* I can feel her anguish like a barb beneath her skin, a nettling pain that won't let her find peace.

"I love you," I assure her, placing my hand atop the duvet, but she pulls away. Retreating ever further from me.

I tiptoe from the room, gently closing the door behind me. I feel myself losing her, my daughter, my most precious gift.

Once it became clear that James and I were not going to have a child of our own, it took me some time to convince him that adoption was our best option.

"But there are alternatives," he'd told me. "Surrogacy, for one."

But the idea of some other woman carrying my baby, *James's* baby, bringing *our* child into this world when I could not, was devastating. "I know, darling, but think of how many children there are in this world who need a home. Imagine the life we could give them."

I started showing him photos from the adoption agency, little boys with golden hair, sweet baby girls in white dresses. And although he looked at each one, I could see, from the detached look in his eyes, that he didn't love them. Not like I did. I'd fallen in love with every photo, imagined each tiny baby in my arms. But when I saw Lily, it was different. I knew she was meant to be mine. Her big brown eyes called out to me, and the way her tiny arms were raised in the photo felt like she was begging me to hold her close, to bring her home.

I set up an appointment with the adoption agency before I even showed the picture to James. I couldn't have withstood it if he'd rejected her like all the others, if he didn't see how special she was. Lily was mine and I was already fiercely protective, ready to shield her from the world.

"She does have a biological brother, you know," the agent explained as we sat in her office, across from her at her imposing desk.

James fidgeted in his chair, but I pretended not to notice him as the woman slid another photo in front of us. Lily with a little boy. A handsome child with a cherubic face and a wide smile. I felt my heart crack open, expanding, widening. Two children. A boy and a girl. The perfect family I'd always dreamed of.

I passed the photo to James. "What do you think?" I asked hopefully.

He ran his fingers over the image, over Theo's face, his wispy curls. "A son . . ." he'd said to himself, wrapping his mind around the idea. I could see his perspective shifting, his heart opening.

"This could be it, James. These children, they could be everything we'd ever hoped for."

"Start the paperwork," he said with a curt nod, his eyes still lingering on the photo of our children.

From the moment I saw my babies, I knew there was nothing I wouldn't do for them, no lengths I wouldn't go to in order to protect the family I fought so hard to build. Madison was going to ruin all of it. It started with my husband, but I could see the venom spreading, poisoning everything around her. Madison was a threat to my family, and, I suspect, her sister may prove to be as well. I will do whatever it takes to ensure that my family stays intact. I always have, and I always will.

23.

MADDIE

BEFORE

"Prokop, party of eight!" the hostess yells, waving a stack of menus over her head.

"That's us!"

The Lobster Shack has been packed all day today, a line of customers waiting for tables building along the sidewalk for most of the afternoon. It feels as though I've been running in circles for hours, taking orders, serving entrées, refilling drinks. We've been working shorthanded, and I'm exhausted by the time the dinner rush finally starts to slow and I find a moment to catch up with Becca.

"You working at Lucky Jack's tonight?" I ask as I join her at the drinks station.

"Nope," she replies, sliding a full glass in front of me, waiting for me to push a lemon wedge onto the rim.

"I'm out of here by nine too. Want to hang out after? Something low-key? Maybe watch a movie, drink some wine . . . Becca? Are you listening?"

Her eyes have drifted over my shoulder, to the customers who just walked in: the Blackwells. Lily waving enthusiastically in our direction, Katherine fingering the pearls at her throat, Theo and James behind them, conferring in hushed tones about something that must be important, given the tension in Theo's jaw.

"Yeah . . ." Becca replies, her voice trailing aimlessly. "Maybe."

I look at her, one eyebrow raised in question, but she doesn't even seem to notice as she watches the Blackwells. They're being ushered to one of our reserved tables, which to my relief is in Becca's section and not mine. Things have started to feel strange at Blackwell Manor, the roles we play beginning to overlap, the line between hospitality and . . . something more . . . starting to blur. It would feel too strange to wait on the family now and then return home to sleep under their roof.

"You okay?" I ask Becca, noticing the vacant look in her eyes, the way she's gone still, as if she's seen a ghost.

"Fine." The edge in her tone catches me off guard. "Sorry," she adds, softening. "I just noticed how busy my section is getting again. I better get back out there." She grabs a tray of waters and walks off, a smile pinned to her lips.

The Blackwells spend a good part of the evening at the Lobster Shack, friends of James's pulling up seats, ordering rounds of drinks, the laughter growing louder, ties loosening as the night wears on.

I keep trying to catch Becca's eye, waiting for another opening to talk to her, to find out what's really going on, but it's as if she's avoiding me. I know she said she was fine earlier, but I could tell she wasn't being entirely truthful. Every time I look at her, she seems to be watching the Blackwells' table, eyeing them with an almost nervous curiosity. Maybe she's just being a good waitress, paying extra attention to important customers, just as Scott directed us to do. But I can't shake the feeling that there's something more going on.

Finally, as the Blackwells and their friends push back their chairs, leaving in a bustle of handshakes and called good-byes, I catch sight of Becca slipping out the back door onto the loading dock.

"You good?" I ask, following her outside.

"I told you before, I'm fine." She looks out over the ocean, at the bands of orange and red stretching across the skyline as the sun takes its final bow.

"So, your place tonight then?"

"Huh?" Her eyes find mine as though she's snapping out of a trance.

"Wine? Movie? I asked you about it earlier."

"Oh, sorry, Mads. I can't tonight."

"But I thought you said you were off?"

"It's not a good night."

"What do you have planned?"

"Can you just stop?" Becca exclaims, throwing up her hands in exasperation. "Just because I'm not working doesn't mean I'm at your beck and call."

I startle at the harshness in her voice. "I didn't . . . I thought . . ." The words feel thick on my tongue, dissolving before they can fully form.

Becca exhales a long, slow huff. "Look, sometimes it feels like you forget that I had a life before you came to town."

"I know you did . . ." I reply lamely.

"Then just give me some space, okay?"

"Yeah . . . okay."

I leave her out there, alone on the loading dock, wondering what the hell just happened.

The sand is cool beneath the soles of my feet, the silver moonlight casting sharp shadows across the dunes that sit like stout sentinels watching over the coast. I don't usually walk home along the beach at night, preferring the protective glow of the streetlights on the main roads, but after the busy day I had today, I found myself craving the solitude, the quiet, that you can only find in a place like this. The beach at night is so different than it is during the day. It somehow feels more fierce, untamed. You begin to notice things at night: the way the ocean blends into the horizon, an endless swirl of black broken only by the quivering reflection of the moon atop the water; the sheer size of it all, the stretch of sand that seems to go on forever, the view unhampered by tents and umbrellas, crowds of tourists come to worship the sun.

As I walk toward Blackwell Manor, the winding staircase that leads up the side of the bluff shifts into view. The crooked planks that scale the stony surface are like creeping ivy rising from the murky darkness. A gust of wind rolls off the water and I brace myself against the sudden chill, wrapping my arms around my midsection, my shoes still dangling from the tips of my fingers. I want nothing more than to crawl into bed and put the day behind me, the argument I'd had with Becca hanging heavily about my shoulders.

Thinking back on it now, it was only when the Blackwells walked into the restaurant that Becca started acting strangely. *I wonder which of them had been the cause.*

I arrive at the bottom of the staircase and begin climbing the zigzagging path to the top, the wooden treads creaking under my weight as I rise higher and higher, nearing the edge of the bluff.

As I reach the platform at the crest and step out onto the lush green lawn of Blackwell Manor, I'm met with something unexpected. Voices. Angry whispers, whittled to razor-sharp points, shooting like arrows across the still night air. It sounds like James and Katherine, but I can't make out what they're saying.

I creep across the lawn toward the pool house. Whatever they're arguing over is surely none of my business. They probably came out here thinking they'd have more privacy, never anticipating that I'd be climbing over the bluff in the dead of night. But as I get closer to the pool house, the sound only grows louder. I can pick up some words now, words I wish I hadn't heard.

"I swear I'll do it, James."

"Enough, Katherine! I don't care anymore."

"You can't just walk away!"

"I can and I am!" His words sound so assured, spit out with unwavering finality. "I can't do this anymore, Katherine."

He's met with silence, his final remark an impassable boulder.

I can hear footsteps now, see a glimpse of James striding across the patio as the outdoor floodlights flick on, Katherine storming into the house. I duck behind a row of shrubs, not wanting to let on that I'd accidentally overheard their argument.

The back door to the house slams, and I risk a look above the foliage. James is digging in his pocket, a flash of silver keys in his hand.

He's leaving. He's leaving me behind.

I creep along the perimeter of the yard, following him in the shadows. I watch as he gets into his car, waking the engine. He turns the vehicle around, and I jump behind a tree, hiding from the sweep of his headlights across the gravel drive.

When I peer around the trunk, all I can see are his tail-lights bumping down the driveway, two glowing orbs of cherry red in the velvety darkness.

The argument between James and Katherine sounded serious, and I don't know where James is going, when he's coming back . . . or if he's coming back at all. *Would he really leave me? Without so much as a goodbye?* Anger begins to roil inside of me. *He can't just walk away from me. Not now. Not when there's still so much between us, so much we've left unsaid.*

I reach into my purse, pulling out my own key ring, the key to Lily's car heavy in my hand.

"For emergencies," she'd said as she slipped the spare key onto my ring. "I hardly ever drive it anyway."

I've never taken Lily's car before, it felt strange that she'd even given me the key. But tonight, all I can see is anger. The image of James walking away, disappearing into the night. Before I have a chance to think it through, I'm darting across the driveway and sliding behind the leather-wrapped steering wheel of Lily's BMW.

I turn the car on and it purrs beneath my feet. I reach to adjust the rearview mirror and my hand freezes on the cool glass. I could have sworn that I saw the reflection of a figure in the front window of the house. A shadowy silhouette, tall and lithe. Katherine, watching me follow her husband.

I have a decision to make. Do I turn off the car, slink back to the pool house, and wait to see if James comes back for me? Or do I follow him, find out where it is that he goes when I see him creeping across the back lawn late at night when he thinks no one is awake to see him leave?

It's rare that one stands on the precipice of a decision with their eyes wide open, understanding that whichever choice they make will change the course of their lives forever. I can see it all stretching out before me, my future playing like a rolling film. And I shift the car into drive.

My life, until I came to Blackwell Manor, existed in a state of equilibrium, lines cleanly drawn, sides carefully delineated. Good from bad, right from wrong. A life in sorted measures. But this decision, to follow James into the dark night, might be the thing that shifts the fulcrum on which my life is balanced. I can already feel the scales starting to tip, the winds changing course, and I'm afraid it's all going to come tumbling down. But it's a risk I know I have to take.

24.

ALEX

I can feel my lungs burning beneath my rib cage, but I push myself harder, pumping my legs faster. I've been here for nearly three days now, and I'm no closer to finding Maddie. Every path I follow seems only to lead to another dead end.

I'm not really a runner. I was never one of those people who found solace in the feeling of the pavement beneath their feet. If anything, I actively hate running. Up until this morning, I never understood why anyone would choose to put their body through this torture unless someone was chasing them. But today I was itching to get out of the pool house, to find a way to vent the frustration, the anxiety, that's slowly been building within me like a pressure cooker. I felt like I was going to explode if I didn't find some sort of release.

I round the curve at the end of Gosling Road, passing a fish mart where the day's fresh catch rests on a bed of ice, unblinking eyes staring skyward. This part of town isn't like the rest. Gone are the luxury shops, the smell of expensive leather and fresh croissants. Here, it's crooked walks weaving through dunes, the black eyes of seabirds keeping watch overhead. It's graying fishing nets hung like garlands over bait shacks, lobster traps in rusty stacks beside a gas pump.

I slow to a stop, bending over to brace my palms on my burning thighs as I catch my breath. I find a bench in the shade and lower myself onto it for a rest. I can't keep running in circles. Figuratively or literally. It isn't getting me any closer to finding Maddie. I swipe at the back of my neck as a bead of sweat slides between my shoulder blades. There has to be something I'm missing. Some piece of the puzzle I'm not seeing.

I close my eyes against the sun and think back to the last time I saw Maddie. After the funeral. After the argument. We'd hardly been on speaking terms, exchanging no more words than required to coexist under the same roof:

"Are you getting in the shower or can I?"

"Did you use the last of the coffee?"

She'd been so distant, so . . . withdrawn. I will myself to go back there, to remember, grasping at any new memory I can pull from the recesses of my mind. And then I see it. Maddie typing away on Mom's old laptop, her fingers furiously flying over the keys.

"What are you doing?" I'd asked. It was the early, gray hours of the morning and the clicking sound of the keyboard drew me out of bed. Although I've always had trouble sleeping, I was surprised to find Maddie in the kitchen, sitting in a square of rinsed morning light that poured through the small window. She sat with her back straight, her hair shaken out around her shoulders.

She slammed the lid of the laptop closed at the sound of my voice, one hand rising to her chest. "You scared the life out of me."

"What are you doing with Mom's laptop?" I was shocked that old thing even worked. Maddie must have found it in the mess that was Mom's room. I hadn't yet been able to bring myself to venture inside.

"Just some studying. I have exams coming up and mine is dead."

It seemed plausible enough at the time, and I hadn't given it a second thought. But Jessie told me that Maddie had taken a leave of absence from school shortly after she returned to the city. Why would she have been awake at the crack of dawn studying for exams she never intended to take?

I need to know what she was doing with that laptop. Maybe it was nothing. Maybe Maddie hadn't yet made the decision about leaving school and she really was studying for exams. Or maybe there's more to the story. I just can't be sure. There *is* one way I can find out for certain, but it would require me to make a phone call I've been actively avoiding.

I nibble at the edge of my thumb. *This is for Maddie. I have to do it.* I pull my phone from my pocket and click on Ben's number.

The phone rings a few times, and I've just about convinced myself that he's never speaking to me again when he answers.

"Alex." It's all he says, my name an exhalation on his lips. I hadn't known what to expect from him. Would he be angry at me after the way I left things? Would he tell me all the ways I'd let him down? But the way he says my name sounds like a sigh of relief. And it feels like coming home.

"Hi, Ben."

"I'm really glad you called." A seagull flies overhead, squalling loudly. "Where are you? Why didn't you tell me you were going out of town?"

"It's a really long story. I know we need to talk about . . . everything, and we will, I promise, but right now I need your help. It's really important." I know that what I'm asking of him, to put his own hurt on hold, isn't fair and I wouldn't blame him for hanging up on me. But I'm not ready to have that conversation with him yet. There's so much I haven't told him, and now things are so complicated between us. I'm at a loss as to how to untangle it all. To explain why I'm here . . . why I left the way that I did. In the moment, I'd told myself it was because I didn't have the same feelings for Ben that he had for me. I was sparing him the heartbreak by making a clean break. But that's not entirely true. Hearing his voice now makes the truth bubble to the surface: I was afraid to let myself fall for him.

"What can I do?" He asks it so resolutely that for a moment I'm overcome with painful affection for him. Even in the midst of what must be his own anger and confusion, Ben is willing to put everything aside to help me, no questions asked.

I'm beginning to realize that I wanted to keep Ben at arm's length so that he would never get close enough to hurt me. Everyone I've ever loved has left—Dad, Mom, Maddie— and I thought Ben would be no different. This thing with him . . . I convinced myself it couldn't last. My world is so small, while his is just opening up. He'll finish law school, he'll get his dream job, and he'll outgrow me. Ben was destined for bigger things than Dogwood Grove, bigger things than me. I pushed him away before I could get too attached. But right now, he's the only one I can turn to.

"I need you to go to my mom's house. Do you remember where I keep the spare key?"

"Yeah, by the back door under the yellow planter."

"Right. I need you to go inside and find my mom's laptop. It's an old Dell. It was somewhere in her bedroom last time I saw it. I need you to look at the most recent browsing history and tell me exactly what you find."

"Okay, I will. But, Alex? Just tell me this: Are you alright?"

"I will be. Just . . . call me back, okay?"

"Yeah, sure," he replies before ending the call.

I stand and put in my earbuds, turning up the volume on my music. Loud enough to drown out my thoughts of Ben, silencing the voice in the back of my head telling me that I made a mistake when I walked away from him.

After I've put a few blocks behind me, my phone vibrates in my pocket and I stop to accept the call.

"Ben? That was fast," I pant.

"You told me it was important. I came right over. It looks like your mom was looking at . . . motels in the Hamptons? That's kind of strange, isn't it?"

"Very." Because of course this wasn't Mom planning a family vacation to the beach. This was Maddie planning her escape. The job at the Lobster Shack didn't just fall into her lap, she was actively looking to get as far away from me as she possibly could after the awful way I'd treated her. She chose to derail her life, to come here, because of me. Wherever she is, whatever's happened to her, now I know it's all my fault. "Thanks, Ben," I say, my voice a vacant echo. "I really appreciate it."

"Alex, please just tell me what's happen—"

But I've already ended the call. I think I've ruined enough lives for one day. Ben is better off staying far, far away from me.

I blink back the tears, the guilt, welling behind my eyes and continue running. I just want to get back to Blackwell

Manor and allow myself to fall apart. *I'm sorry, Maddie. Wherever you are.*

I feel my phone buzzing again, and I debate ignoring it, but I know Ben will only keep calling.

"Listen, I'm sorry I hung up on you, but I'm dealing with a family emergency and—"

"Alex, it's Chief Gilroy."

His wasn't the voice I was expecting to hear. My heart seizes in my chest. *Does he finally believe me that Maddie is missing, that the police should be looking for her? And if that's the case, what's happened to convince him?*

"Do you have news about Maddie?"

"Alex . . . I . . . we found a body."

25.

ALEX

I can feel the sweat drying on my face, the salt from the morning air hardening in my hair, as I push open the door to the county morgue. I came straight here as soon as I got Chief Gilroy's call, running back to my car as fast as my exhausted legs would carry me. I shiver now, in my running shorts and T-shirt, but I can't tell if it's from the cool air-conditioning or the fact that I'm in a morgue that's sent this shudder rolling through me.

Gilroy is already waiting in the lobby, his back toward me, his broad shoulders hunched, his head hanging low. As soon as I let the door fall closed with a bang he whips around, pushing his phone into his pocket.

"Alex. Hello."

His entire demeanor has changed since the last time I saw him. Gone are the jovial smiles, the good-hearted pats on the shoulder. Now his eyes are heavy with a somber weight, the tension in his jaw conveying the gravity of what we've come here to do. A flash of anger washes over me. *Why did it take him this long, until we were standing in a* morgue, *to take me seriously?*

"Where is my sister?" I force the words between gritted teeth.

"We don't know that the person we . . . we don't know if it's Madison yet. I was just getting an update from my team." He pats the phone in his pocket. "Does your sister have any identifying marks? Tattoos maybe?"

"No." *At least I don't think so.* "I guess she could've gotten one without me knowing though. I haven't spoken to her in a few months." Guilt rushes up into my mouth like bile. I haven't spoken to my sister in months, and now she might be dead.

Gilroy nods. "I'm going to take you downstairs to see if you can identify the person we found. All I know so far is that she's a female of about the same age and build as your sister. There was no ID on her when she was found."

"I want to see her." I choke back the tears that prickle at the back of my throat.

"Follow me."

Gilroy leads me into another waiting room, a mirror stretching across one wall.

"On the other side of this mirror is the person we found on the beach this morning. I want you to brace yourself. From what the coroner has told me so far, it looks like her body had been in the water for a few days. If this is your sister, she might not look the way you remember her. That's why I was asking you earlier about identifying marks—she does have a small butterfly tattoo on her ankle and we were hoping it might help in identifying her. The coroner has prepared the body, so it's going to look like she's asleep. She will be under a white sheet, and when you're ready, I'll ask the coroner to lift the sheet and show you her face. I'll need you to tell us if this is Madison. Take all the time you need and just let me know when you're ready."

Nausea churns in my gut. I squeeze my eyes shut, but I'm assaulted with images of Maddie, her bloated body floating in the ocean, her flesh being torn apart by hungry fish, sharp teeth tearing through rotting skin. "I'm ready," I lie.

"Okay." Gilroy presses a button on a small intercom panel beside the mirror. "Dr. Erickson, she's ready."

A light behind the mirror switches on and it transforms into transparent glass. On the other side is a metal table, the shape of a body beneath a white sheet. I try to analyze the size, the contours of the body, to convince myself it couldn't be Maddie on that table.

It isn't her, it isn't her, it isn't her. I repeat the words in my head like a mantra. *It isn't her, it isn't her, it isn't her.*

Gilroy nods and Dr. Erickson slowly pulls back the sheet. The first thing I see is a clump of matted hair, darkened by the sea, as though the ocean had already tried to lay claim to it. Remnants of slimy algae, knots of seaweed interwoven among the tangled locks. My vision starts to blur, and I grip the ledge beneath the mirror with both hands. *I have to get through this.*

Next I see her face. White-blue and mottled, veins straining at translucent skin, her lips a ghastly gray. "It's . . . It's . . ."

And those are the last words I can muster before my world goes black.

26.

THEO

"*Breaking news: In an unexpected turn of events this morning, a body was found on Breaker Point Beach . . .*"

I swerve to the side of the road, ignoring the screech of my tires and the ream of expletives shouted by the driver of the car behind me. My heart bashes itself against my ribs, a pounding thrum that seems to keep in rhythm with the click of my turn signal.

I reach for the radio dial, turning up the sound until it fills my car, assaults me with its presence.

"We're here live with Captain Olsen Barney who made the grisly discovery early this morning."

A man's voice, gruff and weathered, filters through the speakers. "I was comin' out here to set the lobster traps, just as I do every mornin' and there she was, just lyin' on the beach, washed up just near the jetty."

She. They found a woman's *body.* A muscle in my jaw twitches as I try to focus on the rest of the broadcast, pushing away the images that flash behind my eyes like memories.

"I could tell she was dead from the second I saw her. It wasn't like anythin' I've ever seen before, and I hope I never have to again."

The female reporter's soothing voice takes over the transmission. "Sources close to the investigation tell us that the deceased, Rebecca Jones, who most often went by the name of Becca, was a dancer at a local club—"

My phone rings, interrupting the radio broadcast, the sound of the ringtone rattling through the car, Hutch's name on the caller ID.

"Are you seeing this?" he asks, the instant the call connects.

"I just heard."

"I leave town for one weekend and all hell breaks loose."

"Yeah . . ." My mouth feels like it's forgotten how to form words.

"You good, man? You sound . . . off."

"Yeah . . ." I try again, my tongue like rubber against my teeth.

"Do me a favor and swing by Mick's house." He says it as more of a demand than a request, though I don't know exactly when I began taking orders from Hutch. "I've been trying to call him since he ducked out early from your party the other night, but he's gone off-grid. I'm out of town at some bullshit photo op with my dad or I'd go over there myself."

"Yeah . . . I'll go." I check the clock on my dash. I have a little time before I'm expected at the job site. I was on my way to oversee the pouring of the concrete foundation for the new hotel. I spoke to the builders last night, and they assured me that everything is still going to plan and they're finally ready to pour, but I feel a pressing need to see it for myself. I'll check in on Mick, but it'll have to be quick.

"Theo." Hutch's voice has taken on a sharper tone, the edge slicing through the fog. "You're good, right?"

"I told you," I snap back. "I'm fine."

He ends the call, the line going dead in my hand.

I'm good. I'd almost lost myself for a moment there when I'd first heard about a body turning up, but I'm good now. I have to be.

"Pull yourself together, son." I feel my father's words wrapping themselves around me, constrictor tight.

The same words he said to me at my travel baseball championship game. I was twelve years old, last up to bat in the final inning. We had a man on third and we were trailing by just one run. I should have had it in the bag. I had the best batting average in the league by a long shot. I'd heard Father and my coaches already trading comments about the majors someday, or at least an illustrious college career. I had the "it" factor. The thing that set me apart from everyone else. And I knew it. My entire team knew it. So when I strode out to home plate, I knew, without question, that I'd feel the crack of that ball against the aluminum bat in my hand. I knew I'd send it soaring over left field, driving in the last two runs we needed to take home the trophy. I could already feel the weight of it in my hands, imagine my teammates lifting me onto their shoulders, carrying me off the field the same way I'd carry us all to victory. It was going to be my shining moment. And Father was there. Watching from the sidelines. He didn't have time to come to all of my games, but he'd made time for this one. The championships. My golden hour. I smiled as I pulled the batting helmet onto my head, grasped the handle of the bat in my fingers. I kicked at the dirt beneath my cleats, sending up a small cloud of dust. *I've got this.*

All of the best players in the league knew one another.

We studied one another's strengths, weaknesses. For example, I knew that the pitcher on the mound had a wicked fastball, but that his curveballs were inconsistent. He wouldn't dare try it under these conditions, not in the final inning, not with me at bat. And so I braced myself for the speed of his pitch and I timed my swing. But it was a whiff.

"Strike one!" the umpire yelled.

I could hear the murmurs from the bench, from the stands. But I shook it off as the pitcher wound up for a second throw.

"Strike two!"

Another curveball. *How is this possible? Why would he take the risk?* My own arrogance had gotten the best of me. I'd thought I was too good, that he'd be too intimated to go toe-to-toe with me with anything but his strongest pitch. But he had. And I couldn't brush it off so easily a second time. My confidence was shaken. I could hear the gasps from the bench, my own team in disbelief, and I couldn't even bring myself to look at my father.

Instead I held that bat in my hand, focusing on the feeling of the ridges in the tape beneath my fingers. Everything was riding on me.

The pitcher readied himself on the mound. And I readied myself for another curveball. But he threw a slider. A near-perfect pitch that broke just before the hitting zone. I'd never seen anything like it.

"Strike three! You're out!"

I dropped the bat and it fell to the ground with a clang that seemed to reverberate across the field. The other team rushed the mound, the gold trophy shining in the sun over their heads. The pitcher was lifted onto their shoulders, shouts of victory rang through the air. It was meant to be

me up there, hailed by my teammates and coaches. My father was meant to witness my greatest victory, not my most
humiliating defeat. A single tear slid down my cheek, and
before I knew it, a second and a third trailed in its wake. I was
horrified, brushing them from my face with the back of my
leather batting glove.

"Pull yourself together, son," Father hissed into my ear.
I'd been so consumed watching the celebration that should
have been mine that I hadn't even heard him approaching.
"Losing is one thing, but showing weakness is another."

I bit into my trembling lower lip, choked back the remaining tears that threatened to escape. "Yes, sir."

"This is an important life lesson. No matter what happens, you never let anyone see you break."

I've carried those words with me every day of my life.
Never let anyone see you break.

————

I pull into Mick's driveway. It's been awhile since I've been
here in this part of town. Mick never invites us to hang out
at his place, and now I remember why. The house he shares
with his parents is a small New England Cape Cod with a
sagging roof and old wooden windows. When we were
younger I used to love coming here. Sure, it was crowded,
the house brimming with people: Mick, his parents, his
brother and little sister, but it always felt . . . warm. As if they
wanted to be around one another, packed in around the family dinner table. Mick and his brother tossing biscuits like
footballs, his mother yelling at them to stop, her pursed lips
bordering on a disguised smile, his dad telling us animated
stories about his workday, banging on the table as he spoke,
making the mismatched water glasses jump. It was so differ-

ent from what I was accustomed to: dinners prepared by Mariana, eaten separately, whenever our schedules permitted, squeezed somewhere between school, baseball, fencing, debate team. Mick never understood why I'd liked being here so much.

"Let's just go to your house," he'd say. "You've got the better gaming systems, and we won't have to fight with my annoying sister over the remote."

But I didn't gravitate toward Mick's house for video games or watching movies on the biggest screen. It was them I wanted to watch. His family. The way they were together. It all felt so foreign to me, and I wanted to understand it, to try it on, to experience what it was like to be a part of a normal family.

But the house looks different than I remember it. Smaller somehow. The grass is browning in the front yard, burning in the summer sun, and the hedges are overgrown. One of the black shutters is missing from the front of the house, and the bricks of the walkway feel loose under my feet as I make my way to the front door, tufts of weeds pushing through mortar. It never occurred to me, until this very moment, what it must have cost Mick's family to send him to Buckley Prep—what they had to sacrifice, to go without, so that he'd have a chance of someday having more . . . a chance to be one of us. I'd never thought twice about the price of my own tuition. It was a foregone conclusion that I'd go to the best private schools money could buy. I've always been on the path to *more*: bigger houses, impressive degrees, the keys to the kingdom. But that path had to be forged for Mick, his parents fighting through the undergrowth to clear the way, to make him something more.

I cast a glance at the mailbox beside Mick's front door,

letters marked "urgent" in red ink, stuffed into the rusted metal box, and I grimace. The idea of other people's financial struggles has always made me vaguely uncomfortable. Maybe it's because I know this could have been my life. This, or so much worse, had I not been adopted by the right family.

"Mick?" I call, knocking on the door. The doorbell seems to be missing, an exposed wire protruding through the brick wall in its place. "It's Theo. You home?"

"It's not a good time," Mick replies through the closed door.

"Can you open the door at least?"

"No."

No? "Mick, what's going on? Hutch sent me over. He's worried about you."

"Hutch can go fuck himself."

I'm too stunned to answer right away. Mick has always been the agreeable one, the peacemaker in our little group. He's basically idolized Hutch since the first day we met at orientation at Buckley, three scrawny thirteen-year-olds trying to pretend we had the type of confidence we'd need to survive there.

"Did something happen?"

"Are you seriously asking me that?" He's shouting now. Incredulous. His voice seething through the closed door that separates us. "Where is she, Theo?"

"Who?"

He sighs, the flat of his hand slamming against the door. "Maddie! The girl that was staying at your house. Her sister was asking about her at your party."

"I don't . . . Why do you think I'd know anything about that?" *I don't know what he's implying, what he thinks he knows.*

"Just leave, Theo."

"Mick . . ."

"Go!"

I can hear his footsteps fading as he retreats farther into his house, to the warmth of his family, leaving me on the outside.

27.

ALEX

I wrap my fingers around the paper coffee cup, trying to steady my shaking hands on the table. The shock of seeing the body this morning is only just starting to wear off. Even though it wasn't Maddie (*Thank God it wasn't Maddie*), I know the image of that girl, her bloated skin, her blanched lips, is going to stay with me for a very long time.

"Feeling a little better now?" Gilroy asks, as he crosses the interview room and lowers himself into the chair on the opposite side of the table.

A shiver rolls through my body like a wave, and as it reaches my hands, splashes of coffee escape my cup and splatter onto the metal table in front of me.

"It's the nerves," he tells me. "Happens all the time. I'm sorry you had to go through that. We identified the bod— woman you saw this morning. It was Rebecca Jones. Jack's girl. She recognized the tattoo and was able to make a positive ID."

"Becca? Maddie's friend?" My voice escapes my lips, reedy and weak. She must have been the other girl in the photo of Maddie that I found in James's office. I try to conjure that image of her now: young, beautiful, a mane of thick, brown hair. There was no way I could have recognized her earlier, not in the state she'd been in.

"So I'm told."

"What . . . what happened to her?"

"Can't say for sure yet, but it looks like she suffered a head injury before she ended up in the water. Due to the nature of her injuries, we are treating this as a homicide investigation until further notice."

Homicide. Someone killed Becca. I take a sip of my coffee, focusing on the feeling of the warm liquid trailing down my throat, and try to stop the chattering of my teeth. *You can do this, Alex. It wasn't Maddie. Breathe.* "That poor girl."

Gilroy nods solemnly. "Now, the reason I brought you down here, besides, of course, the fact that you were in no state to drive yourself home, was to ask you a few questions."

I nod in agreement.

"What do you know about your sister's relationship with the deceased?" he asks, notepad poised in front of him.

"What do you mean?"

"The other day, outside of Ms. Jones's apartment, you mentioned that Madison and Ms. Jones were close. Do you know how they met? What types of places they may have frequented together? How often they saw each other? That sort of thing."

"I don't know that they were *close*. They met at the Lobster Shack, I think. They both worked there. But that's really all I know."

"I see. Do you know when they might have seen each other last?"

I shake my head. "I have no idea. Like I told you earlier, I haven't spoken to my sister in a while. I don't really know much about her life since she came out to the Hamptons at the beginning of the summer."

And suddenly it dawns on me why he's asking about Maddie and Becca being together. "Do you think Maddie was *with* Becca when she . . . died? Is that why you're asking about all of this?" The questions come tumbling from my lips, tripping over each other in their haste to be heard. "Could Maddie still be out there somewhere? In the water?" I push away from the table, rising to a stand, wild-eyed and ready to spring into action. "Is anyone even looking for her?"

"Whoa, Alex," Gilroy says calmly, his palms up in a sign of surrender. The coaxing tone of his voice is enough to convince me to lower myself back into my seat. "That's not what I was suggesting at all. I'm just trying to get a clear picture of what Ms. Jones's life was like when she was alive. We're going to do everything we can to find out what happened to her. And if she and Madison were friends, then it's possible that Madison might know something that could help us."

I drop my head into my hands. "I don't know where she is."

"See, that's what I find most concerning."

"What do you mean?"

"According to the coroner, Ms. Jones most likely died last Thursday. Which was the same day, according to your report, that your sister supposedly left town. So that has me wondering. Why is it that Madison suddenly disappeared just after her friend was killed?"

I can sense the change in his demeanor like a cold front rolling in off the ocean.

"I don't . . . What are you saying? You think . . . You think Maddie had something to do with what happened to Becca?"

"I'm not jumping to any conclusions here, and you shouldn't either, but the timing does seem somewhat coincidental, wouldn't you agree?"

It's not a coincidence. I'm almost certain that Becca's death and my sister's disappearance are related, but not in the way he's implying.

"I've been at this job a long time," Gilroy continues, "long enough to know that coincidences are rare things indeed. Most of the time, there's more to the story." He crosses his arms over his chest. "And, well, have you ever heard that expression about horses and hoofbeats?"

I shake my head, unsure how the conversation somehow just pivoted from a murder investigation to horses.

"When you hear hoofbeats think of horses, not zebras. You see? Because the most simple explanation is almost always the right one."

"I don't see what any of this has to do with Maddie."

Gilroy leans back in his chair. "What I'm saying is that, sometimes, when a person goes missing, it's because they don't want to be found."

I stand abruptly, jostling the table and spilling the remnants of my coffee. It snakes across the metal surface, staining the edges of Gilroy's fresh notepad. "Maybe you'll actually start looking for her then." If only he'd believed me about Maddie earlier, if only he'd have helped me find her, maybe Maddie would be here to defend herself.

"We certainly will be. And do let me know if you hear from her. I have a few questions I'd like to ask her."

I storm out of the police station.

I have to find Maddie. Before he does.

My foot bounces beneath the table and I press my palms into my thighs willing it to stop. *Maddie is a suspect in Becca's murder. How could this have happened?*

"Anything else I can get you?" the waitress asks as she places my iced tea in front of me.

"Not just yet. I'm waiting on a friend." My stomach grumbles in protest. I haven't been eating much these past days, my anxiety about Maddie making it hard to stomach the thought of food, but I need to keep my strength up. "Actually, maybe just some fries, please."

"You got it, hon."

I check my phone again. April is late. I hope she isn't having second thoughts. I open our text conversation, just to make sure I'm in the right place.

ME: We need to talk. It's about Becca.
APRIL: Not over the phone. Meet me at the Starlight
    Diner @ 7

According to the sticky plastic menu on the table in front of me, I'm in the right place. But April is almost twenty minutes late. *Please show up, April. I need your help.*

I hear the jingle of the bells that hang over the front entrance of the diner, and I twist around in my seat just in time to see her walking in. She looks different without the black Cleopatra wig, her hair falling in chestnut curls that sweep the shoulders of her leather jacket, but I can tell it's her, her stage makeup is still in place.

She slides into the booth across from me, just as the waitress delivers my fries. She pops one into her mouth as I thank the waitress. Neither of us speaks another word until we're certain she's out of earshot.

"Thanks for coming," I start.

April nods. "I felt like I owed it to Becca. What they're saying on the news, that she might have been . . . murdered . . . it's awful." She shudders, her narrow shoulders shaking at the thought.

"The reason I wanted to talk to you was to see if there's anything else you can tell me about Becca. Anything that might help me figure out what happened to her. Or to my sister."

"Aren't the cops supposedly doing that?" She raises a sarcastic eyebrow, biting into another of my fries.

"They think Maddie had something to do with what happened to Becca. But I know, *I know,* that can't be true."

"Typical." She rolls her eyes. "Of course they'd take the easy way out, blame it on the first person they can think of. I bet they aren't looking real hard for other suspects either. Not for a girl like Becca with no real family, no one to ask questions about her. The cops will wanna wrap this up with a neat little bow and forget all about her."

"And that's why I need to figure out what *really* happened. For Maddie, *and* for Becca."

"Look," April says, leaning over the table, her arms folded in front of her, "I didn't mention this earlier because . . . well, I'm not sure if Becca was even a part of it, but there are these parties . . ." Her eyes fall to the table, her fingers toying with the cuff of her jacket.

"What kind of parties?"

"*Exclusive* parties. For *exclusive* customers from the club." Her dark eyes lift, locking onto mine, willing me to understand. "Jack sets them up. I've never been to one, it's not my thing. But I've heard rumors from some of the other girls. There's supposed to be big money in it. If you're willing to do the kinds of things these clients want. I don't know. Becca might have gone in for it. She needed the money. When she first started working at Lucky Jack's, she was sleeping on one of the other girl's couches. Couldn't even afford to rent a room for herself. And then, you know, she seemed to be doing pretty well toward the end. I never knew if it was from the parties, but I guess I always suspected."

"Have you told the police any of this?"

April scoffs. "Of course not. They came down to the club earlier, asking all kinds of questions about Becca. But if they heard that she might have been mixed up in that kind of thing, I doubt they'd bother asking too many more. Besides"—she finishes off the last of the fry in her hand— "I hear there's a lot of high-profile types at those parties. The kind the cops don't look at too hard and who wouldn't mind lying about a dead stripper."

"Where are these parties? At Lucky Jack's?"

April shakes her head. "No, they're always at different locations. And it's invitation only. But I . . . I think Becca might have been involved with someone she met at one of the parties. She mentioned it once, at the club, about how she was seeing someone new, but when we asked her about him, she got all coy about it, and told us he was the kind of guy who 'values discretion.' Refused to tell us where she met him or even his name. I don't know, it just seemed . . . strange. All the girls at the club are always talking about their boyfriends, or guys they're sleeping with or whatever, and Becca is usually the first one to share the sordid details. But this time was different."

"When's the next party?"

April pauses a moment, her hesitation playing across her face. "Tonight."

"Can you get me in?" I can feel my pulse quickening, a cocktail of nerves and excitement coursing through my veins. *I finally have a real lead. Something that might get me closer to finding out the truth.*

"Are you sure you want to do that?"

"I don't think I have any other choice. If Becca was seeing some mystery man, especially someone she felt like she couldn't talk about for whatever reason, maybe the cops will start looking at him instead of Maddie. Please. I know it's a lot to ask, and you don't owe me any of this, but you might be the only person who can help."

She sighs. "A lot of times it feels like no one cares about girls like Becca, girls like me. It's messed up, but it's true. If we don't look out for each other, well . . . most likely no one will. I'll see what I can do. One of the girls owes me a favor anyway. But if I get you this invitation, you'll be careful, won't you?"

"Yeah," I reply. "I'll try."

She rolls her eyes. "Come on, I'd better lend you a dress too."

28.

THE WHARF

He's late. He's never late. But he's going to show. I haven't left him any other choice.

Sometimes I wonder how I got here. How it's come to this. Whether the choices I've made mean I'm no better than he is. But we are not the same. We never have been.

A mourning dove lets out its sorrowful wail, the sound of its coo echoing over the placid sea. It's not typical to hear them at night, but it happens on occasion, usually when there's a predator prowling nearby. But others believe it's a harbinger of hope, the mourning dove a celestial visitor carrying a message from a deceased loved one. In the end, we all see what we want to see. We believe the truths we choose.

I hear him before I see him, in the flutter of the dove's wings, the creak of the old docks. The predator is edging closer. Danger closing in. *Or maybe it's been here all along.* He looks different this time. Shoulders hunched, eyes downcast. None of the usual temerity in his step, as if the ground he walks on owes him something. This time, the figure he cuts against the moonlight is subdued, listless. Broken.

"Here." He shoves another envelope in my direction.

Maybe I should feel bad. Knowing that I've done this to

him, knowing that he trusted me. But I don't. I came here for a reason. This has always been the plan and I'm not going to change course now. Besides, he brought this upon himself.

I take the offering from his hand. Making the extraction as slow and painful as I'm able.

He sneers at me. Something like a growl escaping his lips as he turns to go.

"Wait." He stops at the sound of my voice. I can almost see the anger pumping through his veins as his muscles tense with restraint. I open the envelope, study the contents. "It's not enough."

"It's all I have."

"Then you're going to have to find a way to get more. The stakes have been raised."

I can tell he wants to lash out; he's coiled like a viper ready to strike. But he won't. It won't do him any good.

"Does he know?" he asks me instead, the question hissed through clenched teeth. "Does he know what you're doing?"

"No. And he's not going to find out."

29.

ALEX

I tugged at the hem of April's black dress, shimmying it down over my thighs, trying, in vain, to cover a little bit more of my exposed skin. I felt like a different person, a version of myself I didn't know existed, the moment I slipped into the dress.

"It's perfect," April said.

"Are you sure?" I asked nervously, studying my reflection in the full-length mirror on the back of her bedroom door. "It's . . . a little revealing." My hands automatically rose to my chest, which was barely concealed by the plunging neckline that dipped between my breasts.

"That's kind of the point. And stop picking at your nails. Here." She took my hand and led me to the edge of her bed, where I dutifully took a seat. She pulled a small glass bottle out of her nightstand, swirling the deep burgundy liquid inside, and began to paint my nails. "Gemma said to use her name at the door when you get there."

"And what if they don't believe that I'm her?"

"First of all, I doubt anyone will question you in that dress. Second, it's a masquerade party. Once you have your mask on, no one will know the difference."

"Will Jack be there?"

"I don't think so. She just supplies the girls. She doesn't run the parties."

"Who does?"

"I don't know. Gemma said all she gets is an address and a time to show up."

I let out a shaky breath. The idea of walking into this, completely in the dark, made my heart race.

A silence settled between us as April continued applying the lacquer to my nails. "You don't have to do this, you know. If you're having second thoughts it's not too late to back out. You don't even know if this is going to help you find your sister."

She was right. I knew she was right. I didn't know for sure if going to this party was going to get me any closer to finding Maddie, but maybe it could help me find out who Becca was involved with. If I could give the cops another suspect, maybe it would take Gilroy's focus off Maddie. This party was my only lead, the only glimmering strand of hope I had left.

"I'm going," I replied resolutely, even though I didn't feel nearly as confident as my tone suggested.

April blew on my finished nails, her breath as light as a butterfly's wing as it passed across my skin. "Close your eyes. I'll do your makeup too."

I catch sight of my reflection in my car's window now and I barely recognize myself. The makeup April chose for me is far more dramatic than my usual taste: smoky eyes, thick black liner, bloodred lips, but I have to admit, it works. I look . . . sexy, powerful. It gives me a burst of confidence I've never felt before—like I could make things happen with a flick of my manicured fingers. I tuck a lock of hair behind my ear. All that's missing now is the mask. I lift it to my face, the fine, silky lace as gentle as a kiss against my skin as I fasten it over my eyes. I let out a long breath, standing tall in my heels as I turn to face the house. It's at the end of the block, but I can see the glow of the party inside from where I've parked, the windows spilling rectangular puddles of light onto the darkened lawn in front.

I walk up slowly, steeling myself for what awaits me inside, my heels clicking against the pavement as I draw closer. It's only as I reach the front walk, when it towers over me, that I can fully appreciate the house's size. A sprawling brick mansion with an elegant arched entryway and twin peaked roofs. *I wonder who lives here.*

I raise my hand and grip the brass door knocker, the metal cool in my palm, and let it fall against the door with a thud. As I wait for the door to open, my heart flutters against my ribs as though trying to escape my chest. My newfound confidence is already wavering. *It's not too late to back out.* April's words drift into my ear as though whispered on the wind. Except that it *is* too late. Because the doorknob is turning, the door is creaking open. It's now or never.

A man in a dark suit fills the doorway. He looks at me expectantly.

"I'm . . . I'm Gemma," I muster. "My name is on the list?" It comes out as more of a question than the assertive statement I'd intended it to be. *So much for playing it cool.*

The man nods and moves aside, allowing me entrance into the house. I step into an open foyer, the marble floors slick beneath the soles of my shoes. Overhead, a crystal chandelier twinkles with soft lights, and beyond I can hear the pop of a champagne bottle, the soft murmur of voices.

The man gestures toward the next room with a sweep of

his arm. I find it unnerving that he hasn't spoken a word since he's opened the door, but I lift my chin and stride toward the party as if I belong there.

When I cross the threshold I'm disoriented for a moment. I guess I was expecting something more . . . scandalous—exposed skin, probing tongues—not the finely dressed men in custom-tailored suits, women in black dresses sipping from long-stemmed champagne glasses. At first blush, it appears to be like any other party. Cocktail music wafting softly through the room, drinks clinked together in a toast, small talk made in pockets throughout the space. But then, as though a fog is lifting, I slowly begin to see it as it really is. The men circle the room slowly, predators stalking prey. They're window shopping, a few with women on their arms, but most alone, approaching the girls like me: the ones in the cheap, imitation dresses, clumsy copies of elegant ladies in designer gowns. Suddenly I'm not feeling quite as powerful in April's dress, and what's left of my confidence disperses like smoke. Everything in my body tells me to run, to walk back out that front door before it's too late.

Every little girl grows up with alarm bells in her head. A tinkling chime that sounds when danger is approaching. We're taught from a young age that it isn't safe to walk alone at night, that we need to avoid the shadows and the dangers that might lurk there. We know innately that we shouldn't leave our drinks unattended at a party or that we need to be aware of our surroundings. We walk with our phones in our hands or keys laced between our fingers. I thought it unfair, when I was a girl, that I should have so many rules when the boys my age seemed free of the same burdens.

"This world doesn't treat everyone the same, baby," Mom had said. "It may not be fair, but it's the truth. We women, we need to look out for ourselves, because sometimes, you're all you've got."

Right now, the bells in my head are ringing louder than they ever have before, echoing into my consciousness. But it's not just myself I have to look out for. It's Maddie. I can't leave yet.

I scan the room, instinctively looking for the familiar tint of my sister's hair, the slope of her shoulders. The masks make it hard to tell the girls apart, but I don't think she's here. Not that I really expected her to be. This isn't going to be that easy. But I have a plan. I'm going to show Becca's photo, the one that April texted me earlier, to some of the men here, see how they react to seeing her face, whether they recognize her. It's not a very *good* plan, but it was all I could come up with on such short notice. It's the only way I can think of to track down who Becca might have been in-volved with. Besides, there's something niggling at the back of my mind, something I can't quite bring to the surface, that tells me I'm on the right track, that these parties have everything to do with why my sister is missing.

"Hello, there," a deep voice purrs, a man's warm breath filling my ear, a scrape of stubble against my cheek. "You're new here, aren't you?" He twirls a lock of my long hair around his finger. "I'm certain I'd remember you if we'd met before. Even with this." He traces the edge of my mask with one finger. His skin grazes mine and it sends a hot jolt of fear crackling through my body.

"I'm, uh, yeah. New." I take a step back, but he hooks his arm through mine, pinning me close to him.

"Ah, fresh blood," he remarks salaciously. "Please, allow me to get you a drink." He raises his free hand into the air, and a waiter carrying a silver tray materializes within a matter of seconds. The man lifts a crystal champagne glass from the tray and hands it to me with a flourish.

I take a nervous gulp, feeling the tingle of the bubbles bursting at the back of my throat. "Thanks. I was hoping you could—er—whether you might know my friend?" I hold up Becca's photo, the screen of my phone illuminating the black mask that covers half of the man's face. It reminds me of the Phantom of the Opera's.

"Afraid not. Anyway, my dear, what's on the menu this evening?"

"Menu? I, uh, I'm not sure I know what you . . ."

"Oh, you *are* quite new." The man smiles, a lecherous grin snaking across his face. "The menu. The things you are willing to do this evening. The cost is of no concern to me, and we find it best not to discuss such matters until behind closed doors. But the menu, my dear, is of utmost importance. So tell me"—he leans in close and stares into my eyes, his own dancing delightedly—"what is it that you're offering?"

"I . . . I . . . I have to go." I bolt away from him, doing my best to run in April's towering heels that are half a size too big. I rush to the back of the house, skittering to a stop when I reach the next room.

At the center is another man in a dark suit, his shoulders rounded, his head thrown back in ecstasy. At his knees is a woman, the top of her dress peeled away, the fabric pooled loosely at her waist, exposing her pale breasts. She takes the man into her mouth and he moans with pleasure. The man's eyes lock onto mine from behind his mask and I feel heat rising into my chest, crawling up my neck. He smiles, and that's when I notice the others. Watching. Enjoying the spectacle.

"I'm so sorry!" I back out of the room, colliding with someone in my haste.

It's a woman. With raven-black hair and a matching eye mask, a plume of black feathers gathered at the corner. She holds my elbow, looking at me curiously as she helps me regain my balance. "You all right?"

"Yeah, I'm sorry. I just walked in there and I didn't realize, I mean, I didn't mean to—" The words gush awkwardly from my mouth as though a tap has been turned on and I can't seem to shut it.

"Whoa, slow down," the woman says with a smile. "It's okay. First time here?"

"How could you tell?"

She laughs. "Lucky guess. You must be one of Jack's girls, right?"

"You're two for two."

"Look, I know this can seem"—she makes a vague, sweeping gesture at the house around her—"overwhelming if it's not your thing, but for some of us, it's a haven. A place like this is the only place we can come to be ourselves, where we're free from judgment just because our tastes are . . . less traditional. It can be empowering."

"I don't know . . ." I understand what she's saying, and that may be true for her, but what about the others? What about the women who come here just so they can afford to keep a roof over their heads, provide for their families? From where I'm standing it still looks a whole lot like a room full of entitled, rich men taking advantage of women who don't hold the same level of power. But since I'm supposed to be one of those women, I keep my thoughts to myself.

"Sure, there are a few here who I'd steer clear of," she continues, looking over my shoulder with narrowed eyes toward the cocktail party I'd just come from, "but we're all here because we want to be." She pauses then, considering me, as if the thought has only just occurred to her. "I suppose for some it's more of a business transaction than anything else, but we're all adults. Everything you see here is consensual. It's one of the only rules. No one is going to force you to do anything you don't want to do. My advice? Keep an open mind." She smiles, a scandalous grin stretching ruby lips. "You just might see something you like . . ."

But I can't seem to concentrate on what she's telling me. The room has started to spin, and I feel like I'm going to be sick. "Where is the ladies' room?"

"Up the stairs, to your left." The woman points her long, slim finger toward the nearest staircase.

I turn and flee, running up the stairs as quickly as I can in my borrowed heels. At the top, I'm met by a long corridor that I rush through, struggling to keep my balance and ignoring the carnal sounds that ring out from behind the row of closed doors. I'm growing increasingly dizzy, like I've had too much to drink, but all I've had was half a glass of champagne. Could the man downstairs have slipped something in my glass? *So much for the rules. Can't say I'm surprised that the men here think they're above them.* I drag my hand along the wall for support as I push forward.

Finally I find the bathroom and I sprint inside, locking the door behind me. Leaning against the secured door, I pull off my mask and toss it to the floor. My head is swimming, the edges of the world fuzzy, as I slide to the floor. *Has Maddie been here before?* A wicked voice in the back of my head whispers tantalizingly. Thoughts freed from the darkest hollows of my mind. *How well do you really know your sister?* I push my hands to my ears, willing away the voice, but it lingers, lacing its way between my fingers, infiltrating my head. It's the question I've been holding at bay at the brink of my consciousness, the link I didn't want to see between Maddie and this place. It floats to the surface now, untethered, ringing in my ear as clear as a bell. *Could this be where Maddie got all that money from? Thousands of dollars for the things she might have done behind these closed doors.* The thought makes nausea rise in my gut and I lurch toward the toilet, where I empty the meager contents of my stomach.

Forcing myself to my feet, I brace myself against the sink and splash cold water onto my face, watching as traces of makeup swirl down the drain. I catch my reflection in the mirror above the sink: My complexion is worryingly pale, swipes of mascara are smeared under my eyes, and my hair, which April had trained into spiraling curls, is shaken out around my shoulders. *I need to get out of here.*

My feet are still unsteady beneath me, but I know I have to walk, to push my body forward. I won't be safe until I'm far away from this place. I slip off my shoes, not trusting my balance in them, and pad back down the hallway. My gait becomes quicker, my steps more desperate, until I reach the top of the stairs. The sweeping staircase seems to be undulating, slow waves rolling beneath the treads. I grip the banister with both hands, dropping my shoes to the ground with a soft thud. I don't know how I'm going to make it down the stairs in one piece if the room doesn't stop spinning. But I don't have a choice. I have to get out of this house.

I put one tentative foot on the top step, and the world feels as though it's tilting on its axis. My shoulder collides with the wall, and my breathing becomes shallow. The stairs below me seem to stretch on forever, the exit so far beyond my reach.

Suddenly there's a presence at my elbow, strong arms righting me onto my feet.

"Are you all right?" Silvery words slipping in my ear like minnows. It all feels so familiar, a sense of déjà vu sweeping over me, and I know, somewhere in the back of my muddled brain, that this has all happened before.

I turn to face him, this man who seems to have come to my rescue. My eyes struggle to focus at first, searching his face, the depth of his dark hair, the silky black of his mask, the look of shock in the piercing blue of his eyes.

"James?"

It's the last thing I remember before I collapse into his arms.

30.

LILY

The knock on my bedroom door takes me by surprise. I freeze in the center of the room, my toes curling into the plush carpet. Mother already checked in on me this morning. *The state of you, Lily. I'm making you an appointment with the hairdresser. You cannot possibly carry on like this.* Assuming she hasn't thought of any other grievances concerning my appearance, I don't know who else would be looking for me.

Another rap on the door makes me flinch. "Lily, it's Alex. I need to talk to you." Her voice sounds different. Harder, with a raspy edge. Sort of how Theo sounds after spending a night out with his friends, staggering home after sunrise with his untucked shirt trailing behind him.

"Uh, just a sec." I check my reflection in the mirror above my vanity. Maybe Mother had a point about my hair. It's dreadful. Matted and dull. I'm just . . . finding it hard to care about anything. Now that Maddie isn't here. After everything that's happened, the start of every new day, sunlight streaming through my windows, feels like an affront. An insult. How can life just be going on as usual, as if everything hasn't changed? How can it still be important to brush my hair, assemble an outfit, put makeup on my face? What does any of it matter now? I try to pull my fingers through my hair, but it's too knotted, they get caught up in the coarse locks. *Forget it.* I push it back into a hasty ponytail instead. There's nothing I can do about my face now: the patches of raw skin where I must have been scratching, possibly in my sleep. I don't remember doing it. But my skin looks angry, splotchy. This has happened before; I remember the raised, pink welts. "Stress rash," Dr. Watkins had called it then.

I wish I could call her. For the last two years I've protested going to Dr. Watkins's office, acting as though seeing a therapist was a punishment I was being forced to endure after what I'd done. But if I'm being honest with myself, she was helping me. Helping me understand why I am the way I am, helping me learn to suppress the urges that sometimes feel too big to ignore. Right now I'd give anything to lie on the couch in her office, run my fingers over the pumpkin-colored velvet, tell her everything in the warm cocoon of her office. I can picture her gentle nods, encouraging me to set it all free, to lay myself bare. But then I imagine her pursing her lips, her unspoken disappointment in me at the undoing of all the progress we've made. I hate the thought of being a disappointment to even one more person. But it doesn't matter anyway. Because I *can't* talk to Dr. Watkins. I can't tell anyone the things I know, the things I've done. It's a burden I'll have to carry on my own. It's just that . . . sometimes I'm afraid it's too heavy. That I'll shatter under the weight.

"Lily?" Alex sounds insistent now. Impatient.

"Coming." I pull open the door, tucking a loose strand of straw-dry hair behind my ear.

Alex blinks at me. Adjusting to how far I've fallen in just

a few short days. She opens her mouth, and I wait for her to tell me, just as Mother has, how ill I look. How worryingly thin. I brace myself for the criticism.

"Is your father home?"

It takes me a moment to recalibrate my thoughts. "I don't . . . I don't think so. I heard him up early this morning. Yelling at someone on the phone about pouring the foundation at his new hotel. So if I had to guess, he's probably at the job site. Why are you looking for my father, anyway?" I study her now, noticing the way the ends of her hair soak her T-shirt in wet patches at her chest, the clean scent of soap clinging to her skin. Her face is scrubbed of makeup, making her look even younger than she usually does, with the exception of the purple shadows blooming beneath her eyes like pressed bruises. While the thought of Maddie has pushed me into an almost catatonic state, hours of endless sleep, my mind wiped blank by the little round pills Mother gave me "to help me get through," it seems that Alex has had the opposite problem. She looks as though she hasn't been sleeping very much at all.

"I just need to ask him something." Her eyes shift to the floor. A sign, Dr. Watkins says, that means she's holding something back. "Do you know when he'll be back?"

I shake my head.

"Hey . . . are you okay?" Alex seems to soften, her eyes probing mine. Now it's my turn to look away.

"I'm fine."

"If there's anything you want to talk about—"

"There's not. Was there anything else you needed?" My fingers wrap around the edge of the door, my knuckles pressed white.

"Oh, no, I—"

"I'll see you later then. I have to go."

She opens her mouth to respond, confusion etching across her features, but I close the door before she has the chance.

I watch the shadow of her feet beneath the door, waiting for her to leave, but she doesn't. Not right away. She lingers there a moment, as though she's debating whether to knock again. *Just go away.* I clench my teeth, pressing my forehead to the door, choking back the words that are ready to leap from my tongue. *You need to go before I break.*

Finally she leaves, the sound of her footsteps echoing down the hall. I'm not sure how much more of this I can take. I slide to the floor, my spine scraping against the wooden door as I go. I have to remember what Dr. Watkins taught me. Staying in the moment, taking each minute as it comes, trying not to send myself into a downward spiral about things that are beyond my control. But it seems impossible when it feels as though *everything* is out of my control. Most of the time I feel like I'm standing on the deck of a boat that's lost in the middle of the sea, life tossing me around, rocking me about so violently that it's all I can do to keep from falling overboard, never mind find my balance.

It's a struggle no one understands. How hard I fight to hold it all together. I heard my parents arguing over it. After "the incident" at school my junior year.

"What's wrong with her, James?" Mother lamented.

"We're going to get her the help she needs, Katherine. It's all we can do now." My father, attending to the practicalities, but in no rush to come to my defense.

"I'm . . . I'm frightened of her, James. That she could do something so . . . so *violent.*"

"There's no need for theatrics."

"This wasn't the first time," Mother reminded him. "What about all the others? The so-called accidents . . ."

"We're handling it."

My own mother thinks I'm a monster. Some hideous creature that needs to be managed, fixed, hidden away behind locked doors. I know I'm not what she envisioned when she dreamed of her future daughter. I've never been the kind of girl that she could dress up in pretty dresses, the kind who loves fashion, and shopping, and manicures after brunch. I'm not popular, I'm not charming, I'm not special. I'm not like Maddie.

Mother tells me that as soon as she and Father saw a picture of Theo and me, they knew we were meant to be a family. A boy and a girl, siblings, the missing piece of the puzzle needed to complete the picture-perfect family they'd always wanted. But sometimes, when she's driving me to my appointments, as I sit in the back seat staring listlessly out the window, I wonder whether she regrets it. If she could turn back the hands of time, would she go back to that orphanage, would she choose another baby squalling in its threadbare cot? Would she look past my big, dark eyes and leave me there to an unknown fate?

I couldn't blame her if she felt that way. What I did was . . . awful. I can see that now. In hindsight. But at the time, I was just so angry. I couldn't contain it. The rage that boiled over, covering the world in a hazy, red fog.

It all started with Olivia Davis. And it ended with her too. Olivia was the most popular girl at school. She had perfect shiny hair that swished when she walked, and a perfectly coquettish laugh that filtered through the hallways as she passed with her friends, flanking her like bodyguards. She drank iced coffee, a straw always pressed between her bubblegum-pink lips, and she wore funky outfits that would look mismatched on anyone else, but on her, looked as though they were ripped from the pages of a fashion magazine. Cuffed cargo pants paired with a leather jacket, pleated skirts and high-top sneakers, jewel-toned blazers over dark-washed jeans. Olivia was everything I wasn't, everything I wanted to be. And so it felt serendipitous that on the first day of high school, she chose the seat next to mine during orientation.

"I'm Olivia," she said, through a click of her cinnamon gum.

I knew who she was. Everyone knew who she was. "Lily," I replied, playing along.

"Cool necklace. It's so . . . vintage."

My hand rose to my chest, fingering the silver leaf-shaped charm that always hung around my neck. It was the only item that came with me from the orphanage. A gift from my birth mother, my only tie to the woman I'd never meet. "Thanks."

The orientation dragged on for what felt like hours, the air-conditioning buzzing overhead as it struggled to keep up with the heat rising from hundreds of bodies packing the auditorium. But I hardly noticed. All I could think about was Olivia. The sweet vanilla scent of her perfume, the silvery shadow dusting her eyelids. About halfway through the presentation she passed me the first note, her curly pink handwriting stretching across the page:

This is SO boring!

I wrote back. *Struggling to stay awake.*

She scribbled a reply. *Do you think Mr. Jenkins knows his toupee is falling off?*

I burst into a fit of giggles, clapping my hand over my mouth. Olivia laughed, too, loose and alive.

Mr. Jenkins raised an eyebrow at us, but we couldn't seem to stop.

That was the start of it all. Olivia shoving notes into my locker after homeroom, me writing lengthy replies in study hall, folding the notebook paper into neat triangles to pass to her on my way to biology.

But a few weeks into the school year, the notes had abruptly stopped. I couldn't understand it at first, what had happened, what I'd done to turn her away. But then I started to see. How she sat at the popular table at lunch, surrounded by other shiny girls who dressed like her, talked like her, moved through the world like her. How the older boys had started to notice her, how she had noticed them. How much she seemed to like it.

I was devastated. Didn't Olivia know how much her friendship meant to me? I wrote her a note trying to explain, but when I tried to hand it to her in the hallway, she pretended not to see me. I decided to leave it in her locker instead, my heart poured out on pale blue lines. At the last moment, I took off my necklace, the one she'd loved so much, and folded it inside. I could already picture it around her neck, a tether bonding us together. Surely Olivia would respond to such a meaningful gesture. But she never did. I imagined my letter at the bottom of the hall garbage can. My special necklace lost below the crusts of sandwiches, broken pencils, all the other useless things that the kids at that school couldn't be bothered with.

For the next two years, I did my best to get back into Olivia's good graces. It's hard to explain how it felt being in her orbit. She was special. When she shined her spotlight on you, it was like standing in the sunshine. And when she took it away, well, it was dark and cold in her shadow. In those days, I would have done anything for a few more moments of sun. I went to the school football games to root for her as she cheered at halftime, I stood and clapped when she finished her role as the lead in the school play, I even started dressing more like her and her friends, much to my mother's delight. But nothing seemed to work. It was as if I didn't exist at that school. I doubted anyone even knew my name.

And then, in my junior year, things started to change. Lucinda Gross, one of Olivia's closest friends, plopped down in the seat behind me in Spanish class and poked the back of my neck with the rubbery end of her pencil. "Hey."

I turned around, blinking at her curiously. Lucinda had never spoken a single word to me in all the years we'd been at school together.

"You going to the party tonight?" she asked, gum cracking between her teeth.

"Party?" I'd never been to a party before. I'd never been invited to one.

"Yeah. At Olivia's. Her parents are out of town. Gonna be a rager. Like, the whole school is going."

"Oh," I replied. "Cool. Maybe I will."

"Great! It's a white party, so make sure you wear something white."

"Thanks, I'll see you there."

Lucinda smiled, a saccharine grin. "I can't wait."

I stood on Olivia's doorstep that evening, music thumping from inside, and wiped my sweaty palms on my new white dress. I'd gone out and bought it right after school that day because it looked like the kind of thing Olivia and her friends might wear to a party. *Do I knock? Or do I just walk in like I belong here?* I didn't have to think about it for long, because just at that moment a group of boys from school pulled up in a cherry red Jeep, the top pulled down, stereo blasting. They jumped out of the back carrying cases of beer hoisted on their shoulders and strolled into the yard. I followed them, the sound of the music growing louder as I approached.

Lucinda had been partially right. There weren't nearly as many people there as I had been expecting, but the party *was* raging. Boys I recognized from my classes were doing handstands over a keg, the tap pressed to their lips, girls in short skirts sipped from red plastic cups, their bodies moving to the beat of the music.

And there, at the center of it all, was Olivia. In a white dress, very similar to my own. It was at that moment that I noticed that Olivia was the *only* other person wearing white. *But hadn't Lucinda told me it was a white party?*

"Oh, look!" Lucinda called, turning the volume down on the music. "Olivia, your fan club has arrived!" She grabbed Olivia by the hand and pulled her in my direction.

"I'm . . . I'm not . . ." I stammered uselessly.

"What are you doing here?" Olivia asked through a forced smile.

"I thought it was a party and . . . and . . ." Tears gathered behind my eyes, and the words lodged in my throat.

"She's even dressed like you!" Lucinda howled. "What a freak!"

My eyes darted around the yard. Everyone was staring, amused grins lighting their faces. I could hear the serpentine whispers slithering toward me. "Freak" . . . "stalker" . . . "loser."

I turned to flee, my face burning in shame. But Lucinda wasn't finished.

"'Olivia,'" she whined in a mocking tone, "'your friendship means the world to me.'"

I froze. Anger rising like a tide. These were the words from the letter. The last one I'd written to Olivia. The one she'd never responded to. But, it seemed, she'd shared it with her friends. In a flash I could picture them all at a slumber party, huddled around my letter, reading the lines aloud, cackling with laughter.

"Stop," I said, my tone icy cold.

"'You're my only friend,'" Lucinda continued.

My hands balled into fists, and I spun around to face her, fire burning behind my eyes. It wasn't the first time I'd felt the flames, but it had been so long since the last time I'd let them out.

"Lu, come on, that's enough," Olivia chided, but it was a half-hearted attempt, laughter hovering just beneath the surface of her words.

"But I haven't even gotten to the best part!" Lucinda teased. "Where she tells you how special you are. That's probably why Lily here is your number one fan."

"Shut up!" I shouted. "Just shut up!" I could feel myself losing control.

"'Oh, Olivia,'" Lucinda mocked, as though reading from a script, "'meeting you was the best thing that ever happened to me.' It's like she's in *love* with you or something, Liv!"

"It's not like that," I growled. I could hear some of the others giggling, but my focus was on Lucinda. My hatred strong enough that it felt like it might bore a hole through her. And then I looked at Olivia. She was laughing. *Laughing.* At my most private, humiliating thoughts.

I shoved her. As hard as I could. I wanted to hurt her. I wanted to make it so that she'd never laugh at me again. But I wasn't thinking clearly. I was just acting, my body moving under the control of pure rage. She stumbled backward and tripped on a garden hose, falling hard on her arm. I heard the crack above the music, the bones in her wrist breaking.

"I'm sorry!" I cried, rushing to her side. "I didn't mean—it was an accident!"

"Get away from me, you psycho!" Olivia screamed, cradling her wrist, tears streaming down her face. I could see it in that moment, the way her eyes grew round, the way she edged her body away from mine . . . she was afraid of me. I couldn't stand to look at it, the fear, the horror on her face where once there had been only fondness. I turned and I ran.

My parents handled it. They cleaned up my mess like they had so many others. Money slid under tables, silence bought at a steep price. The same way they had for Theo when he'd gotten that DWI. It's amazing what you can get away with when you're rich. For the right price, you become untouchable. And so I wasn't arrested for what I'd done to Olivia, but my parents pulled me out of school, had me finish my coursework with a private tutor, and they made me start seeing Dr. Watkins every week.

I'd been doing really well since then. Talking to Dr. Watkins made me understand what went wrong with Olivia. That my friendship had been too intense for her, too all-consuming, and that it frightened her. And I learned from that. I really did. I wasn't going to make the same mistakes with Maddie.

And yet . . . I felt myself unraveling around her. Becoming obsessed. I'd just wanted her to like me. She did at first. Maddie was so different from Olivia. Or so I thought. I felt like she understood me, like we'd made a genuine connection. But then . . . then she started to pull away; and the more she pulled, the tighter I clung to her. I borrowed her clothes, her makeup, her mannerisms. I became just like her. I was begging her to notice me, to accept me. But still, Maddie held herself back. She grew distant, secretive. What was once a blossoming friendship was dying on the vine. She made excuses about why she couldn't spend time with me, but I knew it was because of *her*. Becca. Maddie's *real* friend. How quickly she'd traded me in. Left me behind. Just like Olivia had. And those old feelings started to rise to the surface. The rage, the resentment, the desire to hurt her like she was hurting me. After everything I'd done for Maddie, she was going to cast me aside. Just like the others. And I couldn't let that happen.

31.

ALEX

Well, that *was strange.* I stop at the top of the stairs, look-ing back over my shoulder for one last glance at Lily's closed door. She looked terrible, sick. But it was more than that. There's something else that is still bothering me. That was the first time I'd gotten a glimpse of Lily's room, and with-out even setting foot inside, I could tell it wasn't . . . normal for a girl her age. Where was the mess, the scattered makeup, the photos of friends stuck into the edges of the mirror's frame?

I've always believed that a person's bedroom can tell a lot about them—the colors they choose, the items they sur-round themselves with, all of the personal touches—they tell a story about the person who lives there. I think back to the room I shared with Maddie when we were growing up. How it seemed to evolve with us as we grew, a living, breath-ing thing. The dolls and plastic ponies that once lined the shelves gave way to framed photos and bottles of nail polish, then eventually to textbooks . . . and now they're bare. The room already tidied away, packed into moving boxes so the realtor can photograph the space, get it ready for listing. I can still hear the rip of the packing tape as I pulled it off the roll, closing the last box, sealing away the past.

But Lily's room—it was tastefully decorated, like a spread from an interior design magazine, but almost frighteningly impersonal, no fingerprint of the girl who lives there. Peering into Lily's bedroom should have been like holding up a mirror to her, but I saw nothing reflected back. The thought sends a chill shivering through my body.

I need to leave Blackwell Manor. I'm going to find a hotel room today. Now that I have Maddie's cash, I can afford to do it. And after last night, I can't stand the thought of staying for another minute.

I stride through the great room and out into the yard, where sunlight streams into my eyes. I wince, pressing my fingers to my temples.

I woke up this morning with a splitting headache, a shooting pain splicing through the center of my skull. The moment I opened my eyes, I panicked. *Where am I? How did I get here?* I had no recollection of anything that happened after seeing James at the party. I threw back the blanket that was covering me, terrified about all of the things that could have happened to me during the dark gap in my memory, and I was surprised to find that I was still wearing April's dress. I mentally scanned my body. Aside from the headache, I didn't feel any aches or bruises. Nothing to suggest that anything untoward had happened. Relieved, I sat up and surveyed the room. The shoes I'd borrowed from April sat neatly beside the bed, like two obedient pets. At my bedside was a glass of water and a bottle of aspirin. James must have taken me home and tucked me into bed. While I was grateful that I'd made it home safely, the memory of last night—of the things I saw in that place, the shock on James's face when his eyes found mine, the feeling of his hands at my waist—made my stomach lurch. I dragged myself to the bathroom and was sick in the toilet. I wiped my mouth with the back of my hand and switched on the shower. It was only then that I noticed the sunshine filling the bathroom window. *How long had I slept?*

I still don't know exactly what happened to me last night, what poisonous thing was slipped into my drink, but it was enough to convince me that the men who go to those parties are more than capable of harming women. Women like Becca. Women like Maddie.

I'd gone to that party looking for a thread that could lead me to Becca, but it was a connection to Maddie that I found instead. In a sense, I'm glad it was James who found me last night, but it also makes me fearful for what harm could have come to my sister while living under his roof. It makes the photos of her that I'd found in his office feel even more ominous, frightening.

Just as I open the glass door to the pool house, I hear my phone vibrating against the coffee table. I rush to pick it up and find one new voicemail and one unread message.

I swipe the screen to unlock it, playing the voicemail first:

Alex, it's Chief Gilroy. I'd like to get you back down to the station to answer a few more questions. Call me back as soon as possible, please.

His words carried a pugnacious, almost accusatory inflection. I quickly delete the message. I'm in no state to square off with Gilroy right now.

Next I check my text messages.

MADDIE: I tried to warn you. You're not safe there.

I drop the phone as though it's scalded me and it clatters onto the stone path. When I pick it up, I find that there's a web of hairline cracks snaking from the upper corner to the center of the screen, but mercifully it still works. This time, instead of replying to the text, I immediately call Maddie's number. And it *rings.*

After days of getting nothing but her voicemail message, the phone is finally ringing. The sound sends a tingling wave of hope rushing through my body. But then it ends. The call has been sent to voicemail. I try calling again and again, but I'm met with the same recorded message each time: *You've reached Maddie's phone, please leave me a message . . .*

Someone was just there. On the other end of the line. I want to believe it was really Maddie with every fiber of my being, but I just can't be sure. I start texting her, my fingers flying furiously across the screen.

Maddie, if this is really you, tell me a secret.

To anyone else's eyes, the message would seem simple enough. I'm asking my sister to tell me something only she would know, a way for her to prove that she's who she purports to be. But the real Maddie would know that I'm asking for something else entirely.

When we were small, Maddie and I liked to play games of our own invention.

"It must be a twin thing," Mom would say, rolling her eyes good-heartedly at the labyrinth of rules we'd establish, the fantasy worlds we'd create where we'd sometimes lose ourselves for hours at a time. We'd play pirates and scour the woods for hidden treasures, or we'd pretend we were astronauts exploring a strange new planet. But one of our favorite games was one that we never shared with anyone else, it was ours and ours alone, played only as we lay in our matching twin beds at night, stories whispered in the dark:

Tell Me a Secret.

The rules of the game were simple. If you were asked to tell a secret, you had to tell the most elaborate, fantastical lie you could think of. Something so far-fetched that no one would ever believe it was true. But you had to tell it convincingly, without laughing, without breaking character. Sometimes the narrative would stretch on for days, elaborate tales growing, taking shape, over weeks. Maddie was always the best at it. She'd tell incredible stories, describing in intricate detail how she was secretly a mermaid princess, an heiress to an undersea kingdom, who was banished to the human world by her jealous stepmother.

"No, it's true!" she'd insist. "I had the most lovely tail, with shimmering scales of purple and sapphire blue."

"Tell me again about the castle," I'd beg through a yawn.

I'd fall asleep to the sound of Maddie spinning her beautiful tales, her words wrapping around me, keeping me safe and warm in the world she created for me.

I stare down at my phone. Waiting for a response. If the person using Maddie's phone tells me something believable, something real, I'll know, beyond a shadow of a doubt, that it's not Maddie.

Three little dots appear. Maddie is typing. I grip the phone harder, praying for a message of unicorns and rainbows, ships that sail on a sea of clouds, but nothing comes. The dots disappear.

I call Maddie's number one last time, but it goes to voicemail. Whoever was there is gone.

Frustrated, I jam my phone into my pocket and yank

open the door to the pool house. Inside, I begin shoving what few belongings I came with back into my duffel bag. I pack Maddie's things too. The money, the necklace. All traces of my sister now stripped away.

It makes me think of Mom's house. Of the piles of sagging boxes, the dust collecting in empty corners. I'm suddenly hit with a stabbing pain that feels as though it's piercing through my heart. It's interesting the way grief works. How memories can spring themselves upon you seemingly out of nowhere and rip the breath from your lungs. And yet, since Mom died, I've noticed that the colors of my memories have been slowly shifting, muting. After you lose someone, your mind paints over the past in soft pastels. Gone are the slashes of red anger, the deep blues of sadness I'd felt immediately after the funeral. All that remains now are fuzzy-edged visions, faded like old photographs—of Maddie and me wearing matching pink leotards in our living room, of Mom showing us how to hold our arms, how to replicate the poise and grace of her perfect twirls. Maddie had been right. I was choosing to see the worst in Mom, because on some level I think I knew that I was holding on to that anger to fill the void her death had left in my life. Now that I've started to let it go, other emotions have begun to creep in: guilt, regret, loneliness. Vivienne Walker had been larger than life, and in death she left a hole in my heart as big as she was. And I'm not certain I'll ever know how to fill it.

I push away a tear from the corner of my eye and pull the zipper across my duffel bag. I swing it over my shoulder, taking one last cursory look over the pool house. I'm leaving it exactly as I found it four days ago. Four short days that feel like a lifetime. With a frustrated sigh, I shut the door and close the keys in my palm. All that's left to do is drop the keys inside the main house, and then I'm going to leave this place and never look back.

But when I reach the back door of the house, I see something through the glass that I wasn't expecting. Katherine is in the kitchen. I'd planned to leave the keys on the counter, possibly with a note telling the Blackwells that I didn't intend to return, but now I won't be able to do that without walking right past her. And she seems angry. She's gesticulating wildly at a small man in a black polo shirt who is writing down everything she's saying on a notepad cradled in the palm of his hand.

I slip the duffel bag off my shoulder and place it on the ground. Carefully, I crack open the back door, wincing as it makes a slight creaking sound, but no one seems to notice. Katherine's authoritative voice spills out into the yard.

"Mario, I told you, the canapés need to be here by four o'clock. And the floral arrangements need to be in place by at least three. This event is hugely important for James. All of the investors for his new hotel are going to be here. Everything needs to go smoothly. Perfectly. Do you understand?"

"Yes, Mrs. Blackwell. Leave it to me. Mr. Blackwell's party will go off without a hitch. I'll see to it myself."

I slide the door shut, the latch engaging softly. Maybe I'd acted prematurely. If James is having an event here tonight, perhaps I shouldn't leave yet after all. Maybe someone will know something about Maddie. Or, at the very least, it will give me another chance to talk to James. To find out what he knows. What he's done.

32.

MADDIE

I wish I hadn't gone. I never should have followed James last night. It was a mistake. I collect my things from the pool house, tossing them haphazardly back into my suitcase. It's time for me to leave Blackwell Manor. There are certain truths that, once you know them, you can't hide from. The awareness will haunt you everywhere you turn, coloring every decision, entwining itself so intricately into the fiber of your being that it changes you, becomes a part of you. When I looked through that window last night, the lens through which I saw my life shifted. The landscape altered forever. And I can't help but feel that my ignorance truly was bliss.

I had followed James's car as it wound through town. Passing Main Street and the rows of restaurants, fairy lights strung between the trees, sleepy shopfronts nestled down to rest before opening their arms to tomorrow's tourists. He drove out past the center of town, beyond the hotels and beach rentals, into the residential area where the grand houses lumbered like giants rising from the sea. Their windows watched us with hooded eyes as we drove past. Finally, he pulled up to a large Colonial home with soaring pillars and a shiny red door. He turned off his ignition, his taillights fading into darkness. I parked farther down the block, cutting my own headlights and slouching in my seat as I watched him approach the front door.

He knocked and was greeted by another man in a dark suit. They shook hands and James disappeared inside. Curious, I pulled out my phone and dropped a pin to find our current location.

395 Breaker Beach Road.

It sounded so familiar, and yet, I knew I'd never been there before. I mulled it over, rolling the address around on my tongue, until it finally clicked. This was one of the properties that James's company was renovating. I recognized it from his files at the office. *But why would James be dropping in on one of his properties in the middle of the night, and who was the man who answered the door?*

I crept out of the car, curiosity drawing me closer to the house, the red door beckoning me like a siren luring a mariner to his death. But then I heard someone else approaching, the tapping rhythm of stilettos on pavement, and I receded back into the shadows. Two women strutted up the walkway, their hips swaying as they walked. This time, as the man opened the door to allow them entrance, music wafted out of the house, carrying on the soft breeze. *What was going on in that house? Some sort of party?*

I looked down at my work clothes, fingered my hair that was knotted into a messy braid hanging over my shoulder. I had a feeling that the man in the dark suit wasn't going to welcome me in as he had the others. Instead, I walked the perimeter of the property, padding lightly over the springy green grass toward the yard. I lifted the latch of the tall white fence and pushed it open, peering into the dark yard. As far as I could tell, no one was out there. But as soon as I set foot into the yard, a floodlight switched on, filling the space with bright white light. I quickly pressed my back against the side of the house, the wood shingles gritty through the thin fabric of my shirt. I breathed steadily, aware of the rising and falling of my chest, my palms spread flat against the house. Finally, the light turned off. I was more careful after that, only moving along the edge of the house, my shoulder scraping along the shingles as I walked, until I reached a window. Rising onto the tips of my toes, I looked inside.

What I saw sent me staggering back to the safety of the wall, to the shadows that separated me from the people inside. In the center of the room stood a dark-haired woman, completely naked with the exception of a white gag stretched across her mouth, her arms bound behind her back. Her body quivered as a man in a collared shirt approached her, her black hair a curtain around her shoulders. The man twirled a lock of it around his finger, and the woman's body shook. I couldn't tell if it was from excitement or fear. The man circled her, his eyes feasting on the curves of her exposed body as he unfastened a pair of silver cuff links, carefully rolling his sleeves up to his elbows. Then he took a seat in a wingback chair and summoned the woman to him. She complied dutifully, as if she already understood what was expected of her. The man bent the woman over his knee and raised his palm. I heard the *smack* as it collided with her bare skin. The woman cried out, her teeth biting into the fabric straining against her mouth, red lipstick staining the white cloth, and I had to look away. *What was James doing at a place like this?* I'd never known him to be anything but gentle and caring, but this was making me second-guess everything I thought I knew about him.

Instinct was telling me to leave, to run away from this place and never look back, but I had to see James. I had to know for sure. I crept toward the next window, keeping low to the ground as I moved. When I looked inside, I found that there were more people in this room, some of them drinking champagne, some touching, some talking, but they all faded into the background when I finally saw James. With his arms around Becca.

I stood there, frozen in horror, as he dipped his tongue into her mouth, slid his hand to her waist. Becca leaned into him, her body drawn to his. Then James pressed his palm to her lower back and led her toward a staircase. My fingers rose to my mouth. I thought I was going to be sick.

I ran across the yard, not caring about the floodlights, about who might see me. All I cared about was getting away from that place as fast as I possibly could.

————

I lean on the top of my overstuffed suitcase, holding it closed as I struggle to pull the zipper along the sides. I thought James and I had a connection, that I was really starting to get to know the true him, but it was all a lie. He's not the man I thought he was.

I push open the door of the pool house and step out into the yard, dragging my battered suitcase behind me. But one of the wheels catches on a paving stone and the suitcase tips, the old zipper giving way. The contents of my bag pour out onto the ground, and I sink down to my knees, kneeling in the mess I've made of everything. *It wasn't supposed to be like this.*

"Going somewhere?" Theo asks. He seems to have appeared out of nowhere. Towering above me. His figure blocks the sun, which creates a halo of light around his head, but casts his face in harsh, steely shadows. It has the effect of making his features look harder, angrier, his eyes like endless wells of inky darkness.

Ever since the day at the office, when I turned down Theo's advances, he's largely avoided me. The few times we've crossed paths, he'd looked at me with nothing but contempt, resentful disdain.

He doesn't wait for me to respond as I busy myself shoving my belongings back into my bag. "It's probably for the best."

I should let him walk away. But something in me snapped last night when I saw James and Becca together. Something that can't be put back together. I'm not the same girl I used to be. And this new version of me is so full of anger, of disappointment, that it begins to spill over. The words are out of my mouth before I can pull them back. "What's *that* supposed to mean?"

Theo raises an eyebrow, amused. He looks down at me as though I am a bug on the ground, a speck of dirt that's found its way onto his expensive loafers. "Only that I'm not quite sure why you were here in the first place."

Theo doesn't know it, but he's struck a chord. I *did* come to the Hamptons for a reason. I'd become so sidetracked with all of the other noise, all of the subterfuge and sleights of hand that I've encountered here, that I'd nearly forgotten why I came in the first place. I can't leave yet. Not until I've accomplished what I set out to do. "Well, you're wrong. I'm not going anywhere."

Theo's eyes narrow into angry slits. There are few things

more dangerous than men like him. Men whose privilege has taught them that the world owes them a bounty, that it exists simply for them to take from it. And they do, Theo and the others like him, they take. More and more and more. Hand over fist they take. I swallow hard, withering on my knees under Theo's watchful glare, waiting to see what kind of man he will turn out to be.

With a disgusted shake of his head he walks past me. I exhale, the tension in my shoulders draining away. As I watch Theo cross the yard, his long strides cutting a path through the grass, I wonder how long I have until he can't contain that anger any longer.

33.

THE WHARF

I warned him. I told him what he had to do, and yet he isn't here.

I check the time on my phone, the glow of the screen cutting through the darkness. He's twenty minutes late. I'll give him another ten, and then I'll have to assume he's decided to end our little arrangement. I should be used to it, going unseen by him and the others like him. Underestimated time and again. But somehow it still stings.

Behind me something in the water rustles. Probably a bass, a carnivore striking out at its prey. The full moon will have brought them out, turning the otherwise equable night sea into a nocturnal hunting ground. I look up at the moon now, the silver-white disk hanging low in the black-satin sky. It's turned the ocean into something new, a slick of liquid platinum gilding the surface, concealing the violence that erupts underneath. The feeding frenzy, the sharp teeth and torn flesh.

The empty docks around me bob gently with the rising tide. But still he doesn't show. I didn't want it to come to this. Truly I didn't. I'm worried about how this is going to end, about what will come next. But there's no turning back now.

The wheels have already been set in motion. This thing has become larger than me. Taken on a life of its own. But I didn't create it alone. And he could have stopped this. All of it.

I pull out my phone once again, a burner with only one number stored in it, and I send him a message.

Time's up.

I warned him. I wish he would have listened.

34.

KATHERINE

A peal of laughter echoes through the yard. It's Mrs. Remington in her gaudy purple dress that encases her like a sausage, with her head thrown back, mouth gaping like a fish, as though Mr. Fenton has just made a rather hilarious joke. Which I find endlessly doubtful. Mr. Fenton, a small wiry man with a weasel-like face, has as much personality as a slice of burnt toast. I'm simply not in the mood for this tonight.

The party came together nicely though. I survey it all from the private balcony off the master bedroom, like a director standing before her orchestra. String lights hang whimsically from the willow tree, floating lanterns dot the surface of the pool, servers whiz by with platters of hors d'oeuvres—cloudlike crab puffs, fresh caviar on golden blini—and as the champagne flows, the guests have started using the patio as a dance floor. It's all as it should be. And yet I can't bring myself to join them.

These types of things are usually where I'm at my best. Mrs. Blackwell, my leading role. A breeze wraps around me and the drop-diamond earrings James gave me for our tenth anniversary tickle my neck. I've paired them with an emerald green wrap dress and twisted my hair into an elegant bun to make sure they're on full display. But I can't go down there tonight, smile at our guests, make small talk about gardening and luncheons. Not after last night.

I couldn't sleep, so preoccupied was I with planning this event for my darling husband and his godforsaken hotel. Which was how I came to notice the light coming from the yard. I padded to the window and drew the sash. The pool house was shining like a lighthouse in the center of the yard, all of the lights inside burning bright. And then, through the open door, I spied James at Alex's bedside. I was transfixed by the sight of him kneeling at her side, gently pushing a lock of hair from her forehead. The girl was asleep, a vision of youth and innocence, blissfully unaware of the tenderness she'd evoked in my husband. The intimacy of the gesture caused a constriction in my chest, as though a vise had been tightened around my heart.

I'd asked about his evening this morning, over coffee and a platter of fresh-cut fruit. Hoping against all reason that he'd offer a simple explanation for what I'd seen.

"It was fine," he'd replied, hardly looking above the fold of his morning paper. "Nothing of note. Another late night at the office."

"Was it to do with the hotel?" I feigned the kind of doe-eyed innocence that seems to appeal to my husband as of late.

"Of course." A rustle of paper as he turned the page.

He'd made no mention of Alex, of having been in the pool house in the dead of night. But what could he have possibly said to explain away what I'd seen with my own eyes? *It's happening again.*

I watch him now as he glides through his party, shaking

hands and patting backs like a politician on a campaign trail. If James has noticed my absence, if he longs to have me on his arm, he makes no show of it.

This little soirée has drawn an interesting mix of guests. James's investors for the hotel, of course, as this was all for them. To give James a chance to charm his way into their wallets. But he's also invited some of the local players, members of the community, the zoning board. There has been some grumbling about the size and expense of the new hotel. Locals complaining that the construction would cause too much disturbance to protected lands, that it's too modern to fit with the sleepy beach towns they like to pretend the Hamptons still are. James offered these invitations as if to say, "See how good things can be? See how generous I am when you're on my side?"

It makes for an intense dynamic, Joe Burbank from the local conservation society rubbing elbows with Benjamin Blithe, an oil magnate with a net worth in the billions. The tension crackles over the yard like static electricity. And at the periphery of the crowd I spot Chief Michael Gilroy. I've always found him inexplicably handsome, in a way so opposite to my husband. Perhaps that's the appeal. His tanned, weather-beaten skin speaks of days spent at sea, and his blond hair is bleached from the summer sun. I find myself wondering what his hands would feel like on my skin, the rough calluses of his palms such a contrast to James's soft touch. I stop myself, push the very idea from my head, the tips of my ears burning as though Chief Gilroy could read my thoughts. I'd never be unfaithful to James, but sometimes the desire to be seen feels so strong that I imagine stripping bare on a crowded beach, diving free beneath the ocean waves.

What is she doing? Alex has somehow materialized in the middle of the party. She wears a long black dress, the hem brushing the ground, which makes it appear as if she's gliding on air as she strides through the yard. Her long hair has been swept to the side and fixed into graceful waves, giving her the look of a classic Hollywood actress. Seeing her this way, out of her usual denim shorts and oversized T-shirts, is jarring. She bears a shocking, if not eerie, resemblance to her sister tonight. She and James lock eyes and they move toward each other. Their movements appear inevitable, two magnets set on a collision course. He takes her hand in his and pulls her close. I can't hear what they're saying, but I can imagine it. I know my husband, I know the words he will whisper in her ear. This is James at his best, at his most charming: *Would you give me the honor of a dance?*

The memory begins to play, unspooling in my mind, as if projecting a film on top of reality, the two scenes playing out simultaneously.

"I just don't know that I can do it tonight, James." I pressed the back of my hand to my forehead, my temperature climbing, my fingers trembling.

"I'm sorry you're not well, darling. I would stay home with you, but I'm meeting the McClintocks at the theater." James straightened his shirt collar, his strong shoulders flexing beneath the thin white cotton of his shirt.

"Of course. I understand." I tucked myself back under the duvet, willing the disappointment out of my voice. I knew the ballet was a business outing for James, that he'd bought the tickets with the sole purpose of entertaining his newest clients. Though I couldn't help fantasizing about an alternate reality, one in which James picked up his phone: *I'm terribly sorry, but my wife has fallen ill. We'll have to reschedule.*

I'm sure you understand. But I was the one who had to understand. I'm always the one who has to understand.

"You know . . ." James pondered, as if the thought had just then occurred to him, "if you're not feeling up to it, perhaps I'll offer Madison the extra ticket. As a reward for her help at the office these past weeks. She's really taken a lot of initiative. And I'm certain she's never sat in the box seats at the ballet before."

I was swarmed with visions of the ballet through Madison's eyes, the pointed toes dusted with chalk, the lengths of muscle and sinew nimbly propelling the dancers across the stage, the layers of tulle and glittering costumes, and James watching her—drinking in the childlike wonder in her pretty blue eyes.

"What about your daughter?" I tried instead.

James's hand hovered over the knot in his tie. He wasn't accustomed to his decisions being challenged. But he changed tracks quickly. "Lily hates the ballet. You know that. What was it she'd said? Oh right: 'What's the point of a play where no one talks?'"

I rolled my eyes. "She was ten, darling. I'm sure her cultural palate has become a bit more refined since then."

"Still." He tightened the perfect Windsor knot at his throat. "I think it would be a real treat for Madison. Lily can go to the ballet anytime."

I hadn't the energy to protest any further. Not that it would have mattered. Once James has an idea in his head, it's nearly impossible to prize it away from him. In the end, he and Madison would still leave for the theater arm in arm, and all I'd have accomplished would be convincing my husband that I'm a jealous old shrew. *How had it come to this?*

I watched them as they left later that evening, fever and

white-hot rage blazing through my body. It felt as though I was burning alive, a witch tied to the stake. Madison had donned a floor-length black gown, similar to the one her sister wears now, tasteful, elegant, the porcelain-white skin of her back exposed. I wondered whether James had bought it for her.

He used to buy me dresses, lingerie, beautiful, delicate things when I was a younger woman. And when I'd wear them, I could feel his eyes on me all night, biding his time, waiting to ravish me like a wolf who's come upon its next meal. Now I'm surrounded by beautiful things. My closets brimming with designer clothes bought with James's money, but none of it selected by him, none of it chosen because he needed to see me in it. I pictured James picking out a dress that would kiss every curve of Madison's young, nubile body. Running his fingers over the fabrics, fantasizing about peeling it off her, the zipper clenched between his teeth. Time can be inexorably cruel.

I watched as my husband placed his hand at Madison's back, his skin touching hers so casually, as if he owned it, as he guided her to the idling town car waiting to whisk them off into the night. But just before she ducked into the car, she'd turned to face James, his arm still resting protectively at her waist, and she smiled. My husband gazed down at her as if she was everything worth knowing. I felt my heart break, a fault line opening in my center. It was over. I had lost.

And yet, after all I've lost, after all I've done to protect my family, it seems I've still more to lose. I watch James as he twirls Alex around the dance floor now, a vision of Madison, and I realize, with piercing clarity, that I'd never stood a chance.

35.

ALEX

"We need to talk."

James smiles cordially. "We do." He sweeps me into his arms on the dance floor, holding me close as he whispers in my ear, "But this isn't the time or place."

My body follows his lead, my feet tracing his steps as if programmed to follow him anywhere. I can almost imagine what we look like from the outside. James dapper in his black suit, me in the new dress I'd bought specifically for this evening with Maddie's money. I have the strangest feeling that I'm looking down on us from above, that I am both here and nowhere. In this moment and in the next. And before I know what's happened, the song ends.

"James!" a voice calls from the crowd, a raised arm summoning his attention.

"Please excuse me," James tells me before he slips away.

"Wait!" But he's rejoined the party and is quickly surrounded by men in custom suits jockeying for his time and attention. Anger swells within me. Surely he owes me an explanation for what happened last night.

I make my way to the bar. I'm going to have to bide my time until I can get James alone again.

"What can I get for you, ma'am?" the bartender asks.

"White wine, please."

"Would you care for a wine list?"

Of course there's a wine list. "No, that's alright. Anything is fine."

"Very well." He turns and pulls a bottle from a silver ice bucket, yanking out the cork.

"Not really your scene either, huh?"

The sound of a deep, gravelly voice over my shoulder startles me. I whirl around and come face-to-face with Chief Gilroy.

"My apologies. Didn't mean to scare you," he says, pushing his hands into his pockets. "You're a tough woman to get ahold of."

I wonder whether I can lie. Whether he'd believe that I'd lost my phone, that I never received his voicemail or the text he'd sent earlier today:

It's Chief Gilroy again, we still need to talk. Call me.

I'm certain he'd see right through that. And the look in his eye tells me that he already knows I've been avoiding him.

The bartender hands me a glass, condensation frosting the outside, and I take a small sip. "I've been busy," I murmur over the rim.

"Yes, I'd imagine."

"Did you come here to look for me?"

"No, no, nothing like that." He holds up his palms in a show of innocence. "I'm just here as an invited guest tonight. Not in any sort of official capacity. But it sort of comes with the job—you're never really off duty. And now that I've been fortunate enough to run into you, perhaps we could have that little chat?"

"It's . . ." My eyes track James through the crowd. "It's not the best time."

"I see. It's just that, some new information has come to light."

That gets my attention. My focus snaps back to Gilroy. "About Maddie? Do you know where she is?"

"No, that one's still a mystery. But a witness has come forward who claims to have seen Rebecca Jones and your sister arguing the night before Rebecca was killed. Any idea what that might have been about?"

I suck in a breath between clenched teeth before forcing my jaw to relax. "I've already told you, I haven't had any contact with my sister since she came to the Hamptons. I'd have no way of knowing about any arguments she may or may not have had."

"Fair enough," he replies with a slight nod.

"Who was this witness? What did they see?"

"A co-worker from the Lobster Shack. The young lady doesn't know what caused the argument, but she witnessed some sort of heated exchange out in the parking lot. She said it looked pretty serious. I have to be honest with you, Alex, things are not looking good for your sister right now. If there's anything else, anything you haven't told me, now would be the time."

For a brief moment I wonder whether he somehow knows about the money, about the texts I've been receiving from Maddie's phone, but it isn't possible. "There's nothing."

"Very well then. We'll keep looking for Madison. Hopefully she'll be able to give us a few more answers."

From the corner of my eye I see James going into the house. This could be my chance to get him alone. "I . . . I have to go." I dash away from Gilroy, and although I can still feel the heat of his stare boring into my back, I don't turn around.

I make a beeline for the back door of the house, so desperate to catch up with James that I nearly collide with Theo.

"Watch it," he growls without so much as looking up to see who he's almost mowed down. The words come out like icy daggers. It's so incongruous with the usual relaxed charm I've come to associate with him that it makes me wonder whether I've finally gotten a glimpse of the real Theo, the man behind the mask he always wears. I watch as he ducks around the side of the house, away from the party, into the night. But I don't have time to give him another thought. I have to find James.

I slip into the house, where a few guests are congregating in the great room, men loosening their ties, drinking whisky from crystal tumblers. But I don't see James among them. I check the kitchen, which has been taken over by professional chefs and waitstaff, coming and going in a synchronized dance like bees from a hive. Still no sign of James.

I finally find him in the main foyer, pacing the polished floors at the base of the staircase. His shined oxford shoes reflect a constellation of lights from the crystal chandelier as he moves.

"James."

He looks up at me and sighs. "Alex, I told you. We can't do this here."

My fingers curl into my palms, my nails digging into the soft skin. "You know what, fine. You don't want to talk about last night? Fine. But at least tell me about my sister." My voice is growing louder, a dizzying anger taking the reins. "Did you take her to that place? What happened to Maddie, James? Where is she?" My words echo through the open foyer. I imagine them filling the space, drowning us both.

James's eyes widen in alarm. "You need to stop," he hisses. "You don't know what you're talking about, okay? It's best if you just leave matters alone."

Leave matters alone? The rage that rushes through my body curls itself around my neck, digging its claws around my throat, cutting off my ability to speak. I stand there, my body shaking with anger, but I'm unable to find the words to respond.

But, as it turns out, I don't have to.

"Leave what matters alone?"

James and I both look toward the staircase, our heads snapping upward in unison, to find Katherine staring down at us, her gaze glacially cold. She descends slowly, moving like a specter as she floats down the stairs, one hand elegantly gliding along the banister.

"What, exactly, is going on here?"

36.

THEO

I wonder if this is what a heart attack feels like. The thudding in my chest is almost an ache, and my lungs pinch with every breath. I pull my car to the side of the road and climb out onto the gravel-strewn shoulder. My hazard lights blink yellow in the dark, intermittently providing bursts of light along the otherwise desolate road. I bend over, bracing my hands against my knees, and suck in the stale, warm air that tastes faintly of exhaust and salty brine.

I had to get out of there. I thought I could hold it all together, I thought I *was* holding it all together, but evidently I'm not, because here I am, barely able to breathe. I'm hit with a wave of revulsion for this show of weakness despite the fact that no one is here to witness it. Not that it matters. I can picture my father's face as clearly as if he were standing behind me, leaning against the car, arms folded across his chest disapprovingly. *Pull yourself together, son. Never let anyone see you break.*

It's why I had to leave the party tonight. It was all just too much, the smiling, the socializing, the pretending that my life isn't on a fucking crash course bound for imminent destruction. I'm falling apart, but at least no one is here to see it happen.

If I could just go back in time, I know the precise moment I'd go to. The instant the trajectory of my life diverted course. I hadn't known then, of course, that this one, seemingly insignificant decision would change everything. But it did.

I could hear the shouting before I saw them. Voices carry below the bluff, echoing up the rocky crag. I wondered if they knew that. But somehow I doubted it. The conversation seemed private, but there they were, projecting their lines like actors onstage.

It was Madison I heard first. "You're not the man I thought you were!"

"Calm down." Father's placating response. *As if those words have ever served to assuage a woman's ire.*

"I just don't know if I can do this anymore." She sounded broken. Her voice trembling as it reached the peak of the bluff.

I drew closer, edging myself onto the wooden landing of the staircase, straining to hear what would come next. *Had she really just ended whatever was going on between her and my father?* And I knew there was something. We all did. It was if they hadn't even bothered to try to temper the heat that sizzled between them anytime they were in the same vicinity. They were bold, brazen, but perhaps they'd flown too close to the sun. I waited, my breath held in my throat, for Father's reaction. He wasn't a man accustomed to hearing the word "no."

"Don't do this, Maddie." His words coaxing and gentle.

"Don't you dare touch me," she snapped. I could hear the

heaviness of her steps at the bottom of the staircase, and I jumped off the landing, hurrying back toward the house.

I propped myself into a relaxed pose, casually leaning against the house, my phone in my hand, *scrolling, scrolling, scrolling.* I feigned a startle when Madison stomped across the lawn, my head snapping up to watch her. The movement caught her eyes.

"Oh!" Her hand rose to her chest. "I didn't realize anyone else was out here."

"Just got home," I replied breezily.

We stood there a moment, watching each other in the dark.

"I should go," she said, turning toward the pool house.

"Wait!" I don't know why I called after her in that moment. What had taken hold of me. But I knew I didn't want her to leave. This girl. She'd wormed her way into our lives, into our family. She'd used my sister, wreaked havoc on my parents' marriage, humiliated my mother, manipulated my father, and now she was just going to walk away from the destruction she'd caused? Casually step over the debris, the fallen bodies, and disappear into the night? It seemed unjust that it should be so easy. "I was thinking of going out with some friends tonight. Any chance you'd like to join us?"

She looked back toward the bluff, over the expanse of endless black. "You know what? Yeah. I think I could use a night out." Though I'd anticipated an immediate rejection, there was a hardness to her words, a self-destructive determination that I recognized in myself: the drive to drink until your problems dissolved. And I was more than happy to facilitate that.

"This is going to be a night to remember." A winding

smirk cracked across my face, and I hoped that the darkness was enough to conceal the delight that glittered in my eyes.

Lucky Jack's was packed that night, a line trailing around the block. Madison looked nervous. "I didn't realize this was where we were going." She swallowed hard.

"Is that a problem?"

"Er, no . . . I guess not." We both knew it was far too late for her to reasonably object. Hutch and Mick were already waving us toward the front entrance, and I was leading her around the velvet ropes.

I knew why she was hesitant to step into the club, why her pace seemed to slow at my side. Becca. That friend of hers that she was always hanging around with. She worked at Lucky Jack's. "Don't worry. We have a VIP room. It's not like we'll be down on the main floor where all the girls are."

"All . . . All right."

I led her inside, into the dim lighting, the sultry music, the smoky haze that hung over everything, giving it all a dreamlike quality. I'm certain that's intentional. You could almost hear the whispers of the walls: *Reality doesn't exist here, you don't exist here. This is nothing more than a fantasy. Come, give yourself over to this place.*

I grabbed Madison's hand, and she wrapped her fingers around my palm as I pulled her through the crowd to the room Hutch had reserved. Behind the heavy blue curtains, Hutch fell backward onto the leather couch, spreading his legs lazily. The top buttons of his shirt hung open, a smattering of dark chest hair against crisp, white cotton.

"I already called in for a bottle of Dom. Should be here any minute."

Mick chewed the inside of his cheek.

"Don't worry man," Hutch said with an exaggerated roll of his eyes, "I'm paying."

It was dark in the club, but I've known Mick long enough to know that his cheeks were crimson red. He used to be so self-conscious about it. The way his face would flame against his will, making it impossible for him to hide his emotions the way teenage boys are taught to do.

The champagne flowed freely, and Madison went from sitting primly on the edge of her seat to leaning back into the cushions, her long legs folded beneath her like a cat.

"So," Hutch started as he topped off her glass, white foam rising to meet the brim, "I must know more about the mysterious Maddie."

"There's not all that much to know. Certainly nothing mysterious."

"Oh, I find that hard to believe." Hutch slid closer to her on the sofa. He leaned into her neck close enough that his lips could have touched her throat.

Madison shoved him playfully. "And why is that?"

"Well, for one thing, you showed up out of thin air." He snapped his fingers dramatically. "And for another, you're far too gorgeous to really be single. Are you certain you're not hiding a secret boyfriend or something?"

"Who says I'm not?" She smiled coyly, twirled a lock of hair around her finger. *Was she really alluding to her affair with my father right in front of me? In front of my friends?*

"Somehow, I'm even more turned on," Hutch growled as he trailed the back of his hand along the curve of her neck.

I noticed the way she repositioned herself on the sofa, retreating from his advance, but only slightly, gently. Nothing like the instant recoiling, the immediate disgust, she displayed when I merely asked her to dinner. My resentment began to grow. I imagined it taking root in my gut, spreading its poisonous branches into my limbs. Filling me up. If I'd had any reservations about what I had planned, they were long gone.

A rustling of the curtains interrupted Hutch's campaign. "Speaking of turned on . . ." He adjusted himself on his seat, his champagne glass dangling from his fingers over the edge of the sofa. "Let's get this party started."

Something stirred in my stomach. A cocktail of anticipation and trepidation. Mick is always telling me that I take things too far. That I push the limits. He isn't wrong, of course. Sometimes I've felt like it's the only thing I have to offer. If I'm not the life of the party, what use would my friends have for me? Mick would probably stick around . . . but Hutch? I'm less certain. I see the way his eyes light up when I do something reckless, standing on the railing of our balcony at school, straddling death like a tightrope walker, or the time when I'd been caught crashing a wedding and left running down the cobbled roads, my shirttails fluttering behind me. Mick shook his head slightly, a sign that it wasn't too late to change my mind. But it was. I looked over at Madison, innocently sipping the champagne she couldn't afford, and I knew I wasn't going to turn back.

The curtains parted and there was Becca, just as I'd arranged, holding a silver bucket containing a bottle of the club's best vodka. Madison's jaw fell open, but she didn't make a sound. Becca's eyes swept over the room, bypassing Madison as if she was no more significant than a piece of furniture.

"Hello, boys," she said as she placed the bucket on the table.

Hutch yanked out the bottle by the neck, sending a chunk of ice crashing to the table, and took a swig directly from the bottle. He passed it to me, and I did the same. I offered it to Madison next, but she seemed to have folded into herself, staring down into her nearly empty glass of champagne.

The music started to play, and Becca danced for us. Slowly removing one article of clothing after the next, until she was wearing nothing but a silver thong. Hutch and I threw money at her, bills collecting at her feet. But she never stopped moving. Her hips swayed to the music, even when Hutch ran his hands along her body, stuffed bills under the strap of her panties.

"You like that, don't you?" he growled, as he grabbed the bottle of vodka and poured a stream onto her chest, smiling wickedly as he watched a trickle of the clear liquid slide between her breasts. Becca dropped to her knees and tilted the bottle over her mouth, letting Hutch drip the liquor onto her tongue instead. She was good. It was as if she could tell exactly what he wanted from her, exactly how to keep the money flowing. Even Mick tossed her a few dollars, although, always the gentleman, he kept his hands to himself.

Madison looked like she would melt into the sofa if she could. But it wasn't enough for me. I wanted to humiliate her. The way she was humiliating my family. I wanted to show her who was in control.

I pulled Becca into my lap, to hoots and whistles from Hutch. She moved rhythmically against me, and I pulled out a wad of hundred-dollar bills. I peeled one off the stack and slid it beneath her panties, letting my hand linger where it wasn't supposed to, the thin, papery bill the only barrier between us. I thought she'd stop me, but she didn't. We were pushing each other's limits, testing the boundaries. I rubbed the money against her, letting her slide against my hand, until it was nearly inside her.

"Jesus," Hutch said with a laugh as the music ended, "I don't know what the fuck's gotten into Theo tonight, but I think we need to keep this party going." He looked over at Becca. "What do you say, sweetheart? This place is about to close. Should we take this somewhere more private?"

"My father's boat." I don't know why I offered *The Heart's Desire.* Maybe it was one more dig at Madison after I'd seen the way she behaved with my father there, or maybe it was meant to be a rebuke against Father. I knew there was no way he'd have agreed to let us take out the boat.

"Oh, I don't know . . ." Becca replied. It was the first time I looked at her eyes. She looked like she was a thousand miles away. As though someone else inhabited her body when the music started and abandoned her just as quickly, leaving her vacant, empty when it ended.

"We'll make it worth your while," Hutch promised with a fiery grin.

I turned to look at Madison, who appeared as though she was going to be ill. "What about you, Maddie? Will you be joining us?"

"No," she muttered, her voice cracking. "I . . . I want to go home."

"I can take you," Mick offered.

"No way, man," Hutch interjected as he slung his arm over Mick's shoulder. "Don't be so fucking lame. The night is still young. You're coming with us."

I pulled open the heavy curtains separating the VIP room from the rest of the club, and Madison ran out. She rushed by me so quickly that I couldn't be sure, but I thought I saw a trail of tears, silver in the dim lighting, streaking down her face.

I push off my knees and stand up, my head spinning as I lean against the car. I can see headlights rumbling toward me in the distance, and for a fleeting moment I'm tempted to run into the street, to let fate decide if I live or die.

37.

MADDIE

BEFORE

Come on, Becca, just answer me. I dial her number again, but it just rings and rings. It seems to echo out over the expanse of the ocean, an endless bleating.

The marina is empty tonight, almost eerie in its vacancy. The boats moan and whine as they rock in their slips, as if a chorus of ghosts are calling from their hulls. I look up at the sky. A stretch of shimmering stars twinkle overhead, like holes punched through a blanket of black velvet. The moon reflects off the calm waters of the sea, creating a distorted mirror image of the sky above. The sea and the sky. A perfect parallel.

Becca is out there somewhere. With Theo, Hutch, Mick . . . I shouldn't have let her go off with them alone. I don't know if the others saw it, but I did. As soon as she came into the room, when she saw me staring at her, slack-jawed and mortified, she deftly slipped a small pill under her tongue. And after that, she was gone. I watched her float up, up, and away, until all that was left was her body, still dancing and moving under their hands.

I'd almost wished I could join her, wherever she was. I didn't want to watch that, my friend giving herself over to them, like she was an animal in a circus. As soon as I saw her, I wanted to bolt. But then she took that pill and I was afraid to leave her alone, I was afraid things would only be worse for her if I did. I felt trapped, unable to leave but unable to help. Eventually, a sort of numbness settled over me, and I stared into my champagne glass, watching the bubbles rise to the surface and burst with tiny explosions, while my friend was exploited only a few feet away. I knew what Becca would have said if I'd tried to rescue her, if I'd thrown my body over hers, rushed her from the room: "How dare you judge me."

She'd said it before. Last night, in the parking lot behind the Lobster Shack, when I confronted her about James.

"I saw you with him!" I shouted. Becca had avoided me throughout our entire shift, her eyes never meeting mine, our breaks never seeming to align. But I was determined to get her alone. I followed her out to the parking lot at the end of the night. She tried to walk away, but I was insistent, pulling off my apron as I stomped toward her. Becca froze.

"I saw you with James Blackwell," I repeated as I drew closer. "At that . . . that place."

Becca whirled around to face me, fire burning behind her eyes. "You followed me?"

"No. I followed *him*. What was that place, Becca? Why would you go to a party like that? The things I saw . . ."

"How dare you judge me," she spat.

I gasped. Blinking rapidly. I'd never seen this side of her before. "I . . . I . . ."

"You don't know what my life was like, okay? The things I've had to do to survive. And did it ever cross your mind, even once, that I might *like* that kind of thing? That I don't need rescuing? I'm not some . . . some . . . damsel in distress."

"I just thought—"

"No!" she shouted. "You didn't think. You shouldn't have been anywhere near that house."

I could hear footsteps behind us, and we both fell quiet as we watched one of the other waitresses hustle toward her car, head bowed as if she was trying to avoid the shrapnel of our argument. When she was safely out of earshot, I continued, rounding the sharp edges of my voice.

"But you were with James, Becca. How could you?"

She shrugged. "It's nothing personal."

My lips parted in disbelief. "Nothing personal? Becca . . . you knew . . . about me and James. Our relationship."

"If it's any consolation, this thing with James was going on long before you showed up in town. I guess we just fell into old habits. You know what they say . . . they die hard."

"I can't even look at you right now."

"Then don't." She turned on her heels and marched toward her car.

That was the last time I saw her before she was dancing in front of me at the club. I was still angry with her, for the things she'd done, for the words she'd said, but still . . . I shouldn't have let her go off alone in the state she was in. Not after she'd swallowed that pill. I knew she'd taken it because of me. Even if Becca usually had no misgivings about her job, the tension in that room, crackling between us, was too much. I remember what she'd said back when she'd first told me about her job at Lucky Jack's: "It's all on my terms." But tonight it wasn't, and that pill was her escape hatch.

Theo. This is all *his* fault. This was the reason he'd invited me out in the first place. To humiliate me, to dangle my friend in front of me like a puppet on a string. *But why? Why does he hate me so much? Is it possible he knows about . . . James and me?* But how could he? I'd been so careful, and the only person I've told is Becca. I know she'd never break my confidence. Even if she *was* angry with me.

"I'll take it to the grave," she'd said solemnly when I'd first confided in her about our relationship. But then again . . . she never told me about *her* history with James. Maybe I don't know my friend as well as I'd thought.

I wrap my arms around myself, bracing against the cool wind that blows off the ocean. A kiss of salt coats the skin on my face. It seems to permeate everything here. Slowly eroding the town and the people in it. Metal turns to rust under its barrage, wood softens and bends, but the people . . . they grow harder, steelier.

Maybe Alex and I are made of the same stuff. Maybe growing up the way we did made us hardier, like weeds that find a way to push through cement in order to survive, to reach sunlight. I've thought about calling her so many times. I hate the way we left things after Mom's funeral. My sister and I have never gone this long without speaking before. It just doesn't feel right. But this distance between us . . . it's my fault. There's so much I've been keeping from her. I was going to tell her everything, but then I just . . . I didn't. I'd used our falling out as an excuse. I'd let time wedge itself between us, growing, expanding, pushing us apart. The longer I held onto my secrets, the more they became a part of me—and the harder it became to reach out to her. But soon this will all be over, and I'll make things right with Alex. She'll understand. She's my sister, after all. I just need a little more time. To finish what I came here to do. And I won't let anyone, especially Theo, get in my way this time. He thought his little stunt tonight would cause me to crumble, but he was wrong. I'm far more resilient than that.

I just hope Becca is all right. I pick at the skin at the edge of my thumb. I came down to the marina shortly after they left, telling myself they'd be back soon. That everything would be okay. But hours have passed, and they still haven't returned. I'm growing more worried with every passing moment. The guys were pretty drunk. Maybe they lost control of the boat, maybe there was an accident . . . *Should I call someone? The Coast Guard maybe?* But what would I say? Four adults decided to go for a boat ride and haven't come back as quickly as I assumed they would?

But maybe . . . I squint against the horizon, willing my sight to cut through the darkness. *Yes, there's something there.* A boat lazily floating toward the docks. It moves silently through the water, all of its lights dark and cold, like a ghost ship drifting into harbor. As it draws closer I recognize the white sail, the blue hull. *The Heart's Desire.*

Theo, Mick, and Hutch stand on the deck, deathly still. Something's happened. Something terrible. A deep chill settles in my bones when I realize that someone is missing. I don't see Becca anywhere on board. I try to convince myself that she's just inside the cabin, but in my heart I know, from the way the men are staring out over the docks like soldiers returned from war, that she's not.

Hutch's head slowly turns toward me, and we watch each other in the dark as the boat eases into its stall. *Run,* a voice whispers in my head. *Run.*

38.

ALEX

"I asked you both a question," Katherine repeats, frost clinging to every syllable. "What is going on here?"

"Hello, darling," James replies, his movie-star smile making a well-timed appearance.

She levels her glacial gaze at him, unmoved, and the smile falls from his face.

Katherine has reached the bottom of the stairs now, and the three of us stand in the foyer of Blackwell Manor, finally facing the truths that are buried here.

"I was just asking your husband a few questions," I begin. James, wide-eyed with alarm, shakes his head ever so slightly, a doomed man's last wish. But I'm finished with the Blackwells and their secrets. I want to know what happened to my sister, and they are not going to stand in my way any longer. I'll scorch every inch of the ground beneath our feet if it means getting the answers I need. "I was asking him about the sex club he took my sister to."

But for a sharp intake of breath, Katherine's face remains impassive, her emotions impossible to read. "You need to leave our home. Immediately."

"I'm not going anywhere until I know where my sister is. Where is she, James? What have you done to Maddie?"

"I'm afraid I can't help you," he responds, a placating gentleness to his voice that sets my teeth on edge. "I haven't done anything to your sister. If you'll just calm down, I think you'll realize that—"

"I'm done being calm! I saw the photos in your office, James."

"Photos?" Katherine asks, breaking her stony facade for the first time as she looks to her husband, a furrowed crease forming between her sculpted brows. "What photos is she referring to?"

But I ignore her, my eyes boring into James's, the flames of my rage licking across my face. "I know you were stalking her or something."

"I wasn't stalking anyone, I assure you, I hired someone to take those photos. She was living at our home, and I just wanted to be sure—"

"Those pictures look like a whole lot more than a *precaution*, James," I spit.

"It wasn't—"

"Were you in love with her? Was that it? Did Maddie not feel the same way? Is that why she seems to have disappeared into thin air?"

"That's quite enough," Katherine hisses, wrapping her long fingers around my upper arm and squeezing tightly, as though she's ready to physically remove me from their property. But I won't be silenced.

I yank my arm from her grasp. "Or maybe Maddie found out about your dirty little secret."

I turn to face Katherine now, releasing my venom onto her. "Do you know? Where your husband sneaks off to in the middle of the night? The kinds of places he goes, the things he does there?"

39.

KATHERINE

If looks could kill, Alex would be dead on the parlor floor. I glower at her with such white-hot hatred that I'm almost surprised when she doesn't burst into flames.

"Katherine," James starts, his hand reaching out for mine, "I—"

But I hold up my palm to cut him off, the diamond of my engagement ring flashing as it catches the light of the chandelier. I don't want to hear his excuses, least of all in front of Alex.

He must think I'm an idiot. Of course I know about his . . . proclivities. On some level, I think I've always known. Even before I hired the private detective years ago, when the children were still young, to see where it was that he'd started disappearing to. Why he'd come home with that faraway look in his eyes, why he'd stopped wanting me.

Those were difficult years. The children, my perfect babies, were growing older and they'd started exhibiting some . . . troubling behaviors. We'd been warned by the adoption agency that this could happen. That sometimes children who spent their early, formative days in an orphanage might suffer lasting effects. But when we'd first brought

Theo and Lily home, they were cheery, delightful children. Theo, an angel-faced toddler with cheeks as round as apples and bubbly laughter that flowed like a waterfall, and Lily, a quiet, peaceful baby with bowed lips and fawnlike eyes. But as they grew, I started to see the signs.

Theo was desperate for attention. If I took my eyes off him for even a moment to tend to Lily's needs, he'd do something dangerous—climb a tree, curl his toes around the edge of the pool, swaying as if tempting fate to let him fall in. He worshipped James, but punished me. His actions felt like a threat—that he'd injure himself if I wasn't attentive enough as a mother. Lily's problems started later. The lying, the explosive anger.

Between the two children, trying to meet their complicated needs, I was stretched so thin that I thought I might break. I was failing them. I wasn't enough. And as if that wasn't bad enough, that was when James started disappearing. Meetings popping up in the late hours of the night, phone calls going unanswered.

I had my suspicions. Our sex life was all but nonexistent at that point. I was too exhausted, too drained to have anything left to offer my husband at the end of my day as a mother. But James's appetite was a ravenous one, and I thought it possible that he was finding a release elsewhere.

I'd hired a private investigator. Expecting news that my husband was attending sleazy strip clubs or picking up strange women in out-of-town dive bars. What I *wasn't* expecting was the revelation that James was running an exclusive sex club from his vacant properties in the Hamptons. The investigator showed me photos of the things that went on there, the nauseating underbelly of high society. These were men we'd known for years—wealthy men who could pay for the things they wanted behind the closed doors that James provided for them.

It both sickened and pained me to know that this was what James was leaving his family for, that he'd betrayed me so completely. It wasn't just the sex, the disgusting, shameful act that it was. His betrayal cut deeper than that. I was meant to be his wife, his partner, and yet . . . there was this version of James that he'd kept entirely hidden from me. I suddenly felt as though I barely knew him.

"So you *did* know then," Alex retorts, jerking me back to the present. The sneering grin on her face makes me want to reach out and slap her.

"As I said," I reply, regaining my composure. "It's far past time that you leave our home."

James looks as though he's bursting at the seams to unburden himself, to confess what I already know. He's probably in shock that I've known his secret all these years and have said nothing. But the truth is that I don't want to hear all the sordid details. I never have. Though I had hoped he'd be smart enough to have a little more discretion.

My feigned naïvete was my means of taking control. My way of accepting that turning a blind eye to James's . . . extramarital activities at the club . . . was the price of staying married to him, of keeping our family together. It's a cost I've paid for heavily. It wasn't easy, to acknowledge that my husband has a need that I'm unable to fulfill, that there is a dark side to him that he feels he needs to keep from me.

And yet . . . the memory scratches at the back of my mind. Begging me to look at it. To understand. It happened on our honeymoon, as we lay in our hotel room, our bodies still holding the warmth from the sun of the Hawaiian beach. It started the same as it always did, James trailing kisses down my neck, peppering them along my jaw. My body opened to the familiarity of him, wanting more. We began to make love, but something seemed to take over my husband. It was like he was a man possessed. He dug his nails into my skin until I winced, but he didn't seem to notice as he thrust himself against me harder than he ever had before. Though surprised, I went along with it, closing my eyes and moaning as though I was enjoying the pain. But then he clasped his hand around my neck, and my eyes flew open. I stared up at my husband in alarm, his head thrown back in ecstasy. I gasped for air, clawed at his hands, scrambling against him.

"James," I squeaked out. "You're hurting me."

He let go so suddenly, it was as if he'd snapped out of a trance. "Katherine, my God, I'm so sorry. I don't . . . It'll never happen again. I swear to you."

I rubbed my neck, blinking back tears as he pulled me into his arms.

"It'll never happen again," he whispered reassuringly into my hair.

And it didn't. After that night, I remained James's virginal wife. Our sex was polite, cursory. He never brought me into that part of his world again.

"I'm not leaving until I get some answers," Alex insists. "And maybe you'd like some as well, James. Wouldn't you like to know how I found out about your . . . parties?"

I pause, allowing James the space to respond. I'd quite like to know the answer to that myself. But he says nothing. It seems that my smooth-talking husband is at a loss for words, for the first time in all the years I've known him.

"Becca Jones," Alex continues. "The dead girl they pulled out of the water a few days ago. She was a friend of my sister's. And I got a tip that she attended some kind of exclusive parties. So I followed that lead, and there you were." She crosses her arms over her chest. "You know, I find it a little too coincidental that not one, but *two*, women who had the misfortune of crossing paths with you ended up missing. At least one of them dead. So, no, I won't just walk away from this. I know there's something here. I'll ask you again: Were you having an affair with my sister?"

My heart feels like it's clamoring to escape my body. Every muscle beneath my skin stiffens waiting for James's next words. *Will he confess the affair?* He probably thinks I don't know about that either. As if he wasn't carrying on with her right under my nose.

I learned to accept what he did at the club, that dark pressure in him that begged for release, but the affair with Madison . . . that I couldn't abide. With Madison, it wasn't just sex—it was everything. Unlike the women at the club, he didn't leave her behind at the end of the night and return home to me, to his family. He had feelings for her. Real feelings. Madison threatened to take more of my husband than I was willing to share. And then I saw her follow him out to one of his parties.

James and I had been arguing. He was leaving again, lying to me that he'd had to meet with an investor for the hotel. But I knew the truth, and my anger was almost too much to contain. I threatened to leave him if he walked out the door. I hadn't meant it. Not really. But I thought the shock of my words might remind him of all he had to lose. I could feel myself teetering on the brink of going further, of telling him all I knew, of shining a light on the unsightly truth of our marriage. But I refrained. Because I've always understood that once something so ugly was released into our lives, it couldn't be reined in again—we could no longer pretend it didn't exist. But the truth was that I was never going to leave James and the life we've built. I would have done anything to keep my world from caving in. And he knew it. So despite my protests, James shucked me off as casually as an old sweater. He walked away. And Madison followed.

They probably thought they were being so clever in their plans, sneaking off in separate cars for their clandestine affairs, betting it all that I'd be too stupid to notice what was happening right in front of me, but I watched through the front window as Madison climbed into Lily's car and started after him. They disappeared into the night together, leaving me cold and useless behind the glass. And I knew exactly what this meant for my marriage. If James had invited her into that part of his life, it meant she had him fully, completely, in a way that I never have and never will. She was going to ruin everything.

40.

JAMES

Katherine knows. All this time she's known. About the club, about the things I do there. How could she have kept that to herself all these years? She's been carrying around my darkest secret like an ace in her pocket and hadn't given me the slightest indication of her awareness. It's almost chilling, the charade she's been able to keep up for so long. The perfect wife.

And she *is* perfect. In fact, she's obsessed with perfection. I've never met another human being as regimented as my wife. In all the years we've been married I've not once seen her let her guard down. She never has a hair out of place, hell would freeze over before she'd be caught dead in a pair of sweatpants, and she doesn't go a single day without makeup. I can't remember the last time I've seen her true face in the light of day. The warmth I saw in her when we first met, the spark that drew me to her, had extinguished long ago, and all that was left was the cold shell of my perfect wife. It's like being married to a golden statue. Her appearance is unchanging—ever flawless, but impenetrable.

Is it any wonder I sought refuge in the arms of other

women? Women who had the same . . . desires that I harbor. Women like Becca who wanted to do the things that would repulse my wife. She wasn't like the others. Becca was a kindred spirit. A woman who needed to be pushed to the brink of danger and brought back alive. If anything, she was more insatiable than I was. Always begging me to go further, to bring her closer to the edge. Together we explored a world I didn't think I could ever have. She wasn't my wife, and she never sought to be. But she embraced the darkest part of me, the parts I knew Katherine couldn't stand to look at. I could picture Katherine's face if I were to confess my darkest fantasies to her, watch her thin, pink lips curl as though she'd tasted sour milk.

And so I kept the two halves of myself separate. *Or so I thought.* For Katherine, I was the light. I gave her the life I always promised her. And for Becca, I was the darkness. I fulfilled her most forbidden desires. And then Maddie came along. And everything changed.

They're staring at me now. Alex, her arms folded over her chest, her pretty face twisted into a scowl, and Katherine, as unreadable as ever, watching me with her cold, sharp eyes.

"Were you having an affair with Maddie?" Alex repeats.

All this time, has Katherine suspected an affair? My mind reels, and while words are usually my strong suit, this time they seemed to have left me. Ribbons of thought unfurl in my brain, but they all become tangled. I'm unable to find an alternative narrative, an explanation that will appease them both.

"I . . . uh . . . I . . ."

"It's not a difficult question, James!" Alex grows irate. She's shouting now, her hands clenched into fists, her nails digging into the skin of her palms. "You were, weren't you?

You were sleeping with my sister and now she's gone. What happened to her? What did you do to Maddie?"

"No—"

"Did you hurt her?"

"No!" The word explodes out of me. "I never would have hurt Maddie! Never!"

"And why is that?"

"I cared about her, I . . ."

"You were in love with her, weren't you?"

"It wasn't like that!"

"Then how was it?"

"I did love her, but . . ." Katherine and Alex stare at me, the blinding spotlight of their attention shining on me, and it's like a dam breaks inside of me, the truth comes pouring through my lips before I can stop it. "She's my daughter!"

Katherine gasps, and Alex's lips part in shock. My words seem to echo around us like struck glass.

My chin drops to my chest. "Maddie is . . . was . . . my daughter."

Silence blankets the parlor, thick, suffocating, final.

41.

ALEX

"But that's . . ." I croak, "that's not possible." *Maddie? James's daughter?* We had a father, and he definitely wasn't James Blackwell.

I suddenly feel as though I'm in free fall. Alice down the rabbit hole. I've awakened to a bizarre and backward world, a looking-glass version of everything I've ever known.

All my life I've looked up to my sister from beneath her shadow. I wanted so desperately to see all the ways we were similar that I now realize I overlooked all the glaringly obvious ways we were not: the special bond I had with our father, the way our mother doted on Maddie, as though she were a symbol of a better life she might have lived, the deep blue of my sister's eyes—the same blue reflected back at me as I study James's now. Does Maddie have his smile? His sense of humor? We look so much like our mother that I'd never given it much thought . . . where Maddie got the faint dimple in her left cheek, her scalpel-sharp intelligence, her natural athleticism. *Maddie is a Blackwell.*

Now that I see it, I'll never be able to see her as anything else, Maddie was mine: my sister, my blood, the last of my family, the one person I thought I knew better than anyone else in the world. And now she's theirs, one of them, and I'm alone. I no longer belong to anyone. I can feel myself becoming unmoored. *How long has Maddie known? Why didn't she tell me? Why didn't Mom?*

A fresh wave of anger surges through me. So sudden, so strong, that it feels as if it's lancing my heart. Mom lied to me, to us, our entire lives. I can hear the echo of her words, the ones I've carried with me all these years like a mantra, sculpting, defining, shaping me: "Never forget how lucky you are to have a sister. Because that means that you'll never be alone in this world. You'll always have each other." But she was wrong. Because I've never felt more alone than I do in this moment.

"Ah-hem?" A tall, lanky man with a clipboard hovers under the arched entry to the foyer. He chews his lip nervously, peering at James through wide eyes shielded by wire-rimmed glasses. "Mr. Blackwell? Some of the investors have been asking for you. What do you want me to tell them?" He shifts his weight, passing it from one foot to the other.

"Thank you, Brendan," James replies evenly, as though he hadn't just shattered my entire world. "I'll handle it."

Brendan turns on his heel and sprints back toward the yard.

"Look—" James begins, his palms held up in a soothing gesture.

"Oh no you don't," I interrupt. "You can't just walk away from this." The words curl angrily between my teeth like dragon smoke.

"I'll explain everything. I promise. Meet me upstairs in my office in five minutes."

I open my mouth to object, but the words dissolve on my tongue. As hurt, as angry as I am, I still need answers, and James Blackwell might be the only person who can give them to me.

42.

————

JAMES

Alex appraises me cautiously, her lips pressing into a hard line.

"Five minutes," she barks as she turns and starts up the stairs, her heels tapping angrily on the treads as she goes.

Katherine tosses one final, disgusted glance in my direction before she follows behind Alex, the diamond earrings my assistant picked out for her like icicles hanging from her lobes. Surely she's already doing the math . . .

I make my way back to the yard, and the ease with which I'm able to slip back into character is almost frightening, even to me. I wonder when I became this person, when the persona I used to wear like a costume welded itself so firmly to my identity that I no longer know where it ends and I begin. Maybe there's no difference anymore. Maybe I have become my creation. Nothing more than an actor trapped upon a stage he's built.

I weave through the crowd, clapping backs and shaking hands as I pass, and although I look the part, the smile on my face never faltering, my mind is in a different time. Twenty-five years in the past, to be exact.

The first time I saw her, Vivienne, it felt like I'd just landed in Oz; my monochrome existence was suddenly thrown into Technicolor splendor. It was early dawn and I wasn't accustomed to seeing anyone out on the beach so early. The mornings usually belonged to me, long stretches of empty beach, the sand firm beneath the soles of my feet as I ran along the shoreline. But then there she was. And she was dancing— twirling, leaping, pirouetting in the sand, the ocean lapping gently at her bare feet as she landed with small splashes that accentuated her movements. I stopped in my tracks. Watched her from a distance. I was transfixed by the lines of her body, by the grace with which she moved, the raw power that seemed to flow through her and out her pointed toes. She wore a black leotard and leg warmers, her blond hair pulled back into a smooth bun that glowed the most mesmerizing tone of burnished gold under the early morning sun. It felt as though I'd stumbled upon a rare and exquisite bird, and I held my breath as I watched her, fearful that the disturbance of even a tiny grain of sand might send her off in flight, might shatter this most pleasant daydream.

She finished a series of movements, a string of leaps and spins that sent her soaring through the air, and then she propped her hands on her knees, her chest rising and falling with the exertion.

"I'm Vivienne, by the way," she called.

I felt a rising heat claw its way up my neck. *She'd known I was there all along.*

"Mr. Blackwell?" Brendan's voice drags me back to the present. He hands me a microphone.

"Thank you." I clear my throat as I power on the mic. "Thank you all for coming." The crowd offers applause, polite clapping, a few raised glasses. "As you all know, I've invited you here tonight to share in the success of what will

soon be Blue, the Hamptons' newest five-star experience."
This generates more applause, calls of "hear, hear" from
several investors who have already begun counting their
profits from this venture. "Blue will bring together the best
the Hamptons has to offer in hospitality, fine dining, and en-
tertainment." I've rehearsed this speech countless times, but
now the words ring false to my ears. I imagine Katherine and
Alex listening from upstairs, simmering at how performative
it all is, seeing through the smoke to the cold, hard, disap-
pointing reality of the mirrors underneath. "And I've been
looking forward to this evening, to being here with all of
you, but unfortunately, there's been something of a family
emergency." I hear the murmurs from my guests, see the
confusion that passes over their faces. "As you may have noticed, my better half, my wife, Katherine, who was so kind as
to organize this event for us, has been unable to attend. I've
just gotten word that she's quite ill, and I'm afraid that I will
have to take my leave to attend to her." The mutters, the
speculation grows louder. "Please feel free to stay. Enjoy the
food . . . and the open bar." I offer a wink as a shot at levity,
and I'm met with a few strains of light laughter. "But as
those of you who have worked with me before know, at
Blackwell Properties, family always comes first. And I hope
you will all decide to become a part of the Blackwell family."
I give a nod as I hand the mic off to Brendan, and head back
into the house to meet my fate.

———

My footfalls on the stairs feel heavy. A doomed man walking
the plank. And I can't help but think about how I got here,
the series of events that led me to this very moment.

It had been a whirlwind, the affair between Vivienne and

me, a kaleidoscopic explosion of passion and excitement into what had become a monotonous and predictable existence for me. I'd been dating Katherine for nearly two years, and she, and our parents, were breathing down my neck waiting for me to propose. It was the expected next step: find a socially acceptable girl to date, take her for expensive dinners, bring her flowers every Friday, put a diamond ring on her finger, then buy a house with a white picket fence and fill it with children whose lives would follow the exact same blueprint. At first I hadn't minded the cliché of it all, dating the girl next door. Katherine was the most beautiful girl in town, from a good family—she was everything I was supposed to want—I loved her. But after a while it all just felt so . . . predictable. It wasn't Katherine I had been resisting when I turned my head as I walked past a jewelry store, its shop window glittering like ice, as much as it was a rebellion against the expected. I always thought I'd do more, be more, I'd break the mold I'd been born into. And yet there I was, following the path that had been paved for me.

Until I met Vivienne. She was so . . . so . . . different from any of the other girls in my world. She was bursting with life—so full of fiery passion, of unbridled joy. She was unapologetically real, more herself than anyone else I knew. It wasn't long before I started to see my social circle through her eyes: the conformity, the plastic façade of privilege. I knew Vivienne would never fit into my life, not like Katherine did. For one thing, my parents would have hated her. She'd grown up in the Midwest and had never crossed state lines, except when she'd gotten this role with a traveling ballet company. I could just picture the pinched look on Mother's face if I had told her I'd fallen for this gypsy-like ballerina I'd found on the beach. But that was part of the appeal, the deliciously forbidden sweetness of the stolen moments I spent with her, doing things that would have made Katherine clutch at her pearls: making love between the dunes, Vivienne's bare skin glowing white under the moonlight; sharing popcorn in the back row of a drive-in movie far outside of town, licking butter from our fingers; stripping down to our underwear and jumping from the pier, hand in hand, into the icy sea.

I knew I was playing with fire, but I felt invincible with her, like I couldn't possibly get burned. It was the perfect arrangement. Vivienne wasn't needy—she never asked more of me than I could offer. She understood when I couldn't be available to her and never pushed the boundaries. She didn't ask to meet my parents, socialize with my friends. In fact, she seemed content to keep our lives outside of each other completely separate. Vivienne made her own friends easily, with the kinds of people who were far outside of my social circle, and even though it was a small town, when she wasn't performing, she spent her free time in places where there was little chance of us crossing paths—bonfires with the locals, late nights at greasy-spoon diners. We had a mutual understanding of the limits of our arrangement, and Vivienne respected those boundaries. But when I couldn't be with her, I craved her. Thoughts of her consumed me.

Being with Vivienne was like a shot of adrenaline that went straight into my veins, and woke me up from the trancelike state I'd been living in. Before her, I hadn't even realized I was sleepwalking through life: working myself to the bone to get my company off the ground, dating the girl I was supposed to date. At no point was I really *living*, except for when I was with her. And it became an addiction, Vivienne my drug of choice. I couldn't get enough of her, of the heady rush of feeling *alive.* In a way, I think I've been chasing that high ever since, at the club, with girls like Becca, doing whatever it takes to *feel* something again.

But how will I ever explain this to my wife, or to Alex—Vivienne's daughter? I take a deep breath and push open the door to my office. They both glare at me, their eyes hard and angry. For two women who are so different from each other, it seems that they've found common ground in their mutual disappointment in me.

I sit in my office chair, my fingertips pressing into the soft leather arms. "Katherine, I'm so sorr—"

"Just get it over with, James." She waves my words away as if they were gnats. "I'm not interested in hearing any more of your empty apologies."

I swallow hard around the lump forming in my throat. "It was a summer fling. Before we were married. We weren't even engaged yet . . ." I risk a look at Katherine, but the coldness in her eyes is enough to kill, and so I look away, my gaze falling onto my desk blotter. "It meant nothing." It's another lie, but this one is born of kindness. I've already caused my wife enough pain.

"It meant enough for you to conceive a child," she hisses. I can feel the heartbreak behind her simmering anger, that I'd had a biological child, the one thing she'd wanted most in life, with someone else.

"And then you just left her?" Alex interjects. "You had your fling, and you left my pregnant mother to fend for herself at nineteen?"

"No! It wasn't like that!" I pick up a pen from my desk, rolling it between my fingers, as I let my mind go back there. The day Vivienne told me she was pregnant was the same day I was supposed to propose to Katherine. I don't know how it happened; it all felt like a current that I'd been swept away in.

My mother had pulled me aside the week before and handed me a small velvet box.

"It was your great-grandmother's," she'd told me, wrapping her small hand over mine. "She would have loved Katherine. I know she would want you to have this."

I could tell that Katherine knew the proposal was imminent. Maybe my parents had told hers about the ring. I don't know. But something had changed. She was bubbling with anticipation. She smiled constantly, held my hand beneath the table as we had dinner at the club with our parents, brought lunch packed into neat little Tupperware containers to my office. And then my father made us reservations at the nicest restaurant in town.

"Not that it's any of my business, but it would be the perfect time to pop the big question," he'd suggested with a wink. The only problem was that I'd already made plans with Vivienne.

"I'm sorry," I whispered into the phone receiver, the cord stretched into the pantry at my parents' house, the only place I could find a moment of privacy. "I just can't make it tonight."

"But, James, I really need to talk to you."

It wasn't like Vivienne to be so needy, and I found it frustrating. She knew what we were . . . and what we weren't. It was one of the things I loved about her. She never demanded more of me than I could offer. "I can't tonight, okay?" My annoyance echoed down the line.

"I'm pregnant." She said it so matter-of-factly that I thought it was a ploy. Something she'd said purely for the shock value.

"That's not funny."

"Well good, because I'm not joking."

I stared at the sacks of flour, of canned tomato sauce lining my mother's shelves, the labels all facing outward in ordered rows. "I . . . I don't know what to say . . . are you sure?"

"Positive. I took a test."

"Look, we'll talk tomorrow, okay? I promise. I just . . . I need some time to process this."

The line went dead in my hand.

That night over dinner, Katherine barely touched her food. She seemed nervous, sitting across from me in her best dress, her finest pearls, waiting for me to ask her to marry me. *What had I been thinking getting involved with Vivienne? Was I really willing to throw my life away for this woman I barely knew?* If she really was pregnant, there was nothing I could do about that; I'd find a way to make it work. But I knew I'd lose Katherine forever. I panicked—my life spinning out of control. For the first time, I craved the stability of the blueprint that had been neatly laid out at my feet. And so I did the only thing that was in my control. I pulled my great-grandmother's ring from my pocket and slipped it onto Katherine's finger.

News travels fast in the Hamptons. And word of my engagement must have reached Vivienne before I could. Because the next day I came home from work to find a note: *I lied about the pregnancy. It's over between us.*

I called the hotel where she'd been staying, but she was gone. She'd vanished from my life as quickly as she'd come into it.

"So what was it like?" Alex asks, grounding me back in the present.

"I didn't know. About your sister. Not until she showed

up on my doorstep." I recognized her the moment I saw her. The image of her mother at that age, and wearing the necklace I'd given Vivienne during that one magical summer so many years ago. It was like looking at a ghost. Until I realized who she had to be. "She never told me she was my daughter, but I knew."

"What a fool I've been," Katherine sneers.

"You really didn't know before? About Maddie?" Alex asks, her words edged with skepticism.

I exhale, releasing the breath in a slow stream. "I didn't." It was the dementia that did it, the slow erosion of my mother's mind that eventually uncovered the truth. Or most of it, anyway. It was at the very end, when she was losing track of time, when she'd sometimes slip into the past, that she'd accidentally revealed what she'd known all along.

"Katherine is a good woman," she'd muttered as I tucked her into bed one night.

"I know, Mom. She's always liked you too."

"Not like that other girl." Her wrinkled face twisted with distaste.

"What girl, Mom?" I asked it casually, convinced she was referring to a figment of her imagination, an apparition born of her illness.

"That other one. The dancer. The one that showed up at the house claiming she was pregnant with my grandchild."

My grip tightened on the blanket. I could picture it. Vivienne, indignant, pounding on my parents' door, demanding I hear her this time. She'd understood the confines of our relationship, but looking back, I could see how a baby would have changed all of that. How a pregnancy would have tipped the scales.

"And what did you tell her?" I asked, my voice coated

with honey, scarcely daring to breathe. I was afraid of star-tling her back into the present, the truth retreating into the murky recesses of her mind once again.

"I gave her exactly what she'd been after all along: money. Enough money to make the problem go away."

"You paid her? To leave?"

"And to end the pregnancy, of course. You wouldn't be-lieve how quickly she snatched up the cash, James. Couldn't get her greedy paws on it fast enough. A woman like that, a woman willing to kill her own baby for twenty thousand dollars, she would have always been trouble, James. You know that, don't you?"

"Yes, Mom. I know," I lied. But there was so much I hadn't known. Not until it was too late.

I look at Alex now. Vivienne's daughter. "I swear to you. I didn't know Maddie existed. If I had, I would have been there. I never would have missed out on my daughter's life."

The rattle of the doorknob pulls my attention. The office door slowly creaking open.

43.

LILY

"Your . . . daughter? My . . . my . . ." I stammer, but I can't manage to push out the final word, which sits round and fat on my tongue. *Sister.* It ricochets inside my skull, *sister, sister, sister,* until I'm dizzy with it, until it loses all meaning and begins to slip through the crevices of my brain, nothing more than a hiss.

"Lily," Father starts, his eyes brimming with a type of pity that's hard to look at. "I didn't want you to find out this way . . ."

"You didn't want her to find out at all," Mother snaps.

"Don't, Katherine," Father interjects. "Now is not the time."

I hear their bickering, the barbs that spike their words, but I don't care. All I can think about is Maddie. *My sister.*

"Lily?" Alex asks, her eyes wide with alarm as she pushes up out of her seat. "Are you okay?"

It sounds like she's speaking underwater, her voice straining to meet my ears. It's then that I realize I'm swaying on my feet, my vision blurring.

"I'm . . . sorry," I stammer, but it escapes my lips as nothing more than a squeak.

Alex tilts her head, a V forming between her brows. She doesn't understand. Not yet. But she will. Soon, they all will.

"I'm sorry," I repeat, louder this time. More forcefully. "I'm so, so sorry." The tears come now, fast and full, and I pull my hands through my knotted hair, grabbing it by the fistful. Part of me wants to rip it from the roots, to punish myself for the things I've done, but the larger part of me is a pitiful coward and so I let it go and wrap my arms around my shaking body.

"Don't," Mother barks. "Don't say another word, Lily."

But it's Alex's voice that reaches me instead. Gentle and coaxing, it calls to me, leading me through the darkness. "What are you sorry for, Lily?"

"For . . . for what happened to Maddie."

————————

It had gotten so late. Or early, I guess. The hours of the night had already started their march toward dawn, and still Maddie hadn't come home. I knew this because I'd waited up for her. Only because I was worried about her. I'd seen her go off somewhere with Theo, and I wanted to be sure she'd made it home okay. I'd tried texting her, calling a few times, but she never responded. And I was concerned. As any good friend would be.

I spun the friendship bracelet on my arm as I paced over the carpet in my bedroom, pressing the gold starfish into the milky-white skin on the underside of my wrist until it left an indentation. I looked out the window, checking, for the hundredth time, whether the lights of the pool house had come on yet. They hadn't. The yard remained dark, only my own reflection, pale and ghostlike, staring back at me through rain-dappled glass.

It wasn't fair. I'd been such a good friend to Maddie, and yet she was pulling away from me. This was hardly the first time she'd ignored my calls, and lately I'd been getting the impression that she was avoiding me altogether. Telling me she was too tired after work to watch a movie, that she'd had a headache when I asked her to brunch. I'd even begun to notice that the hostess never sat me in Maddie's section anymore when I'd drop in at the Lobster Shack during her shifts. I was beginning to think it was intentional. And it just wasn't fair.

I turned and studied my reflection in the full-length mirror propped against my bedroom wall. My dark locks had been dyed so that when the sun hit my hair just right, you might catch the bronze undertones. I wore a black silk cami, just like the kind Maddie always wore to bed, far more sophisticated than the cotton pajama sets I used to wear. Even my nails had been painted with one of Maddie's favorite polishes. I'd borrowed it from the pool house while she was at work, but I knew she wouldn't mind. We were friends, and friends were meant to do that kind of thing. No, we weren't just friends, I'd become Maddie's *perfect* friend. The shelf behind me was teeming with titles from Maddie's favorite authors, poets, all of the books she'd talked about studying during her time in college, but it wasn't just for show. I'd started reading them, devouring them, as fast as I could. I wanted to know the things she knew, love the things she loved. I wanted to know her. To understand her. And yet, just like the others before her, Maddie was finished with me. Casting me aside like an unloved toy. *Why does this always happen?* I felt a familiar rage brewing inside of me, but I tamped it down. I reminded myself that Maddie wasn't really like the others. She wasn't Olivia Davis. I hadn't fabricated this friendship in my head. Maddie liked me. I could tell. I pressed the metal starfish even farther into my skin.

Suddenly, a flicker of light appeared outside. I rushed to the window and found that the yard was lit up like a Christmas tree. Maddie was home. She must have tripped one of the motion sensors. A wave of relief rushed through me. She was okay. And she'd come back. But then I saw her.

She was walking across the yard, her steps awkward and stumbling. *Was she drunk?* And trailing behind her was a suitcase. The very same one she'd arrived with at Blackwell Manor only weeks ago. The wheels kept catching in the damp grass and she'd roughly yank it free. Maddie was leaving. Disappearing from my life, and she wasn't even going to say goodbye.

I rushed downstairs and out the back door. The night air sent a chill running through me and I shivered against the rain, but I was undeterred.

"Maddie!" I called, but she was already too far ahead.

I started to run, my bare feet slipping in the wet grass. "Maddie!" I yelled again as the rain came down harder, fat drops splattering on my face.

I thought she heard me that time. She seemed to hesitate before taking another step, moving toward the bluff, farther from me. *Had I really meant so little to her that she would leave without so much as a goodbye?* I felt the old anger rising again, dark and familiar, like a slumbering beast yawning to life.

She'd nearly reached the edge of the bluff by the time I caught up to her.

"Where are you going?" I asked, my breath escaping in puffs between my words.

"I . . . I have to go." Her voice sounded muddled, wrong.

"Where were you? Did something happen?"

"I can't . . . I just have to go." She yanked her case with both hands, blades of uprooted grass stuck in the wheels.

"Maddie, talk to me!" I grabbed her upper arms with both hands. Her wet skin felt cool and clammy beneath my fingers. "Don't do this."

She tore her arms from my grasp, my nails raking against her skin. "Don't!" she cried.

"You can't go," I wailed. "Please don't go." A tear streaked down my cheek, mingling with the rain, cold and wet against the night air.

But she ignored me. She picked up her suitcase once again and started toward the bluff. I felt so small, so power-less. Holding back my anger was as futile as trying to push against the tide. But maybe that was always true. It would come in time, no matter what I did.

I shoved her. Just a little. Just enough to rock her on her feet, to cause her to drop her suitcase. But still, Maddie didn't turn around. She never looked back.

And so I shoved her again. With both hands this time. Years of pent-up rage, resentment, and aggression stood be-hind me like a phantom army, lending me their strength, working through my arms. And Maddie fell. Her hair flutter-ing out behind her like a bird taking flight, before she went over the ledge. Out of sight. At first, I felt relief. The soldiers at my back dissolving into the night. And then I realized what I'd done.

I rushed to the edge of the bluff, my bare feet skidding on the graveled ledge, and fell to my knees, peering into the darkness. Maddie had landed on the stairs, on one of the landings that punctuated the winding staircase. She was just . . . lying there. Her skin porcelain white in the moon-light, her hair gently framing her face. She looked like an angel, as though she was sleeping, sweetly dreaming under the stars. It was the truth I wanted to believe. The lie my brain wanted to tell to protect me from what I'd done—the way it always has before. But this time, I forced myself to look. I forced myself to see. And I did.

I saw the blood staining her fair hair—spreading like a hellish halo. I fell to my knees and I screamed, a desperate keening that echoed over the ocean.

"Lily?"

I blink, disoriented at the sound of Alex's voice.

"Lily, what do you mean? What happened to Maddie?"

Mother rushes to my side and wraps me protectively in her arms. Just the way she did that night when I knocked on her door, shaking and crying. She held me close to her as I sobbed, tears and cold rain soaking her silk blouse. For a moment I was a child again and I wanted to believe that my mother could fix everything, that she could make it all okay. But she couldn't. No one can.

"It was an accident."

Alex's fingers rise to her lips. They're trembling. She's starting to understand. My tears come again now. And I'm not sure they'll ever stop.

44.

—————

KATHERINE

It's over. After everything I did, everything I was prepared to do, to protect my daughter, it's over. A lump forms in my throat. I want to find the words to comfort Lily, to set everything right, but there's nothing left to be done. Alex knows, and there's no turning back now.

I can already feel the wheels of justice churning forward, a stony, immovable force. *What will become of my poor, troubled daughter?* A picture forms in my mind, Lily in an orange jumpsuit, the sleeves dangling past her fingertips. My sweet, precious child alone in a cement cell. Locked away with violent thugs. The thought makes my knees buckle. She doesn't belong in a place like that. She wouldn't survive it. But a voice at the back of my head whispers the truth I don't want to hear. *My baby is a murderer.* And I can't even begin to imagine what that says about me as a mother. The bottom line is that this is my fault. I failed her. Somewhere along the way, I failed as a mother.

The shame of it is almost too much to bear. There was a time when I'd watch the news, when the horrors of humankind would pour through my television screen: rapists, gang members, murderers—the worst of society beamed straight into my living room. But these things happened in faraway places to faraway people. I'd tut sanctimoniously, smug in my self-righteousness, as I reached for the remote, wondering what kind of person could have raised such monsters. *Where were their mothers?* And now I know. They were at home. Doing their best to love their deeply flawed children, praying that it would be enough. *It's never enough.*

Lily came to me that night. I awoke to the sound of banging on my bedroom door and found her standing in the hallway, her teeth chattering, mumbling incoherently. I clutched her to me, holding her in a way she hadn't allowed in years.

"What's happened?" I asked, smoothing her hair, feeling the coolness of the night clinging to the strands. "What is it, Lily?"

"Maddie," she choked out. "I . . . it was an accident." I felt her shoulders heave against my chest.

"What was an accident, darling? Whatever's happened, we'll fix it. But you need to tell me everything." My hand rubbed small circles on her back. It seemed to move of its own volition, instinctively calming her the same way I did when she was a baby.

Another sob racked through her body. "No. You don't understand. You can't fix this. Maddie is . . . she's dead!"

I froze, my hand coming to a halt in the center of her back. Perhaps it was the shock, perhaps I hadn't truly processed my daughter's words, but my first reaction was one of relief. Madison was gone. She was no longer a threat to my family. Lily had done what I could not. But reality quickly washed over me, like a deluge of ice water. Lily had *killed* someone. She'd killed someone to protect our family, and now it was my turn to protect her.

"Where is she?" I asked "Mother will take care of everything."

"But . . ." Alex starts, yanking me out of my horrid memories of that night. "Maddie can't be . . . gone. She can't!" Her eyes grow wild, the look of an animal caught in a snare. She's desperate to cling to her delusion that her sister is still alive. "She's been texting me! Maddie is alive! I can show you!"

I slide Madison's phone out of my pocket. Lily had stolen it from the pool house. Another memento of Madison that she couldn't seem to let go of. Though I thought this one might at least be useful and had convinced Lily to turn it over to me. I'd used it to text Alex, to try to frighten her off the trail of the truth, but the moment she sees it in my hand, I watch her face crumble.

Alex falls to her knees, a wounded moan escaping her lips. "Where is she?" she pleads. "Where is my sister?"

45.

THEO

A silver veil of moonlight coats the asphalt as my tires whip over it. I grip the steering wheel as I round the next curve, my speed gaining traction. I tell myself that I don't know where I'm going, that I'm driving for the sake of driving, outrunning the demons that haunt me, but of course I know. I think I've always known. It feels inevitable. No matter what roads I chose to travel, I was always going to end up here.

My phone buzzes in my pocket, but I ignore the vibration against my leg. *I am untethered, beyond reach.* Rubber screeches in protest as the back end of my car fishtails along the road. I straighten it out, my knuckles white on the steering wheel as I push the gas pedal closer to the ground, the red dial of the speedometer climbing higher, pushing further. I'm not certain what I'm pushing, my speed, my luck . . . or both. I feel as though I've been trying to outrun the truth ever since that night, and now it's nipping at my heels like a rabid wolf ready to consume me.

The water was choppy the night we took *The Heart's Desire.* I almost turned back, almost admitted that I had little experience sailing at night, but I looked at my friends, at

Mick lounging on the back deck, at Hutch popping another
bottle of champagne, pouring a fizzing glass for Becca, and I
stopped myself. This wasn't the time to admit my shortcom-
ings. *How hard could it be?* I had plenty of experience sailing
these waterways during the daytime, and *The Heart's Desire*
was fitted with running lights in case I needed them. Besides,
we wouldn't be going too far into open waters. *We'll be fine.*

The music started just as I edged the boat out of her slip,
string lights illuminating the back deck in a warm glow, more
appropriate for a romantic dinner for two than an after-party
with a stripper. I wondered whether Father had ever brought
Madison here at night, whether they'd sat on the deck clinking wineglasses under the stars. The thought burrowed into
my skin like an angry rash as I steered us out of port, toward
the open waters, listening to the sounds of my friends drunkenly singing behind me. I wasn't going to waste any more
time thinking about Madison, or my father for that matter.
I'd gotten my payback, and I was ready to set it aside, enjoy
the rest of the night.

I dropped the anchor and made my way around the rig
toward the back deck.

"There you are," Hutch proclaimed at my arrival. "Let's
get the man a drink!" His words were thick and heavy as he
slung his arm over Becca's shoulders. I noticed he'd switched
to drinking whisky, the dark amber liquid sloshing over the
side of his glass and dripping down his wrist as he raised it in
a toast.

Mick handed me a glass of my own, and I matched
Hutch's gesture.

"To a night we probably won't remember, but friends
we'll never forget," Hutch said. *"Per unitatem vis!"*

"Hear, hear," Mick added.

I didn't know why, but I felt a sense of unease settle deep in my bones as I swallowed the liquor, heat trailing down my throat.

"What was that last bit?" Becca asked. She seemed unsteady on her feet. I wasn't sure if it was the sea or the drink.

"Through unity strength," Mick explained. "Prep school motto."

"Ah, prep school boys." Becca giggled, wrapping her arms around Hutch's neck. "I should have known."

"Oh, you like that, huh?" Hutch growled before thrusting his tongue into her mouth.

Becca pulled away, smiling playfully as she refilled her drink, but I saw something dark pass across Hutch's face. He'd never taken well to rejection.

"Forget that," he said, grabbing the whisky bottle from Becca's hand. "Let's do shots." He pulled a bottle of vodka from the bar cart and quickly filled two thick-rimmed shot glasses. "Anyone else?"

"No thanks," Mick replied.

"Don't be such a pussy." Hutch laughed and pushed a glass into his hand. "Theo? You in?"

I could hardly say no at that point. Even though I wanted to. Even though I knew I'd have to somehow get us all home. I nodded, swiping a full glass from the cart. Hutch gave me a slight nod, indicating his approval, and I hated myself for needing it.

"What was that thing you preppy boys say again?" Becca slurred.

"*Per unitatem vis,*" I replied, and tipped the glass to my lips.

"Why don't you have another?" Hutch asked Becca. He refilled her glass without waiting for her response, guiding it to her lips. A river of liquid snaked down her chin and Hutch quickly licked it away.

"I think she's gone," Mick whispered as we watched Hutch escort Becca to the couch. "Seemed like she was messed up before we even got on the boat." She and Hutch were making out, tongues drunkenly stumbling to find their marks, Hutch's hands sloppily moving over her body, pawing at her sequin halter top until her breasts were exposed under the moonlight.

Becca started to push him away; she tried to stand but fell to her knees on the deck instead. She looked as if she was going to be sick.

"Don't be such a cocktease," Hutch growled.

"Bro," Mick interjected. "I think she's had enough."

Hutch glared at him, his eyes hard, venomous. "Fuck off, *bro.*" He mimicked Mick's voice with a whine. "This is what she fucking came here for."

Hutch pushed Becca to the deck, straddling her legs, pinning her wrists over her head. Her eyes lolled back in her head, her jaw growing slack. "She wants it. She's a fucking stripper, for God's sake."

"I don't know . . ." I started to protest.

"Christ, not you too! You know she's fucking your father, don't you? At those parties he throws."

I froze. *Hutch knew? About my father?* I knew. Of course I did. There were only so many times he could claim he was working late before I grew suspicious. I worked for his fucking company! How stupid did he think I was? It only took a few weeks before I started to grow curious, until I followed him to one of his late night "meetings." But what I saw there, what he was doing with Becca was just sex. Unlike whatever he was doing with Madison. Sex I could ignore. Sex I could turn a blind eye to. But not if everyone knew about it. Not if he was embarrassing our family.

"Maybe that's the problem," Hutch continued, grabbing Becca's face with one hand, shaking her back to consciousness. "You only like it rough?" He slid his hand down to her throat, squeezing tighter. Becca squirmed under his weight, but she seemed too weak to fight him off.

"Just stop!" Mick yelled. "Enough!"

But Hutch ignored him. "Or maybe you only fuck for money." He pulled his wallet out of his pocket and grabbed a wad of bills. He dropped them onto Becca's bare chest. Her eyes fluttered closed and she stopped moving. I wondered whether she was losing consciousness or whether she'd just given up the fight, accepted the inevitable.

"Don't, Hutch," I cautioned, but my words were lost to him as he unzipped his jeans, sliding his hand under Becca's skirt, bunching it up around her waist, exposing her.

Mick shoved him, but Hutch didn't move, his knees still straddling Becca's limp body.

"What's wrong, Mick, did you want a turn first?" Hutch laughed.

Mick shoved him harder, and Hutch rose to his feet, towering over Mick. "All of a sudden you're a big man, huh? After you let me pay for your drinks all night, hell, pay for everything for years, now you're going to step up to me? Over a fucking stripper? Well, go ahead then, take your best shot." He spread his arms wide, challenging Mick to hit him. We all knew he wouldn't.

"That's what I fucking thought," Hutch replied with a derisive chuckle as he turned back toward Becca. "You don't have it in you."

"Do something!" Mick pleaded, looking to me. But I was

frozen. Rooted to the spot. I wondered whether it was because I was too drunk to think straight, whether I was afraid to challenge Hutch, or whether a small, vicious part of me was letting him humiliate Becca the way she'd humiliated my family. "At least get us out of here," Mick begged, and it snapped me out of my trance.

I raced back to the helm and pulled up the anchor. As I dropped the motor into the water, I remembered the words my father had instilled in me: *Real sailors rely on the tide and the wind, not a machine.* But time was not on my side. And my father was not here.

I could hear the commotion behind me as Becca started to regain consciousness. She cried out for Hutch to stop, to get off of her. Mick and Hutch were arguing again, and I heard a crack that sounded a lot like Hutch's fist colliding with Mick's face, Mick howling in pain.

I left the helm, the boat charging forward, as I ran to the deck. Becca was standing now, heaving over the side of the boat, Hutch was on top of Mick, pummeling his body with blows. I charged at Hutch, spearing him off Mick. That's when I felt the boat lurch forward, collide with the sandbar.

I knew those waters inside and out, I'd been navigating them with Father's guidance since I was old enough to walk, but with all of the commotion, I'd forgotten about the sandbar, about Father's warning that we needed to give it a wide berth when coming into port, that the waters above it were too shallow for *The Heart's Desire* to pass through. I rolled off Hutch in the crash, landing hard on my back, just in time to see Becca fall forward, disappearing over the side of the boat, and to hear a sickening thud as her head collided with the hull.

I think the sound sobered all of us. We raced to the railing, peering into the dark night waters as Becca's body slipped below the tide, a wraith retreating into shadow.

My phone buzzes again in my pocket and I roll down my window and toss it onto the pavement, imagining it shattering into a million splintered pieces. I push the pedal harder, my car careening down the deserted road. *This is never going to end.*

After Becca went overboard, Hutch had gone into crisis mode, like one of his father's many underlings managing his campaign. He was going to fix this.

"Fuck!" Mick cried out, his voice disappearing into the vast nothingness of the night. He pulled at his hair. "What the fuck are we going to do?"

"It's fine," Hutch replied coolly. "Everything is going to be fine."

"Fine?" Mick shouted incredulously. "None of this is fucking fine! That girl is dead, Hutch, *dead*! Do you understand that?"

"Of course I fucking understand that." Hutch grabbed Mick by both shoulders, looking him square in the eyes. "But there's nothing we can do to change that now, is there? So all that's left to do is manage the fallout." Hutch let go of Mick and turned toward me instead. "She probably landed on the sandbar. You know these waters better than the rest of us. What'll happen when the tide comes up tomorrow?"

"Hard to say," I replied, swallowing around a lump in my throat. "Depends how strong the tides are. She could be washed out to sea, but a storm is headed our way, and with the swell she might make her way back to shore."

"Jesus," Mick muttered to himself. "I'm going to be sick."

"Here's what we're going to do," Hutch dictated. "I'll go back to Lucky Jack's first thing in the morning. I'll pay Jack, and whichever of her girls might have seen us come in tonight, enough to forget we were ever there."

"What about Maddie?" I asked. My head was spinning, the sound of Becca's skull slamming into the wooden hull still echoing in my brain. I knew she was gone, but it still didn't feel real. I half expected her to climb back aboard, wring the water from her hair.

"You need to handle her. Find out what it's going to cost to keep her quiet."

For the rest of the ride, we were silent. We'd gotten lucky that *The Heart's Desire* hadn't sustained more damage, that I could still get us back to the marina. I steered on autopilot, only the sound of the waves lapping against the boat to interrupt my thoughts about what we'd done. I imagined each break was Becca's fist pounding the hull, demanding we turn back for her.

As *The Heart's Desire* floated back into her slip, Hutch nudged me in the ribs, cocked his head toward the docks.

"Seems we have a witness," he said.

I followed his line of sight to find Maddie standing on the docks under the glow of a streetlamp, shivering against the cool winds as she watched our return.

"Handle it," Hutch growled in my ear as he slipped a small white tablet into my palm. "If she won't take the money, give her this."

"What is it?"

"Something that will make her forget what she saw."

I finally hit the brakes, slowing my speed as I near my destination. *I am here. I've always been here.*

46.

MADDIE

BEFORE

"Money? You think I want *money*? You think there's enough cash in the world to make me 'forget' that Becca didn't make it off that boat?" I'm seething, my chest rising and falling dramatically. I can feel my heart thrashing in my chest like a bird in a cage. "Just go, Theo, get out!"

"Madison, please." He raises his hands in a pantomime of innocence. "Calm down. I'm sure we can come to some kind of agreement if you just . . ."

"*Out!*" I point to the pool house door, my shaking finger betraying my nerves.

But Theo doesn't leave. He walks into the kitchen, a casual saunter to his gait that makes my lips curl. He opens the refrigerator and helps himself to the pitcher of water. I stare, open-mouthed, as he lifts a glass from the cabinet, his back to me, and pours out the water. "Here, have something to drink." He holds it out to me. "Just try to relax so we can talk through this."

I take the glass from his hand and slam it down on the counter. "I don't want water, I don't want your money, and I don't want to talk. I just . . . I just want to go home." My chin starts to wobble, tears threatening to escape my eyes.

"Take the night, sleep on it. What I'm offering you could change your life, Madison. It's not a decision to be made hastily. I'll be back in the morning so we can sort this out."

But I'll be gone. Now that the decision has been made, I see no other way out. I need to run, to leave Blackwell Manor and never look back. And once I'm somewhere safe, somewhere they can't find me, I'll call the police and tell them everything I know about Becca.

Theo backs away, seemingly taking my stunned silence as acquiescence. "Good night, Madison."

My name on his tongue sours in my ears. As soon as the door pulls closed behind him, I get to work. Pulling out my suitcase, quickly packing my life away. I grab piles of clothes from the dresser, swipe toiletries from the bathroom. I am crazed, manic in my haste. A sweat breaks across my brow; my top, the same one I wore to Lucky Jack's, clings to my skin. I grab the glass of cold water sitting out on the counter and drain it in one gulp. And then I go back to packing, stuffing my belongings into my case haphazardly.

I could call Alex. The thought occurs to me as I drop an armful of clothes into my bag in an unfolded heap. I imagine myself dialing her number, the only one I know by heart, telling her I'm coming home. And then I feel the guilt, as familiar as an old friend. *I left Alex behind.* First, when I went to college, when I left her in that house. With Mom, with her drinking, with the sadness I could no longer face. And then I left her one hundred times over. Every time I chose my life in the city instead of going back to that house, every holiday that passed with nothing more than a phone call bringing me closer to home. I hated myself for doing it, but I just couldn't bring myself to go back there. I couldn't stand to be in that house where it felt like time stood still, like nothing could ever change. I'd worked so hard to scratch and claw my way out of there, and I couldn't let it pull me back in.

I wanted to bring Alex with me. I'd told her so many times that she should leave everything behind and move in with me. She could get a job in the city, she could even go to college if she wanted. She could have a life. But her reply was always the same: *Someone has to take care of Mom.*

The shame was almost too much to bear. I'd left my little sister to clean up the mess I couldn't face. "Mom is an adult, Alex, she can take care of herself. You can move out here with me, we'll make it work."

"Maybe," Alex would reply. "I'll think about it." But we both knew she never would. Alex had spent her entire life trying to win our mother's approval, the approval Mom so freely gave to me even though I'd never asked for it. It wasn't fair, but it was the truth.

It drove a wedge between us, both of us standing our ground: Alex refusing to leave, me refusing to return. Except for her birthday. I made Alex a promise when she was ten years old that she'd never have to spend her birthday alone, and I'd kept it. Until this year. When I betrayed her. When I came here to find my father, to find a family that didn't include her.

I should have told her what Mom explained to me just before she died about James Blackwell, about where I'd come from. I don't know what I expected to find here—I didn't anticipate that I'd run into the loving arms of the family I never had—but I wanted to see him for myself, to meet him, to inspect him up close before I decided whether I wanted to let him into my life. Whether I wanted to tell Alex that he existed at all. Alex and I have already had our fair share of parents letting us down; I wasn't sure either of us could take it again. And so I decided that coming here, that meeting James in person, finding out whether it was safe to let him into our lives, was the only way to protect us both.

But that wasn't the only reason for my silence. A part of me was also afraid of how Alex might react if she found out that I had another family. She'd always be my sister, the most important person in my life, but I wasn't sure she'd see it that way—I worried she'd feel as if I, too, was abandoning her. Especially with how tense things had been after Mom's funeral. Our relationship just felt too fragile to withstand the pressure. So I decided to wait until after I had a chance to meet the Blackwells to tell her the truth. I just hope I didn't wait too long, that it's not too late to repair the damage I've caused.

I lean on the top of my suitcase, forcing the zipper along the edges. Clothes drape over the sides, sticking out like a dog's tongue, and I roughly shove them inside, closing the case. Anything that doesn't fit can be left behind. I don't stop to take inventory, to count my belongings, all I care about is getting as far away from Blackwell Manor as possible.

I finish tugging the zipper closed and look around for my phone. *Did I pack it?* I jump up to a stand, ready to search for it, but my head swims, the world around me undulating, pulsing like the blood in my veins. *Whoa.* I push the heels of my hands to my eyes, trying to steady myself, to stop the pounding growing in my head. I shake it off—I have to keep moving.

I pull my suitcase to the door and I'm surprised to find that my fingers fumble at the handle. *What is happening to me?* It takes me a few tries, but eventually I'm able to pull the door open and I stumble out onto the pathway. My legs feel like rubber, and the stars above my head spin and waltz across the sky. *Something is definitely not right.*

I stand on the paved path, a light rain misting around me, and try to think through my next movement. But my brain feels fuzzy now, and I struggle to formulate a coherent thought, let alone a plan. It takes all my effort just to signal my legs to move. I remember that I have to leave, that it's important that I go, but the threads of my thoughts begin to unravel, and reaching for them feels as though I'm grasping at air. *Something happened. An accident. Was it Alex? Is she hurt? Does she need me?*

I swat the thought away. It wasn't Alex. It was Becca. The bad thing happened to *Becca.* I can feel a pit of ominous dread churning in my stomach, but I can no longer dredge up the details of how it got there. I feel myself growing weaker, my vision narrowing. *Go.* It's a hiss. A primal urge called from the deepest recesses of my mind. *Go. Protect yourself.*

I look up at Blackwell Manor, the windows of the first floor lit with yellow light, a jack-o'-lantern's leering smile, and a shiver runs down my spine. *Not that way,* I tell myself. *Anywhere but there.* I head in the opposite direction toward the bluff, toward safety, pulling my case behind me. My feet feel as though they're encased in cement, but I trudge through the grass anyway, wrestling my suitcase behind me as the wheels tangle in the blades of grass.

"Maddie!"

I think I hear my name, but then it stops. Nothing more than a whisper of the wind. I keep moving. Farther away from Blackwell Manor, from the evil, the danger that lurks beneath its roof. I'm only vaguely aware of what the danger is now, why I feel so urgently that I need to leave, just that I do. That if I stop, even for a moment, I will die.

"Maddie!" The manor calls to me again, more urgently this time. My heart hammers in my chest and my steps falter as the rain comes down harder. The house, it won't let me leave. The bluff is my only chance. I push forward, even though I feel as if I'm going to collapse, my head as light as a balloon ready to float away, to dance among the stars.

And then she's here. Somehow she's here. Alex.

"Where are you going?" Alex asks. But she's not Alex anymore. She's Lily. My half sisters shift and bend, sliding into each other and back again.

"I . . . I have to go." My tongue is heavy in my mouth, my words as round as rubber balls.

"Where were you? Did something happen?" Lily-Alex wants to know.

"I can't . . ." I don't know who she is, what she wants. All I know is that I have to escape. I will die if I stay. "I just have to go."

"Talk to me!" she shouts. Her hands are on my arms. And suddenly I remember. Becca, the club, Theo's hands beneath her clothes. The ghost ship sliding into port. "Don't!" I cry. *Don't hurt her. Don't hurt me too.*

"You can't go!"

They'll never let me go.

I stumble in the wet grass. Blackwell Manor pulling me back. But I don't stop. I can't stop.

And then I'm falling. *Falling, falling, falling.* Floating away to dance among the stars.

47.

THEO

I step out of the car, the shattered remains of clamshells crunching under the heels of my leather-soled shoes. Somewhere a fox cries. Its haunting scream drags me back to that night. To the rain, to the blood.

I was pacing the floor of the great room, pondering my next move. Madison had refused the money. It was baffling, her righteous indignation. After all, wasn't that why she was here? Sleeping with a man twice her age? It had to be my father's money she was after. And yet, when I offered her enough of it to change the bleary outlook of her life, she turned it down. I'd managed to slip the tablet Hutch gave me into a glass of water, watched the grainy residue dissolve as I swirled it in my hand. But I couldn't be sure she'd drink it. Or that it would even work. All Hutch had told me was that if Madison drank enough of it, that it would make her recollection of the entire night feel fuzzy. And if that didn't work . . . we'd have to try more "reliable measures."

What if Madison doesn't drink enough of the water? What if she insists on going to the police with what she thinks she knows? I drummed my fingers on the phone in my pocket. Should I call Hutch? I heard his directive in my head: *Handle it*. Madison was my problem. I'd have to fix this, one way or another.

It was then that I heard the scream, a piecing cry that split the still night air. I burst through the backyard, charging through the rain, across the grass. It had to be Madison. *Somehow she's put the pieces together, she knows what we did.* But when I reached the bluff, it was Lily I found instead, her knees bloodied on the gravel where she'd fallen.

"Lily? What are you doing out here?"

She looked at me then, her big, round eyes as dark as the night sky, and as vacant as the void that lay beyond it.

"Theo . . ." Her voice wobbled and cracked. "It was an accident . . . I didn't mean to . . ." She stared over the edge of the bluff, her gaze transfixed on a spot just beyond my line of sight.

I moved closer to the edge, and Lily lifted one shaking finger to show me what she'd done. And there she was, Madison, her clothes soaked through with rain, a pool of black fanning out around her head, shining like onyx under the moonlight.

"Go inside, Lily," I ordered. She didn't move. She just stared down at Madison's lifeless body as though trying to make sense of what she was seeing.

"I think I might have . . . pushed her." She sounded distant, confused. "I can't remember, exactly. But I think . . . I think I hurt her . . ."

I grabbed her with both arms, lifted her to her feet. "You need to go. Right now."

Lily blinked rapidly, her brain coming back online.

"Go!" I shouted, and finally, she ran.

I pulled my phone from my pocket. Dialed a familiar number.

"I need your help. There's been an accident."

———

Father arrived within minutes of my call. I don't know where he'd been. I didn't ask, didn't care to know. He knelt down next to Madison as I explained what Lily had done. He pressed his fingers to her neck and then looked up at me with, much to my horror, a glassy look to his eyes that implied imminent tears. For my entire life, my father had been a beacon of strength, as consistent and immovable as a boulder. To watch him cry over the loss of his mistress brought up a confusing swell of pity, anger, and shame. I knew, in that moment, that I'd never look at him the same way again. The pedestal I'd held him on began to crumble. He was no longer the immortal, godlike figure who loomed over my childhood, always out of reach. He was weak, he was flawed, he was human.

"She's gone," he said, his voice reedy and thin. His vulnerability caused me to look away as if he stood before me fully exposed.

"James? Theo?" Mother jogged across the lawn under a black umbrella. "Lily is hysterical! What's happened?"

She looked over the edge of the bluff, to the platform where Father knelt at Madison's side, and she knew. "Give me her suitcase," she said with a reasoned firmness. "She was obviously planning to leave anyway, we'll make it look as if she did."

Father cleared his throat, taking on his usual authority. "Clear out the pool house too. I'll take care of . . . her." He looked down at Madison with a tenderness that felt like an affront. "And, Theo," he added, his eyes locking on mine, "you and your sister were never here. Do you understand me?"

"Yes, sir," I replied. *I couldn't believe my luck.*

And yet it seems now that luck has run out. I shove my car door closed with a thud and tell myself that it's not too late, that I can still turn back. But I know it's a lie. I've been slowly trudging toward this fate since the night Madison died. Maybe even before that. Perhaps the wheels were set in motion, an inevitable crash course, since the first moment I laid eyes on her. All I know for certain is that it's all come down to this. It all ends tonight.

48.

ALEX

My breath feels as though it's being sucked from my lungs, my palms pressed into the rough carpet of the office floor. The dress I'd so carefully chosen for tonight pools around my knees in a rumpled pile. "Where is my sister?" I ask through wheezing gasps. "Please, I need to know where she is."

James sighs and spreads his hands on the desk in front of him as his chin falls to his chest. It reminds me of a quote Maddie once read aloud to me from a play she was studying for one of her English courses. It was Shakespeare, I think: "Uneasy lies the head that wears a crown." Maddie had loved Shakespeare. She'd loved so many things. And now she's gone. Because of *him*. Because of all of them.

I hate him. My fury so strong, so raw that I feel it could split open the earth beneath his feet. Katherine hates him too. I can tell by the way she glares at him now, her lips pressed into a thin line as she consoles her sniffling daughter, rubbing small circles along her back.

"She's at one of my properties," James replies heavily, each word landing like a fat raindrop.

A memory bubbles to the surface now and bursts in my

mind. It was something Lily had said: "Pouring foundation . . .
new hotel . . ." And I think I'm going to be sick.

I can feel a churning in my empty stomach, bile burning
in my throat. The periphery of the world begins to blur, and
I don't know if I'll have the strength to go on. "No, no, no."
I hear the words, but I don't realize that I'm the one saying
them until they hit my ears. "No, no, no!"

James comes to kneel on the floor in front of me, holding
my shoulders firmly, forcing me to stay upright. "Breathe,
Alex. You need to breathe."

"My sister," I sob, "the hotel . . . the cement." I begin to
crumble again. "Please just tell me she's not under the cement. She hates the dark, you can't leave her there!" A moan
escapes my lips, and despite myself, I allow James to hold me
as my tears seep into the shoulder of his crisp black suit.

"Alex, no, I don't think you understand. Maddie is alive."

49.

JAMES

I drum my fingers on the steering wheel as we travel down the roads I know as well as I know myself. I risk a quick glance over at Alex, who sits in the passenger seat, her slender arms wrapped protectively across her body. I can only imagine what she's thinking, the neurons that must be firing off in her brain, scrambling to find order in a world that I just toppled. I open my mouth to say something—anything to break the anxious silence that presses upon us within the confines of my car—but I think better of it. Maybe it's best that I give her the space to process everything.

After my revelation that Maddie is, in fact, alive and well, the only words Alex spoke were "Take me to her." I nodded once, ignoring the shocked gasps from my wife and daughter. I'm not sure I want to know what *they're* thinking, what they must think of *me*. God, I never meant for things to go so far, to get so out of hand.

When Theo called me, told me there'd been an accident, somehow I knew it was Maddie. That something had happened to her because of me. We'd argued that night. She'd found out about my . . . other life. About my involvement with Becca. She'd been so disappointed. I could see it written across her face as plain as if it were printed in a book. She'd come all this way to find the father she never knew, hoping for a fairy tale, but what she'd found instead was me: a resounding disappointment. She'd never even worked up the courage to tell me who she really was, and in that moment, I wondered if she ever would; or whether she was so repulsed by the man who created her that she would walk out of my life as breezily as she walked into it. I couldn't bear the thought. I loved her. My daughter. *Vivienne's* daughter. The only living person on this Earth with my blood in their veins. And she was . . . perfection. She was transcendent. She was the best parts of her mother that I thought I'd never see again. She carried none of my darkness, none of my flaws. She was light, she was hope, she was everything. And she was hurt.

I rushed to her side, fumbled my shaking fingers along her neck, which was slick with rain, but I couldn't find a pulse. And so I did what I could, what I do best: I managed the crisis. I protected the family I had left. But while they were busy wiping away all traces of the daughter, of the joy I'd finally found, Maddie's eyelids, so pale they were nearly translucent, began to flutter. She was coming to.

"Theo . . ." she breathed, her voice nothing more than a rasp.

"No, darling. It's me. James. Everything is going to be okay."

"Theo . . . Hutch . . . killed her . . . Becca." The effort of speaking those small words seemed to drain her, her eyes falling closed again.

"Hang in there," I whispered as I lifted her limp body into my arms. "Just hang in there, my darling girl. I'm here now."

I bundled her in an old picnic blanket that was left in the

trunk of my car, a relic from happier days that seemed a distant memory, and I drove her out of town to an emergency clinic that welcomed walk-ins and wouldn't question a cash payment or the fake name I gave them for the young woman with a head injury. I wanted Maddie to get the care she required, but I needed to find a place that wouldn't ask too many questions about how she'd been injured, wouldn't insist upon a paper trail. The situation needed to be handled with discretion.

Thankfully, the X-rays showed that Maddie's skull wasn't fractured. She'd need sutures, a cast on her broken wrist, and bed rest while she recovered from her concussion.

"But she's barely conscious! Are you sure it's not more serious?" I twisted the watch on my wrist until my skin burned. "There was so much blood!"

"She did sustain a substantial laceration to the back of her head," the doctor explained. "Head injuries do tend to bleed quite heavily due to the number of blood vessels that are close to the surface of the skin in that area. And with the rain, it probably looked like even more than it was. I'm sure it was rather alarming. But I have to ask"—he adjusted his glasses—"do you know if she'd been drinking tonight? Taken any drugs?"

"Drugs? Of course not! No!"

"We suspect that"—he looked down at his clipboard, checked the fake name I gave him—"Jane may be under the influence of an unknown substance. The results of her physical exam suggest that there may be more at play here than just the injuries we're seeing."

"No, I'm certain she wouldn't have taken drugs. She's a medical student, she wants to be a doctor!"

"I suppose it's possible that she didn't take them by

choice . . . I've seen a few cases like that with girls her age. Terrible thing." He let the implication linger there, hovering ominously between us.

My instincts in bringing her here were right. If someone drugged Maddie, if this hadn't been entirely an accident, that meant she could still be in danger. Especially if Hutch was involved. I never liked that kid. Never trusted him. Or his powerful father, who would shove anything, or *anyone,* under the rug to protect his reputation.

"Once again, I must strongly suggest taking Jane to the nearest hospital for observation," the doctor continued. "One can't be too careful when it comes to head injuries. But if you're going to care for her at home, it is imperative that she get plenty of rest. Somewhere quiet. And make sure she limits her physical activity over the next few weeks."

"I will." I looked over at Maddie, lying motionless in the bed beside me. "I'll take care of her." And I knew just the place to do it.

"Why?" Alex asks, clearing her throat. The gentle sound is jarring as it shatters the heavy silence. "Why didn't you just tell me where she was from the beginning? You knew I came here to find her. And you kept her from me all this time."

"I was trying to protect her."

"From what?"

From the type of men who would kill her to protect themselves. From Hutch. From his father. But there was more to it than that, if I'm being honest with myself. I didn't just do this for Maddie. I did it for my children, my *other* children. For Lily. For Theo. They deserved my protection too. I owed them that much.

I haven't always been the best father to them. I've made

mistakes, I know that. Katherine would say I didn't care enough, but that wasn't true. I loved my children. In my own way. I was hard on Theo because I could see who he would become if I wasn't. How easily he could be lost. I stayed on top of him so that I could make him the best version of himself. So that he could be *more*. Isn't that what every father wants for his son? To see him succeed, to watch him surpass his parents? But perhaps I pushed him too hard, to a place he couldn't come back from.

With Lily, I tried to give her the space she needed to grow, to blossom. She wasn't like Theo. She never sought my acceptance. She shrunk from the spotlight that made her brother shine. And so I tried to give her the distance she wanted. But maybe I should have been paying more attention. Maybe I'd gotten it all wrong. Clearly I had. Because between the two of them, they'd nearly killed Maddie. All because she'd come to find me.

Lily and Theo weren't blameless. They made their choices. But neither of them would have been at the edge of the bluff that night if it hadn't been for me. It was as though all of the decisions I've ever made, all of my mistakes, had all been leading up to that one fateful moment. My children, each orbiting my life in their own concentric paths, collided at that precise moment in time. They were, all three of them, in one way or another my creations. And I knew I owed them all a debt that I could never repay for the many ways I'd let them down. I stashed Maddie away, not just to protect her, but to protect them *all*. In the only way I knew how.

"There's a lot you still don't know. A lot I can't tell you."

Alex sighs. "I just want to see my sister," she grumbles, "and then I want the truth."

What is the truth? When I returned to Blackwell Manor, it

was as if none of it had ever happened. The pool house was cleared of Maddie's things, the blood washed from the deck. And my family went back to their lives as though Maddie had never existed, and I began to wonder if I'd heard her correctly: if my son really could have killed someone and just carried on with life as usual. I felt like I'd been thrown into an alternate reality where the events of the previous weeks had never occurred at all.

But then Becca's body was found. And Maddie began to recover. As she did, her memories of what happened that night began to return. They were broken, disjointed, less like a film reel and more like images, snapshots grasped from the ether: Lucky Jack's, Becca, *The Heart's Desire,* a ghost ship, Theo warning her to be afraid of Hutch, an offer of money to keep her quiet.

I couldn't be sure what had happened on board that boat, but I knew Maddie was scared, and that it would be better for everyone if they thought she was dead. If Theo knew she was alive, if it got back to Hutch and his father, I worried that they'd find a way to tie up that loose end. I'd decided that the best way to protect them all was to make Maddie disappear, to let Theo think it was over. Even if that meant Lily had to believe she'd killed Maddie.

A wave of guilt rolls through me. I've seen the toll it's taken on her—Lily has always been the fragile one—but there was simply no other way. She had to bear the brunt of this plan. She, and Becca.

Poor, innocent Becca who was denied the justice she deserved because of me. *Was her blood on my hands too?* It's the question that's plagued me since the moment I heard her body had been found. It's too much of a coincidence to think that her death on my boat, with my son, isn't somehow connected to my relationship with her, but I still don't know what really happened that night. And it's possible that I never will.

As much as I've wanted to confront Theo, I couldn't ask him to fill in the blank spaces in Maddie's story—a story I was never supposed to know. And so I watched him instead, looking for some sign that he was capable of taking a life, that the guilt was eating away at him. I waited for him to crack, for the truth to spill forth. But it never did. And I'd never been so afraid of my own son. *How much of who he is was caused by the people who raised him, and how much was inevitable? A pattern woven into his DNA before he even took his first breath?*

"We're here," I announce, as I edge the car into the parking lot of a row of townhouses.

"She's been here? So close? All this time?" Alex eyes the complex incredulously.

I'm sorry, I think. "Come on," I say instead.

We both climb out of the car and trek across the parking lot toward unit number 12. It's a silent walk, broken only by the crunch of windblown sand under our shoes. It seems to coat everything out here—the beach, the earth, slowly reclaiming its territory: a constant battle between man's progress and nature's power.

I punch in the door code and the keypad beeps twice, disengaging the lock. I turn the doorknob, the metal cool against my palm, and a chill runs through me. I'm gripped with a sudden, overwhelming sense of dread. *Don't open the door.* Fear hisses in my ear. *Protect her.* It's become so ingrained, protecting my daughter, her secret, at all costs. I shove the voice aside, quiet the alarm bells ringing in my ears. *Maddie is safe. Alex is her sister. She will be fine.*

50.

ALEX

I wipe my sweaty palms against the thin fabric of my dress as James enters the door code, willing my hands to be still. It feels as though my entire body is vibrating with anticipation, stored energy waiting to be released. I don't know what to expect behind that door. *What state is Maddie in? What is the extent of her injuries? Is she being held against her will, or had she chosen to stay? Will she be surprised to see me, or has she been waiting for me to find her?*

After what feels like an eternity, James pushes open the door and I follow him inside, into a small living room. It's sparsely but tastefully furnished, and I wonder whether this was meant to be a rental property. The curtains are drawn, allowing only a hazy gray light to filter through the space. I suppose that makes sense, if you're hiding a girl who was meant to disappear. But there's something wrong. I can sense it as soon as I hear the thud of the front door closing behind me. There's an unusual stillness in the air, and I can't help but think of the glassy calm of the ocean before a violent storm.

"Maddie?" I call out. "Are you here?" My eyes dart around the apartment like a police dog searching for a trail to follow.

Where is she? It occurs to me then what is causing my unease about this place. It's not the shadows or the darkness, it's not even the faint scent of antiseptic that seems to linger in the air. It's the quiet, the deathly silence, that hangs over the space like a thick fog.

"She's probably in the bedroom," James suggests. He nods in the direction of a small hallway. "Last door on the end." But I can hear something off in his voice. A crack in his usual sturdy assuredness. My unease begins to grow.

I take off down the hallway, practically breaking into a jog in my haste to finally see my sister. "Maddie!" I can sense James close behind me as I reach the last door and push it open on whining hinges.

The door bounces off a doorstop and swings back toward me. I stop it with my hand as I survey the room. An empty bed sits at the center of the space, sheets tangled, pillows strewn. At the bedside is a half-empty glass of water, orange bottles of medications. A paperback, its spine cracked, lies splayed open on the floor. But what I don't see is my sister.

I whirl around to face James. "Is this some kind of a joke?"

James stares open-mouthed into the empty room.

"Where's Maddie?" I demand, my hands drawing into tight fists at my sides.

"I don't know . . ." He runs his hands through his graying hair. "She was here. I swear to you she was here!"

I step into the bedroom, inspecting it closer for signs that Maddie had really been here, proof that she'd been alive, living in this very room. I pick up the fallen book and skim the back cover. It's a romance novel, the kind of meet-cute, happily-ever-after Maddie would love. I set it down on the nightstand.

Turning toward the bed, I run my fingers over the flattened pillows and wonder whether I'd imagined the faint scent of blueberry shampoo lifting from the linens.

The pill bottles aren't much more helpful. They're prescriptions for painkillers for someone named "Jane Smith." *Very creative,* I think to myself as I place them back down, letting out a frustrated sigh.

"This is ridiculous," I huff. "Do you have any idea where she could have gone?"

James doesn't respond, which only serves to make me more irritated. "James?" I turn angrily to face him. "Are you even listening?"

But he isn't. He's staring down at a scrap of paper in his hand, his face an ashen white.

"What is it?" I demand.

Again, he doesn't answer. It's as though my voice can't penetrate whatever spell that little piece of paper has cast over him. "James? What is that? What did you find?"

I stomp across the room and snatch the paper from his hand as he blinks back to life. My eyes scan the page hungrily, trying to make sense of the typewritten words as they seem to dance and twirl off the page:

> *If you want to see her again, meet me on The Heart's Desire at 10pm. Bring $2,000,000 in cash. Come alone, or she'll disappear for real this time.*

51.

ALEX

"You'll stay in the car." James says this with a degree of certainty that signals he's not accustomed to having his orders challenged. *Well, that's a real shame for him.*

"Like hell I will!"

"You read the note. It said to come alone. It's nearly ten o'clock already"—he makes a cursory check of his watch and then presses down on the accelerator, his sleek black Lexus growling beneath us—"otherwise I'd drop you off. But since I can't, you'll stay in the car."

We're cutting it dangerously close to the blackmailer's deadline—the pit stop to James's office where he cleared out his safe of all the cash he had on hand set us back. And I doubt it's enough. I don't know what $2,000,000 in cash looks like, but the duffel bag at my feet doesn't seem nearly full enough.

I shake my head. "She's my sister. I can't just sit here and do *nothing.*"

"I'll handle it, Alex."

"Yes, because you've handled this whole situation so well thus far. Excuse me if I'm not exactly brimming with confidence right now." I throw my arms up in exasperation.

"I know, okay? I've made a mess of everything. But I can't risk letting Maddie get hurt. And I know you don't want that either."

I fold my arms over my chest, slouching in my seat. I hate that he has a point.

"We're here," he says, pulling into a dark parking lot dotted with puddles of light from flickering streetlamps overhead.

As James brings the Lexus to park in the shadows, I look around for other cars. There are a few at the far end of the lot, but it's too dark and they're too far for me to be able to tell if I recognize any of them.

"Wait here," James says as he slides out of the car, as if he hadn't just finished lecturing me on that very point.

He doesn't wait for a response, which is probably a good idea considering I hadn't intended to give him one. He grabs the duffel bag of cash and slams the door, striding toward the docks with long, measured steps.

I shift uncomfortably in my seat. *I just wish I could see what was going on.*

I know James had told me to wait in the car, but I don't trust him as far as I could throw him, and right now I can't even *see* him. I unlock the passenger-side door with a click and slip out of the car, closing it softly behind me.

I need to get a little closer, just enough to see what's happening aboard that boat.

I creep off, following the same route I saw James take only moments ago, taking care to stay in the shadows. My heels crunch loudly over the gravel drive—not the most practical footwear for the occasion—and I freeze, waiting to see if anyone's heard me. But the only sounds are the creaks of the docks and my own breath, which escapes in anxious huffs, mingling with the briny sea air.

I make my way onto the dock, which shifts gently beneath my feet, and it takes me a moment to get my bearings. My heels catch between the wooden planks and I peel them off, leaving them behind. Barefoot, I crouch behind a mooring pole, the weathered wood splintered and pocked with age. Barnacles creep up the submerged portion, white and alien-like beneath the water's surface.

I scan the marina from my vantage point and catch sight of James passing under a lamppost, heading toward an impressive-looking sailboat rocking lazily in the last slip. Its wooden hull shines in the moonlight. *That must be* The Heart's Desire.

I sneak closer, moving in an awkward crouch. *If I'd known how the night would play out, I'd have taken a second to change my clothes.* It's not easy creeping around in an evening gown—the hem keeps catching on the splintered wood and I have to yank it free as I move. I duck behind another pole, and watch James climb aboard the boat. *But he's not alone.* There's someone else waiting for him inside the cabin. I squint into the dark, trying to make out the details of the shadowy figure emerging from the cabin, but it's impossible. *Could it be Maddie?*

My pulse races as their voices begin to float toward me. They're too far away for me to make out what they're saying, but I'm almost certain it's a man he's speaking to, the deep timbre of their voices echoing through the night air. It sounds like they're arguing.

Where is Maddie? I need to know who James is talking to. Is this the person who left the ransom note? But maybe James was right. Maybe I'd be putting both Maddie *and* myself in danger if I went charging in there without a plan.

I slide my phone out of my evening bag and click on the latest missed call from Ben. I may not have a plan for once I get onto the boat, but I figure at least one human being on the face of this earth should know where I am in case something goes wrong.

Ben answers on the first ring.

"Alex, thank God. Is everything okay? I haven't heard from you since—"

"Ben," I manage, my voice barely above a whisper. Sending a text might have been the safer route, but I needed to hear his voice. "I can't give you all the details right now, but my sister has been kidnapped, and I'm going to get her."

"Where are you? What are you talking about?"

"Listen, I'm in the Hamptons. At Shore Winds Marina. I'm about to get onto a boat called *The Heart's Desire*. I just wanted you to know in case . . ."

"In case of what, Alex?" Ben's voice strains with panic, desperation.

"In case you don't hear from me after."

There's a beat of silence before he can formulate a response. "Alex, do not get on that boat, do you hear me? You need to call the police!"

"I can't. There's no time." I know I could have used these precious minutes to call the cops, but I also know I wouldn't have waited for them to get here anyway. And this may be my last chance to tell Ben the truth. He deserves at least that much from me.

"This is insane. I'm coming right now." I can hear his car keys jangling, his feet pounding against pavement as he runs, most likely toward his car.

"It'll take you hours to get here. It'll be too late. I just needed you to know where I am, and that . . . I'm sorry, and . . . that . . . that . . ." I fumble over the words I've been trying to find for some time now, the ones I need him to know. *That I think I might love you.*

"I know, Alex. I know."

I get the feeling he does. Maybe he always has.

I end the call, holding the phone to my chest for a moment before dropping it back into my bag.

Still crouched in the dark, the muscles in my thighs burning, I train my eyes on the back deck of *The Heart's Desire*, watching for the right moment to make my move. Minutes that feel like hours slide by; time has become a slippery construct as I wait. James is gesticulating wildly now, and the other man, who's managed to keep his back to me thus far, pushes James hard in the chest, making him stumble on his feet. Then he lunges toward James again, passing through a shaft of moonlight. *Theo.* His face is darkened, and almost frightening, slashed through with angular shadows, but it's definitely him.

I feel my heart drop, my pulse quickening as my hands shake against the rough, wooden pole. *Theo is the blackmailer? But why?* I think back to the few brief encounters I've had with Theo since I arrived at Blackwell Manor—his boldness, the empty coldness of his dark eyes—and it sends a chill down my spine.

I don't know why Theo would want to blackmail his own father—maybe he was jealous when Maddie careened into their lives, a half sibling who might stand to inherit a slice of the very substantial Blackwell pie, or maybe their issues stretched back before her arrival. I can't be certain. But I do know that my sister could be inside that boat at this very moment, at the epicenter of this war between father and son, and I can't stand by any longer and risk her getting caught in the crossfire.

I crawl along the dock, edging closer to *The Heart's Desire*.

"Alex." It's a whispered hiss in the dark. "What the hell are you doing?"

Gilroy. The sight of him drawing closer fills me with relief. *At least I won't have to go in there alone.*

He squats down beside me.

"How did you know where I was?" I ask, as quietly as I can.

"I was out responding to a call when the station radioed me and rerouted me here. Apparently they got a call from your boyfriend."

Ben. I say a silent prayer for him as Gilroy continues. Even from hundreds of miles away he's looking out for me.

"I'm told he was in a total panic, yelling about you getting on a boat, rescuing your sister from a kidnapper. I got here as fast as I could. And you're damn lucky I did. Now, do you want to tell me just what the hell is going on?"

I bring him up to speed as quickly as possible: Lily's story, James's confession that Maddie is his daughter and that he's been hiding her away (for some reason he's yet to explain), the townhouse, and the ransom letter.

"And that's Theo up there with him now?" Gilroy nods toward the boat, his eyes sharp and discerning as he evaluates the situation.

"Yeah. I haven't seen Maddie though."

"She could be inside the cabin. We're going to have to approach this extremely cautiously. The situation could very easily go bad. You should go back to the car. Let me handle this. The fewer people on board that boat, the less risk of someone getting hurt."

I shake my head vigorously. "If one more person tries to tell me to stay in the car, I swear I'm going to lose it. There's no way that's happening. I'm going."

"I had a feeling you'd say that." He rolls his eyes, the whites flashing in the dark. "Come on then. Follow my lead."

Gilroy inches toward *The Heart's Desire*, staying low to the ground, just as I had. I follow in his footsteps, the argument from on board the boat growing louder as we approach. I can catch a few stray words now, punching angrily through the wind:

"*Can't believe . . . daughter . . . liar . . .*"

Gilroy turns to face me, his index finger pressed to his lips. *Shhh.*

I nod my understanding.

He deftly stands and swings his legs over the side of the boat, landing with a thud that silences the men aboard. I rush to follow behind and scramble onto the deck.

Theo and James stare open-mouthed at their unexpected visitors.

"It's over, Theo," Gilroy announces.

But it seems that Theo has other plans. His hand darts to his coat pocket, from which he draws a gun.

I gasp at the sight of it, cold metal catching a glint of silver moonlight. The appearance of the gun has altered the playing field, shifted the balance of power, and the mounting tension is palpable.

"Theo, what are you doing with that?" James exclaims.

Theo looks to his father, his dark eyes as round as discs. "I'm doing what I have to!"

Gilroy pounces on this moment of distraction and charges into Theo, slamming his shoulder hard into his chest. I hear the wind expelling from Theo's lungs, the sound of metal hitting the ground as the gun tumbles from his hand, and I take my chance.

I race into the cabin. "Maddie! Maddie! Are you here?" My eyes dart around the room. The inside of *The Heart's Desire* is nothing like the bright, airy spaces of Blackwell Manor: There's a deep, mahogany bar polished to a high gloss, a leather sofa upholstered in a rich chocolate-brown, and antique rowing oars mounted on the walls. But there's no trace of my sister.

"Maddie!" I shout again, louder this time, my voice cracking with panic. I don't know how much time I have. I didn't stick around long enough to see if Gilroy was able to restrain Theo. For all I know, he could be right on my heels.

A muffled groan from the back of the cabin calls my attention, and my head snaps in the direction of the sound. There are two doors at the far end of the room. Maddie must be behind one of them. "I'm coming, Maddie!"

I push open the first door to find a small bathroom. Grabbing the shower curtain, I pull it open, the curtain rings screeching against the metal rod—but all I find is an empty shower stall, a few half-finished bottles of shampoo. *I chose the wrong door, wasting precious seconds.*

Abandoning the bathroom, I rush to the next door, kicking it open, making up for lost time. My mind glitches, struggling to process what my eyes are seeing. It's a bedroom. The bed is draped with a navy-blue quilt, and atop the bed is a girl: a blindfold pulled over her eyes, a cloth tied across her mouth, hands pinned behind her back, the white plaster of a cast digging into her crooked elbow.

"Mmm!" The girl strains against the gag at her mouth.

I rush to her side, pulling off the blindfold, and her eyes lock onto mine.

"Maddie! Oh my God, Maddie! It's really you!"

My hands reach for the gag, but Maddie kicks and protests before I can grab ahold of it. She yanks her head away, her eyes bulging in fear.

"Maddie, it's me, it's Alex. Let me help you. I'm going to get you out of here."

"Mmmm!" Maddie exclaims again, her scream muffled behind the cloth. She jerks her head dramatically, but I don't know what she's trying to tell me, until I realize that her eyes have grown round with fear and they're locked, not on me, but on something just above my shoulder.

I feel the dread, cold and liquid, shiver through my veins. *Theo must have caught up to me.* I slowly turn toward the doorway, swallowing hard around the fear that's formed itself into a hard lump in my throat.

My shoulders sag with relief as I release a breath. *It's not Theo, it's Gilroy.* "I found her! It's Maddie! Help me untie her!"

But Gilroy doesn't move. And it takes me a moment to register the gun in his hand, the gun pointed straight at my chest.

52.

ALEX

"What . . . what are you doing?" My chin trembles, my teeth chattering in my skull.

He shakes his head slowly. "I'm sorry, Alex. It wasn't supposed to be like this. It really wasn't. But I don't think I have much of a choice anymore."

"You always have a choice, Mike." It's James's voice. He's appeared at Gilroy's shoulder, his palms raised in a peace offering.

Gilroy grabs him by the collar with one hand and shoves him into the bedroom with Maddie and me. It's a small room, and it only feels smaller with so many people crowded inside. The fear rising off our bodies like steam threatens to suffocate me. "You don't have to do this," James continues calmly.

Gilroy huffs. "Just shut the fuck up. You're not charming your way out of this one. You know what they did, don't you?"

"What who did?" James asks.

"That's really how you want to play this? Acting like you don't know that Theo and Hutch *killed* someone? They killed that girl, James. Don't pretend you don't know that. And then they tried to cover it up. I wasn't going to let them take my son down with them."

His son? I don't ask. I'm terrified to draw attention to myself, too scared to so much as breathe.

"Mike, just put down the gun and we'll talk this through." James is still trying to manage the situation, but Gilroy doesn't want to be handled.

"Mick was the only one who wanted to do the right thing. He came to me after Rebecca Jones's body was found, he told me what happened. My son was the *only* one with a conscience! Unlike the monster you raised. Do you know Theo just *stood* there, watched that poor girl being assaulted? But what was I supposed to do at that point? How could I go after Theo and Hutch without implicating Mick for his involvement? He was on that boat, too, he'd been a witness and he'd gone along with the cover-up. I can't even imagine what it must have been like for him: making the decision to turn on his friends, the guys he's tried to fit in with for most of his life.

"Do you know how hard it's been for Mick to try to keep up with Theo, with Hutch, all these years? Have you ever, even once, stopped to think about what it was like for him, for us, to struggle to afford to send him to that fucking school?"

James is silent, seemingly at a loss for words.

"Well?" Gilroy asks again, leveling the gun at James. "Have you?"

"N-no. I . . . I haven't."

Gilroy snorts derisively. "We've known each other since we were kids, James, and our boys are best friends, but you've got your head so far up your own ass that you haven't noticed how deep I'm in over my head, that my house is underwater. I'm mortgaged up to my fucking teeth, while Theo drives around town in his luxury car tossing his daddy's money around like confetti. I've done the right thing my whole goddamn life, and I can't even afford to send my kids to college. Tell me, how is that fair?"

"It's not, Mike, and I'm sorry for that, but—"

"You're sorry? You're *sorry*? I really don't think you are. All those times you've used your money, your privilege, to get your kids out of trouble. Greasing a few palms to get Theo out of that DWI, Lily walking away from a potential assault charge in high school without so much as a slap on the wrist. But my son wouldn't have the same rich-boy escape hatch. Not this time. Not when a girl is dead. Theo and Hutch would have walked away scot-free, I've seen it happen, and my kid would have been left holding the bag. So I decided to make them pay another way. Why shouldn't we be on the receiving end for once? And Theo was happy enough to keep the money coming, as long as I kept his secret. Then Alex here showed up."

Gilroy swings the gun in my direction again and every muscle in my body tenses, my hands shaking uncontrollably.

"As soon as she told me her sister was missing, that she'd been staying at Blackwell Manor," Gilroy continues, "I knew her disappearance had to be related somehow. It was too much of a coincidence, and I don't believe in those. Not in my line of work.

"That's when I started paying more attention to the Blackwell family. Keeping tabs on your comings and goings. And I noticed something very strange—that you visited one of your rental properties almost every day. Going into the same unit day after day. I didn't see anything special about this particular apartment, so I decided to take a look inside for myself. All I had to do was watch you punch in the door code and use it myself after you left. And"—he lets out a low whistle—"I couldn't believe what I found.

"I knew who Maddie was the second I saw her. She's the spitting image of her mother. I knew Vivienne that summer, too, you know, the summer you met. You seem to forget that I'm a local boy too. That we lived in the same town. Even if our parents weren't in the same social circles. You rich people, it's like you don't even see the rest of us. We're just here to serve you. But Vivienne saw me. I was a busboy at the diner that summer, and we became friends. She told me she'd been seeing you—I tried to warn her against it, but she wouldn't listen. I hadn't seen her in years, not since that summer, but then there was Maddie—a clone of her mother—in one of your properties, and well, it wasn't too hard to put the pieces together.

"Maddie was so happy to see me, or, more likely, the badge pinned to my shirt. As soon as I walked into the apartment you'd been locking her away in, she told me everything—what she knew about Rebecca Jones, what she'd seen. It was like she couldn't wait to lift the burden of truth off her chest. But I couldn't be the one to help her. I had to think of my son."

"So you took her?" James asks, his voice as soft as a whisper.

"That wasn't the plan. Not at first. But I had to. Everything started to fall apart. Theo couldn't come up with the money I needed, when I was so close to paying off my debts. He said he didn't have any more to give. And I knew the rest would have to come from you. I went back to the apartment while Maddie was asleep. I blindfolded her and brought her here as leverage. She was never supposed to see me."

He points the gun at James again, and I feel a flood of relief that I'm no longer in the line of fire.

"I knew you'd do anything to protect your son. And Maddie—your daughter. I wasn't going to hurt her. I just needed to make sure you'd come. That you'd bring the money and find a way to convince her to keep quiet about what she knew.

"But Alex wasn't supposed to be here. She wasn't supposed to know about any of this. I warned you to come alone! Why couldn't you listen?" His voice grows manic and a drop of sweat rolls down the side of his face, disappearing under his collar. "I told Theo too. I showed up at your party earlier as a final warning. I cornered him and told him to come here tonight. That it was his last chance. I wasn't sure he'd show after he took off running. But turns out he can follow simple directions, unlike his father."

The gun swings like a pendulum back to me.

"No one else was supposed to be here, no one else was supposed to know." Gilroy presses his fist—the one not aiming a gun at my chest—to his temple. "Alex shouldn't be here. I thought we could make a deal. You, me, and Theo. That we all had something to lose, that it would be in all of our best interests to keep this under wraps, but now it's too late, it's too late."

"It's n-not," I stammer as I crawl onto the bed, huddling close to my sister. I can feel her body shaking beside me as Gilroy tracks my movements with the gun. For some reason, in this moment, it's Ben that I think of. And it dawns on me, like a crashing wave, that he's the only other person in this world who cares about me—who, I suddenly realize with an aching desperation, I want to fight to get home to. I can feel the weight of his hand in mine as if he's here with me now, a reassurance that I can do this. That I can keep Gilroy talking. That I can make it back to him. *You got this, kid.* "It's not too late. Just let us go and I won't tell anyone. I promise I won't." My voice comes out like broken glass.

"I'm in over my fucking head," Gilroy says, more to himself than to anyone in the room. I can see his internal struggle playing out across his face. He doesn't want to do this, but his finger hovers dangerously over the trigger.

"Please don't," I whimper.

"I'm so sorry," he says, and he begins to squeeze.

I clench my eyes shut, waiting for the crack of the gun, waiting for darkness, for whatever comes next.

"No!" I hear instead. I risk opening my eyes to see James standing at the foot of the bed. His arms spread wide, shielding Maddie and me as best he can. "I can't let you do this."

"I have to," Gilroy replies solemnly.

I am back there, in the last memory I have of my family together, happy. I can hear the soothing sound of Maddie's voice as she reads to me under our blanket fort, see the image of my mother spinning through a frosted cloud of perfume in her shimmering gold dress, feel the stubble of my father's cheek against my own. I am far away, wrapped in the warmth of a glittering memory, as Gilroy fires off a shot.

———————

I press my palms to my ears to try to stop the ringing that pierces through my skull. *I'm alive. Somehow I'm alive.* So is Maddie, who presses her forehead into my shoulder, her tears wet on my skin.

And so is James, who still stands at the end of the bed, his arms stretched open as if nailed to a crucifix.

But how? And where is Gilroy?

I look around this new, soundless world, the incessant ringing burying all other noise like a thick blanket of snow. There's a bullet hole in the wall beside the bed. *Gilroy must have missed. But how?* And then I see him. Standing in the doorway is Theo, a wooden oar in his grip, as if he's positioned behind home plate, frozen in a practiced baseball stance.

"Dad?" he says, his voice cutting through the silence. It wavers like a small boy's, begging for his father's approval.

"It's okay, son," James replies, "you did good."

It's then that I finally see Gilroy lying in a heap at Theo's feet, the smoking gun still in his hand.

53.

ALEX

Beep . . . beep . . . beep

The sound of the monitors strapped to my sister interrupt the silence. It's so strange to see her this way. Maddie has always been such a large presence in my life, but she looks so small, so fragile in the hospital bed, her skin pale against the stark white sheet that's pulled over her.

It took a lot out of Maddie to tell me her story. Mom's final confession just before she passed. The truth about where Maddie came from. She takes a sip of water from the Styrofoam cup on her tray table.

"You really never told James who you were?" I ask when she places the cup back down.

Maddie gives her head a small shake. "No. I didn't want him to know who I was until I was ready. That's why I deleted all of my socials before I came out here too. I didn't want him to put the pieces together. I just . . . I wanted to get to know him on my own terms. Without any added pressure or sense of obligation on his end."

"I guess that makes sense."

"I was going to. Eventually. I just . . . hadn't gotten there yet."

I shift in my seat and something digs into my thigh through the pocket of my jeans. I reach in to retrieve it. "I almost forgot. I found this." I hand Maddie Mom's necklace. The V charm dangles through my fingers, swaying on a thin gold chain.

Maddie reaches out and closes it gingerly in her palm. "She gave me this when she told me about James. He'd given it to her."

"And she'd never taken it off. All these years. I can't imagine what it must have been like for her, keeping this secret inside for so long. Do you think . . . did Dad know?"

Maddie nods. "I asked her about that. He knew from the beginning. Mom wanted another child. Remember, it was just the two of us. Mom's parents disowned her when she got pregnant so young and refused to give up the baby—me. She had to drop out of her ballet program. Apparently they didn't have much money, but they'd put everything they had into Mom's dream of becoming a dancer. They were so disappointed with her for ruining her chance after they'd sacrificed so much to give it to her. And it was clear that the Blackwells weren't going to be involved, so . . . well, I guess Mom was worried that someday . . . when she was gone . . . that I'd be all alone in the world, with no one to call family. So she was determined to have another child, and then she met Dad.

"They met at the bar where she was singing at the time, while he was traveling through town. They'd formed something of a friendship where they'd spend time together whenever he was in town. According to Mom, it was the closest thing she had to a relationship since James. She had a young baby at home, and she was working every hour she could just to keep us afloat. I imagine she didn't have much of a dating life. Anyway, eventually they made an agreement.

Dad was going to give her the child she wanted, and he was going to have the family his lifestyle didn't really allow for. Without all the traditional pressures. He could come and go as he pleased.

"It seemed like the perfect arrangement for both of them. Until things got complicated. Mom said he loved me from the start, treated me like I was his own, but when you were born . . . well, he was enamored. He started to stay in town longer and longer, giving up jobs so he could be home with us. But it was never supposed to be that way. He and Mom started to argue all the time. He'd never wanted to be a real family. And I guess . . . I guess he couldn't handle it."

I quickly swipe a tear from my eye with the back of my wrist. Maddie looks away, giving me the kindness of pretending not to have noticed.

"What about the money?" I ask, eager to change the subject to something less painful. "Where did you get all of that money I found in the pool house?"

"It was the money the Blackwells gave Mom. To leave town, and . . . you know."

I sit up straight, my eyes wide. "She never spent it?"

Maddie shakes her head. "No, she kept most of it in a safe deposit box. She spent only what she needed to find a place for us to live, and she put the rest away."

"But . . . we barely scraped by most of the time. There were days we couldn't even keep the lights on. And she had thousands of dollars just . . . sitting there?"

"It was 'blood money' she said. She told me she'd have begged on the streets to feed us before relying on a dime of the money that was meant to kill her baby. You know Mom, she was nothing if not stubborn. She saved the money to give it to me someday, so that the Blackwells could pay for my life instead of my death I think it felt like some sort of justice to her."

"Wow." It's all I can muster. For so long I thought of our mother as weak, a woman prisoner to her addictions, but she was stronger than I ever knew.

"I just wish you would have been honest with me from the beginning," I say, "when Mom first told you about James."

"I know, I should have been. I should have known we were strong enough to face it together. But after the funeral, when we had that argument . . ."

"I'm so sorry. I said some things—a lot of things—I shouldn't have. I was just . . . I don't know . . ."

"You were angry." As usual, my sister can read my emotions better than I can. "And you had every right to be. I'm sorry that I wasn't around more. I had my reasons for leaving, but I could have done more to help, I could have been there for you."

"How did we get here?" I ask, leaning forward in my chair to fold my arms on the bed beside her, resting my head atop them.

"We forgot what it meant to be sisters."

I reach out and squeeze her hand. She squeezes back.

"Now enough about me," she manages, her voice dry and cracked. "Tell me about you. Who is that you keep texting with when you think I'm not looking?"

A warm blush floods my face. "Ben."

"Oh, thank God." Maddie exhales dramatically. "That's finally happening?"

"What do you mean 'finally happening'?"

"It took you two long enough to figure it out," she says with a knowing laugh, "but I could tell you had a thing for him since the day you met."

"Not possible."

"Totally possible. Just by the way you talked about him."

"He's here, actually. Outside in the waiting room. Things are a little messy at the moment. And we definitely haven't 'figured' anything out, but I think I want to try?"

Maddie settles back into her pillow, a small smile playing about her lips. "I'm glad. You deserve to be happy, Alex."

I roll my eyes.

"No, I'm serious. You've spent so much of your life looking out for everyone else. You always say I took care of you growing up, but you took care of me too. Me, *and* Mom. It's about time you took care of yourself, let yourself be happy."

"You know," I reply, "a wise person once told me that life is all about choices."

Maddie groans and covers her face with her palm. "I was insufferable."

"Oh, completely. But you also happened to be right. I want to choose to put myself out there, to let Ben in and see where it goes. After everything you and I went through as kids, I think I closed myself off. I'm going to choose to do things differently."

Maddie smiles contentedly.

"And what about you?" I ask. "What about medical school? What about James?"

"I'm going back to school as soon as I can," Maddie answers definitively. "I'm done putting my life on hold.

"But as for James . . ." She shakes her head slowly. "I haven't decided yet. Things are just so . . . complicated. Part of me wants to have a real, open conversation with him now that the truth is out, but another part of me wishes I'd never met any of the Blackwells."

"You have the rest of your life to make that decision," I assure her.

Maddie nods slowly, her eyelids growing heavy. I can tell she needs her rest. She's been through so much in the past few days. The doctors say she'll be fine, but they're keeping her here for monitoring until she regains her strength.

"Do you want me to put on the TV?" I ask.

Maddie nods again, though her eyes are nearly closed already.

I grab the remote and click on the television. It's tuned in to the local news:

The investigation continues into the death of Rebecca Jones. Sources close to the case tell us that several witnesses have been brought in for questioning, including the son of Governor Remy Hutchinson; the son of local property developer, James Blackwell; and the son of chief of police Michael Gilroy. Arrests are expected to follow, and the hashtag JusticeForBecca is already trending on social media in anticipation. Meanwhile, Chief Gilroy, who is currently in a coma following a near-fatal head wound, is also being investigated for his own alleged involvement in a kidnapping scheme meant to—"

I click the TV back off. I think I've heard enough. Eventually Maddie and I will have to talk about what happened on that boat. We'll have to face a future in which my sister will forever be entwined with the Blackwell family. But for now, I'm content just to be here, in this moment with her.

I have my sister, and we'll always have each other.

THE END

ACKNOWLEDGMENTS

There are so many people I want to thank, but I'd like to start with you, the reader. Because of you, I get to do what I love and call it a job. I truly feel so fortunate to be doing what I'm doing every day and so thank you, from the bottom of my heart, for allowing me to share my stories with you.

I also owe a huge thanks to my amazing agent, Melissa Edwards. Melissa, thank you for taking a chance on me and my books, thank you for being a wonderful advocate, and thank you for your endless advice. But most of all, thank you for always being a text/email/phone call away to talk me off a ledge when I'm panicking about something that probably doesn't require panicking. The road to publication isn't always an easy one, but it certainly felt like it with you in my corner.

I'd also like to thank Jenny Chen, my fabulous editor, for all of her hard work in making this book what it is today. Jenny, when I got the call that you were interested in working together, you made a dream come true for me. And working with you has been exactly that: a dream. Thank you for your enthusiasm about this book and for all of your invaluable insight that helped make it the best it could be.

Thank you also to Mae Martinez for all of your assistance along the way.

There is so much that goes into taking a book from an idea to the reality that you're holding in your hands. It truly takes a village to get it done, and mine is the best. Thank you to all the folks at Penguin Random House and Ballantine Bantam Dell who devoted their time and talents to making this book a success. From the cover art to the final edits, you have been incredible to work with. A special thanks to Kathleen Quinlan and Vanessa Duque for the fantastic marketing as well.

Thank you to Addison Duffy for your representation of the film and TV rights for this book. I'm thrilled to have the opportunity to work with you, and I can't wait to see what comes next for us!

Thank you to my critique partners, Shelby Holt and Tanya Berzinski. Your input during the writing process helped me cross the finish line and finally get to type those two little words that every author loves the most: "The End."

These acknowledgments would be incomplete without also recognizing my personal cheering squad. Lauren Izzo, thank you for the late nights spent plotting. I couldn't do this without you. Wolfpack forever. Jessica Ostrowski, thank you for always sending me your most insane ideas. You never know what's going to spark inspiration. I hope you noticed that one of your wild ideas made the ending of this book possible! And to Lisa Prokop, thanks for pouring the wine while I stress over deadlines. You will always have a stool at my kitchen counter.

Last but not least, I have to thank my entire family. You have all been so wonderfully supportive and excited about this book, and it means the world to me. Mom, thank you for always being by my side. From being my first reader to bullying all of your friends into buying my books, your faith in me means more than you know. Ali, thank you for believing this book (like all my others) was my best one yet, and for forcing me to be your sister against my will. And to my brothers, Steven and Michael, thanks for answering the strangest of questions as I researched this book. I may have written a book about sisters, but it turns out that having brothers isn't too bad either.

Giancarlo, thank you for always encouraging me to reach for the stars and for never wavering in your belief that I could reach them. Your faith in me makes it all possible.

And to my daughters, Christina and Juliana, I love you endlessly. This one is for you.

THE PERFECT SISTER

STEPHANIE DECAROLIS

A READER'S GUIDE

QUESTIONS AND TOPICS
FOR DISCUSSION

1. One of the recurring themes in *The Perfect Sister* is how the same relationship can be viewed in different ways. What instances of this did you notice throughout the story? How did they affect the plot?

2. As you read, what did you think happened to Maddie? Did your thinking change as events unfolded?

3. What was the role of nature versus nurture in this story? What impact do you believe the parents in the story had on their children? In what ways does a parent's past affect later generations?

4. Were you surprised when James revealed the truth about his relationship with Maddie? As you think back on the story, do you recall any clues that foreshadowed the ending?

5. Who did you think was the narrator of The Wharf chapters? Did that ever change as the story progressed?

6. Which narrator was your favorite? Which was your least favorite? Why?

7. How did Alex's character evolve over the course of the story? Were there any other characters who changed over time?

8. Complicated family dynamics played a major role in this novel. How did the relationships between the members of the Blackwell family and the members of the Walker family drive the story?

9. What role did economic disparity have in the story? Do you think it would have played out differently if the Blackwell family had not been wealthy?

10. Almost every character in this story was hiding a secret. How did each of their secrets play a role in the plot? Why do you think each character felt they couldn't share their secret? How did your perception of certain characters change after you learned what they were hiding?

STEPHANIE DECAROLIS is the *USA Today* bestselling author of *The Guilty Husband* and *Deadly Little Lies*. She is a graduate of Binghamton University and St. John's University School of Law, and currently lives in New York with her husband and their two daughters.

X: @StephDeCarolis

ABOUT THE TYPE

This book was set in Dante, a typeface designed by Giovanni Mardersteig (1892–1977). Conceived as a private type for the Officina Bodoni in Verona, Italy, Dante was originally cut only for hand composition by Charles Malin, the famous Parisian punch cutter, between 1946 and 1952. Its first use was in an edition of Boccaccio's *Trattatello in laude di Dante* that appeared in 1954. The Monotype Corporation's version of Dante followed in 1957. Though modeled on the Aldine type used for Pietro Cardinal Bembo's treatise *De Aetna* in 1495, Dante is a thoroughly modern interpretation of that venerable face.

RANDOM HOUSE BOOK CLUB

Because Stories Are Better Shared

Discover
Exciting new books that spark conversation every week.

Connect
With authors on tour—or in your living room. (Request an Author Chat for your book club!)

Discuss
Stories that move you with fellow book lovers on Facebook, on Goodreads, or at in-person meet-ups.

Enhance
Your reading experience with discussion prompts, digital book club kits, and more, available on our website.

Join our online book club community!

f **g** randomhousebookclub.com

Random House Book Club ™

Because Stories Are Better Shared

RANDOM HOUSE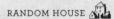